Twenty-six-year-old Josie Lloyd grew up in Essex, before going to Goldsmiths' College where she graduated with an honours degree in English and Drama. After a brief time training traders in the City, she embarked on a career in the Sales Promotion industry. After a year, she decided to write *It Could Be You*, gave up her job, and worked as a waitress and freelancer. She now lives with her piano in Ladbroke Grove and is working on her second novel.

IT COULD BE YOU

Josie Lloyd

An Oriel Paperback
First published in Great Britain in 1997 by Oriel,
a division of Orion Books Ltd,
Orion House, 5 Upper St Martin's Lane,
London WC2H 9EA

Second impression 1998

A CIP catalogue record for this book
is available from the British Library.

Typeset at The Spartan Press Ltd,
Lymington, Hampshire.

Printed and bound in Great Britain by
Clays Ltd, St Ives plc.

ACKNOWLEDGEMENTS

This book would never have been written if it weren't for my friends who have put up with me, held my hand and not let me give up, especially my top girls Harriet, Laurel and Katy. A special thanks goes to Dawn for having faith in me and putting the manuscript in front of the right people; to Sadie for her encouragement from the start and to Tom for coming up with the title. I'd also like to thank Steb, Ruth, Jonny and Matt who helped me follow my dream, and all the people who have kept the wolf from the door whilst I was doing it – Ian, Claire at Stop Gap Marketing, Mands and all the gang at BBL. Thanks also to Fraser who rescued me from post-it note hell when I had lost the plot, Chris Crosbie who told me jokes, Victoria who coped with the printing crises, Anna and Ray, and Mark and Lizzie for their excellent yoga teaching.

I feel immensely grateful to Rosie Cheetham, my brilliant editor who has never stopped inspiring me and has supported me through all the re-writing. I'd also like to thank my wonderful agent, Vivienne Schuster at Curtis Brown, my copy editor Jan Boxshall, Charlotte Hobson and everyone at Orion.

Most of all, I'd like to thank my hugely supportive family, especially my sister Catherine, Mum and Dad for letting me know that I'm doing the right thing.

BOOK
I

'Do it!' said Charlie Bright as she wriggled her bottom back in the chair, her face breaking into a cheeky grin.

David looked at the glossy picture of an actress sprawling across a velvet armchair in the open magazine. 'Like that! Are you sure?'

Charlie's large blue-grey eyes met his in the mirror. 'I want it . . . *Please*.'

David appraised her porcelain fair skin dotted with freckles across her high cheek bones. Her brown hair tumbled in messy curls over her shoulders and, with her exceptionally long eyelashes, she would have looked naive if it weren't for her full mouth which always looked as if it was going to burst into a smile at any moment.

David sucked in his cheeks and rested his hand on his hip, before nodding. His pierced nipples strained against the latex T-shirt as he bent down to her in the chair, so that his face was level with hers. 'You're right. Blonde will be a knock-out.'

Charlie's eyes sparkled with excitement. After all, if the actress could get a new bloke by going blonde, so could she.

It was six o'clock on the first hot Tuesday of summer. Outside, number 52 buses queued on Kensington Church Street, their fumes mingling in the balmy air. Charlie slipped her sweaty feet out of her Pied à Terre slingbacks, tipping her head back into the nook of the sink and letting David's assistant work the fragrant shampoo into a soft lather.

She wiggled her toes, excited by the prospect of a new look. The only problem was that she ought to have started her get-fit régime back in April. She'd kept meaning to buff her cellulite, drink detox herbs and do a hundred sit-ups every day, but somehow she hadn't managed to find spare time between the office, *Brookside* and the pub.

She thought of the white legs beneath her grey bootcut trousers and the wobbling triceps hidden by her French Connection T-shirt, and bit her lip. She wasn't ready to expose herself in those little summer dresses, most of which were compacted at the bottom of her laundry basket waiting for the day when she finally did her handwashing.

That's it, she thought, as she agreed to a scalp massage. Starting tomorrow, she'd stop drinking and smoking altogether, make vegetables her staple diet (as opposed to toast) and renounce bacon butties, home-delivered pizza and chocolate for ever.

From now on, she would get up at six a.m., meditate to some Gregorian chant and then eat a bowl of fresh fruit salad. No, no, no. Better still, she'd get up and go for a five mile run first. She imagined what it would feel like to be thin and to wake up without the aid of two alarm clocks and an emergency BT call. She saw herself flinging back a smooth, clean duvet and stretching her tanned, vibrant body, her thoughts positive, her teeth gleaming. White muslin curtains would flutter into her Zen-inspired, minimalist bedroom and she'd pull on some state-of-the art trainers and power off to Battersea Park.

On the other hand, she thought, running is bad for your legs. She didn't want premature arthritis and anyway, didn't the guy who ran the London marathon just die of a heart attack? OK. New plan. She'd go straight to the gym and do one of their crack of dawn aerobics classes. Then she'd have an invigorating shower with one of those skin buffing mitts she'd buy from The Body Shop and then drink at least a litre of mineral water.

She sighed contentedly at her plans and held the towel turban on her head as she sat back down in front of the mirror. The future was Bright, she thought, laughing at Rich's pun on her name. She would be a sorted and independent woman. She'd give up praying at cashpoint machines and become financially responsible. She'd arrive early for work, keep a neat and tidy filing system and show everyone at Bistram Huff, the sales promotion agency where she worked, just how supremely capable she was.

And once she'd clinched her long-awaited promotion to account director, firmed up her bum and got a suntan, then surely she couldn't fail to pull him. It had been so long since she'd fancied anyone like this. Not since her last boyfriend Phil and it was nearly a year since they'd split up. She allowed herself to think back to the relationship for a moment and the agonising pain of the heartbreak. She breathed deeply at the memory, but the scar must have healed without her noticing. In fact, thinking about it now, she could see for the first time that Kate, her best friend, had been right about Phil. He was egocentric, weak and, although she had elevated him to God-like status, he was after all only a bloke. She'd been so eager to please him, laying down her personality as his doormat. What had she been on?

She watched David as he cut her hair and slathered purple peroxide all over it, neatly wrapping the dyed strands in strips of foil. She felt so different now. Ready to start afresh, ready to fall in love again, though this time she wouldn't shackle her heart to a commitment-phobic like Phil. But then *he* was nothing like Phil. He was strong and capable and . . .

Her mobile phone interrupted her thoughts and Charlie fumbled to find the armholes in her gown. The foil bundles crackled as David carefully parted them so that she could get the phone next to her ear. It was Rich.

'What are you doing? You sound like you're in a hurricane.'

'I'm having my hair done.'

'You've really done it? Blonde?'

'Uh-huh.'

3

'Oh.'

Charlie raised her eyebrows and looked at the ceiling. 'Don't sound so pleased.'

'I liked it before.'

'How can you say that? It was a permanent bird's nest. Anyway, it's all gone.'

Rich knew arguing was pointless and he hid his disappointment well. 'So how are you feeling?'

Charlie softened at his placatory tone and winked at David. 'Nervous.'

'*You're* nervous. What about me? I'll have to live with it.'

'Ha bloody ha.'

Rich chuckled. 'Listen, I'm just leaving. Shall I meet you somewhere for a drink?'

'I'm not drinking.'

'And I'm the Virgin Mary.'

'No, seriously. This is it, I'm on a new summer régime.'

'I'll see you in the 51 then.'

Charlie rolled her eyes and smiled. 'All right. Just the one. I'll see you there at eight.'

'Boyfriend?' asked David curiously as she squeezed the red button on the phone.

'Rich? God, no! He's my flatmate.'

'He sounded like your boyfriend.'

'No way. I've known him all my life. He's sort of like a big brother.' She replaced the phone on the counter and smoothed the black gown on her knees. 'You're looking at the most single person on the planet.'

'I can't believe that.' David had always been gay but, as Charlie shrugged, he realised she didn't have a clue how much her earthy beauty, cheery manner and the mischievous light in her eyes turned men on.

'Well, you won't be for long with this hair,' he warned.

'That's what I'm hoping.'

David opened one of the foil bundles to check the progress of the peroxide. 'Anyone in particular?'

Conjuring up his image, Charlie felt as if she was sitting on a hot water bottle. She remembered how his graceful, strong

4

hands had flipped through the pages of the directory. He'd been choosing a model to feature in the car campaign they were working on. He'd stopped at a picture of a stunning blonde girl and his tanned index finger had stroked over the page before he turned to look at Charlie with his smoky brown eyes. Her stomach had flipped over.

'Maybe,' she said, and picked up the magazine to avoid further scrutiny.

Charlie peeked at herself in the rear-view mirror as she stopped by the traffic lights on King's Road. Her tangled curls had been replaced by a sleek crown of bright blonde hair shaped around her face in the latest style. It made her look older, more sophisticated, and she felt more sexy than she ever could have imagined. She turned up the latest Ministry of Sound tape and tapped her hand against the tattered steering wheel of her ancient Fiat Panda.

Of course, now she had a new haircut she would have to sort out her car and her wardrobe. As the Panda lurched and stalled in the traffic jam on the way to Battersea Bridge, Charlie looked into shop windows. Why was everything designed for stick-thin girls with no waist and no hips? Only people like Kate managed to look fantastic in those clothes and Charlie wondered whether she would ever be as funky as her friend.

Ever since they had studied English together at London University, Charlie had been in awe of Kate. She was gutsy and strong and wore sexy clothes with a 'don't mess with me' attitude that Charlie admired. Kate always got what she wanted. She'd blagged her way into a glamorous job as a magazine journalist and what's more she was going out with Dillon. And let's face it, Dillon was cool.

Charlie, Kate and Rich had first met Dillon three years ago when he was converting the grotty pub across the road from Rich's flat. By the time the wrought-iron sign saying 'the 51' went up above the glass doors, the floorboards stripped and polished and the high ceiling fans wired to the control panel behind the bar, they'd become fast friends.

Dillon's overnight success with the 51 was due partly to the big smile and laid-back manner which he'd inherited from his Jamaican mother and partly to the flair for modern British cooking inherited from his English father. The bar was filled every night with the Battersea crowd drinking trendy beers and New World wines, listening to Dillon's specially compiled reggae and funk tapes and eating his state-of-the-art pub grub.

It had become Rich, Charlie and Kate's hang-out, where they met after work and enjoyed long leisurely breakfasts on Sunday lunchtimes. When he shut up for the night, Dillon would sit chatting with them over a bottle of wine and sometimes, when Rich wasn't there, he rolled a joint and Kate and Charlie got stoned with him. That was when Charlie noticed that Dillon and Kate were falling for each other.

Yet when Charlie suggested to Kate that she fancied Dillon, she'd been outraged.

'Dillon? Give me a break! He's ugly, hairy, stubborn . . .' She'd trailed off, trying to muster up insults. 'Half the time I want to hit him.'

Charlie laughed. 'What are you like? Dillon is gorgeous.'

'You go out with him then, if you think he's so bloody wonderful,' Kate retorted.

'You'll see,' predicted Charlie, astonished that for once Kate couldn't see what was so patently obvious.

It had been a hot summer's night last year when they finally got together. The doors of the 51 were wide open and the tables on the terrace were crowded. Inside, Dillon was lounging by their table, his arms full of glasses as he leaned over and offered his unflattering opinion on the layout of Kate's latest article.

'You don't know anything,' said Kate, her small dancer's frame tensed in defiance, her dark eyes, a legacy from her Chinese grandmother, narrowed into slits.

'I'm not criticising you. I was only saying what I thought. If you don't want my opinion, don't ask.'

'I won't, I don't need it,' she snapped, angrily snatching up the magazine.

Dillon flicked long dreadlocks back over his huge shoulder. 'You're so touchy!'

'Don't worry, I won't be staying on your account,' said Kate, then turned on her heel and pushed her way out between the crowded tables. Dillon's distinctive green eyes widened as he watched her depart and then he looked at Charlie.

'What did I say?'

'Go after her,' Charlie urged, arching her eyebrows and nodding at Kate. It took a split second for Dillon to make up his mind and then his athletic six foot three frame galvanised into action. He dumped the glasses on the table and reached Kate in a couple of strides, grabbing her arm and twirling her round. They looked at each other for a moment and then Dillon kissed her. Charlie remembered how she had clapped her hands and everyone started cheering as the kiss went on, relieving months of sexual tension, until Kate came up for air, giggling and blushing in Dillon's embrace. And that had been the start of their tempestuous relationship.

Now, even though they had been going out for a year, Charlie was convinced that Kate was in denial about her feelings, but maybe she was just being cool. It certainly worked. Men fell around her feet and Charlie longed to have Kate's knack of treating 'em mean and keeping 'em keen. In Charlie's eyes, her friend was everything a nineties woman should be: she travelled on her own, was never afraid of confronting people in power and could spend Sundays all by herself without ever getting lonely.

Charlie was so impressed that she couldn't admit her own dreams for the future involved an idyllic country cottage with a big kitchen table, a Labrador with a thumping tail and a couple of Siamese cats. She pictured herself mooning around in a floral apron with flour on her cheeks, throwing scraps to her hand-reared geese in the yard and breeding beautiful babies. The fantasy was far too uncool. Anyway, that was way in the future. Right now she wanted to live a little.

Now Dillon gawped as Charlie walked towards the high

7

chrome bar. She did a twirl for him and his huge lips widened into a smile.

'Is it really you?'

She giggled and propped her elbow on the bar. 'Yep, the new improved version.'

Dillon tucked a white cloth into the waist of his leather trousers and put his hands on his hips, his muscular chest visible beneath the tight V-neck T-shirt. 'I hardly recognised you.'

Charlie peeped at herself in the mirror between the bottles at the back of the bar and finger-combed her fringe. '*I* hardly recognise me.'

'What's brought this on?'

'I just felt like a change. It's summer time.'

'Don't I know it,' he said, uncorking a bottle of Chardonnay and pouring her a hefty glass. 'This place has been heaving and I've hardly seen Kate.'

'Oh dear.' Charlie frowned, knowing that Kate would be cross.

'She'll be down later,' said Dillon, clinking his beer bottle with her glass. 'Cheers.'

Charlie fumbled in her bag to get some money.

'Don't. It's on the house. Looking like that you're bound to attract the punters.'

She blushed and looked around for Rich. 'Is his lordship here?' Dillon nodded to a corner table below a high ceiling fan. Rich was reading the pink pages of the *Evening Standard*, his suit bedraggled, his Austin Reed tie loosened at the neck. His usually pristine white shirt was crumpled and his floppy brown hair fell in his face.

Charlie smiled at Dillon and tiptoed towards the table. 'Can I sit here?' she asked in an American drawl.

Rich looked up briefly. 'Go ahead,' he mumbled, as he resumed reading. Then he looked up suddenly.

'Oh my God!' he said, his tortoiseshell glasses slipping down his nose.

Charlie grinned. 'You like?' She swivelled her hips into the corner chair and looked inquiringly at him.

8

'You look so . . . so different.'

'I shall take that as a compliment,' she said, her eyes challenging him over the top of her wine glass.

Rich sat up straight, his English propriety returning. 'Of course it is. You look lovely,' he said, staring at her. 'It's very . . .' he paused, groping for a word, 'modern.'

Charlie grimaced. 'That's the kind of thing Dad would say!'

Rich didn't smile and Charlie pushed his arm playfully. 'What's wrong with you, misery guts?'

Rich folded up the paper and shook his head. 'Rotten day, that's all.'

She cocked her head sympathetically. 'Still no better?'

He took off his glasses and rubbed his eyes. 'It's this case I'm working on. I know when it eventually comes to court we're going to win it.' He put his glasses on the table and looked at her with his speckled blue eyes, the wrinkles around them owing more to stress than his thirty years.

'I thought that was the point. You're a lawyer,' said Charlie, slipping off her shoes to curl her legs underneath her then, deciding her feet were too smelly, putting her shoes back on. She must remember to put foot spray on the Boots list.

'If people were just honest from the start, I'm sure they'd get what they wanted in the end. Instead they get a piece of information they think they can profit from and go charging ahead, stamping on anyone who happens to be in their way. It makes me sick.'

'But surely that's what you're there for, to make sure the best man wins,' said Charlie.

'The one with the best law firm and the most money wins,' corrected Rich. He took a sip from his pint. 'Anyway, it's boring. You don't want to hear about it.'

Charlie bent towards him. 'Of course I do. I hate to see you working this hard. You must stop caring so much. You're such an old softie.'

Rich snorted. 'These guys in court aren't going to think so. I've got enough evidence to see them go under once and for all. The guy I'm defending is evil, but the prosecution hasn't got the money to prove it.'

'You shouldn't have so many scruples.'

'I'm beginning to think that too,' said Rich. He took another gulp of his pint. 'So what's it like to be blonde?'

Charlie grinned and tapped her hands on the table. 'Good. I'm on a new summer health drive, I'm not going to drink, smoke or anything.'

Rich raised his eyebrows and looked at her wine.

'Well, cut down at least. You're going to see a whole new me.'

'I'm already seeing a whole new you. How was your day?' he said, changing the subject.

'Busy. I've planned all the point of sale for the car campaign, we've got another brief for a collector scheme with a cigarette company, and the Up Beat promotion has to be planned. I don't know how I'm going to get all the work done with Philippa going on holiday tomorrow.'

'I thought you'd be overjoyed.' Rich was used to being a sounding board for Charlie's angst about her hyper-critical boss, the much feared Philippa Bistram.

'I am, but I've got this horrible feeling that something will go wrong.'

'How can it? As you've said yourself, sales promotion isn't exactly rocket science and without Philippa breathing down your neck every two seconds you'll be laughing.'

Charlie sighed. 'That's what I'm hoping, but she makes me feel so inadequate. She picks holes in everything I do and overrides my decisions all the time. Everyone else in my team is lazy, except Bandit, but then he's always wheeling and dealing and going out for lunch. I can't trust any of them to help me out in a crisis. Maybe I'm not good enough to be an account director.'

Rich tutted. 'Rubbish. Of course you are. You just need a chance to prove yourself. It's all about confidence.'

Charlie nodded but her attention was caught by Kate, who stood at the door pushing her blue sunglasses to the top of her head so that her long raven-black hair swooshed down her back. She was wearing the latest Whistles hipsters and a cropped baby pink T-shirt which showed off her tight torso and pierced belly button. She squealed when she saw Charlie, and bounced over in her platform trainers. She patted Charlie's hair approvingly. 'Love it!' she gushed. 'You look amazing. Who did it?'

'David.'

'It shows. It's a beautiful cut,' she said as she kissed Rich on the cheek and, seeing that she had left a deep plum lipstick stain, wiped it off with her thumb.

'Drink?' She nodded to their nearly empty glasses.

'I'm on beer, but blondie here is guzzling the white. I'll join you if you want.' Rich started to get up, but Kate restrained him.

'Stay put. I'll get a bottle.' She swung her Prada knapsack off her back and, dumping it on the table, undid the tie and retrieved her purse and pack of Marlboro Lights. She glanced up and grinned. 'Might as well start as we mean to go on.'

'Oh God,' said Charlie as Kate wriggled her way through the crowd to the bar. 'There goes my healthy night.'

Within a minute, Kate was back with an ice bucket and three glasses. Rich chuckled and shook his head as he watched Kate deposit a large lump of gum in the ashtray. She put a cigarette between her lips.

Rich picked up the bottle and looked at the label. 'Very nice.'

'Peace offering from Dillon,' said Kate, her voice muffled as the cigarette wagged between her lips. 'Want one?' She offered the pack to Charlie.

'I shouldn't,' she muttered, glancing at Rich as she pulled one out of the packet.

'You said you'd given up,' he recriminated.

'Shut up, you old fuddy-duddy. A girl needs her vices,' said Kate, flicking her Cadillac lighter. She lit Charlie's and her own cigarette and inhaled deeply before grinning at Rich.

'How is Mr Virtue?' she asked, cupping her hand on his knee affectionately and leaning towards him. She looked at his face and frowned. 'You're looking a bit peaky, mate.'

'He's working too hard,' said Charlie.

'Thank you, Mother.'

'A holiday and a shag, that's what you need. All work and no play makes Rich a dull boy,' scolded Kate.

Rich shook his head. 'Is that what you advise your readers?'

Kate grabbed the wine bottle and filled up their glasses. 'Absolutely. I've been writing an article that's right up your street. It's on how to flirt properly.'

'Thanks, I'll remember to buy my next issue of *Just Teen*,' said Rich. He took a sip of wine. 'Life on the cutting edge of journalism is as challenging as ever, I see!'

Kate puffed out her cheeks. 'It's as dull as watching paint dry. I want juicy stories that involve a bit of scandal and delving about. I want something serious for a change. I'm determined to get a new job this summer. Mind you, if the weather stays like this, I know I won't get my act together to get interviews. I'd rather hang out and do lunch.'

'I hope it does stay like this. I'm desperate for a suntan,' said Charlie.

'Go on a sun bed then.'

'I did.'

'When?' asked Rich.

'Lunchtime.'

Rich set his glass down on the table. 'You vowed never to go on one again after that time you went to Microwave Beach, or whatever it's called, and got burnt in stripes from your neck to your ankles.'

Charlie inhaled on her cigarette. 'I know, but I went on a stand-up one, they're much better for you. Anyway, I don't want a serious tan, I just want to take off the blue.'

Kate stubbed out her cigarette. 'Since when did you turn into such a vain old tart?'

Charlie sat back in her seat and looked out of the window on to the street. 'I'm not! I told you, I want a change of image, that's all . . .' She trailed off and blushed.

Kate and Rich exchanged a look. 'Who is he?' demanded Kate.

She looked at them shiftily. 'There is no "he" involved.'

Kate put on Rich's glasses and fixed Charlie with a stare. 'Come on. Out with it.'

Charlie paused for a moment and then exhaled dramatically. 'It's Daniel.' She put up her hands defensively. 'I know. I know I'm being ridiculous and there's no way he'd ever fancy me but . . .'

'Isn't he the new creative director you were talking about?' interrupted Rich.

Charlie nodded. 'Daniel Goldsmith.' She put her elbows on the table and covered her burning cheeks with her hands. 'He's just so gob-smackingly amazing and he hasn't even noticed me. I keep smiling at him, trying to be in the lift when he is, telling witty anecdotes in earshot, that kind of thing, and I land up feeling like a prat. Short of doing a naked tap dance on the boardroom table, I don't know how I'm going to catch his attention.'

'If he's doing that good a job of ignoring you, which isn't easy, why do you want him at all?' asked Kate, looking confused. She'd never seen Charlie in the throes of such a serious crush.

'All the girls at Bistram Huff fancy him and I don't want him to think of me as just another frumpy account handler. I want him to see me as . . . oh, I don't know.'

Kate laughed. 'You're gorgeous and he must have noticed you. He's just playing hard to get.'

'No. He's way out of my league.'

Kate looked at her friend, astonished. 'Charlie, he's just a bloke! Sorry, Rich.'

'I know. But this is different. My palms go clammy when he walks in the room. He's got these dark mysterious eyes and smooth olive skin that you just want to rub your cheek against.'

'Goldsmith. That's a Jewish name,' pondered Rich.

'That would make sense. Jewish men are always sexy,' said Kate as Charlie, oblivious to them, stared into the distance.

'He's got this air about him – like he's a free spirit and his mind is on nobler things and then suddenly he looks at you and it takes your breath away. It's like the world could be falling down around him, but the only thing that matters to him is looking into your eyes and you feel so naked – as if he can see into all your filthiest fantasies.'

Kate looked dubious. 'One moment you're saying he's not noticing you and the next he's riveted to the spot scanning through the crinkled pages of your Nancy Friday collection.'

Rich was amazed. 'So that's why you dyed your hair?'

Charlie sighed and started to peel the cardboard beer mat. 'You wouldn't understand. He's . . .'

'Charlie. Charlie. Earth to Charlie, do you read me? Come in please?' laughed Kate. She nudged Rich. 'I think we've lost her.'

But Rich was gazing straight at Charlie, his face solemn.

'Rich?' said Kate.

He jolted and smiled wanly. 'Absolutely! We'd better have another bottle of wine.'

Charlie squinted at the digital display of her alarm clock, trying to focus on the swimming numerals. Seven. Seven five zero. Seven-fifty. Ten to eight. Ten to eight. TEN TO EIGHT! She trampled off the stained duvet and sat up abruptly, holding her head and yelping as her hangover kicked in. As usual, the quiet drink at the 51 had turned into a session and when she staggered home arm in arm with Rich in the small hours, she'd been too pissed to remember to drink any water.

She'd woken up at the time she was supposed to be arriving at work. Why did that always happen? Philippa would be furious. Never again. No more booze, she vowed, rubbing her eyes with the heels of her hands.

She groaned as she looked around her room. Her jacket and trousers lay in a crumpled heap at the foot of her bed, the rug bore a dry tea stain and an empty mug on its side. Last week's Sunday papers were scattered over the floor, along with odd shoes and abandoned damp towels. T-shirts and leggings lolled over the sides of the drawers, one of which was completely off its runners, balancing on the clutter and housing a tangled snake-pit of tights and holey socks.

She flopped out of bed and lurched to the window, tugging the string of the blind which rolled up at an angle. Stumbling away from the brightness of the day she grabbed her threadbare dressing gown, hanging upside-down on the back of the door, and staggered into the living room.

The flat, on the second floor of a Victorian mansion block, was large and south-facing with two floor to ceiling windows. The curtains were partially drawn and the filtered sunlight illuminated a column of dust stretching from the flaking ceiling rose to the worn Habitat rug. A shabby sofa, covered in an Indian cotton throw, and two squashy armchairs were clustered around an old trunk which was caked with dried wax. One wall was covered in book shelves below which a scratched table housed a bunch of yellowing newspapers and blackening bananas. Between the windows Channel Four's *Big Breakfast* was blaring from the huge TV.

In the corner, Rich was ironing his shirt and eating a piece of toast at the same time.

'I'm late,' Charlie croaked, scuttling across the shabby carpet to the bathroom.

'Good morning to you too,' said Rich as he set the hissing iron to rest on the metal plate and headed for the kitchen. He tickled Kevin, their cat, under the chin.

'Shall we make her some tea?' he asked, as Kev paced on the kitchen table. Rich lifted down Charlie's favourite china mug from the hook above the sink and plopped a tea bag in it.

In the bathroom Charlie gazed in the mirror above the sink. Yesterday's mascara streaked down her face making her look like a heavy metal groupie. As predicted, her hair was a disaster. One side was plastered in a flat rosette against her head, the other stuck out at an electrostatic ninety degrees. Stepping into the shower, she jumped as the trickle of water ran scalding hot and then freezing cold. She shook the shampoo bottle vigorously, but it was nearly empty, so she squeezed it under the stream of water and it spluttered as it took in water. She huddled under the shower covered in goosepimples and held the bottle upside down over the crown of her head, but the nozzle was pointing in the wrong direction and the shampoo squirted over the mouldy shower curtain.

She picked up the wafer-thin remnant of soap and, vowing to do a bumper shop in Boots at lunchtime, shaved her armpits with Rich's razor, before dripping on to the bathmat. She wrapped one hand towel around her head and one around her body and sprinted to her room, lunging for her alarm clock as it squawked into life from its extended snooze mode, spilling the mug of tea that Rich had left for her and knocking a half-eaten apple under the bed.

Swearing, she flapped her scalded hand in the air and hopped on to the upturned plug of the hairdryer. Her eyes smarted as she limped across the room to find some knickers.

Charlie was irrationally superstitious about her underwear, attributing bad clothes purchases, failed relationships and exam successes to the particular knickers she was wearing at the time. She rummaged through the drawer and found a pair of grey Marks & Spencer cotton high-tops. Practical and comfortable, but associated with seeing her ex-boyfriend Phil two weeks after they'd split up, losing all her dignity and begging him to come back to her. No-pride knickers, she thought. Not a good idea if she was going to see Daniel. She pulled out a white stretch lace pair. They were vaguely associated with the Panda failing its MOT, but she couldn't be sure. She'd risk it.

She listened to the breakfast show on the radio, thinking as always that she ought to tune into another station to get away from the adverts which were one of her pet hates. Hearing that the time was already eight-fifteen, she yanked open her wardrobe and gawped at the laden hangers in despair. Typical, she thought. She had *absolutely nothing* to wear. Today was a tricky day. Although she didn't have any meetings, she would see Daniel and so she had to be sexy, yet smart. She looked down at her legs and ran a hand over the shins, then pulled out her favourite Kookaï suit with its short A-line skirt and little tailored jacket. No, she couldn't wear it

– she hadn't shaved her legs so she'd have to wear tights and she knew she didn't have a clean pair. She heaved back the hangers on their rails and riffled through the clothes, chucking un-ironed, mismatching outfits on the bed in panic.

Eventually, in desperation, she decided on the first option and slipped into the red skirt, twisting it round her as she did up the zip. She pulled open another drawer, shook out a tight black T-shirt and pulled it on. She could get away without wearing a bra, after all her perfectly rounded breasts were showing no signs of sagging, but then she remembered she'd forgotten her deodorant and stretched the neck of the T-shirt as she tried to reach her armpits with the roller-ball.

She winced as the radio DJ told Sharon, a dental nurse from Peckham, that she'd just won £25,000 and Sharon let out a piercing scream, followed by a series of deeply irritating squeals. Charlie hurled the deodorant at the radio.

'Tights, tights,' she muttered, dragging out a limp, baggy pair from the laundry basket. She sniffed them gingerly before dousing them with Issey Miyake and pulled them on. Then she flung the wet towels and piles of clothes on the bed to find her handbag. She spotted its strap under the duvet and tugged it out, delving in its depths to find her hairbrush, which was covered in loose tobacco from the broken emergency cigarette it had spiked.

Feeling dizzy, she brushed her hair and plugged in the hairdryer. She tried to style her hair straight, but she couldn't coordinate the movement of her arms and the brush in the mirror, so she gave up, tipped her head upside down and blasted her hair with hot air. There was no way she could replicate David's sleek style. As she stood upright the blood rushed to her head and she had to steady herself against the radiator to stop herself falling over.

She peered in the mirror. Her hair looked terrible, sticking out in clumps, and so did her face which was pale and blotchy. She looked worse than she had done when she woke up. She scrabbled in her top drawer, found some styling mousse and squirted it into her hand, but the pressure had gone and a white sticky mess trickled into her palm. She slapped it on to her head and tried to make amends, brushing her hair and blowing it with the dryer at the same time, until she growled in frustration and tossed the hairbrush over her shoulder.

Rich knocked softly on the door and poked his head round. 'I'm off,' he said.

'Hang on a minute. I'm coming with you,' said Charlie, dropping to her hands and knees and trying to locate her other shoe under the bed.

'Charlie,' said Rich impatiently, averting his eyes from her laddered gusset.

'I'll be a nano-second. I'll give you a lift to the station.'

Ten minutes later, when Rich had finally located her car keys under a cushion in the lounge, Charlie was ready.

'Philippa's going to kill me,' she wailed, as she darted across the road to the car.

'I don't see why it takes you so long to leave the house,' said Rich. 'You flap for Britain.'

'I don't,' said Charlie defensively, getting into the car and swiping the *Marie Claire* minus its front cover, the empty sandwich carton, crushed cigarette packet and selection of broken cassette cases from the passenger seat into the footwell. She leaned across and yanked up the lock. Rich got into the passenger seat. Charlie dumped her handbag on his lap and tried to start the engine.

'I knew I should've taken the bus,' said Rich as the engine turned over with a bronchial wheeze.

Charlie ignored him and pumped the accelerator. 'Come on, baby, you can do it,' she coaxed, gripping the steering wheel.

'Do you want me to have a look?'

Charlie gave him a withering stare.

Rich raised his eyebrows sceptically and opened the door to get out, just as the car coughed into life.

Charlie grinned at him. 'You see. You're such a panicker.'

The District Line train screeched to a halt in the black tunnel, silent commuters jolting against each other as they lunged for the overhanging rails. Rich could feel the tension of a hundred minds cursing their fate. Luckily he'd got a seat, but that was only because he'd slipped in before the grey-haired man, who now stood glaring down at him in silent Tube rage.

Rich shrank behind his open copy of *The Times*. This was all he needed. If only he'd taken the bus and hadn't waited for Charlie, he'd have been at his desk by now; not that he particularly wanted to be there. But where did he want to be?

Rich had done his A-levels, got into Bristol University and, still at a loss as to what to study, he'd plumped for law as a safe bet. He'd reasoned that a law degree would always be useful, no matter what he decided to do with his life. Then, before he knew it, he'd finished his articles.

At first he'd been ecstatic when he landed a job at Mathers Egerickx Lovitt. In law circles they were considered to be one of the top five firms for commercial litigation. Back then, he'd been enthusiastic about the challenge of complex law suits and had set himself a personal target of making it to partner level by the time he was thirty.

However, his glittering career had not progressed as planned. For the last two years he'd been doing tedious back-up research on the PWL case, sifting through thousands of company files to find evidence against a huge multinational company. The work was mundane and painstaking and his enthusiasm had dwindled along with his chances of promotion. He was hopeless at office power play and petty politics and he was disgusted that the partners favoured his colleagues with more aptitude for arse-licking.

Each day he became more embroiled in the twisted, tangled task. He resented the work bitterly, but knew that he had too much pride to give up. And he'd started thinking more often, what was it all for? Even if they won the case, who would benefit? There might be a write-up in the paper and a shaky couple of days on the FTSE 100 Index, but it wouldn't affect anyone. And where was the justice in him earning a fortune to churn through paperwork?

Sweat prickled on the back of his neck as the Tube grew more stuffy. The commuters shuffled nervously and Rich looked down at the fake Rolex which Kate had brought back from Thailand. He wished he could press a button on it like Captain Kirk and beam himself down to a paradise island with a gorgeous babe. Kate was right, he could do with a holiday and a shag, but only older women of the nymphomaniac divorcée type fancied him. At office Christmas parties, the only people who flirted with him were the partners' wives. He was beginning to think there must be something wrong with him.

Maybe he should change his career. Yet what else could he do? In his secret fantasies, he imagined himself as a pop star, wooing the crowds with pelvic thrusts and ground-breaking guitar riffs. Yet despite the air guitar sessions he performed in front of the bathroom mirror, Rich knew he could only play the opening bars of *The Pink Panther* on the real thing.

He'd love to crew a racing yacht around the world, but he didn't have enough experience and he was too old to start right at the bottom as a deck hand. Maybe he could start his own restaurant? No, he didn't have enough money, and anyway most restaurants in London folded in the first year. He'd have to work every night and he only had to look at Dillon to know he didn't have the ability to cope with the stress.

The Tube jolted once again and was on its way, rumbling along the dark tunnel to Blackfriars. Rich shook out the newspaper and read the predictions for a hot summer ahead. Maybe he was destined for this. Maybe this was his lot in life – stuck in a rut in London. He should stop complaining and get on with it.

He thought of Charlie and her eternal optimism and wished he could be supportive about her career in sales promotion, yet he felt angry that she too had followed the wrong path. She'd completely cut off her creative side and her natural flair for drawing. She'd always been brilliant, ever since she was old enough to pick up a fistful of crayons, and now she wouldn't so much as step inside an art gallery. Rich put her loss of self-confidence down to the summer when Charlie finished her A-levels.

It was the year that he got a job as a bartender in Browns and he and Charlie hung out in her parents' house in Brighton all summer. They'd had a ball. That was, until the letter came.

'They've turned me down, I haven't got in!' Charlie thrust the letter towards him, her hand shaking indignantly. Getting into the foundation course at St Martin's had been everything she dreamed of. She'd pulled out all the stops with her art A-level and had planned her portfolio with military precision. Now she realised that the shimmering castles of her future were nothing but a rapidly evaporating mirage.

Rich swung off the sun lounger. 'I don't believe it! They're mad!'

Charlie snatched the letter from him and paced on the crazy paving, rubbing her head in confusion.

'They've made a mistake. They can't mean it,' she reasoned, picking up the phone that they'd stretched out to the garden table.

'What are you doing?'

'Ringing them up to find out why.'

After hanging around on the switchboard, Charlie was put through to the senior tutor and her bravado deserted her. She took a deep breath as she waited while he looked her up in the file.

'I'm sorry. As you know there's fierce competition for places on the foundation course and this year in particular we've had a number of outstanding applicants . . .'

She listened, feeling numb, and Rich could hear the tutor's voice as Charlie slowly replaced the handset, cutting him off.

'What did he say?' asked Rich.

'He said that I'm not good enough.'

On her way up to the seventh floor of Bistram Huff's stylish Thames-side offices, Charlie tweaked her knickers from her bum, ruffled her hair in the tinted mirror and squeezed her lips together to smooth out her unfamiliar red lipstick. She felt nervous about what her colleagues would think of her overnight change of image. All sales promotion agencies, like advertising agencies, operated purely on gossip and she knew she'd be talked about all day. She looked at her watch and made a face. It was only five to nine, but still she felt anxious as she jabbed the button again, catching her worried reflection in the mirror.

Charlie hated letting people down, especially Philippa, but no matter how hard she worked, no matter how late she stayed in the evening, she always felt that somehow it wasn't enough. She constantly dished out praise and encouragement, but never got any herself. Lately she'd felt totally taken for granted.

It hadn't always been like that. When Simon Huff left BKF, the huge media giant, three years ago, he'd taken their best account team to set up a rival break-away agency and the coup had dominated the marketing press for months. With the financial backing of Philippa Bistram, who had been marketing director with one of his main clients, Si had created Bistram Huff and in just eighteen months had expanded to become one of the top five below-the-line marketing agencies in London.

Charlie had been temping at BKF at the time Si was hatching his plans, in a post-university financial crisis. She had warmed to his frenetic Australian charm and helped him in his subterfuge, never expecting that he would recruit her as his first junior account handler in the new agency. She had blossomed at Bistram Huff, learning all she could from Si so that very quickly he came to rely on her judgement and her ability to see a job through. When she had earned it, he'd promoted her to account manager and she relished the responsibility, helping Pete and Toff, the junior executives, to shine.

However, in the last eighteen months things had changed. Si had decided on a massive expansion plan. He wanted to make Bistram Huff a through-the-line agency and had acquired bigger accounts, pitching for direct marketing and advertising briefs as well as the big promotions for which the agency had a good reputation. In order to help him, he'd persuaded Philippa Bistram to pump every last penny of her private fortune into Bistram Huff and to take an active role in the company.

On the day she'd arrived, Philippa had demanded the hands-on role of client services director so that she was ultimately in charge of running all the accounts. Si hadn't been able to argue and Bistram Huff had changed for ever.

Charlie had been friendly and eager to please her new boss, but Si was in the office less and less, and it quickly became clear not only that Philippa wanted to run her own show but that she didn't value anyone else's opinion. It wasn't long before the two best account directors resigned and went back to BKF. Ever conscientious, Charlie worked twice as hard to meet Philippa's exacting standards, but when Philippa brought in her own accounts and recruited new staff, she'd expected Charlie to cope without any support.

Charlie had – just – but now she was in a Catch 22 situation. She'd been given the worst clients to contend with and there still wasn't an account director for the team. There was the guy from Coca-Cola who rang her at five o'clock on a Friday night demanding a promotion plan for one of his brands by Monday morning, then changed his mind after she'd worked all weekend. Then there was the woman from the cereal conglomerate who insisted on running promotions on the back of cereal packets but never approved the copy until the last moment. These two were just the tip of the iceberg.

Charlie had to admit she did quite like the pace of the work. It always came in fits and starts and she loved the pressure as a deadline approached. She would be deluged by phone calls, a mound of contact reports to write, documents to compose and faxes to send. These would pile up in her in-tray as she ran around like a headless chicken – arguing with printers whose schedules had been disrupted, cajoling clients into making decisions, beating down suppliers who demanded extra costs for producing miracles at short notice. And then it would all be over and she'd have quiet times when she could chat to her friends and go out to lunch, before they won another pitch and the process started again.

Yet she was determined to get promoted. If only she could make it to account director, she'd have the authority to make the team more organised and Philippa wouldn't boss her around so much.

The lift pinged open and Charlie stepped on to the thick pile carpet, smiling at a client who lounged on the leather sofa, talking into his mobile phone. A motorcycle courier, clad in dirty leathers and a huge helmet, was stuffing a package into his black sack as his radio crackled incomprehensibly. Behind the smooth curve of the high reception booth Sadie, the blonde receptionist, surveyed the view of the Thames while buffing her long nails. 'Good morning, Bistram Huff. Hold the line one moment. Good morning, Bistram Huff,' she sing-songed into the mouthpiece of her reception apparatus, the liplined red pout barely moving in her young, blemishless face.

Charlie picked out her faxes from the in-tray on the counter and smiled at Sadie, who pointed to her hair and gave a thumbs-up sign. A blast of ringing phones, whirring printers and the jubilant roar of Pete Martin replaying Manchester United's latest goal escaped into the reception area as she pushed open the double doors into the chaotic open-plan office.

'Yo,' Charlie said, slapping Pete's upturned hand. His thinning hair lifted briefly in the air wave. He wore a zip-up jacket and a Chemical Brothers T-shirt, jeans and blue converse. Charlie liked Pete, knowing that his sexist bravado was only a laddish front and that underneath he was a pushover, bullied by his pregnant girlfriend Sharon.

'Check it out!' He wolf-whistled as she passed him. 'Babe alert! Babe alert!' he shouted as the others looked up. Charlie blushed.

She carried on towards her desk and noticed Tina, slumped in her chair beside the giant cardboard cut-out of Doctor Spock. Tina was usually miserable about something, but today she looked particularly grim.

'What's up?' asked Charlie, touching her fat leg sympathetically.

Pete pounced to her side. 'PMT. The incredible story of a killer period. All over the West End from Friday,' he rasped like a cinema announcer.

'Fuck off!' snapped Tina, her grating Scottish accent even more surly than normal. She shuffled her black legging-clad thighs under the desk.

'You know what PMT is, don't you?' said Pete. He nodded smugly. 'Pre-meditated tantrum.'

'Ignore him,' said Charlie, a laugh in her voice as she swung her bag on to the cluttered desk and opened a drawer to find her bumper box of Nurofen for Tina. She must tidy it up, she thought, as she rummaged through loose business cards, recipe fridge magnets, dog-eared Cup-a-Soups and out-of-date Slim-Fast sachets, chewed biros, pencil flakes from the broken tub sharpener, the wacky calculator with musical buttons, the half-empty bottle of perfume, fluffy tampons, dead marker pens and broken nailfiles.

She pulled out the painkillers triumphantly from the back of the drawer and handed them to Tina, whose pale, spotty features shifted momentarily into a smile. 'Your hair looks nice,' she said, popping two pills out of the blister pack.

'I haven't got the hang of styling it yet.'

'I wish mine would do that,' said Tina, lifting a floppy clump of her mousy hair.

Charlie smiled apologetically and turned back to her desk, wishing that she could say something to stop Tina being so miserable. She looked over at Toff, who was rooting about in the grey filing cabinet, and noticed that his customary pin-striped trousers were going threadbare.

'Have you seen that tranny of the baseball caps from the shoot we did the other day?' he asked.

'Organisation, Toff, is what it's all about,' she said, taking the plastic folder of precious transparencies from a pile on her desk and frisbeeing them over to him.

'He couldn't organise a piss up in a brewery!' interjected Pete, catching the folder in mid-air as Toff gawped at Charlie.

Behind the glass in the corner office, Philippa Bistram was perfectly manicured for her imminent first-class departure to the British Virgin Islands. She was dressed in an elegant cream suit and expensive-looking patent snakeskin heels which emphasised the bullet-hard calves she'd acquired from her daily work-out at the same gym Princess Diana used. She was leaning over a pile of papers on her black lacquered desk, her pointed face set into its usual frown, and even from the other side of the glass Charlie could see the deep crease in the thick foundation on her forehead.

As if sensing her gaze Philippa looked up, her razor-sharp black bob swinging perfectly into place. Charlie waved a hand in greeting, but half an hour before her departure, Philippa had dispensed with any display of grace. She turned her wrist and glanced at the diamond-encrusted Tag Heuer before beckoning Charlie into her office.

'Hi! Excited about your holiday?' gushed Charlie as she slipped through the door.

Philippa inspected Charlie up and down, noting her new look with a contemptuous elevation of her eyebrows. 'No. I've been here since six-thirty doing the forecasts,' she said.

Charlie shrank at her rebuff, feeling the familiar rush of guilt from the pit of her stomach and berating herself for oversleeping as she perched on the black leather chair. Philippa towered above her on the other side of the desk, scanning through a mound of documents before picking up her Waterman fountain pen, the diamond ring on her right hand glinting like an evil eye in the silence.

Eventually, Philippa scribbled on the top sheet. 'Sort this out,' she commanded, pushing the paper across the desk without looking at Charlie, who blanched at her officious manner. Within ten minutes, a stack of paperwork was piled on the desk and her mind reeling with all the instructions she had to remember.

'OK. That's about it,' said Philippa, snapping the lid back on her pen, her cold blue eyes meeting Charlie's at last. 'You're absolutely sure you're happy sorting out the presentation for Up Beat?' Her thin mouth was set in a warning.

26

'Fine,' said Charlie, irritated that Philippa didn't trust her.

'As you know, it's fairly routine, but I don't want any hitches.' Charlie gathered up the papers and tapped them on the desk, trying to appear professional. 'There won't be, not if I have anything to do with it.'

It was more than her job was worth to make a mistake on the Up Beat account. Up Beat, Philippa's 'baby', was the UK's leading high-street record retailer. It was also Bistram Huff's largest client and income source.

'Just make sure you keep an eye on Daniel. I want variations on the theme of what we did last year. Clean, simple, lots of print,' continued Philippa. She ran a manicured hand through her sleek hair.

Lots of margin, thought Charlie. Philippa always charged Up Beat a fortune for the cheap promotions they ran, frightening Nigel Hawkes, the marketing director there, into signing the invoices. Charlie knew that Bistram Huff should create more imaginative promotions for such a high-profile client, but Philippa always persuaded Si that the bottom line was more important for a growing agency.

'Don't worry, everything will be fine. Just enjoy your holiday. You deserve one,' soothed Charlie, hating herself for pandering to her boss's diva ego.

Philippa managed a flicker of a smile as she picked up the phone.

Back at her desk Charlie logged on to her computer and repaired the ladder on her inner thigh with a dab of Tipp-Ex, before spotting Bandit walking across the office dispensing bite-sized chocolate bars that the direct marketing team were using in a teaser campaign.

David Delancey had earned his nickname, Bandit, for a number of reasons, but mainly because he had a knack of hijacking business from rival agencies. Charlie watched him swaggering in his dog-tooth suit and pyschedelic silk tie and thought how boyishly attractive he was, despite the fact that he was so short.

Philippa had employed him as account manager a year ago and at first Charlie had been wary of him. He was a born wheeler-dealer and could probably sell ice to the eskimos, with his gift of the gab. Yet although he made loads of noise, usually to cover for his laziness, Charlie was fond of him.

Bandit stopped dramatically when he saw her and Charlie tipped her head, making a face in the spotlight of his attention.

'Boys!' he exclaimed, chucking chocolate to Toff and Peter. 'We have a goddess in our midst!'

Charlie laughed.

'No, really. I love it. It makes you look sophisticated in a very . . .' he groped for words . . . 'well, in a very *fuckable* sort of way.' He sat on the edge of her desk and ripped open a chocolate bar with crooked teeth, his hazel eyes teasing her.

'Flattery will get you nowhere,' said Charlie, enjoying his attention.

'What did Her Highness say?' He flicked his head in Philippa's direction.

Charlie shrugged. 'Oh, you know. She said it made me look sophisticated in a kind of fuckable way.'

Bandit laughed. 'Do you think they'll actually *let* her into the British *Virgin* Islands?' he stage whispered, referring to Philippa's reputation which was mostly of his own invention.

'She could bully her way in anywhere, believe me!' She stood up and moved around her desk. 'Caw-fee?' she asked Bandit in a Brooklyn drawl.

'Dollface, I thought you'd never ask,' he replied, loosening his tie and undoing the top button of his shirt.

As Charlie made her way to the kitchen, Bandit stuck his head around Philppa's door. 'Can I have a word?'

Philippa glanced down her sharp nose as he pulled the door shut behind him. 'Yes, but I haven't got long.'

'Gorgeous suit,' he said, flopping casually into the chair.

Philippa put her hand on her hip and looked at him. 'David, what do you want?' she asked with semi-impatience.

He spread his hands out on the desk. 'I was wondering whether you'd think about my promotion while you're away, that's all.'

Philippa stroked her Estée Lauder enhanced cheek and

laughed shortly. 'Forgive me, David, but I have better things to do on holiday than contemplate your career.' She flicked open the catches of her buff leather briefcase.

Bandit sat up in his chair. 'But you know it's time I became an account director.'

She ignored him and he paused, watching her. 'Look, I'll tell you what, while you're gone I'll bring in some new business.' He scratched the back of his closely clipped hair.

'Really!' Philippa's tone was sarcastic.

Bandit bounded out of the chair and leaned on the edge of her desk. 'Hang on a minute. You don't know what I have in mind.'

'What do you have in mind?'

'Well, I know I can get something in from the *Reporter*,' he tempted.

Philippa pursed her thin lips and looked into the space above his head. 'You might have a point. It's about time we got our teeth round some big newspaper accounts.'

Bandit beamed at her. 'So if I get a newspaper deal, you'll sort out a promotion for me when you come back?' He spelled out the deal like a born salesman.

'We'll see.' Philippa snapped the case shut.

Bandit punched the air. Her answer was as good as a yes.

Philippa picked up her Louis Vuitton handbag and placed it carefully over her shoulder pad. She looked up into Bandit's delighted face as she walked past him to the door.

'Hold the fort for me while I'm gone,' she said with a half smile.

'Consider it done!' Bandit tapped the side of his nose and restrained himself from whooping with glee as she swooped out.

In the office kitchen, the coffee machine gurgled in the corner as Charlie, her head still fuzzy, glanced mindlessly at the notice board. It was covered in curling photos of the agency Christmas party with stuck-on speech bubbles, the summer softball league table and over-photocopied jokes.

She poured the coffee into Bandit's favourite 'Same Old Shit, Just Another Day' mug as Lisa from the promotions team stood by the door looking her up and down with barely concealed awe.

'You look incredible,' said Lisa, peering up at Charlie through wire-framed glasses, her frizzy ginger hair corkscrewing in all directions. 'Have you got a new boyfriend or something?'

Charlie smiled. 'Not yet.' She offered the coffee pot and Lisa thrust out the cup in her hand. 'Talking of which, how is Gavin? Are you two still together?' Lisa was in a permanent state about slippery Gavin in the accounts department, who couldn't ever quite leave his wife.

Lisa screwed up her small features into a scowl. 'Men! The fuckers.'

'No change there then,' laughed Charlie.

Lisa hunted through the cupboard for the biscuit tin, which was plastered with a huge notice saying 'Hands Off, Client Biscuits Only,' and pulled out a custard cream.

'You should find yourself someone new,' said Charlie, watching her carefully put back the tin.

Lisa hooked off one side of the biscuit and raked the cream with her teeth. 'I tell you what. I wouldn't mind a bit of Daniel. Have you seen him today?'

Charlie blushed as she piled an extra sugar into her coffee. 'I've got a brainstorm with him this afternoon.'

Lisa smiled. 'You bitch. He's wearing the most divine jeans. Phwah, what a bum.'

'Lisa!'

'He's all come to bed eyes and gone to bed hair. Mind you, he'd never fancy anyone around here. I expect he goes out with models and actresses.'

Charlie wrinkled her nose. 'I expect so,' she agreed, looping her fingers through the mug handles and making for the door. 'See ya!'

'I'm going on a toast run,' said Pete as she slumped in her chair and pressed the backs of her fingers on her burning cheeks.

Pete's pencil was poised above his Post-It pad. 'You want the usual?'

Her stomach, activated by the thought of Marmite on toast, growled. Perhaps it would be best if her diet started tomorrow, once she'd got over her hangover.

The creative department of Bistram Huff was situated on the first floor and, as Charlie nervously knocked on the open door, the thud of a dance music station blared from a bank of stereo equipment. Poppy Raid, the creative assistant, wobbled on patent platforms and twisted one plait round her index finger, noisily chewing gum. She was wearing multicoloured over-the-knee socks and a bored expression. Most people assumed she was a lesbian, but Charlie noticed that her gaze didn't leave Daniel's bum as he leaned over the desk.

'Hi,' said Charlie as she stepped into the room.

Daniel swivelled round. 'Come in, come in,' he said, beckoning her over to the large round table in the middle of the desks. At one end of the room, Will Wilmot sat at a huge Apple Macintosh screen.

'Turn that down, Will,' shouted Daniel. Will slid off his high stool and pressed a button on the stereo and the bright room was quiet, apart from the muffled blast of a barge slithering along the Thames below them.

'You've changed your hair,' said Daniel softly. He smiled as she met his stare. 'I like it.'

Thank you God, thought Charlie. He likes it! She wanted to can-can on the desk. 'Thanks,' she mumbled, sitting down at the table. She breathed in Daniel's knicker-melting scent and tried to calm her racing heart.

Oblivious to her inner turmoil, Daniel turned back to the open job bag on the desk. He flicked through the last two years' promotional work for Up Beat.

'Bandit will be here in a sec,' Charlie blurted, opening her pad and underlining the words Up Beat Brainstorm in her thick pen.

Daniel nodded. 'Would you like some coffee?'

'I would,' said Bandit, pushing through the doors. 'Mine's black, one sugar.' He winked at Poppy who slouched to the kitchen.

Bandit flopped on to the seat opposite Charlie and rubbed his hands together. 'What do you think, Daniel?'

Daniel flipped through the plastic sheets, looking at the in-store posters and tent cards. 'This is shit,' he said. 'These "money off" and "two for the price of one" promotions are so dated. It's a record store, for Christ's sake, not a supermarket.' He pushed the work away in disgust.

'Well, Philippa wants the same kind of thing this time,' said Charlie. 'By yesterday.'

'What's the story with Up Beat anyway, can you fill me in?' asked Daniel, his direct gaze making a tingling sensation flutter in Charlie's stomach. She lowered her eyes as she carefully explained the history of the account and how Philippa made a huge mark-up on all the printing.

'You're the creative director, can't we do something a bit more imaginative?' interrupted Bandit.

Daniel strode towards the window and ran a hand through his hair. Poppy clonked Bandit's coffee on the table. 'You're right. I think we should do something different,' Daniel announced, turning round, his face lit up by a boyish grin. 'What do you think, Charlie?'

He was so good-looking that her stomach somersaulted and she quickly cleared her throat. 'Putting Philippa's wishes aside for a minute, let's go back to the original brief,' she said, taking a stack of papers from under her folder. 'We're trying to drive people into the stores, to make it worth their while buying CDs from Up Beat and not from anywhere else.'

Poppy snapped a bubble. 'Surely that's impossible. People have so much choice these days. At the end of the day it's all about convenience.'

'You're right. We need to get the Up Beat name out there. Get people talking about it,' said Bandit.

Charlie brushed her hair behind her ear. 'Then maybe we should take a different approach. Up until now, all the promotions have been focused on rewarding the people who already buy their music from Up Beat.'

'So?'

'So, we're missing out on a huge opportunity. I think we should take the appeal wider. This promotion should be about communicating with people outside the shop environment.'

'Yes, but it's not an advertising brief,' said Daniel.

'I know,' continued Charlie. 'But if the ultimate aim is for Up Beat to sell more CDs we have to get people who wouldn't normally shop at Up Beat into the stores.'

'Surely the best way to do that is to tie up with a third party,' said Bandit. 'Do you remember the holiday voucher promotion we did?'

Charlie twisted her lips as she thought. 'Good idea, but I think we need something more direct, something that has an immediate reward.'

'You mean offer free CD tokens with tea bags or washing powder?' Daniel looked sceptical.

'No, I was thinking bigger than that.'

'Go on.'

She was winging it now and she shrugged as she looked at Daniel and Bandit. 'Why don't we add a competitive element?'

Daniel sat back on the desk as they fired suggestions round the table and Charlie forced herself not to look at his taut buttocks. She made sketchy notes in her book, her fingers longing to caress Daniel's lean thighs.

'I think Charlie was on the right track earlier,' he said eventually. 'We're going round in circles. We should make the promotion more fun.'

'Like a scratchcard or something,' mumbled Charlie.

Daniel held up his hand to stop the others talking and looked at Charlie. 'What did you say?'

She was astonished by his intensity and blushed as she noticed everyone staring at her. 'I said, what about a scratchcard promotion? People are receptive to them because of the Lottery Instants. We could run a national promotion and if people rubbed off the right codes on their cards they could go to Up Beat and claim a free CD.'

'Go on.'

She looked at him coyly as he stood up. 'It would be a good way to use the budget,' she said. 'If we could do it.'

Daniel put one foot up on the chair and leaned towards the table. 'And we'd still get all the print and we could tie up with a publishing group. Think of the exposure for Up Beat. They'd love it.'

Charlie felt a warm glow of pride.

'What do you think, Will?' Daniel asked.

'It sounds like a great idea, but what magazines would you target?'

Charlie thought for a moment. 'I think a newspaper would be better,' she said. 'Perhaps we could run a national promotion over a weekend in one of the tabloids?'

Bandit shot out of his chair. 'Yes! Yes,' he interjected. 'Tom Johnson at the *Reporter*!'

'Who?' asked Charlie.

'Tom Johnson, my mate. He's the director of promotions there. Don't you see? This kind of promotion will be right up his street.'

Daniel stroked his smoothly shaved jaw as he mulled over this latest suggestion. 'The *Reporter* would be cool. I can see it now. Every reader would have a card and, say, a one per cent chance of winning a CD. Simple. We'll call it "Up Beat's Groove on Down", or something. I refuse to have one more promotion called Music Mania!'

Charlie shook her head. 'It would be a great promotion, but Philippa won't like it. She'd freak if we agreed something like this.'

Bandit crossed his arms smugly. 'No she wouldn't.'

'That's all very well for you to say, but you wouldn't be the one in the firing line,' she retorted.

'Scaredy cat.'

'I'm not scared, I'm being practical.'

'Charlie's right,' said Poppy. 'I've seen Philippa go mad about changes to the Up Beat plans. That was half the reason why the last creative director got sacked.'

'Who's presenting the proposals?' asked Daniel.

'Si is, in a fortnight.'

'OK,' Daniel turned to face Poppy. 'Can you and Will do the visuals for the presentation as Philippa wants them and I'll sort out the new concepts? We haven't got much time, so let's get cracking.' He hooked his thumb into the back of his jeans pocket, dimples appearing as he smiled.

Charlie stood up, wanting to rip open his shirt and bury her face in the ruffle of dark hair. She'd have to pull out all the stops with Si to get him to agree to the plans, but she couldn't back down now. 'I'll talk to Si,' she said uneasily.

Daniel winked at her. 'I'm sure you'll persuade him. After all, you're not just a pretty face.'

Charlie rolled her eyes at his corny comment, but she was glowing with his compliment as she pushed open the door.

Rich was in a café in South Kensington, spending his lonely Sunday washing down a full English breakfast with a gallon of tea, brooding on the fact that Charlie had been working for the last two weekends. Furthermore, she'd been totally preoccupied with this Up Beat promotion she was preparing and when he had seen her, all she'd done was swoon around the living room extolling the virtues of the *gorgeous* creative director. Rich was sceptical. Daniel sounded like an arrogant tosser, if you asked him.

Pushing his empty plate away he settled back into the green plastic seat. His breakfast hadn't shaken him from his grumpy mood. Rich never, ever got angry, but today he was feeling irritated. So far, he'd been the victim of three of his pet hates: all the inserts from his Sunday paper had scattered over the wet pavement as soon as he stepped out of the news-agent's, one of his egg yolks hadn't been runny and the couple at the next table were talking to each other in baby voices. He picked up the travel supplement and shook it out, but the glamorous destinations just added to his gloom. What he needed was a break, something exciting to happen to him.

He put his elbow on the table, humming along to the Crowded House CD which was playing, and resting his cheek on his fist, he stared out of the window. It was still raining outside, but hopefully the downpour would cleanse the dirty streets and lift the oppressive, overcast muggy weather of the past few days.

At the next table, the girl had started her baby-voiced whining again and he was just thinking that he was glad he wasn't in a relationship when he heard the door open and a short girl ran in. She shook herself in the doorway and brushed off the carrier bag she'd been using as an umbrella. She looked around the crowded café before making her way to Rich's table and the three spare seats surrounding him.

'Mind if I sit here?' she asked, hunching off her leather jacket.

When Rich pictured himself with a woman she was either a Charlie look-alike, or a Fiona-type from Fulham with a cookery qualification and a fine assortment of Alice bands. But he was fascinated by this green-eyed urchin who slipped into the seat opposite and started scribbling notes in a black sketch book. He observed her from behind his *Observer* and when she sucked the end of her biro, Rich decided there was definitely something sexy about her.

He was about to start a conversation when he was overcome with shyness. Instead he picked up the review section and hid behind it. He was hopeless at approaching girls. Charlie said that Rich had 'I AM NICE. TELL ME YOUR PROBLEMS' tattooed on his forehead. Usually when people had an 'It's so nice that I'm your friend and not your lover' conversation, you could guarantee they'd be rutting like rabbits within two hours. In Rich's case, when girls said 'It's so nice that I'm your friend and not your lover,' they meant it. He only ever received signed Valentine cards.

He risked another glance at the girl. She was looking straight at him, trying to read the upside-down headlines. Blushing, Rich turned his paper round, cursing himself for being so un-cool. She laughed.

'I'm always doing that,' she said in a lilting Irish accent.

The waitress approached the table and took Rich's empty plate. 'What can I get you?' she asked the girl. She picked up the laminated menu and flipped over the pages. The waitress waited impatiently for her order.

The girl nodded to Rich's plate. 'What did you have?'

'The breakfast special.'

'Any good?'

'Filling.'

'Good. I'm starving. I'll have a vegetarian one of those,' she said.

Rich looked at her. She was so small, he wondered how she would manage it.

'I'm Maria, but everyone calls me Pix,' she said, finishing off the sentence in the book with a stabbed full stop. She smiled at him, revealing overlapping ivory teeth.

'I'm Richard, but my friends call me Rich,' he said. 'Not that I am,' he added, trying to fill the space that had been created by her open stare. He took in her fresh face and clear skin and imagined that without the nose stud and with long hair, she was the kind of girl who'd be chosen to advertise soap.

Rich held her gaze, realising that she was listening to the conversation on the next table and he laughed when she pulled a face in disgust as 'Pooky' and 'Mr Fluffy' got up to pay their bill.

'What's that?' he asked, breaking their stare and nodding at the incomprehensible squiggles and odd sketches on her book.

'Ah, nothing, I'm planning out my final year project,' she said, glancing down at the page.

'What's it about?'

'Photography,' stated Pix. 'To be honest, it's the oldest trick in the book. It's entitled "Appearances and reality as explored through the photographic image". She put inverted commas round the title with her ink-stained fingers. 'It sounds grand, but everyone on the course is doing pretentious stuff on post-modernism or media exploitation, so I figure this will seem refreshing.'

'Go on?'

Pix looked at him as if sizing him up to tell a secret, then launched into an explanation of her project.

Rich listened, worried about his stubbly chin and surreptitiously trying to see whether his armpits were damp while meeting the occasional glance of her earnest eyes with reassuring nods.

'How does it sound?' she asked, as the waitress arrived with a loaded plate.

'I'm no expert, but I think I got the gist of it. To be or not to be and all that jazz?' he ventured.

'Exactly!' Pix beamed. She ruffled her boyishly cropped hair. 'Maybe I'm being a little long-winded, you know what I mean, like?'

'Not at all,' lied Rich.

'Ah, it'll have to do. I've got too much other work on.' She pulled the plate of food towards her.

Rich sipped his tea. 'Like what?'

Pix nodded, trying to chew her mouthful before she spoke. 'I design flyers for clubs.'

'That sounds very trendy. Do you go clubbing a lot?'

Pix shook her head, piling up her fork with fried bread and, Rich noticed, gloriously runny eggs. 'Sometimes, but it's usually too noisy. I'm more of a Van Morrison and an early night girl.'

Rich laughed. 'A woman after my own heart.'

By the time Pix had devoured her breakfast and Rich was shaking with caffeine overload, the rain had stopped and, without thinking, he asked if she fancied a walk. To his surprise, she agreed.

In Hyde Park, the grass was still wet but the air was clear and warm, filled with the tangy, sweet smell of tarmac after rain. They strolled past Kensington Palace, dodging roller-blading maniacs whose tracks snaked across the drying paths.

Pix shifted her knapsack on her back. 'Let's play a game. You ask me a question, any question, and then I'll ask you one. You start. Ask me anything!'

Rich breathed in, looking across to the pond and the kids with their miniature yachts. 'OK. What's the worst thing you've ever done?'

'That's easy,' she said, and Rich found himself choking with laughter as she described her severance from the

Catholic faith which involved giving her then boyfriend a blow job in the confession box of Father Ryan's church.

Pix turned round and skipped backwards along the path as she looked at him.

'OK. My turn. Where do you live?' she asked.

'Battersea. It's a bit grotty, but it's home. You?'

Pix breathed in and looked about her at the fertile trees, their leaves shining in the sunshine. 'I know all about grot. I've got a place in a housing community in Vauxhall.'

'You mean you share cups of lentils?'

Pix pulled a face at his gentle mocking, but gradually she told him about her home life and then about her dreams of a shutter-clicking future in which she belly-crawled through war zones to capture images of human suffering that would break the heart of the world.

When Rich asked her about her relationships, Pix was quite matter-of-fact. He was half expecting her to declare her state of gay liberation, but to his surprise she listed a run of disastrous relationships with 'New Age' men.

'Ah, men are men.' She shrugged. 'Nothing will change them. Marriage, time, money, women . . .'

'We're not all that bad!'

'Maybe not. I guess I'm waiting to be surprised.'

They'd reached the bandstand and Pix sat in a deckchair in the sunshine, peeling off a jumper from her skinny frame. 'So tell me about you. I want to know more.' She tucked the jumper behind her and leaned back.

Rich observed the smooth undulations of her small breasts beneath the fabric of her khaki vest and, although he preferred more curvy women, decided he certainly wouldn't kick her out of bed for farting.

She put her arms above her head and basked in the rays of the sun while Rich looked at her hairy armpits. He scanned through his repertoire of anecdotes and found none that would do. He thought about making up some stories about getting lost in Tibet and discovering the secrets of the universe from a wizened old monk, but he knew that Pix would see right through him.

'Well? I'm waiting.' She opened one eye.

Not for the first time, Rich realised that his life was boring. He skipped over his grammar school education and uneventful middle-class youth in Brighton, quickly using up his supply of travelling and 'women that got away' stories. He trailed off.

'So. What do you know about?' asked Pix, cocking her head at him.

He shrugged. 'Nothing much.'

'Rubbish. Blokes know about all sorts of stuff. I call it bloke knowledge. Things that us girls don't have a clue about.'

'Like what?'

'Well, you're born knowing the rules of cricket and how to put a bicycle chain back on, who's in the premier league . . .'

Rich laughed.

'And you know about plumbing. All men know roughly how a washing machine works. To me all that stuff is as daunting as tampering with the ignition system of a rocket.'

'Yeah, I'm quite good with cars, but you know about girl stuff which is far more interesting and deeply mysterious.'

'You mean like gussets and deniers and needlework?'

Rich passed his hand over the top of his head making an aeroplane noise. 'You're a different species.'

Pix smiled at him. 'Love life?'

'Hopeless.'

'So basically, what you're telling me is that you're a single, meat-eating, middle-class, conservative male,' said Pix, punctuating his five qualities on her fingers.

'That sounds awful!'

'Harsh, but fair. One thing's for sure – we have nothing in common.' She looked at the empty bandstand. 'Still. You need livening up and I need a bit of culture, so I think we should hang out for a while.'

'So that's settled then,' said Rich, feeling like he had stepped unwittingly into the pages of *Generation X*.

'I should be making tracks,' said Pix later, as they neared

the gate of the park. She groped in the pockets of her army trousers for a pen, eventually emptying them on to the path.

'What's this?' asked Rich, picking up a stone.

'It's my moonstone. It must be working.'

Rich turned it over in his hand. 'What's it supposed to do?'

'Moonstones are great. They attract people and good things to you.' She closed his hand around it. 'Why don't you have it? Ask it to bless you.'

'You don't mind?'

'Not at all. If you have a crystal they're not supposed to touch the ground, so I'd have to cleanse it anyway. You might as well keep it.'

'Thanks,' said Rich, clutching it like a lucky charm. 'I'll tell you what,' he added, with a flash of inspiration, 'I'll take you out if you like. How about going to a concert?'

'You're on, but only if I can take you out too. I'll show you my London. A Pix O'Reilly mystery tour. You'll love it, I promise!' Rich couldn't help smiling back at her.

'You should smile more often. You've got a cracking pair of chops,' she said and Rich felt a warm sensation rush through him. He spent so much time paying attention to other people that he'd forgotten how amazing compliments made him feel.

Pix wrote his numbers on the back of her hand before they parted and as she bounced down the street in her black boots, Rich kept looking over his shoulder at her retreating figure. He clutched his moonstone and felt happier than he'd done in weeks.

The atmosphere at Bistram Huff was always lighter when Philippa was on holiday, but Charlie almost wished she was back. Her colleagues used the absence of the dictator as an excuse to put their feet up and when Charlie walked in on Monday morning, she encountered Bandit standing on a chair tampering with the office phone system.

'What are you doing?' she asked.

'We've decided to change the music on hold,' he explained as he inserted a new CD into the machine and leapt down from the chair. 'OK. Ready,' he shouted across the office, and one of the guys picked up the phone. Within seconds a group had gathered and were sniggering around the earpiece.

Charlie sat down at her desk, smiling as Bandit strutted towards his admirers and put the phone to his ear, then roared with laughter. She picked up her phone.

'Sadie, can you put me on hold for a moment?' she asked, curious about the boys' prank. The voice of a banned American soul singer pulsated with lurid sexuality through the office telephone and Charlie laughed and shook her head at Bandit who was now pelvic thrusting around the desk.

She flicked open the Bistram Huff directory and checked Daniel's extension number which she already knew off by heart, cradling the phone against her ear. Should she call him and greet him with a friendly 'hello', or invent an excuse to have a meeting with him?

Sadie came back on the line and the music stopped abruptly, rousing Charlie from her daydream.

'The triple M is in five minutes,' Sadie announced.

'Thanks,' mumbled Charlie, mentally pulling up her socks and starting on a list of the team brainstorms that needed to be planned. A wave of panic and guilt swept over her – she should have prepared for the Monday morning meeting last night. Thank God Philippa wasn't in.

In the boardroom Pete's peeling nose was the subject of discussion. He'd been given a green card by his pregnant girlfriend Sharon and had been out with the boys all weekend. His bragging was in full swing as Charlie entered the room, but he still had time to slip in his latest sexist joke.

'What's the similarity between a woman and a tiled floor?' he quipped.

'Don't know,' said Toff.

'Lay them right the first time and you can walk all over them for the rest of your life!'

'Old joke, old joke,' nodded Bandit as he grabbed a toffee from the bowl in the centre of the table and crammed it in his mouth.

Charlie called the meeting to order. 'OK everyone, it's going to be a bastard of a busy week. We need to know everyone's schedule. Toff, you start,' she said, stirring her coffee with a ballpoint pen.

Marcus Deyton-Smith fidgeted with his mangled notebook. He had been nicknamed Toff because of his public-school accent, but unfortunately his trust fund had not stretched far enough for him to pursue a career as a jockey, or his intelligence far enough to be a racing journalist. Instead he had fallen into sales promotion by accident, adding a touch of old school City style to the agency with his tailored pin-striped suits and red braces. He infuriated Charlie with his incredible lack of common sense.

As usual Toff's top-line work commitments drifted into a stuttering speech about disastrous suppliers and petty problems. Charlie tried to listen and be sympathetic, but after fifteen minutes, when his pontificating showed no signs of abating, she started to doodle. 'Charlie Goldsmith', 'Mrs Daniel Goldsmith', she scrawled, before drawing a square. In it she wrote 'Mr & Mrs Bright invite you to the wedding of their daughter Charlotte and Daniel . . .'

'Charlie?' Bandit slapped her knee with a rolled up copy of *Campaign*. She jolted, embarrassed that she had not been paying attention.

'Your turn,' said Pete, anxious to get on with the meeting so that he could discuss football. Charlie looked around her at the expectant faces.

'Si is at the meeting with Up Beat this morning, so we'll know what we're doing for the next few months,' she informed her colleagues.

'How were the visuals from the hunk of the creative department?' asked Bandit.

'Fine.' Charlie stroked a lock of hair behind her ear. 'Daniel did a great job.'

'Aha! Do we detect a slight flutter of the old hormones? You're not going to fall prey to his charms like everyone else in this building, are you?' Bandit teased, folding his arms.

Pull yourself together, Charlie reprimanded herself, stung by his words.

'He's not my type,' she said, brushing Bandit's feet off the table.

'Yeah, right.'

Simon Huff was at least two feet too short for his weight. His balding head was permanently beaded with sweat, mainly because his office, known as 'the Jungle', was heated to a stifling tropical temperature. It overflowed with a large collection of ferns and rubber plants, which he claimed reminded him of his Australian homeland.

Behind the dense foliage, a gimmick cuckoo clock which was one of Si's favourite toys pounced into action. 'It's three o'clock, wise guy,' chirped the electronic bird in the clock's doorway as Si called Charlie and Daniel into his den to announce that the meeting with Up Beat had been an unmitigated success.

'Nigel Hawkes was leaving a trail of slime as usual, but fortunately the European group director was there. He loved the whole concept of the scratchcard promotion. You and Daniel definitely make a winning team,' he gushed.

'That's wonderful, but won't Philippa be furious?' asked Charlie, trying to steer Si towards the reality of the situation. 'You know how protective she is over Up Beat.'

'The group director is the ultimate boss and the man from Del Monte – he say yes!' Si's belly wobbled beneath his pink shirt as he chuckled and rubbed his chubby hands together. 'We're going to make a fortune, so Philippa can't complain, can she?' He grinned and nodded at Daniel. 'With your visuals and Charlie's brains . . .' he thrust his hands out like a preacher . . . 'the world is our lobster.'

Daniel turned his cheeky glance on Charlie. 'Our success is only due to the fact that Charlie trusts her intuition.'

Charlie cast her eyes down away from his intimate look, frightened that she would leap across the space between them and ravish him until he begged for mercy.

'And I trust it too,' said Si. 'I've got high hopes for you, young lady.'

'I'll second that,' said Daniel.

Charlie felt herself blushing.

'I certainly look forward to working with you more in the future.' Daniel looked directly at her breasts.

'Oh you shall, you shall,' said Si, heaving himself out of his chair. He reached up, dark circles of sweat under his arms as he put a hand around each of their shoulders. 'Starting now. We have work to do.'

'Charlie?' Daniel took her arm gently as Si blustered away to a meeting. She turned to face him and Daniel rubbed his hand on the back of his neck. 'I'm glad it's worked out.'

She shook her head. 'You did all the hard work, the promotion would never have worked without you.' She stopped abruptly, realising she was gushing and that Daniel's eyes were scanning her mouth and moving up her nose to her eyebrows, as if he were mentally kissing her.

'We've still got to find a newspaper willing to run it,' she stuttered.

Daniel teased her with his eyes. 'You'll sort it out,' he said. 'I've got this feeling you always get what you want.'

He knows! He realises that I fancy him, thought Charlie. She wanted to run away, but Daniel was not setting her free and she felt as if she was being drawn into his gaze. She met his eyes. 'Not always.'

He reached forward and stroked her cheek briefly. 'Where there's a will, there's a way.'

Seconds later Charlie was on the phone to Kate. 'He fancies me, I'm sure he was flirting with me,' she squeaked after she'd relayed the conversation in an excited whisper. 'And he wouldn't unless he felt something too, would he?'

Kate laughed. 'Stop being such a stupid cow and calm down.'

Charlie whimpered.

'He probably does fancy you, but are you sure you're not reading too much into the situation?'

Charlie exhaled and sat back. 'You're right, I'm projecting my desires. I've read *Women Who Love Too Much*.'

Kate tutted. 'Stop right there. You don't have to spiral into pyscho-babble. If you're so sure the sparks are flying, why don't you ask him out tonight. Strike while the iron's hot and all that?'

'I can't,' hissed Charlie, sitting forward on her chair. 'Everyone will know. Anyway we've got the agency softball match tonight.'

'Chat him up there then.'

Charlie tapped her lips. 'I'm not sure he's coming. He's a bit too sophisticated for that kind of thing, but maybe I could get Bandit to fix the teams so he'd have to come.'

'Charlie?'

'Hmm?'

'Be cool.'

Charlie laughed as she delved inside her jacket to check her sweating armpits. 'Me? Cool? I'm a fucking iceberg!'

'That's my girl.'

Charlie squeezed her memory foam stress toy as she explained the latest Up Beat developments to the team.

'I didn't think that newspapers did instant-win scratch-cards,' said Toff, miming a cricket bowl.

'They do now,' said Bandit. 'Time to call Tom Johnson, I think.'

Pete, who was adding one more paper-clip to the long chain that was draped over his lamp and decorated with football cards, was surprised. 'You've kept that contact quiet!'

'Waiting for the right moment,' said Bandit, flicking through his card index.

'Do you really think you can sort it out, just like that?' asked Charlie.

Bandit retrieved the white card and looked at the number. 'Do bears shit in the woods?'

Charlie watched him chatting into the phone, his feet on the edge of the desk. 'OK, Friday at ten. Sounds fantastic. Yeah, and we'll get a window for lunch. Our shout. Of course. We'll do a lunch visible from space. Yeah, fantastic. See you then. Cheers!' He plopped the receiver back and grinned, his hands behind his head.

Charlie looked around the team and they all turned to Bandit, impressed.

'Now then. Who shall we have in our softball team?' asked Bandit, ostentatiously ignoring their stares. 'I'll e-mail the females, shall I?' He sat up and clattered the keys on his keyboard. 'Boys?'

Charlie laughed at him. 'Don't forget the creatives, you know how snotty they get when they're left out,' she said as flippantly as possible and meandered back to her desk, glad that Bandit couldn't see her burning cheeks.

Bob Grafton was the main print buyer for most of the sales promotion agencies in London and he knew everyone. As well as being jovial and friendly, he was an excellent source of gossip and could always be cajoled into playing for Bistram Huff's softball team, usually turning up late in his clapped-out rusty Mercedes with a bootful of beer. He looked like an off-duty Santa Claus as he slouched on the home base in ridiculous shorts, swigging beer.

'Come on now. Don't let that blonde hair stop you concentrating,' he teased Charlie as she stood in front of him.

'Shut up, Bobby, or I'll clout you with this,' she said, gripping the wooden baseball bat and laughing.

'Did anyone ever tell you that you look fantastic in shorts?' he asked as the pitcher slapped the hard white ball into the leather glove.

'That's more than can be said for you!' She giggled, and prepared herself for the pitch. Above her the clear blue sky stretched out over Regent's Park. This was a crucial run. If she missed this ball, or it was caught, the team would be out and she would be to blame. Watch the ball, she thought. Focus.

Suddenly she'd hit it, the ball soaring up towards the orange sun, suspended above the tree tops. She flung the bat down and could hear Lisa screaming at her to run.

At second base, Paul from the direct marketing team tried to get in her way, but she dodged round him. She could see Will in the outfield overarm the ball towards the square, but she kept on running. Her team were yelling now from the baseline, 'Go, go, go!' She sprinted into the base, just as the ball flew through the air towards Bob, who was looking in the opposite direction.

'Bob!' screamed Bandit.

Bob dropped his beer, arms and legs flailing as Charlie skidded into him, knocking him over before he could catch the ball. She'd made it. Her team had won. Breathless, she stood up and smiled at Bob, who was lumbering to his feet.

'I'll get you next time,' he chuckled as the team cheered her home run, and she playfully stuck her tongue out at him.

Charlie slapped Lisa's hand and flopped down next to her. Across the dry expanse of grass other teams were playing and Charlie lay down and closed her eyes, listening to the muffled cheers drifting in the breeze and pointing her face into the sun as she tried to catch her breath. Then she heard the crack and fizz of a can being opened near her face and opened her eyes to see Daniel, who handed her a beer.

'I didn't know you were here,' she said, sitting up hastily and straightening her T-shirt.

'And miss a winning run like that? You must be joking.'

'You saw it?'

'Of course.'

Charlie grinned as he sat down beside her.

Daniel took off his baseball cap and smoothed down his hair. He looked breathtakingly gorgeous in baggy blue shorts and battered sneakers, stretching out his long, well-defined legs on the tufty grass. 'I had no idea you were such an athlete.'

'Luck.' She sipped her beer. 'I've got hopeless hand-to-eye coordination. Great hand-to-mouth coordination, mind you.'

'That sounds good to me,' said Daniel suggestively.

'New game, new game,' shouted Bandit. 'Charlie, over here.'

She stood up and turned back to Daniel. 'Are you going to play?'

'It's not really my scene, but I guess there are advantages,' he said, looking at her legs.

Charlie smiled and brushed the dry grass from her bottom. 'Come on, then.' She held out her hand to pull him up and their eyes met, his handsome face caught in the sinking sun.

Bandit took the softball league very seriously and this was an important warm-up game, if he was going to pick the best Bistram Huff players for the match against Rectangle Marketing.

'OK, Daniel, you can play on Charlie's team, but someone will have to sit out.'

'That's not fair,' said Charlie.

'I'll sit out,' volunteered Tina, who was shaking tomato ketchup on to a hot dog from the makeshift buffet.

'Thanks, Tina. Now, Bill, you're first in to bat. Let's play ball!'

Daniel was watching Tina. 'Maybe I should sit out and let her get some exercise,' he said.

Charlie put her hand over her mouth. 'You can't say that!'

'I can. It's disgusting that a girl allows herself to be overweight. Hasn't she got any self-respect? I mean, what bloke in his right mind is going to look at her?'

Charlie nudged him in the ribs. 'Don't be so unkind. Someone will probably fancy her. It takes all sorts. Anyway, maybe she's happy being single.'

'No-one likes being single.'

Charlie was about to say she did, but she stopped herself. It wasn't true. She looked at her hands.

'Have I hit a raw nerve?'

'Not really.'

'So you're single?'

She nodded, feeling as if she were admitting a terrible crime, but she didn't have time to explain because Daniel was next on to the pitch.

'This one's for you,' he said as he brushed past her and socked the ball as if he were trying to hit it to another galaxy.

Charlie shook her head. 'Show off!' she said, but she couldn't tear her eyes off him.

*

49

Charlie looked down from the glass lift to the palm trees in the atrium below. The headquarters of the *Reporter* were housed in a towering glass monolith in Canary Wharf. Bandit offered Charlie some chewing gum as the lift ascended noiselessly towards the tenth floor.

'You'll like Tom Johnson. He's a good geezer. Really. I've got a great feeling about this,' he said.

But Charlie's feelings were anything but great the moment she saw Tom. He was only just taller than Bandit with a flashy linen suit and over-Brylcreemed black hair. His skin was sun-bed orange and pock-marked from adolescent acne and Charlie noticed him checking his reflection in the glass as he approached them.

'Hey, buddy,' Tom said, shadow-boxing with Bandit.

'Looking good,' said Bandit, slapping Tom on the back and walking with him towards a large meeting room. Ignored by them both, Charlie trailed behind feeling disgruntled.

It wasn't until they were seated at the table and Tom and Bandit had exhausted all their gossip that the meeting finally begun. Tom leaned back in his chair and looked enquiringly at Bandit and Charlie.

'So? What's the story?' he asked.

Charlie seethed inwardly as Bandit snatched the presentation away from her, explaining that they wanted the *Reporter* to run Up Beat's scratchcard promotion, embellishing his own contribution to the package and pretending that the idea had been his in the beginning.

Tom nodded before pulling out a calculator. 'So. Five mill scratchcards. Not bad. I guess we could consider it. Obviously you'll have to print the cards and supply them to us in time.' He jangled his wrist, shaking the chunky silver bracelet under his shirt.

'How does your sign-off procedure work?' asked Charlie.

Tom looked at her as if astonished that she had a voice. 'Well, sweetheart, I'll have to look at the opportunity and discuss it with a few people,' he said. 'I'll check the schedule. We've got quite a few promotions coming up.'

'What I mean is, do you have the authority to give us the go ahead?' said Charlie more pointedly, infuriated that he was being so patronising.

Tom Johnson waved his hand. 'Sure, sure.'

'We'll leave it with you then,' said Bandit, glaring at Charlie.

'What about Teddy Longfellow?' asked Charlie, ignoring him. She knew the reputation of the newspaper magnate who controlled every move on his papers. Bandit stood up quickly but Charlie remained seated, her hands clasped together on the table.

'Yeah. I'll have to run it past him, but Teddy and me, you know, we're like that,' he said, holding out crossed fingers.

Exactly, thought Charlie, you cross your fingers in the hope he won't sack you.

'How long will that take?' she asked through gritted teeth.

'He's kind of tough to get hold of, but I should get a window with him in the next, say, week or so. No hang on, he's away next week, so it will be the week after.'

Bandit shuffled impatiently, but Charlie simply furrowed her eyebrows at him. 'I'm afraid that's too late. We need approval sooner than that.'

Tom Johnson stood and put his hand up. 'Hey babe, no sweat. When I say it's sorted, it's sorted.'

Charlie wanted to hit him. Condescending little prat.

'So, where are we going for lunch?' he asked, turning to Bandit.

Bandit smiled ingratiatingly. 'I've booked a table at the OXO Tower.'

'I'm afraid you'll have to count me out,' said Charlie, gathering up the presentation. 'I've just remembered that I have to get back to the office.'

Neither Bandit nor Tom looked particularly upset.

'No problem,' said Tom. 'I'm sure we'll manage to amuse ourselves.'

Charlie was fuming as she walked into the lift. Bandit had promised that Tom had the authority to approve the promotion straight away, but clearly he didn't. Up Beat had approved the idea and she had to get it moving, and fast, but by the sound of things it would take Tom weeks to get it agreed at the *Reporter*. The door closed on the lift and she pressed the presentation case against her legs.

She couldn't go back to the office. She couldn't let Daniel down, or stand for Bandit making her look such a fool. It would take ages to start negotiations with another newspaper group and she cursed herself for relying on Bandit. Why did she always have to clear up the mess? She couldn't let the opportunity pass. The *Reporter* was perfect for the Up Beat promotion and she had to find a way to get them to agree. She thought of Si. What would he do? How many times had she heard him say, 'There's only one way to get things sorted in this business. Go to the top.'

I can't, she thought. She couldn't just barge in on Teddy Longfellow. He would never see her. But then she thought of Si again. 'Where I come from, there's no such word as can't. You should know that by now.'

Would Si be angry with her for taking a risk? What if the plan she was forming backfired? She would look even more of a fool. But then, if she was going to get promoted, she had to prove that she could take the initiative. Maybe it was just what she needed to get herself noticed. She started to sweat in the lift and, steeling her nerves, jabbed the top button for the executive suites.

Teddy Longfellow was on the phone when Charlie eventually blagged her way past the secretary into his oak-panelled office. Tensing her knees to stop them trembling, she stood by the door willing herself to be calm. She thought of Kate, who never got frightened in these situations. She knew what Kate's advice would be: 'Think of him in the nude.'

Viewed like that, Teddy Longfellow was much less scary, but she still felt panicky as she observed him. He was everything his name suggested. He was tall, and had short brown curly hair with day-old stubble poking from his chin. He flexed enormous fingers as he put down the phone and looked her up and down. Charlie forced her face into her friendliest smile.

'Mr Longfellow, I'm Charlie Bright,' she said, her voice catching in her throat. She had to be strong. This was her only chance. 'I'm very sorry to intrude on you like this, but I won't take up very much of your time.'

Teddy Longfellow's eyebrows raised in amusement and surprise as he shook her hand. He offered her a seat on the other side of his glass desk. 'To what do I owe this unexpected pleasure?' he asked.

Charlie took a deep breath. Don't think, she thought. Just do it. 'I have a proposal that I think might be of interest to you,' she said, smiling at him as she unzipped the case and took out the presentation.

'Then I'm all ears,' he said, leaning back in his leather chair.

Charlie stood up and spread the visuals on the desk, explaining the Up Beat promotion as succinctly and professionally as she could.

Teddy Longfellow nodded and was silent for what seemed like an eternity. 'It sounds like a good idea,' he said. 'But I'm intrigued to know why you didn't go to my promotions department.'

Charlie rested her hands on the edge of the desk. 'I did.'

'And? They said "no", right?'

'Not at all. Tom Johnson was very enthusiastic, but at the risk of sounding impertinent, I'm aware how long this kind of promotion takes to sign off and I really don't have much time.'

Teddy Longfellow tapped his fingertips together. 'I see.'

'I thought I'd find out whether you'd be interested before I took the promotion to the *Mail*. They're very keen to run it, but obviously the *Reporter* would be our first choice.'

His eyes locked with hers for a moment before he shifted forward on his chair. 'Is that so?'

She crossed both her index fingers behind her back. Please, please, just give me a break.

Teddy Longfellow flicked through her presentation document as she stood to attention on the other side of the desk, not daring to breathe.

'Well, I don't see why we can't run it. I'll get the necessary people to give you the go ahead.'

Yes! She tried to control her grin. 'Thank you, I appreciate it. I'm sure it will be a very successful promotion for the *Reporter* and, of course, for Up Beat.'

'I'm sure it will be too,' said Teddy Longfellow as she packed up the presentation and headed for the door, her feet barely touching the soft buff carpet.

'Oh, Miss Bright,' he said.

She turned around to face him.

'Just for the record. I own the *Mail* too and I know for a fact that they wouldn't take this promotion.'

Charlie blushed, her heart thumping. She'd blown it! How could she have been so stupid?

He laughed at her embarrassment. 'Don't worry,' he said. 'You can have your promotion. In fact, you should come and work for me. I like a woman with balls.'

Bandit staggered into the office at four-thirty, stinking of red wine and cigarette smoke.

'Tom's a great guy,' he slurred. 'He asked me to put in a good word with you.' He winked dramatically at Charlie. 'You could do worse.'

'Really!'

'I don't care what you do. I'm just passing on the message.' He waved his hand drunkenly. 'I told him you were an ice maiden, but anyway, as a special favour, he'll get approval for us, no problem.' He burped and slumped into his chair.

Charlie bit her lip. She had to tell him what she'd done. 'Bandit?' she began nervously.

Pete interrupted, jogging the back of Bandit's chair. 'Come on. Si wants us all in the meeting room.'

'Coming, coming,' said Bandit, holding on to the desk for support.

'Pull yourself together,' said Charlie. 'Si will freak if he sees you in this state.' Bandit smiled at her, his eyes bloodshot, and draped his arm around her shoulder. 'It's just as well I've got you to look out for me then.'

In the meeting room, Si wiped the sweat away from his forehead with an oversized white handkerchief. When everyone had settled down he cracked his knuckles and looked out of the window.

'I suppose Charlie has told you all about the Up Beat promotion,' he began. There were affirmative noises. Charlie sat on her hands and bowed her head as Si spoke. She closed her eyes for a moment, knowing what was coming and what it would mean.

'You'll be pleased to hear that Teddy Longfellow at the *Reporter* has approved the promotion and that it'll be going ahead next month.'

Bandit bolted upright. 'What? How . . .?'

Ignoring his outburst, Si continued. 'Charlie here showed some remarkable initiative this morning.'

Charlie's heart was beating fast. She should have told Bandit. She avoided his gaze as Si explained what she'd done.

'You did *what*?' hissed Bandit furiously. 'How could you? You've gone right over Tom's head.'

Si patrolled the view for a moment longer and stopped behind Charlie's chair. 'As you know, things have been gathering momentum round her and I know we've all been busy.' He looked around the faces of the team and put his hand on the back of the chair. Charlie's stomach tightened in nervousness.

'I think this is an appropriate time to announce that we've decided to put some more structure in the team,' he said, moving to the head of the table. 'I'm pleased to tell you that we've decided to promote Charlie to account director.' He thrust his hand towards Charlie like a music hall compère.

Charlie put her hand over her mouth. 'Oh my God,' she gasped as the team gave a spontaneous round of applause.

'That's great,' enthused Pete.

Toff smiled, 'Congratulations, Charlie.'

She looked over at Si, her eyes wide with shock.

Bandit stood up, his face contorted in an angry grimace as he supported himself on the edge of his chair. 'Well, well, well,' he sneered.

Charlie looked at him. 'Please, Bandit,' she began. 'I had no idea. It's not like you think.'

Si looked at him sternly and Bandit held himself in check with difficulty. 'Well done,' he said. 'What on earth will Philippa say?'

Charlie looked at Si for reassurance.

'She suggested it in the first place,' he lied.

Charlie put down the phone to Rich as a new e-mail flashed up on her screen. 'Congratulations,' it said. 'I think we should celebrate. Love D.'

Love D. Love? Love! She opened a new e-mail message. 'What do you have in mind?' she typed and clicked on the send button. She imagined Daniel sitting by his computer and a thrill of anticipation swept over her.

'Are you free tomorrow night?' the simple message came up. She touched the screen as if she could fondle the letters of the proposal she had dreamed about.

'Maybe,' she typed. She'd have to get out of her Friday night session with Rich in the 51, but this was so exciting! She stared at her computer screen waiting for the reply.

'Then you're coming out clubbing with me. No excuses. I'll pick you up at ten.'

Charlie pressed the pre-programmed button on her phone to Kate's direct line.

'Bingo!' she said, not waiting for Kate to say hello.

'Let me guess, um . . .'

Charlie squeaked with impatience. 'Durrr. Daniel.'

'He asked you out?'

'Yep!'

'Oh my God. What did he say?'

'He didn't.'

'What do you mean?'

'He e-mailed me!'

Kate laughed.

'You've got to help me. I'm going clubbing with him, so we have to shop. Oh, and I've been promoted,' gushed Charlie, standing up as she saw Si beckoning her.

'Wait,' said Kate. 'Slow down.'

'I gotta go. Later.' She dropped the phone in its cradle and squeezed her cheeks which were aching from grinning so much.

'Come with me,' said Si, guiding her out of the office to the lift.

'I managed to get it all arranged quickly,' he whispered, as they stepped out of the lift in the underground staff car park. He gestured to the green Mazda MX5.

Charlie gasped and, forgetting professional etiquette, hugged him. He patted her as she gushed with thanks.

'You deserve it,' he said, handing her the keys. 'You'd better take it for a spin around the block, see if it's to your liking!'

Charlie ran her fingers over the walnut dashboard and gripped the steering wheel like a Formula One racing driver.

Si laughed and shook his head. 'You have fun,' he bellowed in the echoing car park.

She sped into the bright sunshine. It was time to convertible flirt. Hitching up her skirt, she reached into her handbag for her sunglasses before tuning in to Radio One and turning up the Spice Girls.

Laughing with glee she drove along the Embankment, carving up a black cab driver who looked furious until he peered down at her bare thighs and wolf-whistled.

'Boadicea, check out my chariot!' Charlie yelled to the bronze statue, before wheel-spinning away at the traffic lights by Big Ben.

She sped around Parliament Square, blowing a kiss to the statue of Winston Churchill. 'Cheer up, Winnie,' she laughed, not noticing the fluorescent-vested cyclist wobbling on his racer in her wake.

Revving up into a higher gear, she passed Buckingham Palace and saw that the flag was flying.

'Hello, Liz.' She waved and breathed in the smell of freshly cut grass from Green Park. She two-wheeled round the block to Trafalgar Square, waving at Nelson on his column before gliding up the Strand, winking at a City gent who was crossing to Simpson's.

Things have changed so much, she thought as she slowed down to cross Waterloo Bridge. This was her favourite view of London. The sun beat down, making the Thames sparkle like her eyes. She looked out at the turrets of the law courts and thought of Rich. He'd been so pleased about her promotion and she couldn't wait to show him the car and tell him about Daniel. These must be lucky knickers, she thought as she looked over to the grey dome of St Paul's against the clear blue sky.

She breathed in, intoxicated by the air of the capital city that she adored. 'I love this place,' she said aloud. 'Nothing will ever make me leave.'

Rich rearranged the candles on the kitchen table, wondering whether it was too early to light them.

'Best to wait,' he said to Kev, who was treading purposefully across the lino towards the oven where Rich's lemon chicken was roasting. Rich picked an olive from the bowl on the table and went through to the lounge, his ears on tenterhooks for the sound of Charlie's key in the door.

He had come home early to cook her a surprise celebratory meal, knowing that she was over the moon about her promotion. Champagne was chilling in the fridge along with the oysters he'd bought from the fish market, and he'd even made her favourite garlic potatoes. She'd love it. He smiled to himself and looked at his watch. Where was she? Even if she'd gone out for a drink after work, she should be home by now.

He put a tape in the video to record *Brookside* and went back into the kitchen to open an expensive bottle of New Zealand white wine. He was pouring himself a glass when the phone rang. 'That's her now,' he told Kev.

But it wasn't Charlie, it was Pix.

'I'm about to have a bath,' she explained. 'And I wrote your number on my hand in indelible ink, but after my bath it will finally be gone, so I thought I'd call to check you still wanted to go out.'

Rich was flustered by her forthrightness. 'Yes. I . . .' he stuttered.

'It's just I was thinking about you. I know there's all those rules, like you're supposed to wait for a bit and then be cool, but I'm so impatient.'

Rich couldn't help softening at her refreshing honesty. 'I've been thinking about you too.' He put his leg over the back of the sofa and slid down on to the cushions.

'I'm not being pushy, I know what you English men are like. You're very delicate.'

Rich laughed. 'Don't worry, I can handle it.'

'I had such a good time the other day and I'd like to see you again, so you ought to know that I'm free on Tuesday.'

'I guess it's a date then. I'll get tickets for something.'

'You don't have to.'

'I want to. Where would you like to go?'

'Surprise me. Let's do something you like, something you care about.'

'OK.'

'Now then. My pips are going, but I have to ask you something.'

'Go on.'

'It's an ego thing.'

Rich laughed. 'You have an ego?'

'Of course.'

'Go on.'

'I need to know whether you would have called me, that's all.'

'Why?'

'Because I'll start obsessing that I've thrown myself at you.'

Rich shook his head and laughed. 'I would have called you, OK?'

'And now you think I'm mad.'

'Yes, but that's because you are.'

Pix had a smile in her voice. 'Good. Just checking.'

Charlie shuffled out of the changing room in Hype DF, her jeans bunched around her ankles. The tight black dress hugged her cleavage, scooped in her waist and flattered her shapely legs.

'That's more like it,' said Kate as they looked at Charlie's reflection in the mirror.

Charlie breathed out and, turning sideways, ran her hands over the clinging fabric. 'I can't wear this. Just look at my stomach! I look fifteen months' pregnant.'

Kate pulled a face at her. 'You do not.'

'*And* these mirrors make you look thin. Just think what I'll look like in the club. Daniel will hate it.'

'It'll be dark. Anyway, it's a perfect FTD.'

Charlie delved in the scooped neck of the dress and hitched up her breasts. Kate was right, with a Plungebra it would be a fantastic tit dress. She sucked in her cheeks and scrutinised herself again.

'So what's the story with Daniel?'

Charlie pulled at the hem of the dress. 'How do you mean?'

'Relationship history, girlfriends, family?'

Standing on tiptoe, Charlie looked over her shoulder to inspect her rear view. 'I don't know.'

'But I thought you chatted him up at softball the other night.'

'I did. Do you think my bum looks too big?'

Kate groaned. 'It's vast. I'm surprised you can fit through doorways.'

Charlie wrenched off her shoes and trampled out of her jeans to get the full view of her legs.

'What did you talk about then?' asked Kate.

'Work and stuff. Don't worry, I'll find out everything soon enough,' said Charlie, realising Kate was right and that she hadn't discussed Daniel's life beyond Bistram Huff.

'What shoes would you wear?'

Charlie cocked her head. 'You should be able to tell me that. You're the Imelda Marcos of SW11.'

'How about some of those sandals you tried on.'

'But they cost a fortune.'

'So? You've been promoted and you want to seduce him, don't you?'

Charlie turned back to the mirror. 'Are you sure I won't look like a tart?' She caught Kate's eye in the mirror.

Kate shrugged. 'SAS.'

Charlie laughed. 'Good point.' She fiddled with the buttons on the back of the dress. 'A shag's a shag, but it's not exactly easy access though.'

'All good things come to those who wait,' said Kate, picking up the bundle of carrier bags. 'Talking of which, where's that bottle of vino collapso you promised me?'

'OK OK,' said Charlie, shuffling back into the changing room. 'We'll go and pick up Rich.' She struggled out of the micro-dress and looked at her belly in the mirror. There was so much to do before the big date tomorrow night. She would have to get new knickers, zap her bikini line, paint her toenails and find new earrings to go with the dress. She was exhausted just thinking about it. She held up the dress as she emerged from around the curtain.

'Are you sure? It's very short?'

'Positive!' Kate grabbed her by the elbow and frog-marched her to the till.

Charlie took the Visa card out of her wallet and kissed it. 'Come on, baby, just one more "wafer thin" dress.'

Kate laughed. 'Don't worry, you're in charge now. You can afford it.'

'Famous last words,' said Charlie, handing over the card.

At ten o'clock the next night Charlie was in a panic.

'I stink of garlic,' she groaned, cupping her hand in front of her mouth, her eyebrows furrowed with worry. She hadn't been able to resist Rich's delicious garlic potatoes when she had finally made it back from shopping.

'You don't. You've gargled an entire bottle of Listermint,' said Rich.

'Do I look OK?'

'Terrific.'

'I can't believe Kate let me buy this dress,' she muttered, inspecting herself in the mirror for the fiftieth time. Rich was about to reply that he could when the door buzzer went.

'That's him!' screeched Charlie, darting into the bedroom to find her jacket, but she had already put it on the back of the sofa and Rich held it out for her patiently. She grabbed it from him. 'Wish me luck.'

'Be careful. Remember: just say no.'

'No is not in my vocabulary,' she teased, blowing him a kiss and racing towards the door.

She had heard that Orgasm was *the* place to be in London, but its reputation as a private members club for the rich and famous meant that she had never dreamed of going there herself. Yet here was Daniel leading her through the pearly gates, the colossal security guards patting him on the back, guiding them like VIPs past the queueing clubbers. Charlie felt nervous and out of her depth as the simpering blonde in the pay kiosk waved them on.

I shall remain cool, thought Charlie as she walked through the club's bubble-gum pink silk entrance, the enticing throb of dance music growing louder. After all, she had done her fair share of clubbing in London. Yet these thoughts vanished as the doors to the first room of Orgasm slid open.

In golden cages suspended from the ceiling, girls with fur boas and high latex boots gyrated to the thudding club music while colossal cherub statues with projector eyes beamed rainbow-coloured lasers around the walls. Daniel looked at Charlie in the bizarre light as plumes of green dry ice shot out in front of them. 'Come on.' He smiled, taking hold of her hand. 'This is just the doorstep. Let's go and get a drink.'

The Inner Sanctum of Orgasm was for members only and was reached by a transparent plastic lift. As they arrived, a girl with brutally cropped dark hair planted a kiss on Daniel's cheek, leaving a deep plum lipstick stain. Charlie coughed, feeling territorial, and Daniel dismissed the girl. 'Don't worry, babe,' he said. 'You just stick with me and you'll have lots of fun!' He put his arm around her and steered her down the pink fur steps.

But Daniel's comforting embrace was soon withdrawn as he was engulfed by eager clubbers. Charlie felt alone and bewildered, hearing the 'Moi, Moi' of theatrical kisses and snippets of conversation: 'Ya, lunch at Quag's . . . Vicki's at the Met bar . . . she's modelling in the West Indies . . . Shoot in Zanzibar at Christmas . . . Bambi's got the contract . . . Troy is opening up in D'Arblay Street . . .'

She pushed her way forward and reached Daniel's side just as two handcuffed men, body painted and naked except for gold loincloths, wandered up to them.

'Hey, Dan,' drawled one with an American lisp, 'who's the little lady?' He nodded to Charlie.

'This,' said Daniel, taking Charlie's hand, 'is my partner in crime.'

'Yet another string to your bow, dear boy,' said the other body-painted American, his voice high and camp.

'Stop being bitchy, Manolo. Now, run along you two,' said Daniel, as if reprimanding school children. 'Charlie is my special guest, and I would very much like to get her a drink.' He looked into Charlie's face as if she were the most captivating person in the world.

The bar and all the surrounding stools were in the shape of huge pairs of red lips and Charlie felt clumsy as she hoisted herself up. Giles, the barman, shook Daniel's hand. 'Good to see you, Daniel,' he said, his huge black hand gesturing to the rows of coloured bottles behind him. 'What's your poison tonight?'

'The usual, thanks.'

Giles turned to Charlie. 'And for your guest?'

'After all that lot, a cup of tea wouldn't go amiss!'

Daniel laughed. 'Here, try this.' He handed her his glass and she took a sip. Her eyes widened in appreciation as she let the champagne cocktail fizz over her tongue. 'Another one, please Giles,' said Daniel and Giles nodded with approval.

They leaned on the bar, their heads close together to talk above the throbbing music. 'So,' said Charlie, in her best chat-up voice, 'Do you come here often?'

'Well, yes, I suppose I do. It's a nightmare trying to get membership, but a few people owed me some favours.'

Charlie was impressed. 'I've read about this place. Apparently everyone comes here.'

Daniel smiled and started to gossip about some of the members making them seem like personal friends as he name dropped, but Charlie couldn't take it all in. Just watching the contours of his face and his lithe body beneath his open shirt made her ache with desire.

'Come on,' said Daniel, draining his second glass. 'Let's go upstairs and party.'

Charlie jolted back to reality and downed the rest of her cocktail. Daniel held her around the waist as she slid off the stool. She stood in his embrace staring up at him, feeling as if she had just begun a bungie jump. Her mouth was so close to his. Surely he was going to kiss her?

'Great tits!' he said, moving away from her.

Charlie looked down at the objects of his admiration, relieved that even if he wasn't going to kiss her yet, the dress had the desired effect. A small square of folded paper nestled in her cleavage.

'Some Charlie for my Charlie,' he said.

She stared at him for a second in bewilderment, then realised what he meant. Rich was always reading out terrifying statistics about drugs. Thanks to him she knew all about neuro-fibrillary tangles and premature strokes. She'd told him off for being so straight-laced and teased him that recreational drugs were just what he needed, but he'd always been adamant that it wasn't worth the risk. Although she didn't admit it, she agreed with him.

She'd had Ecstasy once before and had been sick, but she couldn't refuse Daniel now. He would think she was such a prude. Her head was light with champagne and suddenly she thought that a little cocaine wouldn't hurt. What harm could it do? She'd have a laugh and drink cranberry juice all next week in penance.

Sod Rich and his frumpy ways. She was only young once and she might as well have fun. She smiled at Daniel. 'Excellent,' she said.

'It looks like the start of *Doctor Who* on the telly.' Charlie couldn't hide her amazement as she followed him through the swirling black starlit tunnel to the upstairs dance floor. At the end of the tunnel they emerged on to a platform and Charlie gasped as below her a sea of flung-out arms and turned-up faces greeted them, the wall of sound, heat and smoke hitting them full force.

'They're not looking at us,' shouted Daniel like a tour guide stepping into the noise of a welding factory. 'The DJ's platform is just below. Come.'

He led Charlie down a scaffolding staircase and through a hidden door to the back of the DJ's box.

Charlie gazed at the jumping columns of green lights in the DJ's booth. OJ, the DJ, had a huge reefer in his mouth and one side of a large set of earphones jammed between his right ear and shoulder. As his foot tapped, his fingers rested on one of the spinning discs in front of him. Charlie saw his eyes close as he started to push up one of the sliding knobs on the deck, letting go of the record as he did so. His timing was perfect. A crashing, thumping new sound exploded into the mix and a huge cheer rose from the crowd below.

OJ lifted a fist in the air, acknowledging the adulation from the dancers. Huge gothic pillars rose from the floor while suspended platforms hung from the ceiling where the dancing elite posed. Girls in sequinned bras whirled next to a troupe of black acrobats. Lasers, light shows and projected fantasies lit up the billowing backdrops.

Daniel put his hand on OJ's shoulder in greeting as he led Charlie to the sofa against the wall. He ran out long equal lines of cocaine on a record cover using his gold Amex card. Charlie pressed her knees together to stop them shaking as Daniel handed her a rolled £50 note and she snorted the line of powder. Handing back the note to Daniel, she sniffed and rubbed her nose, the coke making her throat numb. She blinked and watched him finish his line.

'This stuff tends to knock your socks off, so I think we ought to go and dance!'

He was right. On the dance floor Charlie lost track of time, her mind and body absorbed in the music. People emerged through the dry ice to exchange nods, winks and hugs with Daniel. In the bone-melting heat, rivulets of tingling sweat ran down her back as she swung her arms in the air with the crowd to the beat of the music.

'Here,' said Daniel, popping half a pill in her mouth and handing her a bottle of warm water. 'These Es are the best!'

Charlie nodded and pushed it round in her mouth. To swallow or not to swallow, that is always the question, she thought. She took a slug of water and knocked it back, smiling to herself as she remembered Kate's advice that the way to a man's heart is always to swallow. Maybe she would keel over, but at least she'd go out happy.

Later, Daniel pointed her in the direction of the toilets and she strutted up the stairs to them, her vision like a steadicam. In the crowded preening parlour, a beautiful girl sat by a table of make-up. Feeling dizzily euphoric, Charlie smiled at her and picked up a huge powder brush, dabbing her sweating face.

She blundered into a cubicle and crouched above the toilet, cocking her head and trying to read the graffiti on the back of the door, but her vision blurred. Her heart pounded as the drugs rushed through her veins. She stood up and steadied herself against the loo-roll holder. 'Woah. Easy, tiger,' she murmured. She looked down at her knickers twisted around her shoes, too dizzy to bend down to pull them up, trampled them off and kicked them behind the toilet. 'Who needs knickers anyway?' she said, leaning down on the flush handle.

As she washed her hands, the cold water made her skin tingle. She smiled at the girl next to her and smoothed down her skirt before rubbing her fingers under her eyes to remove the smudged eyeliner. She wanted to patter her feet on the floor with excitement and giggle with glee that she was with Daniel. She looked at herself again. Going blonde was definitely the right decision. She felt completely different. Her jaw stiffened and she realised she was grinding her teeth together. The girl next to her handed her a piece of chewing gum.

'Having a good time?' she asked.

'Un-fucking-believable,' Charlie said to her reflection.

As she wobbled back towards the dance floor, she looked over the balcony and spotted Daniel. In her absence, he was clearly the centre of attention. Smiling, she stopped to watch him dance, enjoying being a voyeur. She tapped her feet and swayed her hips in time to the music, savouring the fact that any minute she would be back dancing in front of him. Then she noticed a man with silver blond hair and a black cape walking towards Daniel. As he moved through the crowd with the grace of a ballerina, the dancers stood aside for him, clapping their hands on his back and smiling.

Charlie moved towards the stairs, wanting to get back to Daniel. When she next looked up she saw the blond man opening his arms and embracing him. She shivered as he kissed Daniel on the mouth. Daniel pulled back and looked around him and the man turned quickly and strode away. Daniel followed him and grabbed his arm, but the man brushed him off and walked from the dance floor.

Hurrying down the steps Charlie shouldered her way through the glistening bare midriffs twisting and rocking in her path. Yet her fears were allayed as soon as Daniel saw her. He pulled her forward and she toppled towards him. He caught her and gently pushed her away, then continued dancing.

'All right?' he asked and Charlie nodded, forgetting the man she had seen moments earlier as the music seeped into her core and she was helpless to fight her dancing body.

'Are you coming up?' asked Daniel. She grinned and nodded. He winked at her and smiled back, taking her damp hands and sqeezing them as her head spun with the effects of the Ecstacy. She chewed the gum, her chest thumping with elation as she danced. After a while Daniel took her in his arms and hugged her and she groaned with joy. Maybe he fancied her after all!

She strained towards him, but he released her and took her hand in his, massaging her fingers gently. She wanted him so much! He was so sensual and even though his face was glistening in the coloured light, she thought he was the most beautiful man she had ever seen. She was about to pull him to her when one of the girls standing nearby crashed into them and flung her arms around Daniel. She put her mouth to his ear and Charlie shrank back.

'Back in a minute,' shouted Daniel, walking away with the girl.

Charlie's fuzzy brain crowded with doubts. Where was he going? Was that girl his lover? What if he left her on her own? She carried on dancing, afraid to move from the dance floor in case Daniel came back to look for her. Couldn't he tell that she fancied him? It would be impossible for her to flirt more, so why didn't he make a move? Was she too short? Too fat? Not glamorous enough? Or maybe he was just stringing her along, waiting for the right moment to make his move.

Well two can play at that game, she thought. Maybe she should play hard to get. Maybe she should just chill out and leave the decision to fate. One of the guys next to her steadied her.

'Are you OK?' he shouted.

She nodded vaguely and gave in to the music, joining the group dancing next to her and trying not to search the crowd for Daniel.

It seemed ages before he came back. He sniffed and brushed his nose with his hand.

'Do you want to sit down?' he asked, catching the eye of the guy who'd spoken to Charlie.

She took Daniel's hand as he led her through the crowd and into a huge chill-out room. The floor was covered with people sitting on low bean bags, smoking and staring up at a huge screen showing flickering images from cult movies. Charlie trembled with excitement as he steered her to a corner cushion.

'Enjoying yourself?' asked Daniel, as she squeezed next to him.

She nodded, mesmerised by his eyes. He put his hand on her cheek and gazed at her.

Kiss me, kiss me, she yelled in her head, her lips puckering and her eyes closing, but Daniel simply laughed and pulled away from her. Reaching in his pocket he pulled out some

Rizlas and began rolling a joint with the dexterity of a Cuban cigar lady.

'Let's just chill out for a while,' he said, teasing her with his eyes as he licked the sticky edge of the paper and rolled the tobacco and grass into the paper. Charlie racked her brain for something to say to him. What should they talk about – Bistram Huff? The Up Beat promotion? Her conversational powers seemed to have deserted her.

'OJ is superb,' she said with difficulty, her mouth sticky and dry.

Daniel patted her knee and lit the joint. 'Shh. Don't worry, you'll be fine in a bit.'

He turned away and touched one of the men on the seat near them. He turned round, his face lighting up when he saw Daniel. He thinks I'm boring, thought Charlie, politely nodding hello when Daniel introduced her to the man. Soon she was surrounded by people discussing last Sunday night at The End, the club that went on until Monday morning. Charlie pressed her clammy hands between her knees. Last Sunday night she'd been in bed at ten o'clock, tucked up with the latest Jilly Cooper.

One girl sank on to the cushion next to Daniel and folded her long legs underneath her, pouting. She had finely bronzed skin and a skimpy bra barely covered her pert breasts. Charlie hated her on sight. She looked as if you could lick her lips and stick her to a window. She kissed Daniel on both cheeks.

'Got any coke, Dan?' she asked.

'I've given it to Marissa,' he said, holding the twisted end of the joint and shaking it. He nodded his head in the direction of a girl on the other side of the room. Through the smoke, Charlie recognised the girl who had taken Daniel away earlier. 'You'll have to buy it off her.'

'How's Angelica, by the way?' she asked.

'Fine. She's in St Tropez.'

Charlie stiffened. So Daniel did have a girlfriend.

'Why didn't you go with her?'

Daniel lit the joint. 'New job,' he explained.

69

The girl waved to him with her fingers as she moved over to Marissa, her fingernails stained with sparkling polish. Another girl sat in her place and started talking to Daniel as they shared a joint. Charlie bowed her head, wishing that she didn't feel so off her head.

'Come on, I love this mix,' said Daniel suddenly, standing up and making back for the dance floor. 'Are you OK?' he asked Charlie.

'Fine,' she said, smiling lamely, and followed him back to the floor, disappointment crashing into her buzzing head.

It was six o'clock in the morning by the time they left Orgasm. Blundering into the bright Saturday morning sunlight, Charlie shivered as her body adjusted to the loss of the club's dense smoky air which had enveloped her like a duvet. She had thought that the drugs were wearing off and her mind was clearing, but in the cold light of day she felt more disorientated than ever.

'Come on, let's go and get a coffee,' murmured Daniel, something about the daylight making whispering necessary. They made their way through the dimly lit streets towards Soho on wobbling legs, passing the street sweepers in their green jackets, busy at work on the empty pavements. A circle of pigeons cooed in the morning mist. Charlie looked up at the neon signs in Piccadilly Circus, shining out with unusual intensity.

'God, that's bright,' she said, shielding her dilated pupils. Daniel led her to the statue of Eros, sitting her down on the black step.

'Stay there.' He leaned close to her face. 'I won't be a moment.'

Charlie felt too dizzy to argue and shivered as she watched him walk away.

A red bus and a black cab went past and she cuddled herself, aware of the loud ringing in her ears. She looked up at Eros, the sunlight starting to glint on his arrow as she tried to make sense of the night. The logical side of her brain kick-started into action when she saw Daniel striding towards her, scattering the pigeons in his path, and her heart jumped.

He stopped in front of her, his cheeks flushed from his brisk walk, and held out his hand to pull her up from the step. 'Don't look so forlorn. I've got a present for you!'

He put his hand in the pocket of his jacket and pulled out a pair of cheap sunglasses, the rims of which were patterned like the Tube map.

'Ta da!' he said, placing them on Charlie's face. 'All out of Raybans, I'm afraid, but these look gorgeous on you!'

Charlie giggled. 'Excellent!' she exclaimed, turning her face once more towards the Coca-Cola sign. 'Where on earth did you get them?'

'An old friend runs one of those tourist kiosks up by the Tube. He gave me a key.'

Daniel pulled out his Armanis and put them on.

Outside Bar Italia, Charlie and Daniel sipped cappuccinos watching Soho wake up. Over the sweet-smelling aroma of coffee and fresh pastries, a jovial white-aproned Italian swept cigarette butts into the gutter. A couple of old grey-faced tramps shuffled to their daily pitch taking with them a complex bundle of carrier bags, string and cans of Tennant's Extra while a trio of musicians huddled together, their bow ties undone and their waxed hair dishevelled.

'How are you doing?' Charlie looked over the rim of her coffee cup at Daniel.

'Fine. Still fairly out of it, I suppose. How about you?'

'Superb.'

Daniel watched a stall owner from Berwick Street market push a cart bulging with buckets of bright flowers past a row of shiny Harley Davidsons and sniffed the air.

Charlie looked into her coffee cup, and blew a hole in the creamy froth to reveal the brown liquid underneath. She didn't know what to say. She didn't want to leave Daniel, but he obviously wasn't interested.

'I guess I should go home,' she said, wishing that he'd disagree with her.

'I'll give you a lift, if you like. The car's round the corner.'

'God. I don't know how you can drive, I can hardly see!'

Daniel laughed. 'You did get a bit out of it.'

'Sorry.'

'Don't be silly. As long as you had fun.'

'I did, but I could do with a hot bath.'

'Me too,' said Daniel. 'It's nice having the bathroom all to myself, for once.'

Charlie looked at him quizzically.

'Angelica,' he said. 'She's such a slob.'

Charlie wanted to cry. 'Have you lived with her for long?' she asked, trying not to sound suspicious.

'All my life.' He drained his coffee cup and pulled out his Porsche keys. 'We have a sort of love-hate relationship.'

'I see.'

'Isn't it always like that with sisters?'

Sisters? Angelica was his *sister*?

'Come on, I'll take you home,' he said.

Rich was emptying a milk bottle full of water into the weeping fig when Charlie hobbled in.

'What time do you call this?' he asked, looking at the video clock as Charlie collapsed on to the sofa. 'And where on earth did you get those glasses?'

Charlie put her hand up slowly and held on to her glasses protectively. 'I blew it.'

Rich picked up the debris from his night home alone. He squashed the empty pizza box, crushed the beer cans and threw a cushion at Charlie. 'What happened?'

She hugged the cushion to her. 'He thinks I'm a dork.'

'It can't have been that bad.'

Charlie put her hands on her throbbing head. She was so embarrassed, she couldn't possibly tell Rich that she'd taken far too many drugs. 'The club was brilliant, but I acted like such an idiot. I was completely paranoid about Angelica, who turned out to be his sister, and I had nothing to say to his friends. They were so intimidating and they were all stick thin models. It was awful.'

'But you looked amazing.'

Charlie flung her arms out. 'I didn't.'

'You're much more sexy than those stick insects. You have to remember, Marilyn Monroe was a size sixteen.'

'Thanks very much. That makes me feel a whole lot better.'

Rich chuckled. 'You're like a work of art.'

'Yeah. More jelly botty than Botticelli.' Charlie wriggled her feet free of her shoes. 'And these bastards chewed up my feet and spat them out the other side.' She pointed a blistered toe at Rich.

Rich picked up her shoe. 'All that pain and he *didn't even kiss you?*'

'Shut up!' said Charlie, smiling despite herself as she swiped at him with the cushion. She collapsed back with the exertion.

'He's never going to fancy me and now I'm going to feel like a complete fool on Monday.'

Rich sat at the other end of the sofa and lifted her feet on to his lap. 'Stop being such a drama queen,' he said, gently massaging the ball of her foot.

Charlie sighed, her eyelids drooping. 'Is there something wrong with me that someone's not telling me?'

'You're being ridiculous.' He pressed his thumb into the arch of her foot.

'You would tell me, wouldn't you?' she said sleepily.

Rich shook his head, a grin on his face. She smiled and closed her eyes. 'Shh,' he soothed, gently rubbing her feet until she was asleep.

Philippa was back. The cloying smell of Poison hung in the air, along with an undeniable sense of oppression.

In Si's office, Philippa stood with her hands on her hips. Si reclined in his large chair stroking one of the ferns in the bank of tropical plants behind him. His foot wagged like a dog's hind leg being tickled.

'Look, Pips, give the girl a break,' he said.

Philippa scowled, her eyes narrowed like angry spiders. 'So you promoted her, just like that! Don't you think it would have been polite to ask me first?'

'Well if you'd been here, I would have, wouldn't I?'

Philippa's eyes flashed angrily. 'That's not fair and you know it,' she retorted. 'I can't leave you alone for five minutes. Last time I went away you brought in Daniel at vast expense, and now this.' She paced in front of his desk. Philippa had been furious when Daniel joined the agency and Si had spoiled her for a couple of weeks to calm her down.

'It's only a small promotion,' reasoned Si. He cupped his face in the palm of his hand. 'I thought you'd be pleased. Charlie is diligent and hard-working and she can take some of the pressure off you.' He knew he was moving along the right track. 'As for Daniel, he happens to be working out very well. The Up Beat presentation was bonza. And Charlie?' He smiled at Philippa and thrust his sweating palms towards her. 'She's as happy as a pig in shit. I gave her one of the new cars and I took the liberty of ordering a Merc for you as a little welcome home present.'

He knew her well. Philippa exhaled, her anger deflated by his bribe. She smiled, shaking her head slowly. 'You get away with murder, you really do.'

'It's my job, honey bunch.'

Charlie was dunking a tea bag in her mug when Philippa strolled into the kitchen.

'Good idea,' Philippa said. 'I'm dying for a coffee.' She made no effort to move towards the coffee machine and Charlie felt herself smiling automatically. She lifted down one of the posh china cups.

'How was your holiday?' she asked.

Philippa's permed, lacquered and highlighted new haircut failed to move as she shook her head briefly from side to side in her self-congratulatory way. Her skin was mahogany brown.

'Well it wasn't exactly a holiday,' she said. 'I had so much work to do, I had to take some with me. I came back via Paris for some meetings.'

'Really?'

Philippa waved her head in frustration. 'Paris was hot and heaving with tourists,' she said as if she were a disgusted native.

74

'But how were the Virgin Islands? Gorgeous, I expect?'

Philippa was unable to resist gloating. 'The Virgins are nice, but ten years ago things were different. I stayed there for a couple of months once with an artist and it was much more remote and romantic,' she said. 'Still, I managed to top up the tan.'

In her office, Philippa swivelled her hips and relaxed into her chair, smiling briefly. Charlie held on to her hot mug, not wanting to risk a circle mark on the immaculate desk.

'Si said the meeting with Up Beat went well,' said Philippa.

Charlie looked at her. Did Philippa know about the *Reporter* promotion?

'Yes, we're all delighted,' she said cautiously.

Philippa nodded and looked in her diary. She started to write something. 'He also said that he'd announced our decision to promote you. Congratulations.' The displeasure in her voice was masked by the cold-eyed smile she now gave Charlie. She looked like a doctor writing out a prescription for a hypochondriac.

'Thanks, Philippa. I really appreciate it. I'm very excited.' Charlie hated herself for sounding so pathetic.

'Excitement is all very well, but as I'm sure you're aware there is a lot of work involved. I want to make a start straight away.'

The sleek phone on Philippa's desk buzzed, cutting the tension, and she placed the receiver to her ear so that it didn't dislodge her discreetly expensive earrings.

'Philippa Bistram,' she snapped. One of her most bitched-about habits was that she never acknowledged Sadie, the only person who put through calls to her. 'OK, tell him to hold for a second.' She put her hand over the mouthpiece, her polished white-tipped nails pointing like syringes towards Charlie.

'I'll take this call and then I want a full brief on Up Beat,' she demanded, knowing that this would give Charlie only a few minutes to gather her thoughts.

'Put him through,' she barked down the phone. Charlie nodded and stood. As she turned, Philippa's personality underwent a total metamorphosis.

'Hi,' Philippa cooed. 'How lovely to hear from you!' Her voice was light with feminine charm as her mouth formed a glossy smile. It must be a client.

'Yes, it was lovely. Good to get away from it all,' she giggled.

Charlie walked out of the office cringing. Behind her she could hear Philippa's shrill laugh.

'Oh God, yes I know. Launching is a *nightmare*. When I was directing the launch of Sligo's we had a TV and press campaign breaking simultaneously all over Europe. I didn't sleep for weeks . . .'

Charlie looked at Pete who was taking off his jacket and could also hear Philippa speaking.

'You could land a harrier jump jet on those shoulder pads,' he said.

'How's the point of sale artwork coming?' she asked Bandit.

He shrugged. 'I'm off to talk to Will down in creative now.'

'Can you ask him if he can dig out the visuals Daniel did for Si's meeting and bring them into Philippa's office?' She grimaced at him. 'She wants a full run-down in five minutes.'

Bandit pointed his fingertips at his chest and snorted a contemptous laugh. 'Excuse me, but you're mistaking me for someone who gives a fuck!'

'Please, Bandit,' she begged. 'I'll owe you one.'

Bandit put his tongue in his cheek. 'OK I'll bring them in. By the way, what did Philippa say about your promotion?'

'She was delighted,' she lied.

Philippa was far from delighted when Charlie re-entered the office. Her face was drawn with anger, her knuckles white as she replaced the receiver.

'Shut the door.' She spat the words at Charlie who skidded into panic, like a needle across a record.

'I think you've got some explaining to do,' said Philippa. 'That was Nigel Hawkes. It appears that my instructions for the presentation were deliberately and quite conclusively ignored.'

76

Charlie felt her cheeks burning. 'We did follow your . . .' she started.

'There was no "we" involved,' Philippa interrupted. '*I* gave *you* specific instructions.' Her mouth was a fuchsia slash of anger.

'We presented your ideas. Only Daniel worked up an idea for a scratchcard promotion. Si said that the group director loved it and I got it approved by Teddy Longfellow at the *Reporter*.' The words caught in Charlie's throat. She had expected Philippa to be angry, but not this angry.

'Of course Daniel is going to work up ideas,' she snapped, her sarcasm making Charlie flinch. 'That's what we pay him for. It's your job to deliver to the client what is required.'

'I know, but . . .' said Charlie, desperate to explain.

'There are no "buts"!' Philippa's voice lowered menacingly. 'I wanted the same ideas as last year because *if* you hadn't noticed, Up Beat is our largest client. It has stayed that way because *I* have made sure that we get maximum revenue from the printing.' She jabbed her finger on the desk to emphasise her fury. 'How dare you agree a promotion behind my back?'

'That's just the point. We have got the print for this job,' began Charlie.

There was a knock on the door.

'Come,' shouted Philippa and Bandit entered carrying visuals that had been presented to Up Beat. He saw Philippa's face and looked at Charlie.

'Welcome back,' he said, his voice loud with fake enthusiasm. 'Isn't it great about the *Reporter*? I told you I'd get a big newspaper promotion.' He looked Philippa in the eye. 'I'm sure you'll agree with Charlie that these visuals are great.'

'Leave them on the desk,' said Philippa through gritted teeth, averting her eyes.

'I'll catch up with you later then,' he said. He was nearly out of the door.

'David?' Philippa made no effort to sound pleasant. 'You don't know anything about the office phone system, do you?'

'No, why?'

Charlie marvelled at his convincing innocence.

'Because a client said that there was some disturbing music on our waiting system while I was away,' she said, fixing him with her icy stare.

Bandit shrugged. 'I don't know what you're talking about.'

'Maybe not. However, I'm sure you'll agree it's important that we present the right image. I'd appreciate it if you'd sort it out.'

Charlie silently cursed him. She was furious that he was such a good liar and had claimed the victory for getting the promotion into the *Reporter*.

'I know I shouldn't have to tell you this,' said Philippa when the door had shut. 'However, it's your responsibility to control the team. It would be in your interest to make sure that incidents like this don't happen again.' Her words bit into Charlie's confidence. 'Now let's continue. What were you saying about the print?'

Charlie coughed, trying to clear the excuses that welled in her throat. She thought of Daniel. He'd never let Philippa talk to him like this. She must stop being so weak.

'It's a big job. We'll have to arrange the printing of all the scratchcards. I'm sure we'll make just as much money as we did last year, if not more,' she added, feeling more assured now that Philippa was listening to her.

'How big?'

'Five million scratchcards and all the supporting materials,' said Charlie. 'I'm sure there won't be a problem.'

'There'd better not be. Our expansion plans are reliant on the profit from Up Beat. Let's go through the timing plan, shall we?' asked Philippa abruptly, changing the subject and sitting down.

Charlie recoiled from Philippa's mood and slid the plan across the desk to her. Philippa scanned the document before picking up a red fibre-tipped pen.

'No, no, no,' she said, crossing out most of the neatly typed page. 'You'll have to get approval sooner than that and . . .'

Charlie watched, humiliation sweeping over her while Philippa marked her work as if she was a backward pupil.

'I could give you a hand on this,' said Philippa finally, handing Charlie back the desecrated plan and indicating one section circled in red. 'But I think the rest of it is down to you. I'm extremely busy.'

Charlie looked at the timing plan and realised that her workload had just tripled.

'Oh, I see.'

'Don't let me down,' Philippa warned.

'I won't.' Charlie smiled feebly and left the office, her spirits deflated, surprise tears smarting in her eyes.

The owner of the busy Soho sandwich shop tapped his long knife on the white board. 'What's it to be, darling? Ciabatta? Brown? French? Toasted?' He looked at Charlie over the high glass counter as she scanned the rows of fillings in oval steel bowls and bit her lip.

She'd rung Daniel earlier to talk about the Up Beat plans, but he was directing a photography shoot and she'd agreed to come over to meet him when he finished at lunchtime. In her post-drugs blues, compounded by the return of Philippa, she needed cheering up and she was desperate to apologise to him for her behaviour on Friday night. Yet when she arrived at the studio, Daniel was engrossed in arranging a shot and waved her away saying he'd be ready in ten minutes. She'd lurked in the shadows watching him re-position the balloons on the set and admiring him. She was lost in fantasy land when he'd turned and given her a blistering smile.

'I'm starving,' he said. 'Can you pop out and get me a sandwich?'

Charlie crushed her disappointment along with the plans for an intimate lunch. 'What would you like?'

'Anything.'

Now this was turning into the worst dilemma in the world. What should she get him that was impressive yet tasty? Smoked salmon was too risky, brie too girlie and she didn't have that much money. Daniel hadn't offered her any, but she'd have to buy two sandwiches so that she could eat hers with him, and then there were drinks.

'How about bacon and avacado?' suggested the sandwich man, starting to lift out the tray of gooey mixture.

'No, wait!' she said suddenly, remembering that Daniel was Jewish. She tapped her lips, wishing she would stop being so pathetic.

'It's for a friend,' she said lamely, as the tray went back in its slot. The queue was now stretching out of the door of the small shop and she was running out of time.

'Shall I come back to you when you've made up your mind?'

'No. I'll have that,' she said in a panic, pointing at the mixture nearest her. It looked like spinach, ricotta cheese and something else. She could just make it. 'Ciabatta.'

'At last,' muttered the man, spooning the mixture on to the bread. Charlie watched, feeling nervous. It looked as if it had too much mayonnaise in it.

Feeling flustered, she clutched the brown paper carrier bag and ran back up the road to the studio. She should have got a different sandwich, so that she could swap with Daniel's if he didn't like this. This was a disaster.

Rob, the photographer, was arguing with Daniel when Charlie slipped back into the shoot and it took ages for him to notice her. Daniel ran both his hands through his hair and tensed his face in mock irritation.

'How's it going?' she asked.

'We'll have to redo the shots and Rob is going mad. Do you mind if we skip lunch?'

'No, no, don't worry,' Charlie gushed, handing over the sandwich. 'I hope you like it.'

'Have you got two there? I'll take one for Rob, he'll be starving too.'

So much for her lunch!

'Listen. I'm up to my eyeballs for the rest of today, is the Up Beat stuff urgent?'

'Yes, but all I need is a chat about it.'

Daniel unwrapped his sandwich and bit into it, taking no

80

notice of the filling. He was looking over towards the shoot, his attention distracted.

'Why don't you come over to mine later?'

'Your house?'

'It's the only time I'll have and I doubt if I'll be going back to the office.'

'Are you sure?'

Daniel smiled at her and she blushed. 'Of course,' he said, leaving the sandwich on the stool.

Philippa slammed the door of her new Mercedes, the sound reverberating around the concrete pillars of the underground car park.

'I'd like a word with you,' said Bandit, who was waiting by the lift. He put his hand in his pocket and jangled his keys as Philippa approached him.

'What is it now?' she asked, jabbing the lift button.

'Take a wild guess,' he said, his voice malicious. 'How dare you promote Charlie? You promised me.'

'I promised nothing of the sort.'

'But the newspaper promotion! The business in the *Reporter*, it's worth a fortune and we wouldn't have won it if it hadn't been for my contacts. I *deserve* a promotion.'

'I'm well aware that your contact was next to useless,' said Philippa as if the whole issue bored her. 'Simon and I thought Charlie was a more suitable candidate for promotion at this stage.'

'Jesus, why her? I've worked my bollocks off for this agency,' he ranted, his anger echoing around them.

Philippa held up her hand. 'If I were you, I'd shut up now. You work no harder than anyone else, David.' The lift doors opened. She turned to face him before stepping in. 'When, or should I say, if, you prove yourself to be the asset to this agency that you think you are, then we'll review your status.'

'That's so unfair!'

'Who said life was supposed to be fair?' said Philippa stepping into the lift just before the doors closed.

Bandit kicked the air in front of the lift, his pent-up anger escaping in a growl. Then he straightened up and pulled at his jacket.

'Well, fuck you. Fuck you all!'

Rich paced by the main ticket desk in the Barbican waiting for Pix. He had spent hours deciding what to wear and, looking down at his pressed chinos and checked shirt, he wished that he'd been more adventurous. He played with the bar of Belgian chocolate that was going soft in his grip and decided Pix would think he was boring and straight. He looked around him and groaned. The place was heaving with clusters of middle-aged people discussing cycling in the Loire and HRT over their G&Ts.

'Ladies and gentlemen, please take your seats in the concert hall. Tonight's performance will commence in three minutes.' Rich tapped the programmes against his legs and looked around, trying to spot his impish companion. Then he saw her staring at the theatre posters and reading the blurb about the summer season. I knew it. I should have got tickets for the theatre, Rich said to himself, plunging into doubt about the success of the evening.

Perhaps Charlie was right. He was far too serious, but he was still cross with her after their argument in the supermarket last night.

'It's probably the come-down from the weekend,' she'd said grouchily, chucking chocolate biscuits in the trolley.

Rich looked up from his carefully prepared list. 'What do you mean?'

'Nothing.'

He looked at her grey face and comprehension swept over him. 'What did you take?'

'You don't want to know.'

'Ecstacy? Cocaine? Dope? What was it?'

Charlie was silent.

'Well?'

Charlie nodded bleakly.

Rich stopped the trolley. 'Charlie!'

'Stop being so judgmental. I didn't tell you because I didn't want a lecture and I don't want one now.'

'I have every right to be judgmental.'

'No you don't.' Charlie glared at him angrily.

'I thought you had more respect for yourself. No wonder you slept all weekend and feel like shit.'

She should have known that Rich wouldn't understand.

'I don't want you getting wrapped up with people who take drugs.'

Charlie grabbed the trolley. 'Just leave me alone,' she said, grunting with frustration as the wobbly wheel jammed and she skidded off to the dairy section.

They'd only started talking at the checkout, when Rich was loading up the bags and Charlie caught his eye.

'Stroppy bitch,' he teased.

'You're the stroppy one!' she gasped, thwacking him with the celery.

'No, you are.'

'No, *you* are.'

He shook his head. 'Am not.'

'Aren't.'

'Am.'

'Ha! I won,' laughed Charlie.

Pix turned and looked down the wide staircase. Rich waved the programmes at her and watched her skipping down the stairs towards him, her dangling ethnic earrings tinkling as she approached.

'I've never been here before,' she said, her eyes shining. 'It's brilliant, there's so much space.' She stretched out her small arms. 'Do you know, there's a botanical garden here that's second only to Kew, and a huge library. There's loads going on, it's so cool.'

Rich let her excitement seep into his consciousness and drown his doubts as he guided her to the stalls in the concert hall.

She wore a simple cotton dress which exposed a tattoo on her left ankle. Rich was fascinated. There was something about tattoos that made him assume that the host had a torrid

83

past, dabbling in underworld crime and unmentionable acts in public toilets.

'I was seventeen,' she said, as if that explained everything.

'Why did you do it?'

Pix rubbed the panther head affectionately. 'I was trying to show off to a bloke I fancied. This was a desperate attempt to get his attention.

'And did you?' asked Rich.

'Yes,' she laughed. 'He had to carry me home from the tattoo shop when I fainted with the pain!'

As the orchestra tuned up and the lights in the auditorium dimmed, Pix settled back in her seat, folding her legs underneath her, and gazed up at the stage like a child watching a Punch and Judy show. The conductor entered regally to polite applause and bowed on the podium, before introducing the piano soloist. Pix turned to Rich, her eyes dancing with anticipation, and he put his hand on her arm.

It was ages since Rich had been with someone so uneducated in cultural etiquette as Pix. He had to rugby tackle her to stop her giving a solo standing ovation between movements of Mozart's Twenty-First Piano Concerto. But what endeared him to her most was that her face expressed every emotion she felt without censorship and during the slow movement, she turned to him, her eyes wide. 'It's giving me goosebumps,' she whispered, showing him her forearm.

At the end of the concert, she clapped until her hands were scarlet and they were still red when the time came to say goodbye. Rich offered to get a cab and take her back to Brixton, but Pix was adamant and insisted on catching the Tube.

'Thanks for asking me, it was a good crack,' she mimicked his sincerity. 'The concert was amazing. I'm sorry if I babbled on at you all night.'

'I loved listening.' Rich smiled back at her. She was so fresh. So unconcerned with aspiring to be something she wasn't.

'It's my turn to take you out next,' she said.

'I'm all yours.'

'Then I'm taking you to a festival, OK?'

'What kind of festival?'

Pix stroked his cheek, as if trying to wipe away his sceptical expression. 'Lighten up. Trust me.'

In the street light, he looked at her upturned strawberry lips and kissed them briefly before he hugged her.

'You're brilliant,' said Pix, putting her ear against his shirt.

Charlie scanned up and down the rows of wine in Oddbins and chewed her cuticle. What had happened to her decision-making abilities? Trying to impress Daniel was causing more stress than she could possibly have imagined.

She hated choosing wine and the labels were unhelpful. They should say, 'This medium dry wine is great if you're trying to impress a potential shag' or 'Don't be fooled by the posh name. This gives the impression that you've grabbed the only bottle left over from your last party.' No such luck. She dithered on the fiver divide. She could simply buy an expensive bottle, but then it might look like she was trying too hard and her Switch card probably wouldn't work. And then there was the red or white conundrum. Daniel might prefer white considering it was such a beautiful evening, but then if they had dinner, red might be a safer bet. She exhaled with exasperation and plumped for a bottle of expensive Australian Chardonnay, hoping for the best as she wrote yet another rubber cheque.

The mews was an oasis of old-fashioned tranquillity nestling among palatial Georgian mansions in a leafy north London suburb. She folded up the page she'd torn out of the office copy of the A-Z and parked the Mazda at the end of the street. As she walked down the cobbles looking at the cared-for window boxes bathed in the evening light, she felt a pang of nervousness. If this was where Daniel lived, what would he think of the flat in Battersea? It was so scummy in comparison.

She checked the piece of paper Daniel had given her and pressed the doorbell by the Mediterranean blue door, breathing in the heady scent of honeysuckle which trailed over a trellis on the white-washed bricks.

Daniel came to the door with a beer can in his hand. His hair was tousled and he was wearing a T-shirt and a pair of faded jeans. Charlie noticed his tanned feet with clean pink nails and wanted to kiss them. He was so beautiful. He smiled at her, his lips glistening in a sexy Brad Pitt sort of way.

'Welcome to my humble abode. Be careful of Benson,' he said, easing open the door.

'Benson?'

'My Rottweiller,' he explained and disappered behind the door.

Great. Meeting a psychotic hound was way down there on her list of 'fun things to do' along with netball and the dentist.

She tentatively jabbed the door which swung wide open. Daniel was crouching down, grinning as a chocolate brown Labrador puppy skidded around the polished floorboards licking his outstretched hand and panting in excitement.

Daniel looked up at her, watching relief and embarrassment spread over her face.

'You pig!' Charlie blushed as she marched into the hall. 'I was terrified!' She pushed Daniel so that he fell over backwards, laughing. Benson raced towards her, tripping over his front feet, and Charlie scooped him up into her arms, getting paw prints all over the new turquoise sundress she'd bought in an emergency flap around Jigsaw a few hours ago.

'Come on, I'll show you round,' Daniel kicked the front door, which shut with a homely thud.

The 'humble abode' was worthy of a whole edition of *Homes and Gardens*. IKEA eat your heart out, thought Charlie as she peeked into a room on the way to the kitchen. Shafts of coloured light fell from a stained-glass skylight on to the white furnishings giving the room the serenity of a chapel. In the corner, she spotted a cast-iron spiral staircase and with a lurch of excitement wondered whether it led to his bedroom.

In the kitchen, Charlie let Benson slither out of her arms and hoisted herself on to a chrome stool as Daniel unwrapped the wine she'd bought. He looked at the label, opened the fridge and put it next to the milk, before offering her a beer.

'How did the shoot go?' asked Charlie, resting her elbows on the polished high wooden counter. She suddenly felt nervous, as if she shouldn't have come.

Daniel pulled out a dog chew and gave it to Benson. 'We got it done. What's going on with Up Beat?'

Charlie explained Philippa's caution and told him the designs would have to be completed by the end of the week in order to meet the deadlines, apologising profusely for the extra workload as they chatted.

'No sweat,' said Daniel. 'I'll sort it.'

Charlie stared at him with unashamed desire. Seeing him in his own home made him seem so real. She followed him into the lounge and watched him pick up a sleek remote control from the glass coffee table.

'I'm sorry about the other night. I'm not used to taking so much in one go.'

Daniel pressed a button on the control and the slimline stack of stereo equipment burst into life. 'It doesn't matter. As long as you enjoyed yourself.'

He ushered her through French doors into a walled garden. 'This is brilliant. It's such a suntrap.' She sat down on a swinging wicker chair with Benson at her feet. Purple clematis covered the wall.

'It's nice, isn't it? I like it because it's private and I can sunbathe in the nude.'

Charlie sighed to herself at the thought. 'Do you do that often?'

'Sometimes. You'll have to come and join me one of these days.'

'I might hold you to that.'

'Is there anything else you wanted to discuss about Up Beat?'

She sat up in her seat, flustered. Daniel had pulled the conversational rug from under her feet by talking about work.

'No. As long as we sort it.' She paused. 'How are you enjoying Bistram Huff?'

Daniel shrugged. 'It's OK. The office is cool and my salary keeps me out of mischief. How about you?'

Charlie was reluctant to discuss her job, but as they relaxed in the evening sun, Daniel coaxed out all her insecurities.

'The team are OK though, aren't they?'

Charlie laughed. 'Yes. They're all football crazy at the moment though.'

Daniel got out of his seat and ruffled Benson's ears. 'Don't you like football?'

'It's OK. I can think of things I'd rather do.'

Daniel sat next to her on the swinging chair. 'Like what?'

Charlie shrugged, alarmed by his closeness. His arm was behind her now and he was watching her intently. He reached forward and stroked a lock of her hair. 'I bet you're a real sensualist,' he said.

She cocked her head. 'Aren't you?'

'What do you think?'

This was it. An open invitation. She couldn't wait any longer. She leaned towards him and kissed his soft lips, closing her eyes as her senses buzzed with the smell of his aftershave and the pressure of his strong arms which now drew her into his embrace.

She pulled away. 'I'd say you were fairly sensual,' she whispered.

'Only fairly?' He bent his head and kissed her again. This time her knees trembled and she held her breath as he nibbled her lips and his tongue danced with hers. He was the best kisser she'd ever encountered.

'Daniel, Daniel,' she muttered as he kissed her nose and her eyelids and she heard him moan with desire.

Then abruptly he stopped. 'What's wrong?' she asked in alarm.

Daniel looked at his Rolex. 'It's time for the match. I'd nearly forgotten.'

'What match? What?' She stood up, feeling utterly confused.

'I've got a few mates coming round to watch the semi-final. I'll see you tomorrow,' he said, walking through the kitchen and opening the front door. He smiled and tapped her on the nose. 'See you,' he said, and suddenly Charlie was out in the mews, looking back at the blue door and wondering what on earth had happened.

In the Crown and Sceptre, Bandit put the pints on the table, holding two packets of crisps between his teeth. Bob Grafton smiled up at him and rubbed his forehead.

'You'd better tell me what's happened,' said Bandit, scrutinising Bob's worried face.

'Oh, it's nothing.'

'And I'm Mary Poppins!'

Bob pulled on the pint and licked his lips. 'I dunno. It's work and stuff.'

'And?'

Bob looked at him sheepishly. 'Amanda.'

'Ah, I see.'

Amanda, Bob's wife, was the most hard-done-by spouse in London.

'She's all arsy because I haven't been paying her enough attention,' he said, taking a huge glug of beer. 'She's got a point. I've been on a bit of a bender, to tell you the truth.'

'Quel surprise!'

'You know how it is. I went to Amsterdam with the boys at the weekend and then it was a leaving do with CJZ on Monday and a launch celebration with BKF last night. Jesus, we got ratted. Landed up getting thrown out of the Light of Nepal about three. Monstrous.'

'So what's new?' Bandit slapped him on the shoulder. 'You don't have to look so glum, you're well practised.'

Bob avoided his gaze. 'You're right.'

Bandit sipped his beer. 'So what's bothering you?'

'Nothing. It doesn't matter.'

'It obviously does.' Bandit put his hand on Bob's shoulder. 'Look, we've been mates for years. If there's something you want to tell me . . . get off your chest . . . then fire away. I'd never say anything. You know that.'

There was a short silence. Bandit smiled sympathetically, but when Bob looked away, Bandit knew something was eating him up. 'You've been a naughty boy, haven't you?' he said slowly.

Bob put down his glass and covered his face with his hand.

Bandit smiled. 'Look, it's not that big a deal. You can tell me. You might as well now, I've as good as guessed by the look of things.'

'You promise you won't say anything?'

Bandit rolled his eyes. 'Bob!'

Bob looked up, his cheeks white. 'If this ever gets out, I'm dead. If Amanda found out, it'd be the end of our marriage.'

'That bad?'

'That bad!'

Bandit shuffled closer as Bob shook his head and stared at his half-empty pint.

'I've been such a git.' He took a deep breath and exhaled wearily. 'You know Caroline from Rectangle?'

Bandit nodded. Rectangle was an agency famous for its babes and he'd missed Caroline at last week's inter-agency softball game. As he recalled, she always wore a pair of cycling shorts that went right up her cute butt. 'Come to think of it, I do remember her.' He smiled.

'She's pregnant.' Bob watched as Bandit spluttered, choking on his beer.

'Don't tell me?' Bandit's eyes nearly popped out of his head.

Bob nodded, his jolly face miserable. 'I shagged her after that boat race party at Dynamic Marketing,' he admitted.

'*You* shagged *her*?'

'You promise you won't ever say anything?' he checked once more with Bandit, who crossed his heart. 'You're the only person who knows.'

'Never, I promise. Jesus! Pregnant?'

'She wants to keep it.' Bob rubbed his eyes.

'Fuck!'

'Exactly.'

'What are you going to do?'

Bob finished his pint. 'I don't know.'

Bandit touched his arm in consolation. 'Don't worry, mate, we'll find a way out.' He gestured to the pint and Bob nodded. Bandit went to the bar.

After several more pints and much commiseration, they finally came round to the subject of business.

'We've got a big promotion with Up Beat coming up,' said Bandit. 'We're doing a scratchcard promotion in the *Reporter*.'

Bob sniffed. 'How many scratchcards?'

'Five million.'

Bob whistled.

'We need a competitive quote. Do you think you could do it? I'd love you to get the business. You could do with a break.'

'Leave it with me,' said Bob. 'I'll do my very best.'

Charlie sat at the kitchen table, her face covered in mud pack as she flicked through a magazine. 'I've decided. I'm going on the food combining diet and then I'm going to have colonic irrigation,' she said.

Rich was on his hands and knees, searching for the washing liquid ball under the sink. 'Good idea. At least that might stop you being so full of shit,' he said, banging his head as he came up.

'Don't make me laugh,' giggled Charlie, holding her face. 'It hurts.'

Rich bundled his dirty shirts into the washing machine. 'You're being completely paranoid.'

Charlie stared at him through the khaki holes of the mask. 'I'm not. He doesn't fancy me because I'm too fat and too ugly. Why else would he chuck me out? Maybe my breath smells as well.'

Rich tutted, not having found the washing ball, and slopped the thick liquid over the shirts. 'It doesn't.'

'You don't understand, it's so humiliating. I threw myself at him and he rejected me. He couldn't get me out of there fast enough.'

Rich slammed the washing machine door and fiddled with

the programme button. 'Maybe you've got it all wrong. Maybe he didn't want to jump on you because he wants to develop the relationship. To let you get to know each other first.'

Charlie broke a piece of chocolate from the bar on the table and tried to put it in her mouth, but the mask was drying and it cracked, making her wince. 'Come off it. Men don't think like that.'

Rich pressed the 'on' button and stared through the frosted plastic at his washing. 'You've been talking to Kate too much.'

'What do you think I should do then?'

He eased himself up as the machine started filling and sat opposite her. 'Relax for starters. Let things happen in their own time and stop being so impatient. Give it a couple of months.'

'Months! I'll have sealed up by then.'

Rich sighed in exasperation. 'Then the best way to make him sleep with you is to reject his advances. Play hard to get.'

Charlie nodded and looked up at him. 'Do you think he could fall in love with me?' she asked, her mouth pinched by the drying mud.

Rich laughed at her affectionately and took her hand. 'If he saw you now? Probably not, but then again, I guess that's what love's all about – adoring someone even when they're insecure, covered in mud and sucking chocolate.'

'It'll never happen.'

Rich dropped her hand and looked away, his heart churning like the washing machine. 'Don't forget your bath,' he said, wondering why he still hadn't found the right moment to tell Charlie about Pix.

Charlie looked up at the wall clock in the office. 'God, is it that time already?' She'd been so busy finishing the final copy for Up Beat that she hadn't noticed it was already five o'clock on Saturday afternoon.

'I'm going to miss the footie results,' whined Pete.

'Get outta here, boy!'

Pete picked up his car keys. 'You're not staying much longer, are you?'

'No, I'm going to finish off the copy and fax it through to legal so that they get it first thing Monday morning and then that's it! Thanks so much for your help. I'm glad I can rely on you.'

Pete smiled. 'I know Bandit's being horrible, but he'll get over it. His bark's worse than his bite.'

'I hope so,' said Charlie. She'd been trying to make up to Bandit for the fact she'd been promoted, but he was still being obstructive and surly and she could tell he was brooding.

'See you then,' said Pete, heading for the door.

'Oh, Pete?'

He turned in the doorway.

'What was the score from the match on Thursday night?'

'What match?'

'The European championship semi-final or whatever it was.'

Pete shrugged his shoulders. 'You must have made a mistake. There were no matches on Thursday and the semi-final isn't for ages.'

Charlie rested her chin in her palm and looked out of the window feeling perplexed. Why had Daniel lied to her? Maybe Rich was right, he'd just made an excuse to play for time. And he knew that she'd find out about the lie because it was so obvious. She should relax. Daniel obviously wanted the first time anything happened to be special. She must revel in this important stage and not sleep with him under any circumstances, then when they did it would mean so much more.

She dialled home to talk to Rich and smiled at the stupid message she and Rich had recorded over the theme tune to *The Man From Uncle*. She left a message and rang Kate for a chat, but she was out too.

Typical. Everyone else is having a life, she thought as she went over to the printer, smoothing down her denim mini-skirt.

'Hey, gorgeous,' said Daniel, creeping up behind her. His arms were laden with scans and mock-ups.

Be cool, be cool, she cautioned herself as she turned to face him. 'I thought you'd gone ages ago,' she said.

'These took me longer than I thought, but as you well know, talent cannot be rushed!'

Daniel grinned at her and she rolled her eyes at his arrogance. 'In that case we'll go into the boardroom to have a look,' she said, leading the way. How dare he be so gorgeous!

Daniel laid out the designs on the glass table and stood behind her as they chatted. Yet soon, she felt him rest his hand lightly on her waist, his mouth tantalisingly close to her ear.

'Are you sure that everyone has gone?' he asked.

She jumped at his touch, too excited by his closeness to speak. She nodded, her hand fluttering to her throat.

'Good.' He took out a packet of cocaine and wagged it in front of her face. 'I've always wanted to do this on the boardroom table.'

Charlie looked around her. 'We can't.'

'I thought you were my partner in crime,' he said, challenging her.

She bit her lip. 'You're so naughty.'

Daniel laughed and ran out two lines on the table. 'This is just the beginning.'

Charlie watched him, longing to run her fingers into his hair. Her heart thumped with excitement and fear, but she loved her role as Daniel's partner in crime. When the cocaine hit her, she suddenly felt reckless and she moved towards Daniel. Couldn't he see she was burning with desire? She tried to remember her resolution to be cool, but to Charlie the chemistry between them almost crackled and she turned to steady herself on the table.

'Now then, I'd like to make my designs clear to you,' murmured Daniel, circling her waist from behind.

'Really?' she croaked.

'Uh huh,' replied Daniel.

This can't be happening. Stop him, play hard to get, she thought, but her knees were weakening and she heard herself moaning as he kissed her shoulder, his hands sliding under her T-shirt like silk.

She stiffened with the thrill of his touch. 'Trust me, you'll like them,' he whispered, wriggling his fingers under the elastic of her cotton vest top and feeling the soft curve of her breast.

'You haven't disappointed me yet,' she breathed, too terrified to break the moment. Her nipples were screaming for his touch and she strained towards him as he found them, rolling the hard nubs in his fingertips.

Slowly Daniel turned her around as she grabbed his face, trying to kiss him.

'Ah, ah,' he teased, brushing the papers out of the way. Looking her in the eye, he slipped off her shoes and pushed her backwards until she was sitting on the table, her arms behind her.

'Daniel!' she warned, as he pushed her skirt up. What if they were caught? They would both lose their jobs. But Daniel raised his eyebrows at her, daring her to protest.

'Don't you want to know what I have in mind?' he asked, still looking at her as he bent down and kissed the inside of her thigh. 'I'm sure you'll love the concept.' He moved further up her legs and she tensed with anticipation. 'The thing is, with my favourite concepts, I like to put the effort in,' he murmured between kisses.

Despite herself, Charlie felt her fears melting with each electrifying touch of his lips, the cocaine making her brain buzz and her senses zoom into the sensation. Her legs were trembling as he reached the line of her cotton knickers. Daniel smiled and stopped.

'I'll show you,' he said, smirking with delight as he surveyed her open legs, and she thanked God that she'd done her bikini line last night!

Daniel took his pen from his pocket. Taking off the lid, he started to draw up the inside of her legs, talking about his designs. Charlie closed her eyes as the pen tip caressed her, exciting her into a frenzy. She opened her eyes and tried to grab him and pull him towards her, but he drew away, easing the lid back on the pen. She looked down and laughed as she saw the crude drawings of copulating couples.

'What I want to know is how far you'll go to support my designs?'

This was it. She couldn't back out now. She slid towards the edge of the table, grabbed his face and kissed him.

'How far?' murmured Daniel.

She undid his belt and the top button of his trousers and felt the tip of his hot penis straining against the elastic of his boxer shorts. He was magnificent. At her touch, Daniel closed his eyes and started undoing the rest of his fly, but Charlie wriggled free of his grasp.

'Ah, ah,' she said, slipping off the table and turning around, swaying her buttocks against him and teasing his hardness with the soft fabric of her knickers. She pulled the designs in front of her on the table.

'Before I commit to your designs, I have to see them properly,' she said, pulling the boards towards her. She pushed back and rubbed against him, her elbows on the table. 'Well?'

'You're absolutely right.' Daniel hooked his finger inside the side of her knickers and she felt him slide them down her legs. His hands caressed her buttocks and her heart raced. What was she doing?

Daniel cleared his throat and she heard his trousers and boxer shorts slip to the floor. Then he leaned forward to explain the designs and she gasped as she felt the tip of his penis catch between her legs. She closed her eyes and held her breath. His skin felt so firm and soft.

Charlie broke away, her heart pounding as she turned round to face him.

'Does that make what I have in mind clear?' he whispered.

'Very.' She pushed him back against the sideboard, sinking to her knees and licking his long shaft as he trampled his trousers away from his ankles.

He held her hair for a moment, before moving away from her. 'I want to watch you,' he rasped. 'Get on the table.'

She looked at him for a moment, surprised, but she knew she would do anything. She crawled on to the boardroom table while Daniel fixed her with his stare.

'Show me,' he said. 'I want to see you touching yourself.'

Charlie's cheeks were burning as she lay exposed in front of him, her fingers rubbing her own soft flesh. She felt so brazen, yet this was better than her most outrageous fantasies.

He shook his head, his breath shuddering as he watched her. 'I've imagined you doing this since the first time I met you,' he said. 'You don't know what you do to me.'

She slid to the edge of the table and reached out for him, drawing him close as their mouths met in a passionate kiss, teeth clashing and tongues dancing as they pressed themselves together.

'I thought you didn't want me. The other night . . .?'

Daniel kissed her again. 'I thought I was going to jump on you and you'd be offended.'

'Offended,' she gasped, ripping open his shirt, running her hands over his divine chest, burying kisses in the soft hair and licking his erect pink nipples as her senses filled with the smell of him. 'I'd have loved it!'

Daniel grabbed her skirt and pulled it off, before lifting her T-shirt and vest top over her head. With a satisfied moan, he took her breasts in his hands and bent down to kiss them.

Charlie wrapped her legs around him. 'Oh Daniel, Daniel. Please.'

He stopped kissing her and for a moment they were eye to eye, locked in each other, their surroundings forgotten. Then he pushed into her, his mouth opening in a silent gasp. She held his gaze, knowing this was too dangerous, knowing that she was being irresponsible, but the sensation was too amazing, and her need for him too great for her to care.

She closed her eyes as he thrust into her, kissing her and sucking her lips, and she heard her own moans through the sound of their union.

'You love it, don't you?' said Daniel, grabbing her bottom

and picking her up as if she were as light as a feather. 'Come on.' He waded out of the boardroom towards Philippa's office.

There, he leaned her up against the door and Charlie trembled, grabbing his hair. He pushed into her body and her mind, the sweat breaking out on his forehead as their probing tongues played together.

Breathless, Charlie let her legs drop to the carpet and, disengaging herself from him, tiptoed over to Philippa's desk. Shoving the leather chair aside, she bent over the desk. 'Take me,' she begged, and Daniel was there, spread-eagling her over the desk and sliding inside her from behind.

Taking one of her arms, he guided her hand so that she could play with herself and feel him sliding inside her. He fell forward, leaning down so that his front pressed against her back, their skin kissing as he reached round and caressed her breasts.

About to come, Daniel pulled away and sat back in Philippa's large leather chair, his hands behind his head. 'Sit on me,' he said and Charlie straddled him, grabbing the back of the chair as she slid on to him, her knees sinking into the soft leather. It was as if she had been transported to a new planet of sensation in which only she and Daniel existed.

Suddenly, Daniel put his finger to her lips. 'Shh,' he warned. They stopped, their ears scanning the building for sound, but it was silent. Then Daniel lunged at her breast, taking it in his mouth and rocking deep inside her so that she arched towards him.

'I'm going to come, I'm going to come, I'm going to . . .' she cried, her senses orbiting into pleasure like an astronaut somersaulting in space.

Daniel smiled as her face relaxed and he stroked a damp lock of blonde hair away from her face.

'You're amazing,' she whispered.

'No, you are.' He twitched inside her.

'No, you are.' She smiled, kissing him and wriggled off him.

'Your desk,' he said into her tousled hair, but before they got there Daniel sank to his knees and, pushing her back against Pete's desk, opened her legs and buried his face between them. Charlie cried out, grabbing on to the desk behind her and dislodging Pete's red in-tray which crashed to the floor as Daniel's hot mouth made her burn with ecstasy.

On all fours she crawled into the kitchen, Daniel chasing her with his tongue. Panting, she hoisted herself on to the counter by the coffee machine. Daniel stood in front of her and pushed inside her. They rested their foreheads together, their sweat mingling. Charlie reached to her side and turned on the tap, gathering a pool of cold water in her palm and slapping it on to his chest. He gasped as the icy trickle tingled down to his navel. Then he splashed her, drenching her hair as the water fell over her nipples and coursed towards her clitoris.

'Reception,' Daniel's voice was gruff. 'I'll race you,' he said, withdrawing from her and running towards the door. Charlie chased after him in delight until he turned to catch her and pushed her up against the reception booth.

She bit his shoulder as he moved inside her, her nails running down his back. Exhausted, they sank to the carpet and she gave in to his dominance. Sliding her legs around his back and then around his neck, he held her hands high above her head, pinning her against the carpet. Daniel looked at her.

'Yes . . . yes,' he gasped, his eyes narrowing and then closing as he came and Charlie cried out, their voices echoing around the empty office.

She slid her legs around Daniel's back as he collapsed on top of her, stroking his back and kissing his shoulder, bathing in the red glow of the sunset. 'About your designs. I think they're fantastic,' she said.

BOOK

II

'I don't believe it!' The exclamation went up from Bandit as he slammed down his phone, jumping out of his seat like an excited foreign exchange dealer.

Pete was impatiently prodding the keys on his calculator. 'Spill the beans then,' he said, banging the calculator on the desk.

'X marks the spot,' announced Bandit. He threw up his pen into the air so that it twirled round, the smile on his face as bright-eyed as the kipper on his tie.

'What Xs?' asked Toff, rubbing a spotty patch on his temple that Clearasil never reached.

'*The* Xs!'

'These Tipp-Ex crosses?' asked Pete, pointing to the mark on the side of his desk.

'Yes, my dear boy. The very same. I know the meaning.' Bandit tapped his pencil on his desk.

'What Tipp-Ex crosses?' asked Charlie, amused, as she staggered towards the filing cabinet behind Bandit's desk, her arms full of folders. She'd had a busy morning, comparing print costs from old promotions, knowing that her figures for the Up Beat job had to be faultless before she presented them to Philippa. She dumped the folders on the floor and was about to stand up when the meaning of Bandit's words hit her like a punch in the stomach.

'I've just been on the blower to Poppy down in creative,' he was saying. 'She says that Daniel was shagging someone all over the office at the weekend. Apparently, there's a Tipp-Ex cross in every place he did it.'

'He's got a nerve,' laughed Toff, shocked by Bandit's revelations.

'And that's not the best bit,' continued Bandit, delighted that he was drawing the attention of the group of aghast listeners. 'Apparently there's a cross on Philippa's desk!' He slapped his knee and laughed with the others.

Charlie stood up slowly trying to stop her knees shaking. She turned round to see Pete rubbing his hands together like a tabloid editor who'd just got the story that will ruin the Prime Minister.

'So who was Daniel with?' asked Charlie, her voice catching in her dry throat, blood rushing to her face. Pete smiled, the possibilities flashing through his head.

'Maybe he's been banging Philippa?' suggested Bandit, turning his nose up at the thought.

'No,' chipped in Sadie, who was struggling to open a roll of fax paper with her teeth. 'It couldn't be Philippa, she was out with that City bloke she's been seeing.'

Pete looked over his shoulder at her. 'I bet it was you, you old tart!'

Sadie looked down her nose at Pete. 'No, Daniel's not my type,' she said, ignoring his comment. 'He's given me the come-on before, but men like him are all Porsche and no trousers. I go for the more mature man myself.' She stared into the distance as if she could conjure up the image of her dream man.

'I should introduce you to my dad then,' said Pete.

'Oh, grow up,' scolded Sadie, sticking Sellotape to the thinning hair on the back of his head. 'You wouldn't know the first thing about sex appeal!'

Jeremy from one of the other teams sat on the edge of Pete's desk. 'Well it might not necessarily be a woman. Rumour has it that Daniel's bisexual,' he said, throwing in a juicy bit of gossip.

'Ah, that explains it,' said Bandit. 'It was Will all along.' He laughed and limped his wrist.

Pete pursed his lips. 'Or what about the security guard? He's got a fantastic arse and he's camp as a row of pink tents.' He walked over to Bandit's desk. 'Lean over the desk, boy,' he rasped, pretending to be Daniel and grabbing Bandit around the waist.

'Yes, oh yes, fuck me, fuck me,' quipped Bandit as the two boys simulated sex over the desk amidst raucous laughter.

Charlie abandoned the files on the floor, grabbed her mobile phone and rushed to the toilets, cupping her hands under a gush of fizzing water at the basin, sending a fountain of splashes over the mirror. She threw it over her face as if it could wash away the last five minutes, but as she stared at her dripping face in the tinted mirror, snippets of the conversation she'd just heard stabbed her brain. 'X marks the spot . . . He's come on to me before . . . Rumour has it he's bisexual . . .'

'It's not true,' she whispered to her disbelieving reflection. She staggered into a cubicle and shut the door, slumping on to the closed toilet seat. The thin plastic buckled beneath her as she dialled Kate's work number, but she was out at a meeting and her mobile was on voicemail.

She brought her knees up, resting her feet on the edge of the seat, and hugged her legs, feeling desperate. There seemed to be no possible explanation. Tears welled up, unspent, held back by the horror that Daniel could have betrayed her. Catatonic, she stared at the closed toilet door and its notice urging employees to place sanitary towels in the bins provided. What was she going to do?

Pull yourself together, Charlie told herself. What they were saying about Daniel was untrue. There was no way he would have painted crosses everywhere they'd been on Saturday and he certainly wouldn't have told Poppy. She mustn't show how upset she was, otherwise they would all suspect her and if they did . . .? The consequences were too horrendous to contemplate. She'd be the laughing stock of the whole office and, come to think of it, the whole industry.

She stood up and flushed the toilet unnecessarily then returned to the mirror, where she pinched her pale cheeks to revive some colour in them. Taking a deep breath, she walked back into the office.

An embarrassed silence greeted her. Bandit had his head down at his desk as if he'd been told off. He was pretending to read *Marketing* and not making eye contact with anyone. For a moment, the only thing audible was Toff's portable radio which he kept permanently tuned in to the cricket commentary. Then she heard the commotion.

Philippa was pacing back and forth in Si's office and the venetian blinds were banging against the glass panelling. The black wooden door remained firmly shut, but the whole office was listening. With a growing sense of dread, Charlie slipped behind her desk.

'What's going on?' she whispered to Toff, noticing that his face was still flushed from a bout of giggling.

'Philippa's going ballistic,' he whispered back. 'This Tipp-Ex cross business has got right up her nose. By the sound of it, she's going to string Daniel up by his balls!'

'How ridiculous,' mumbled Charlie, glad that no-one was noticing how fragile she felt. The tension was unbearable.

'This is an agency, not a playground,' she heard Philippa screaming at Si, before the door of his office was wrenched open. Philippa loomed in the doorway, her yellow silk blouse pulled in a taut line across her breasts as she stood with her arms akimbo glancing around the desks.

Then she stormed out of Si's office and into her own, grunting as she yanked the door from its jamb and slammed it shut. The glass rattled in the partitions as if there had been an earth tremor. With the force of the slam, a jacket cloaked in plastic slumped to the floor like a shot body. Half-way up the outside of the door was a Tipp-Ex cross and like a fire extinguisher being released, the office erupted into laughter.

Charlie's hands were shaking as she dialled Daniel's mobile phone. It rang and rang before he answered, the roar of the engine and the thumping CD making conversation impossible. 'Stop the car and talk to me,' she hissed.

'What?' Daniel shouted down the mouthpiece so that Charlie had to hold the receiver away from her ear to avoid being deafened. 'Who is it? I can't hear you,' he repeated, then she heard the sound of brakes and a horn being blasted.

'Up yours too, mate!' Daniel screamed down the phone, followed by a string of obscenities. Then 'hang on,' and Charlie heard the mobile phone dropping into his lap as he swerved the car and pulled over.

At last, Charlie had his attention.

'Yo. Daniel.' His smooth voice oozed like melted chocolate through the airwaves.

Charlie fought back her tears. Was this the same voice that had tried to seduce Sadie? 'It's me,' she said, and even Daniel could hear the pain in her voice.

'What's up, babe?'

Charlie felt as if a bowling ball had become lodged in her oesophagus.

'Everyone knows. There are Tipp-Ex crosses, everywhere, everywhere that we, we . . .' Her voice faltered as an angry suppressed tear leapt from her eye.

'Whoa,' soothed Daniel as if taming an unbroken filly.

'I can't say anything. I have to talk to you. Can I meet you for lunch?'

'Sure,' said Daniel, confused. 'Where? You name the place and I'll be there.'

'It's got to be obscure, somewhere no-one will find us,' said Charlie. 'Where are you?'

'Knightsbridge.'

'OK, I'll meet you on the steps of the Natural History Museum at one. Don't be late.'

'I'll be there,' said Daniel. 'You sound like you're in a Bond movie, meeting me on the steps. What are you going to do, stage a killing?'

'Yes. Yours, probably,' said Charlie, but as she dropped the receiver back into its cradle she knew that confronting Daniel was not going to be easy.

Through the blur of her misery, she saw him dodging through

the traffic to cross the Cromwell Road. As ever, he looked gorgeous in a baggy navy shirt over cream trousers, the gold frames of his sunglasses catching the sun. Charlie was prepared to face the fact that he'd betrayed her, but despite her anger, she felt the familiar jolt through her loins as his smooth face bent towards her and he kissed her tenderly.

She folded her arms, resisting his kiss. 'You're late.'

Daniel slid his glasses down his nose and looked at her. 'Now is that any way to greet your lover?'

Unable to keep his gaze, Charlie twirled round and headed up the steps. She had already bought some tickets and Daniel followed her through the entrance barriers. He towered above the school children, drawing attention from mothers and teachers who gawped at his model good looks.

Daniel caught up with Charlie as she stormed into the main hall and swung her round to face him, gripping her by the shoulders.

'What's the matter?' he asked, shocked at her blazing eyes.

'You're a liar, a cheat and a bastard! That's what's the matter!'

'Excuse me?' coughed Daniel, dropping his hands from her shoulders and recoiling.

Charlie's eyes welled up with tears. 'Everyone knows that you've been fucking someone in the office,' she levelled.

'Don't be so ridiculous,' retorted Daniel, looking at her as if she had gone mad.

'Well how do you explain the fact that there are crosses in all the places we were on Saturday?' Her eyes were scalding. This had to be a bad dream and there must, there simply had to be an explanation.

Daniel ran his hand through his hair. He looked into Charlie's eyes and his brow furrowed into an uncomprehending wrinkle, then he rubbed his chin slowly and was silent for a long moment.

'So what you're saying is that you don't trust me. Is that it?'

Charlie felt her anger faltering. 'How can you explain it then?' she asked, her voice breaking as tears started to dribble down her cheeks.

Daniel looked at her aghast and, putting his hands on his hips, turned away from her. He walked towards the giant skeleton and Charlie felt her panic rising. Daniel's shocked and hurt reaction was not what she'd been expecting. There could be a logical explanation after all. She looked up at the huge diplodocus which seemed as vast as her despair.

'Daniel. Wait.' She caught hold of his arm. 'What am I supposed to think? No-one else could have done it!'

'So it had to be me, right?'

Charlie let go of his arm. 'Tell me otherwise!'

'You think I'm such a good actor that I could lie about the way I feel about you or make a joke out of it when we make love? Is that what you think? Is it?'

Charlie went silent, looking at her hands. Daniel was clearly offended and despite the fact that she was the one who'd been betrayed, she now started to feel guilty. As if sensing this Daniel continued, each word whittling into her resolve to be angry.

'What about me? How do you think I feel about this? I thought you trusted me, Charlie. I thought we had something special at the weekend, but you're ready to cast the first stone just like everyone else as soon as there's one little rumour that might damage your precious reputation . . .'

'Stop it,' sobbed Charlie. 'I do trust you, but what would you think if you were me?'

'Despite the fact that the whole thing was probably caught on security cameras and Poppy is seeing one of the security guards,' muttered Daniel, turning away from her.

'What? What did you say?'

'It was probably the security guards. They must have caught the whole thing on the security cameras and decided to play a joke on me. They've been trying to get me back since I fleeced them at poker!'

'Security cameras. What security cameras? I've never seen any.'

'You're not supposed to see them,' said Daniel sarcastically. 'They're hidden. Someone's played a practical joke that's backfired, that's all.'

Charlie felt a capsule of relief burst inside her, flooding through her veins like a drug. She followed his gaze to the skeleton, her mind whirring as she rubbed her forehead. 'But everyone will know about us.'

'No one will find out. They wouldn't release your name or the tapes. They're private contractors. Even Si and Philippa wouldn't be allowed to see them. I'll slip Jack a few quid and no-one will be the wiser. And I'm sure Poppy knows she'll be out of a job if she opens her mouth,' he said. 'You know what agencies are like, they'll create gossip out of nothing.'

It all made sense. Daniel was as much a victim as she was. Charlie stared at a group of children who had been listening to their public conversation. They giggled and ran off in their maroon school hats and grey blazers towards the Creepy Crawlies exhibition.

Daniel stared at the diplodocus, his hands in his pockets. 'You know the thing that pisses me off?'

She shook her head, but he ignored her.

'I thought that after the Up Beat promotion we could tell everyone that we're together and I could have a proper relationship with you. Now I can't, not only because of this, but because you're not as serious as I thought.'

Panic ran through her. How could she have been so stupid? 'That's not true,' she gasped. 'I didn't know about the security cameras.'

Daniel stared at her, his eyes narrowing with hurt. 'I can't believe you thought it was me.'

'I didn't, I . . .' Charlie stammered and fell silent, dread creeping over her. She must have been crazy to accuse him.

He shook his head at her and snorted contemptuously.

'Daniel, please. I'm sorry. I didn't think. I couldn't think. I'm so sorry,' she said, reaching out to grip his arm. 'Please don't be angry with me.'

He shrugged her off. 'I guess I was wrong about you.'

Charlie's heart was thumping and her cheeks started to burn. 'You weren't. I want a relationship with you more than anything.'

'You could have fooled me.'

He thought she was a slag! 'Daniel,' she begged. 'I've been desperate for you. You must know that. I want you so much.'

'Do you?' he asked, staring into her eyes. 'Do you really?'

'Yes, yes,' she cried, wanting to shout out the words. 'Can't you see I'm crazy about you? I've been dying to go out with you ever since I first saw you.'

'I see.'

'Please, Daniel,' she sobbed, throwing herself into his arms. 'I'm so sorry. I'll make it up to you.'

'Shh,' he said. 'Calm down. It'll all be OK, you'll see.'

In the attic gym in Chelsea, Charlie and Kate lay back against the hard blue floor mat for the sit-up section of Gerry's Powerhour. The supersonic fat-burning routine was, apparently, a 'miracle cure for legs, tums and bums'. It must work, because amongst the forty or so sun-bed orange girls, there was not a square millimetre of cellulite to be found.

Gerry was yelling through the mouthpiece of his headset to make himself heard over the thumping dance music and Charlie tilted up her pelvis and squeezed in her abdominal muscles. She stared at the ineffectual ceiling fan whirring above her. 'Five, six, seven, eight,' yelled Gerry. Charlie looked over at Kate lying on the next floor mat and they winced at each other as the crunches continued.

Gerry was a black muscle-bound instructor who pulsated fitness and sported what looked like a car trailer attachment down the front of his stripy cycling shorts. 'Yes, and squeeze. That's right now, seven, eight. Last eight,' he lied for the fifth time. 'OK now, double time, and squeeze, come on girls, keep those abdominals in and *breathe*.'

Charlie's leotard was soaked with sweat, but she forced herself to continue. After seeing Daniel today, she was more convinced than ever that she had to be in top shape to keep him.

'Never, ever, again,' complained Kate, clutching her flat stomach as Charlie drove them to the 51 after the class. 'From now on, you're on your own.' She rested her unscuffed trainers on the dashboard.

'I quite enjoyed it,' said Charlie.

'You are *such* a liar. You hate exercise. I can't believe you wanted me to collude in this fitness fad of yours.'

'It's not a fad.'

'You enjoyed it because of Gerry's lunchbox. You spent the whole class ogling it.'

'I did not!'

'You did! You're just D and G.'

Charlie put up her hand. 'For your information, I am no longer desperate and gagging.'

'You've finally got it together with Daniel?'

Charlie put her tongue in her cheek and nodded.

Kate screamed and knelt up in the passenger seat, waving her hands up in the air. 'She shagged him! She shagged him!' she yelled, drawing attention to them both.

Charlie blushed and slapped her down, veering across lanes as they passed over the bridge in the sunset.

'Drive!' commanded Kate, pointing her fingers over the top of the windscreen. 'I need a drink for this.'

As soon as two pints of beer were on the table and Kate had passed one of the two lit cigarettes in her mouth to Charlie, she began. 'Details, details,' she urged, shaking out the match and leaning close.

'What do you want to know first?'

'How big?'

Charlie laughed and took a drag of the cigarette. 'Huge! Circumcised of course, but lovely.'

Kate grinned. 'Lucky girl. OK, from the beginning. Tell me everything.'

Charlie took a deep breath. 'Well. I was in the office on Saturday . . .' she began, and Kate sat back as Charlie launched into a fifteen minute monologue.

'How does he do on the checklist?' asked Kate, when Charlie had finished. Over the years, they'd formulated a checklist of no-go men that expanded as each new relationship failed. 'We know he's not an actor, which is brilliant news. They're all bastards. So what's next? Does he have a lurking girlfriend?'

'I don't think so,' laughed Charlie, taking a gulp of beer which would undo all the good of Gerry's gruelling class.

'We'll find out,' said Kate with mock impatience. 'Has he just finished a relationship?' She counted through the checklist on her fingers.

'No.'

'Recent death in the family?'

Charlie shrugged, shaking her head.

'How is the relationship with his mother?'

'OK,' said Charlie and paused. 'Actually, I don't know. He hasn't mentioned his family much. He has a little sister.'

'And he's great in bed. Well, the boardroom table, so that's good. What about contraception?'

Charlie screwed up her face.

'Charlie!' scolded Kate. 'There are thirteen forms of contraception and this isn't one of them.' She held up her crossed fingers.

'I know, I know. I'm going to take the morning-after pill.'

'Oh well, that's really responsible!'

'Don't lecture me. I feel bad enough as it is.'

Kate eyed her suspiciously. 'Are you absolutely sure about the Tipp-Ex cross business? You're positive it wasn't Daniel?'

Charlie smiled, her face radiant with affection. 'No way. He really cares.'

Dillon came up to them with a huge bowl of nachos dripping with melted cheese.

'I thought you might be needing these after your exercise class,' he said, smiling. 'What are you two gossiping about?'

'She's in lurve,' said Kate, twisting a nacho and lowering it, complete with a smooth mound of yellow cheese, into her mouth.

'I knew it wouldn't take long with that hair,' said Dillon. 'Who's the lucky geezer?'

Kate blew out and flapped her hand in front of her mouth as the cheese scalded her tongue. 'Daniel. You know, the one from work.'

'Who?'

'Daniel,' translated Charlie shyly.

Dillon raised his eyebrows. 'You be careful. He's got to be pretty special to deserve you.' He pinched Charlie's cheek, but she knew that Kate had told him all about her obsession with Daniel in less than favourable terms.

Kate rolled her eyes affectionately at him as he left. 'Come on. Tuck in.' She pushed the bowl towards Charlie.

Charlie patted her stomach and blew out her cheeks. 'No way. It's bad enough drinking beer. I must shift this weight.'

'What weight?' asked Kate with her mouth full.

'My flab.'

'You're right. It's best to turn into a fucked-up skinny girl. Blokes like them best.'

'I know.'

Kate stared at her wide eyed. 'Charlie, I was *joking*.'

The next day Charlie could hardly move, her calf muscles solid with lactic acid, but she didn't care. She sat at her desk dreamily gazing at a fluffy vapour trail streaking across the clear blue sky and wondered whether it was possible that a man could be so perfect. She had loads of work to do, but she still pinched Tina's *Daily Mail* from her desk and read Daniel's horoscope, smiling smugly to herself at the prediction that the planets were all geared for him to fall in love. Knowing that it was in the lap of the stars she dialled his extension, her heart pounding with anticipation.

'Take off all your clothes,' Daniel answered with a deep rasp after only one ring.

'How did you know it would be me?'

'I didn't,' he gloated.

'Oh!'

He heard the alarm in her voice. 'I've been beaming you vibes all morning, kind of the reverse of a voodoo doll. Where've you been?'

'Meeting with Nigel Hawkes at Up Beat,' said Charlie, elated that he had been thinking of her.

'Well, I need your help.'

'What's up?'

'My cock,' said Daniel. 'I've got this huge stiffy just

thinking about you and no matter what I do, it won't go away.'

Charlie blushed, shocked that he was being so provocative in the office, yet despite the danger of the conversation, she felt a surge of happiness. 'Well, I really don't know how I could possibly help,' she said, pretending to be prim.

'I do and what's more, I have a cunning plan,' said Daniel. 'I'll meet you in the copying room on the third floor in two and a half minutes. That's if I can walk with this huge thing in my trousers.' He put down the phone before Charlie could say anything.

She replaced the handset as if it was scalding. Feeling as conspicuous as if she were nude, she looked around her, her pulse thumping in her veins as she rose to her feet. This is ridiculous. She hesitated, sitting down. She brushed her hair out of her flushed face as if trying to dismiss Daniel's proposal.

But two and a half minutes later, Charlie closed the door of the copying room behind her and stood against it letting out a hot breath of relief and excitement. Daniel was standing by a large grey copier in the corner and he opened his arms to receive her in his embrace. Their mouths met as if their lips were magnetised and Daniel's tongue pushed into her mouth to find hers.

'I have to have you,' he apologised, pulling up the short skirt of her suit. She gasped as his hand plunged between her legs and ripped off her white lacy G-string. He kissed her face with passionate urgency as he undid the buttons of her blouse and bent down to suck her pert nipples, igniting the sensation fuse which burned through her to set her loins on fire.

'Daniel,' she gasped, trying to push him away, terrified that they'd get caught, but before she knew it he'd lifted up the lid of the photocopier and bent her over the cold glass plate.

'Don't you want me?' he asked.

'Yes, oh yes,' she murmured, savouring the delicious moment as she felt him pushing into her.

Without warning, the door of the copying room swung open. Daniel stopped moving. Charlie was hidden from sight behind the lid of the copier, but his rigid penis was still inside her tense body as Alison from the accounts department moved to the photocopier near the door.

Daniel pressed a hand into the small of Charlie's back to tell her not to move and then jabbed the copy button. She squeezed her eyes closed as the band of sharp light passed across her body, shuddering with excitement and fear. What if Alison saw her? Her heart was like a metronome at top speed. She would spontaneously combust with embarrassment if they got caught. How on earth would they get out of it?

Alison's photocopying seemed to be taking an age. Florid images of gagging her and bundling her into the Porsche then taking her to the top of a dodgy bungie jump and swearing her to secrecy loomed up in Charlie's imagination. Eventually the whirr of the machine stopped.

'Bye,' said Alison as she departed with her enlarged spreadsheets.

'Bye,' said Daniel, withdrawing his enlarged penis from Charlie.

'Don't you think we should stop?' She twirled round to face him. 'What if we get . . .' But Daniel's kisses stopped her questions and she moaned as he sank to his knees, lifting up one of her legs and burying his mouth into her, making her come.

Charlie grabbed his hair in both hands, pulling him to his feet, kissing him as he plunged inside her once again. Lost in frantic passion, she groped inside the back of his T-shirt.

'Where shall I come?' he breathed and she pulled away from him, sinking down to take him in her mouth as he came, his hot sperm shooting into her mouth.

Daniel lifted Charlie and sat her on the glass of the photocopier. They looked at each other's flushed cheeks, their breathing fast and heavy.

'Wow,' gasped Charlie, her trembling fingers trying to do up her buttons before anyone caught them.

'Hello,' said Daniel, kissing her and pressing the copy button once more. By the time Charlie realised what he had done it was too late to move.

Daniel laughed and picked up his A3 copies. 'Your genitals are quite photogenic,' he teased, looking at the copies from different angles.

Charlie pounced after him. 'Give me those!'

He held them out of her reach. 'No. They're for my bedroom wall, for when you're not around,' he said, watching her blush.

'You'd better bloody well keep those hidden.'

Daniel looked at them again. 'Very interesting,' he pondered. 'Rotund.'

Charlie looked at him and grabbed her bum. 'Do you think my bum's too big?'

He cupped one of her buttocks and gave it a playful squeeze. 'I like my women with a bit of meat.'

Daniel obviously thought she was too fat!

'Please rip them up,' she begged, trying to grab the papers once more.

'Don't you trust me?' Daniel trapped her arms by her sides.

'Of course I do.' She looked up into his eyes, 'It's just that it'll spoil everything if people find out. Anyway, I wouldn't want to ruin your reputation as the office Casanova.'

At that moment a photocopier repair man in a cheap grey suit entered the room and they sprang apart.

'I'll speak to you later,' said Daniel, folding up the sheets of paper. Charlie nodded, her cheeks staining vermilion. She walked out of the copy room towards the lift.

'Oh, Charlie.' Daniel had followed her.

'Yes?'

'I believe these are yours.'

He thrust the G-string into her hand before ambling towards the stairs, running his hand through his hair. Even though his back was turned, Charlie knew he was smiling.

'My house. Tonight. Nine p.m. Don't be late. Love D' was all it said. Charlie smiled at his irresistible arrogance, yet she knew that she would call Rich and wriggle out of her plans to spend the evening with him. She must remember to keep these knickers. She realised that her buttons were done up wrong just before the lift opened, catapulting her into reality and Sadie's inquiring look.

The private view of Anabel Constantin's 'Urban Myth' in Pierre Derevara's Clerkenwell art gallery was already crowded when Charlie and Daniel arrived.

'That's Pierre,' said Daniel, pointing out an exceptionally good-looking man in the middle of the crowd. Charlie stared at him then up to the high skylights of the converted warehouse in awe.

'He owns this place?' she asked.

'Of course,' said Daniel, waving to his friend.

Pierre glided towards them. He was slightly taller than Daniel with cropped, immaculately tousled blond hair. He was wearing oblong tinted glasses, a pair of tailored plaid trousers and a theatrical ruffle shirt which showed off his wonderfully proportioned body to perfection. He grinned at them, a bulging leather book clutched in one tanned, manicured hand and a glass of champagne in the other.

'Well, well, well!' he exclaimed as Daniel introduced Charlie. 'A beauty, Dan my boy, a real beauty. You must come in and meet everyone.'

He led them into the vast room and when they both had glasses of champagne, Pierre nodded towards a girl with long blond hair and a snub nose, being chatted up by a fat man in a tweed suit and spotted bow tie.

'Anabel's already got three commissions. Three. It's hilarious!' Pierre's astonishing eyes bulged dramatically and he walked towards her across the whitewashed floorboards.

Charlie looked around her at the 'Urban Myth'. A green council dustbin was suspended from the high ceiling and spun slowly like a disco ball over the crowd. Dotted across the huge white brick walls were various canvases with bits of rubbish glued to them, each surrounded by a small cluster of people admiring it and looking through the glossy programme. At one end of the room a projector spat images of detonated tower blocks on to a torn sheet and a dreary voice droned over the Brit-pop soundtrack.

'I've got to speak to a few people,' said Daniel, hurrying after Pierre and slapping his back as he talked to the immaculate guests. Charlie recognised a few of them from Orgasm and felt like a tramp in her linen trouser suit.

She folded one arm across her and sipped champagne, looking around her at the exhibition. On the canvas next to her, a crushed Cola can was stuck with the word 'Pain' airbrushed underneath it. It was about the most pretentious thing she'd ever seen. She could do so much better. If you could get an exhibition with this pile of rubbish, she might as well give up Bistram Huff and start all over again as an artist, but she quickly stamped out the idea. She couldn't leave Bistram Huff, especially now she was with Daniel.

She looked around the gallery, wondering how she would ever be able to afford such a cool place to live. Daniel's friends all seemed to have such style. A glass escalator rose to another level which was obviously the living quarters. As if reading her mind, Daniel waved to her.

'I'll show you upstairs.'

'Won't Pierre mind?'

Daniel looked at her as if she was crazy and took her hand.

Pierre's apartment was made up of frosted glass screens and looked like a Japanese art gallery.

'What do you think of the exhibition?' asked Daniel as she admired a wrought-iron sculpture of a torso rising out of the middle of the room.

'It's, um, interesting.'

'Come off it. It's bollocks! Pierre owes Daddy Constantin a favour, so Anabel gets the exhibition. Nepotism all the way. That's the way it works.'

Charlie was stung by his condescending tone. She should have told the truth and now Daniel thought she was as stupid as everyone else in the room.

'So, where's the snow then?' asked Pierre, walking through the automatic sliding screen.

Daniel flopped down on a white leather padded bench and crossed his legs, putting a small package on the kidney-shaped frosted glass table.

'Can I use your loo?' asked Charlie.

'Through there,' said Pierre, waving his hand at a blank wall and sitting next to Daniel by the coffee table.

Charlie approached the wall and touched it tentatively, starting as it slid back to reveal Pierre's astonishing bathroom. The toilet was a steel pedestal on a raised tiled platform and Charlie looked at it sceptically, laughing at herself that she'd so recently had sex with Daniel, but was paranoid about him hearing the sound of her pissing.

Pierre's shelves were stacked with pristine designer products. No wonder he looked so preened. She was staring at the moisturiser and buffing lotions when she felt the toilet move beneath her. She sprang off it and it flushed automatically, then she heard Pierre and Daniel sniggering like schoolboys. She stumbled across the gigantic tiles past the spotlessly clean chrome shower room.

'Don't you love it?' asked Pierre, the screen sliding back just as Charlie got her trousers back up. 'It's my latest import from Japan. You can adjust the height, warm up the seat and it's even got a sprinkler that will spray your ass. And it's all remote control. Very convenient.' He laughed and demonstrated. 'I have great fun with all my guests.'

Daniel put his arms around Charlie and kissed her. 'Don't look so worried.'

She smiled, embarrassed that he was being so open in front of Pierre.

'You two are so sweet,' said Pierre, looking at them in the mirror as he fiddled with a strand of his perfect hair.

Daniel smiled and clasped his hands behind Charlie's back. 'She's a babe, isn't she?'

'One of your finest. Now you two come and join me. I have to get through this ghastly exhibition somehow and you are going to be my accomplices,' he said. He pulled Charlie away from Daniel and led her through the screen to the table. 'Ladies first,' he said, sitting close to her and handing her a thin silver tube and, despite all her good intentions and promises to Rich, Charlie took it from him.

Rich was getting pissed. He sprawled in his surfers shorts on a threadbare patch of grass in Gabriel's Wharf, his head resting on Pix's thigh. A matted mongrel wandered past, its pink tongue dripping in the afternoon sun.

'There's Khalin, she's a mate of mine,' said Pix, waving towards the stage where a band was setting up for the next set. 'She's married to an Indian prophet.'

Rich hauled himself up on to his elbows and followed her gaze through the milling crowd. On the stage, a bare-foot girl with henna patterns swirling round her ankles and a green plastic jewel in the middle of her forehead was tapping the microphone.

'She always says that if you call yourself mystic you can get away with singing out of tune.'

Rich laughed and looked back at her. He took her chin between his thumb and forefinger. 'You look so funny, upside-down. This looks like your nose.'

Pix looked down at him and smiled. 'You're a big kid, d'you know that?'

'No I'm not, I'm a serious lawyer,' he mocked in a gruff voice.

Pix started to massage the area between his eyebrows in circular movements with her thumb. Rich closed his eyes and sighed.

'This is one of your seven energy centres,' she informed him.

'It feels great, can you do my other six?'

Pix ignored him. 'The Indians believe that your energy lives like a serpent at the bottom of your spine. You can awaken it and channel it to uncoil through your body,' she said.

There's certainly a serpent uncoiling through my body, thought Rich, glancing downwards at his shorts. He sat up and grabbed Pix who giggled as he pulled her on top of him. She straddled him in her Indian cotton skirt and Rich looked up into her sunlit face, wondering whether she could feel him stiffening through the thin cloth of his shorts. The beer and the sunshine were making him feel incredibly horny.

'What do you think of me, Pix?' he asked, wanting to gauge her feelings before he attempted to snog her.

She closed one eye against the glare of the sun and thought for a moment. 'I think that for someone so full of dreams, you're the least impulsive person I've ever met,' she said.

'How can you say that?' he protested. 'I'm very impulsive.'

'Come on then, give me an example.' Pix placed her palms on the ruffle of hair on his stomach where his T-shirt had ridden up.

'I don't know. All the time,' said Rich, feeling the ache in his penis subsiding.

'Rubbish. You've got a big gut full of instincts which you ignore!' She patted his stomach to make her point.

Rich pulled a face and looked past her at the stage. The drums flooded the square with an infectious rhythm and on the stage, Khalin turned and nodded to the percussionist and sitar player who embellished the beat. She closed her eyes and stood by the microphone rotating her wrists above her head like a snake charmer.

Suddenly Rich lumbered up and pulled Pix to her feet, yanking her into the centre of the square where he began to dance. Pix jumped up and down with glee and clapped her hands as she belly-danced round Rich who jerked to the music, hunching his shoulders and lifting up his hands and feet like a spiderman stuck in gunge. When Khalin started singing, Rich grabbed Pix and improvised a dance, throwing in every move he knew from *Come Dancing* to 'Greased Lightning'. Pix laughed as he took her hand and she twirled away from him, before he swooped her up in his arms in his own version of a jive. Soon the jugglers were juggling in time and the face-painted kids, excited by the atmosphere, jigged around and played tag as more people joined the happy crowd.

As the set finished, Rich puffed a hot breath towards his brow and beckoned Pix to sit down.

'You were great,' she laughed, putting her hand on her

chest and gasping for breath. 'You got everyone dancing! Khalin will be delighted.'

Rich flopped on to the grass. 'You see I can be impulsive,' he said. He breathed in, smelling the wafts of smoke from the barbecue by the Greenpeace tent. He was glad that Pix had challenged him and he remembered what it felt like to be himself rather than a suited, Tube-travelling zombie.

'Shall we go back to mine and have something to eat?' he asked, taking a final swig out of the warm can of beer. There was no way he could stomach a veggieburger. 'Are you hungry?'

Pix smiled at him. 'I could eat the hind leg off the lamb of God.'

On the other side of town, Daniel was in a hyper mood, the music blaring out of the Porsche as he roared around Hyde Park Corner, weaving through the Saturday afternoon traffic.

'Where are we going?' asked Charlie, but Daniel just grinned at her and accelerated down Buckingham Palace Road, screeching to a halt outside Victoria station. He bounced out of the car. 'Come on, I've got to show you something. You said you had useless hand-to-eye coordination, so this should sort you out.'

Charlie stumbled after him as he disappeared inside a huge arcade, sliding his sunglasses to the top of his head. It was full of schoolboys glued to the noisy machines, roaring round imaginary race tracks and fighting computer demons, the summer's day outside forgotten as they immersed themselves in their virtual reality world.

'What happened to discos and girls?' asked Charlie, nodding at the group of lads who were concentrating all their efforts on a noisy computer car race.

'This is much better,' said Daniel, leading her through the coloured lights, clashing jingles and simulated applause to a large black machine with two guns mounted on the front.

'Do you want to be pink or blue?' he asked, pulling some change out of the pocket of his Calvin Klein khakis.

Charlie looked at the screen and the jerking computer men in combat gear. 'Blue of course.'

'OK, shoot everything that's blue,' said Daniel, gripping hold of his gun and training it on the screen as he dropped the money in the slot.

Suddenly they were drowning in noise. Computer generated images plunged them into underwater worlds, mountain combat and space wars as she fought against Daniel. Eventually the scores flashed up.

'That wasn't too bad for your first attempt,' said Daniel, looking impressed.

'Can we go again?'

He smiled and kissed her. 'Of course. Have you got any money?'

By the time they stumbled out of the arcade and back to Daniel's house, three hours had passed and Charlie yawned, her head buzzing and her eyes tired from concentrating on the screen.

She couldn't believe how fast time went when she was with Daniel and how easily she had slipped from her single life into being his girlfriend. She almost felt like she was on holiday and she hugged her knees as she sat engulfed in one of Daniel's midnight blue bath towels identifying the gorgeous aroma surrounding her as a mixture of aftershave and fabric softener. She hummed to herself as she surveyed Daniel's bedroom. A dark duvet was thrown over the cast-iron bed, an antique wardrobe stood in the corner next to a pine trunk which she presumed was filled with love-letters. She felt herself itching to spy.

As she had imagined, the bedroom was in the gallery of the main room and she flopped back on the bed basking in the sunshine falling through the stained-glass skylight. Daniel, who had been feeding Benson, padded up the spiral stairs carrying a bottle of water and Charlie stretched out on his bed before him like a cat. He peeled back the towel as if it were the velvet wrapping of a diamond necklace. She breathed in as he gazed down at her naked flushed body and kissed the gentle undulation of her stomach.

'You're beautiful,' he said.

'You're not so bad yourself,' she said as he lay down next to her on the duvet.

'I'm going to have my wicked way with you all weekend,' he said. 'I'm not letting you out of my sight.'

Charlie leaned up on one elbow. 'You'll have to. I'm going to my parents for Sunday lunch tomorrow.'

'Then I'll come with you.'

Charlie looked at him dismayed. It was too soon for him to meet her parents.

'What's wrong? I thought you wanted me to be your boyfriend.'

'I do,' she said, rolling over to straddle him and looking down into his face. His hands reached up, taking each of her breasts into his hands.

'How do you feel?' asked Charlie, joy radiating out from her bones.

Daniel weighed her breasts as if testing the edibility of soft peaches. 'Like this,' he replied, twitching his hard penis towards her, so that it gently slapped her buttocks.

'Oh, I see,' said Charlie, raising her eyebrows.

'Hop on,' he said.

Charlie scanned his face, wondering what to do. She longed to feel him inside her, but there was no sign of any condoms by the bed. She was about to say something when Daniel pushed himself into her and she gasped. She knew she was being stupid, but she couldn't stop now. Daniel watched her as she trembled with suspense.

'Don't worry,' he whispered, kissing her with such passion that it was as if his presence filled her brain, leaving no room for sensible questions.

Pix and Rich had decided to walk most of the way home, strolling hand in hand along the Embankment, browsing at the book stall under Charing Cross rail bridge where Rich bought her his two favourite novels and she bought him a beginners' guide to Feng Shui. By the time they reached the flat, the moon was lingering like a fingerprint in the sky.

Pix sat cross-legged on the Formica counter. 'You enjoy cooking,' she said as she watched him at the stove. Rich lifted the saucepan lid and prodded the pasta with a fork.

'It puts me in touch with my feminine side.'

Pix rolled her eyes at him and jumped down to look at the photo-covered pinboard by the fridge.

'It makes quite a change,' continued Rich. 'I can't be bothered to cook when I get home and Charlie can only cook beans on toast and tuna bake. It gets a bit boring.'

'Is this Charlie?' Pix asked, intrigued. Nearly every photo showed Rich with a beautiful girl.

The wooden spoon stopped briefly in the creamy sauce. 'Uh huh.' He sprinkled chopped coriander into the pan.

'She's very pretty.'

'She is there, but she's gone blonde and it doesn't suit her.'

'What's she like?'

'Difficult to describe really,' said Rich, licking his finger. 'When you know someone that well, it's hard.' He trailed off and shook the saucepan full of pasta.

'Is she funny?' urged Pix, peering at the photos.

'She's funny all right,' said Rich, staring into the steam. 'She's funny peculiar and funny ha-ha and she likes tea in blue china mugs and bacon sandwiches with mayonnaise.'

Pix turned, astonished by the affection in his voice, but her attention was caught by a birthday card that Charlie had made Rich.

'This is great,' she said, lifting it down and studying the cartoon drawing of a space man. 'Where did you get it?'

Rich took it from her and looked at it before chuckling. 'Charlie drew it. She always says that I'm on a different planet.' He handed it back to her.

'It's great. I'm doing a flyer for Space Odyssey and it would be a perfect illustration.'

'Borrow it then.'

'Are you sure?'

'Charlie won't mind. Anyway, it's my card. I'm always saying she should draw more. She's so talented.'

'She should do flyers. Judging from this, she's got the eye for it.'

Rich wrinkled his nose. 'She's too wrapped up in her job.'

'Where is she tonight?'

Rich served up the pasta on to two plates. 'She's got this new bloke and she's spending all her time with him.' He poured the sauce over the pasta and sprinkled chopped herbs on top.

Pix sat down at the table and started tossing the salad. 'You don't approve?' she asked, popping a cherry tomato in her mouth.

'It's none of my business,' said Rich bitterly, placing the steaming pasta in front of her. 'There you go.'

'Wow, this looks incredible. I haven't eaten posh food for weeks.' She grinned, sniffing the aromas rising from the plate.

'Dillon, this chef we know, runs the bar over the road. I get all my tips from him.' Rich sloshed white wine into her glass. 'It's amazing how much you can charge for some sun-dried tomatoes and a packet of rocket from Sainsbury's,' he said, spooning parmesan over his plate.

'It smells delicious and I'd rather be here than in a restaurant,' laughed Pix, raising her glass to Rich.

By midnight, three empty bottles stood on the table and Pix was dipping her fingertips in the pool of wax around the squat candle on the table and moulding it into small cups as she told Rich about all the places she wanted to travel to. Suddenly Kev flopped through the cat flap in the back door.

Rich, unsteady on his feet, swooped up and picked the green burrs from his ears.

Pix stared at the cat. 'He has a good aura.'

'You hear that, Kev, you've got a good aura, mate.' Rich grinned at Pix. 'I'm just going to ask Kev's advice on something.' He pretended to turn away and held the cat close to his ear. 'Do you think I should ask Pix to stay the night?' he stage whispered. 'She doesn't want to traipse back to Brixton in a cab. What do you think?'

Kev licked his ear and they both laughed.

Rich turned to Pix, keeping his face straight with mock seriousness. 'Kev wants to know if you'd like to stay the night?'

Pix walked over to Kev still in Rich's arms. 'I'd love to.' She stroked the cat under the chin before Rich put him down.

'Watch him, he's a right old flirt,' said Rich as Kev circled Pix's ankles.

'It takes one to know one.'

He took her in his arms and hugged her. 'You can use the bathroom first if you like,' he said, leading her out of the kitchen towards his room.

Rich noticed the answer machine flashing and pressed the button as Pix shut the bathroom door. He stood motionless, his heart raging as he listened to Charlie's message.

'Hey Superman, it's me. I just wanted to say hi and I hope you're having a good day. Listen. I'm going home for lunch tomorrow. Do you want to come? Mum and Dad would love to see you. Anyway, I'll call you. Big hugs, bye bye, my love.'

When Pix came out of the bathroom, she found Rich curled up in bed. She smiled and watched him as he feigned sleep. Then she crawled under the cold duvet and curled up against his back. He didn't move as her arm slid around his waist like a tentacle. He felt her kissing his shoulder and resting her nose on the soft fabric of his T-shirt.

'Night, night, Pix,' he whispered, his eyes wide open in the dark.

Pix relaxed back on to the pillow, breaking contact with him. 'Aye. Sweet dreams,' she said.

'Who's she?' Angelica Goldsmith's hostile voice punctured Charlie's sleep. At the foot of Daniel's bed, Angelica levered off her gold stilettos and threw them towards the staircase so that they clattered against the cast-iron banister.

Charlie sat up in bed, duvet clutched to her chest. Angelica's piercing blue eyes had the same intensity as Daniel's and they glowered at Charlie from her deeply tanned face.

Her thick blonde hair, highlighted by the sun, swept in waves over her slim shoulders as if she had just stepped out of a top hair salon.

Charlie turned to Daniel, but his face cracked out of sleep into an open grin.

'Babe!' he croaked, opening his arms.

Angelica grinned back at him and Charlie could see what she must have looked like as a child. She flopped on to Daniel's side of the bed and embraced her brother, her eyes scratching over Charlie's face as she stared over his shoulder.

Daniel pulled away and kissed his sister on the forehead, holding her cheeks in his hands. 'When did you get back?'

Angelica stood up, yanking off her earrings and chucking them on the bedside table. 'The flight got in at about nine last night and we went clubbing,' she said. 'I'm exhausted. St Tropez was soooo hot.'

'Did you dump that prat Rufus?' he shouted after her as she flounced into the bathroom.

'God yes. I bumped into Thierry Derevara, Pierre's cousin. Fucking *gorgeous*! It must run in the family!' Her voice was drowned by the gushing of water in the bath.

Charlie sat reeling from the unwelcome intrusion.

Daniel laughed. 'Angelica,' he said in explanation. 'Isn't she a blast?' He pecked Charlie on the cheek and threw back the duvet. 'I'd better go and make some breakfast. She'll be starving.'

Charlie gawped at him as he sprang out of bed and hauled on his tartan boxer shorts.

'Oh,' she muttered, her voice reflecting how peeved she felt.

'What's the matter?' Daniel asked, looking down at her.

'Nothing,' stammered Charlie. 'She gave me a shock, that's all.'

'Don't mind Angel, you'll get used to her.' He jogged down the stairs to greet Benson. 'Hello boy, Mummy's home,' she heard him say to the excited puppy.

'Some angel!' Charlie pulled on her jeans, her body still warm from Daniel's night-long embrace. Wishing that she could use the bath, she scowled as she heard Angelica yelling from the bathroom.

'Can someone bring me a clean towel?'

Charlie bristled with anger. She opened Daniel's laundry basket and started to pull out a dirty towel, then thought better of it. She ought to start off relations with Daniel's sister as amicably as possible. Taking a thick blue towel from the pile that Daniel's cleaning lady had laundered, she opened the door of the bathroom a crack.

'There's one here, I'll leave it outside the door.'

'Bring it in,' commanded Angelica as if addressing a servant.

Charlie opened the door. The huge slanted window in the beamed roof was glistening with steam and the antique enamel bath underneath it filling with bubbles. Angelica groaned with pleasure as she sank into the tub like Cleopatra and Charlie looked up at the state-of-the-art surround sound speakers in the ceiling as the slow beat of some jazz funk filled the room.

'There.' She placed the towel over the chrome rail.

In the kitchen, Daniel was whistling. Charlie went up behind him and put her arms around his waist, pressing her cheek into the warmth of his back. He removed her arms gently, breaking out of her embrace.

'Careful, I'm cooking,' he said, throwing pancake mixture into a sizzling frying pan.

Charlie backed away and Daniel swirled the batter around in the pan.

'You haven't forgotten that we're going to my parents for lunch, have you?'

Daniel left the pancake bubbling on the stove. 'Of course I haven't forgotten. Come here.'

She put her arms around him, clinging for reassurance as he stroked her tangled hair. 'That's my girl,' he said as if sensing her submission. She put up her lips to him and he kissed her, his open eyes keeping a check on the pancake. It wasn't long before Angelica burst in to the kitchen wearing Daniel's favourite T-shirt.

'Don't mind me,' she said. Daniel immediately broke away from Charlie.

'Angel, meet Charlie.' He waved a spatula between the two women. Angelica looked Charlie up and down. 'Hi,' she said with a false smile, before picking a grape off the bunch in the fruit bowl and biting into it.

'How was your holiday?' asked Charlie.

Angelica hoisted herself on to the kitchen counter and swung her long brown legs. She looked as if she were a model waiting for a photo call. 'Fine,' she said, making it clear that it was none of Charlie's business. 'Dan my man, give me all the news, gossip and scandal.' Angelica leaned on the counter looked indulgently towards her brother.

'How could there be gossip with you out of town? I've been keeping a low profile.'

'Oh dear.'

'No. I've loved it. I've been having a great time,' he said, smiling at Charlie.

'Oh?' Angelica looked surprised, realising that Charlie was not one of the one-night stands she was used to finding in Daniel's bed on a Sunday morning. 'Where did you meet?' she asked, staring at Charlie as if she were a Martian.

Charlie bristled with indignation.

'We work together,' said Daniel, not noticing.

'Dan! Sowing your seed in the work place – ha!' Angelica threw her head back and screeched.

Charlie wanted to slap the bubbling pancake on to Angelica's smug face.

'I suppose everyone knows, don't they?' She slipped off the counter and raised her eyebrows at Charlie.

Charlie shook her head, not daring to let herself speak.

Angelica threw her a 'don't be so naive' kind of false grin. 'I wouldn't like to be in your shoes,' she said, putting her arms around Daniel as Charlie had done earlier. 'Discretion has never been a quality possessed by my darling brother. In fact, the more sordid the little secret . . . well, I shan't say.'

Daniel didn't seem to hear her. Instead he lifted up one

of her arms and kissed it. 'Great tan,' he said. 'Was anyone fun out this year?'

Angelica broke away from him and sat on a stool, waiting for her breakfast.

'*Everyone!* And we all missed you,' she said. 'Tamara was there.'

'Oh. Is she OK?'

'You'd find out if you bothered to talk to her,' said Angelica, scolding him. 'Her dad's just bought that big château on the hill in Monte Carlo.' She pressed the back of her hand to her forehead dramatically. 'Yet money means nothing to her without you.' Daniel slid the pancake on to a plate.

'Honestly, Dan, do you have to leave a trail of heartbroken women all over the world?'

'She'll get over it.' He put the plate down beside his sister.

Charlie stood up, pushing her stool back. Benson was scraping at the back door wanting to be let out.

'Listen. Why don't I leave you two to catch up?' she said, her heart pounding, lowering her hurt eyes away from Daniel. 'I'll walk Benson and then take him home. You can come and pick us up in a while, if you want.'

'You hear that Benson, you're going for a *walk*,' gushed Angelica, whisking Benson into a frenzy of excitement.

'No pancakes?' shouted Daniel over the noise Benson was making.

'No, I want a bath. Thanks anyway.'

'I'll pick you up about eleven-thirty, is that OK?' he asked, dropping a knob of butter into the frying pan.

'You're not going out, are you?' Angelica clattered down her loaded fork. 'I wanted you to give me a lift up to Oliver's, he's having an all-day party.' She stared at Daniel with crestfallen eyes.

'Sorry hon, but we're going out. I've got Sunday lunch at Charlie's parents.' He shrugged.

Angelica pouted. 'Don't be mean. I've been away all summer and as soon as I'm back, you're going out. Anyway, you hate Sunday lunches and all that parents bit.'

Charlie looked furiously at Daniel, but he put Angelica's forkful of the syrup-dripping pancake into his mouth to avoid making a comment.

Benson looked like a slow motion film of a galloping horse as he strained at his leash, pulling Charlie over the crossing to the local cemetery. Angry tears smarted in her eyes. 'How dare they,' she muttered, thinking about all the smart put-downs she should have thrown back at Angelica.

'Cheer up, darlin', it could be worse,' said a guy leaning out of an open-topped jeep at the traffic lights.

Could it, she wondered, scowling at him.

Daniel hadn't even kissed her goodbye and her heart twinged with foreboding.

She strolled along the cracked concrete path between crumbling gravestones. The sun shone through the trees overhead and she passed an old woman, pruning a bowl of roses on a grave. Charlie nodded to her and watched as she talked to the old marble headstone, thinking how dreadful it must be to lose a loved one. What if she lost Daniel? What if Angelica turned him against her? What if he went off her and back to the glamorous Tamara? She couldn't bear the rejection. By the time she'd reached the flat, she'd realised that however upset she felt, she mustn't show him. She couldn't risk it.

She'd never had a visiting pet in the flat before and Benson was intent on making his mark. Within seconds Kev launched into the air, his fur on end, hissing at the curious puppy.

'Calm down,' said Charlie, frightened of Kev, who spat and flexed his claws, lashing out at Benson as he scampered into the living room.

Charlie rugby-tackled the cat, seizing the rigid animal and holding him out in front of her she elbowed open the door of Rich's room and backed in, kicking it closed behind her.

'Sorry Rich, Bens—' she said looking towards the bed, but her jaw dropped as Pix raised her head above the duvet.

Rich, who'd forgotten that Pix had stayed the night in his bed, sat up and looked between the two women.

'Sorry,' mumbled Charlie, dropping Kev like a hot potato and groping for the door handle. The concept that Rich could, or would, have someone to stay had never entered her head and her heart pounded as she closed the door. Reeling with shock she stumbled towards her room and sank to the floor by her bed.

Benson nuzzled her, raising her from her stupor, and she ruffled his soft ears. 'What's going on?' She grabbed the phone off the table by the bed and punched in Kate's number.

'I'm having a crisis,' she said, her voice shaking.

'So am I. I'm waxing my bikini line,' replied Kate. 'Hold on, this is the last strip.' There was a ripping sound and Charlie winced as Kate swore down the phone.

'OK. Talk me through it.'

Charlie crumbled as she recalled the events of the last two hours. 'I don't know what's wrong with me,' she ended, wiping a tear from the corner of her eye.

'Angelica is a bitch. Rise above it, babe.'

'But Daniel should have stuck up for me,' lamented Charlie, her voice choked with self-pity.

'Angelica is his sister and he didn't *have* to do anything. You wanted him to be more attentive, but let's face it, you're forgetting the one crucial point.'

'What?' asked Charlie, already knowing the answer and starting to smile.

'He's a man!' they chorused.

'Chances are he didn't even notice what she was doing.'

Charlie let Kate's words diffuse reason into the situation.

'That's not the worst of it. What shall I do about Rich?' she asked. 'He didn't even tell me he was seeing anyone.'

'So? Give him a chance to explain.'

'He's had plenty of chances to explain,' shot back Charlie, astounded by how angry she felt.

'Really?' Kate knew that Charlie had been neglecting her friends. 'Come on, this isn't like you. Where is the cool, calm, sophisticated girl I once knew and loved? You don't have to be like Angelica and get all territorial.'

'I am *not* like Angelica,' screeched Charlie like a spoilt child, and they both laughed. 'Oh Kate, what would I do without you?'

'Go completely off the rails. Now then. Shall I do my toenails vamp, baby blue or red pepper?' She put on her bimbo voice.

'Red pepper. Vamp is out and blue is so . . . common!'

'Ha! I caught you out. You can still make decisions, so there's hope for you yet!'

Charlie laughed. 'Oh God, I'm being horribly selfish. How are you? Where's Dillon?'

'Out there in cyberspace, somewhere.'

'What?'

'He's gone to the Surf Café to cruise the Internet for salad dressings.' Kate's voice vibrated as she shook the nail varnish bottle. 'He's been putting it about on the World Wide Web for the definitive dressing. So far he's got an orange and vodka one from Vladivostok or somewhere.'

'You're joking.'

'I'm not. And you think you've got problems!'

Pix was in the kitchen pulling a box of herbal tea bags out of her knapsack. When she saw Charlie she put it down and smiled, her green eyes crinkling.

'Hi, I'm Pix,' she said. 'Sorry, did we give you a shock?'

Despite herself, Charlie felt herself smiling back. 'You did, but I'll get over it. I'm Charlie by the way,' she said, moving forward to shake Pix's hand.

Pix rubbed her hand on her purple dungarees before taking Charlie's. 'I know. I've heard a lot about you.'

'Really? That's strange because I've heard nothing about you.' Charlie glared at Rich who was sloping into the kitchen.

'You've met then,' he said, rubbing the back of his neck where it had been scorched by the sun the day before. His eyes were bloodshot with hangover. 'What's the story with the dog?'

'He's Benson. Daniel's puppy.'

'He's a cutey,' said Pix, ruffling Benson's ears.

Rich bristled. 'What's he doing here?'

133

'I took him for a walk. Daniel's sister turned up and I wanted to come home and get ready,' said Charlie. 'I'm taking Daniel home for Sunday lunch,' she added, her smileless face fixed firmly on Rich.

'I see,' said Rich. 'Well in that case, please give my love to your parents.'

Charlie turned away from him and filled up a bowl of water. She knew she was being spiteful, but she felt so betrayed that Rich hadn't told her about Pix. And anyway, it was far more important that Daniel met her parents. Rich had met them hundreds of times. She placed the bowl on the floor for Benson.

'So, Pix. What do you do?' she asked, trying to lighten the proceedings.

'I design flyers for clubs, but at the moment I'm a student. Photography,' she said, her eyes darting between Charlie and Rich who both looked at her with fake interest, the tension between them almost visible.

'Oh? Where?'

'St Martin's.'

Charlie felt her back stiffen with indignation. How could she still feel jealous after so long? It was as if Rich was deliberately trying to taunt her. 'St Martin's is supposed to be the best,' she said, putting her hands in the back pockets of her jeans. She bit her bottom lip, catching Pix's confused look. 'Look. Sorry to be rude, but I'm running late.' She ducked out of the kitchen, astonished that her eyes were filling with tears.

'She seems upset,' Pix said to Rich, who was watching the space left by Charlie's departure.

'Don't worry about her,' he said, looking as if he had just seen a ghost. He turned his attention to Pix. She smiled and moved towards him, her face full of affection. Rich panicked. He didn't want her here. Charlie must have thought that he'd slept with Pix when nothing had happened.

'Would you like some breakfast?' he asked, dodging past her and flinging open the fridge. 'How do you like your eggs?'

'Unfertilised,' said Pix, laughing at the oldest feminist joke in the book.

Daniel sniffed loudly and ran the back of his hand under his nose. 'I couldn't get rid of Angelica. I'm sorry if she was a bitch, she doesn't mean to be,' he apologised as he climbed the stairs of the flat. He hugged Charlie and she put her head on his chest, listening to his heartbeat which seemed unusually fast.

'Don't worry. I was pissed off because I wanted a lie-in with you,' she said, staring up at him with large eyes, her prepared speech forgotten. Daniel kept his sunglasses on and stroked her cheek with unexpected tenderness.

'So did I,' he said.

Benson wagged his tail at their heels, whimpering for attention as Daniel flicked his tongue into Charlie's mouth in a passionate kiss. She smiled and closed her eyes while Daniel planted noisy kisses on the sleek soft curve of her neck.

'I have to have you,' he said in an Italian accent as he started to sink to his knees. Charlie opened her eyes and suddenly pushed him away. Rich was standing in the living room watching them.

Daniel held out his hand. 'Hi. You must be Rich, right? The lawyer?'

Rich's smile was rigid. 'Yes, that's right. And you must be Daniel? The boyfriend,' he said, hating him on sight.

Daniel laughed, not noticing Rich's stony expression.

'This is Pix,' said Charlie as she appeared from the kitchen, 'Rich's new . . .?'

Pix pulled a face. 'Girlfriend,' she joked.

Daniel pushed his sunglasses to the top of his head and looked her up and down. He ran his tongue around his teeth. 'Hi, sweetheart.'

Pix blushed and moved behind Rich as if for protection.

Charlie turned to Daniel. 'We'd better make a move.'

He put his hand on her shoulder. 'Here goes. Big parental meeting.' He grimaced at Rich and Pix as if he was nervous.

'They're lovely people,' said Rich.

135

'Right. Well. See you around.' Daniel raised his hand like a film star getting into a limousine. Benson raced down the stairs ahead of them to take up his position on the rug on the back seat of Daniel's Porsche.

When the front door slammed, Pix burst out laughing. She ran her hand through her cropped auburn hair mimicking Daniel. She stood in front of Rich and looked him up and down, undressing him with her eyes.

'Well hello,' she drawled.

Rich laughed. 'What a wanker!'

'He's very good-looking, but I can't see why Charlie is with him,' said Pix, shaking her head.

'Neither can I. Is he really that attractive?'

'No way! Attractiveness has nothing to do with looks, it's about the whole package. Daniel isn't even in the same league as you.' She reached up and kissed him on the lips.

Rich put his arms around her and kissed her back, allowing her to take his mind off Charlie.

Pix broke away from him. 'No, no. Don't kiss me like that,' she said dragging Rich to the sofa. 'Since I'm your new whatever, I'm going to give you a kissing lesson.' She sat him down and knelt over him. 'What is it with English men? They never know how to kiss.'

Rich was upset. 'I've never had any complaints before,' he said, but Pix silenced him, coaxing him into an embrace. With murmurs of encouragement she kissed him over and over again, teaching him not to thrust his tongue, but to kiss her lips, gently sucking so that their mouths created a vacuum in which their tongues met. Rich felt as if his brain had gone into tunnel vision, focusing on the oasis of sensation, and he heard his own murmurs mingling with her.

He wrapped her in his arms, smelling her petuli oil scent, and they rolled off the sofa on to the rug with a gentle thud. Pix giggled and for a moment they lay on their backs looking up at the flaking ceiling rose.

She turned her head towards him. 'Let's do it.'

Rich nodded, his hands already fumbling under her T-shirt. Yet as soon as Pix's small hand fluttered towards his fly, to his horror he felt his hardness melting. He tried kissing her more vigorously, but it was hopeless. He sat up, breaking away from her.

'What? What is it?' she asked, sitting up beside him.

How could this happen, when every morning he woke with a thumping erection?

'I don't know. I'm really sorry. Would you mind if we waited, Pix?' he asked, looking at her with flushed cheeks.

Pix hugged him.

'I feel so stupid.'

She held him more tightly. 'Shh. It's OK,' she whispered. 'I understand.'

'Darling!' Hazel Bright threw her arms around her daughter and Charlie kissed her mother's soft cheek, apologising for being so late. Hazel held her daughter's shoulders at arm's length. 'Look at you,' she tutted, touching Charlie's hair. Then she moved away and appraised her figure. 'You're losing weight. Are you eating properly?'

Charlie gave her a warning look. 'Mum, I'd like you to meet Daniel,' she said, turning round to gaze at him with uncensored pride. Hazel, flushed from her Sunday tipple of sherry, plumped up her colour-rinsed curls and shook Daniel's outstretched hand.

'Delighted to meet you, Daniel. You're very welcome.'

Charlie cringed as they trooped into the kitchen. She could tell her mother was putting on her best Cheltenham Ladies' College accent. Moreover, she was shamelessly scrutinising Daniel's face for any obvious traces of a first-class degree from a respected university, which she felt should be the minimum prerequisite of any man attempting to date her daughter.

Daniel greeted his lover's mother's gaze with a smooth self-assurance that made Hazel blush.

'Daddy is in the sitting room,' she chirped. 'I'll give him a shout. Do make yourselves at home. She untied her Liberty print apron, flinging it over a pine kitchen chair, and made for the door, nudging Delilah the ancient tabby off the Welsh dresser on the way.

'Donald. Charlie's here,' she called, checking her lipstick in the hall mirror.

Charlie clapped her hands together. 'Drink?' she asked Daniel with the authority of being in the place she still described as home.

Daniel didn't answer. He was studying the gallery of family photos adorning the kitchen wall. 'Check out those flares!' He pointed to an eight-year-old Charlie in full seventies glory.

'Don't look,' squealed Charlie, rushing to his side. 'They're so embarrassing.' She put her hand out to cover the pictures, but Daniel caught hold of her and started tickling her.

'Pipkins.' Charlie's father arrived in the kitchen. He took off his half-moon glasses and peered at his daughter.

'Hello, Daddy,' said Charlie, the laughter still in her voice.

'Oh I say, blonde, eh? Whatever next? I hope that's not permanent!'

He smiled as Charlie tiptoed to kiss his cheek.

'And this is your new young fellow, I presume,' he said, looking at Daniel with the down-the-nose stare of a vicar studying a wayward parishioner who smelt of urine.

'Daddy, this is Daniel.' Charlie reached out to Daniel and beckoned him forward.

'You've been keeping her safe in that contraption of yours have you, Daniel?' asked Charlie's father. He'd been roused from the golf page on Ceefax by the arrival of Daniel's Porsche which had scattered the carefully raked gravel in all directions.

'Safe as houses,' levelled Daniel as he shook Donald's hand.

Donald nodded and grunted. 'Who's for an aperitif?' he asked, leading the way to the sitting room. Nervousness flooded over Charlie and she wished she hadn't called her parents to warn them that Daniel was coming. If Rich was here, Hazel would be up to her elbows in the garden and Donald would have been lighting the barbecue, wearing his floppy denim hat.

'Should I have worn a blazer?' teased Daniel, standing next to Charlie at the mahogany drinks cabinet.

She shook her head, worried that he felt out of place as Donald poured gin and tonics and passed a bowl of peanuts to Daniel.

'I thought we'd eat in the dining room, it's *so* much more comfortable,' Hazel announced, ushering everyone through the double doors.

'Mother,' hissed Charlie, suffering a clang of gloom. She hated her parents putting on a show. Daniel wasn't a visitor, he was her boyfriend.

Sure enough, the table was set for royalty. Great Aunty Betty's Royal Doulton dinner service was crammed on to the lace tablecloth along with Donald's prized Edinburgh crystal glasses and silver-plated cutlery.

'Where shall I sit, Mrs Bright?' asked Daniel, holding on to the back of a chair. 'Oh call me Hazel, please,' she replied. 'Anywhere is fine.' She waved her hand in the air as if the dinner was a slapdash affair and hadn't taken her all morning to prepare.

'Thought we'd have some Australian red,' announced Donald. 'Big fan of the New World wines. Big fan.' He showed the label to Daniel, who took the bottle from him.

'Go ahead and open it,' said Donald, handing Daniel the ancient corkscrew with the tree bark handle. It broke before the screw was half-way into the cork.

Hazel flapped to Daniel's side. 'That always happens.'

Charlie tried to control her irritation. 'Why don't you throw it out then?'

'We can't throw it out. We've had it since we were married,' said Hazel.

Donald took his Swiss army knife out of his pocket. 'Here.' He reached for the bottle and removed the offending corkscrew. 'Marvellous invention these,' he said, his voice strained as his hand gripped the red handle of the army knife and pulled out the cork. He untwisted it from the metal spiral. 'Have you got one of these, Daniel?' he asked, clearly pleased with himself.

Charlie covered her face with her hands. Of course Daniel didn't have a Swiss army knife in his pocket! This was a big mistake. She grabbed the wine from her father.

'Let Daniel taste it,' he said jovially as he picked up the carving knife and sharpened it.

Charlie dutifully poured half an inch of wine into Daniel's glass, giving him an 'I know, I'm sorry,' look.

'Fuck me,' he mouthed in reply, his eyes teasing her as she blushed. He swilled the wine around the glass and sniffed it.

'That will be lovely,' he said, placing it down untasted.

Charlie smiled as she poured the wine. Hazel handed round the perfect roast potatoes while Donald distributed the beef and eventually they were ready to eat. Then the genteel form of torture that Charlie's parents had been perfecting all their lives began.

'So, Daniel, what do your parents do?' Donald was first off the mark with his favourite missile. Charlie's eyes flashed a warning at her father, but he ignored her and raised his eyebrows towards Daniel.

'My father recently retired from the Diplomatic Corps,' offered Daniel, 'and my mother was a ballerina.' He looked down at his plate.

'Dancing eh!' said Donald, missing the 'was' in Daniel's last sentence. 'Hazel and I love dancing. We still do "Rock around the Clock" every Christmas. Can't say it gets any easier though!' he admitted, chuckling to himself and rolling his eyes in his wife's direction.

Hazel tutted at her husband and turned her attention to Daniel. 'Where does your family come from?' she asked.

'All over the place, but my father lives in Scotland now,' replied Daniel.

'*Scotland!* Mary Rose lives in Scotland,' exclaimed Hazel, as if she lived in the same street as Daniel's father.

'How is Mary Rose?' interjected Charlie.

'Bonkers as usual,' grumbled her father.

'Don't be such a bully,' scolded Hazel. 'She's fine. Busy on the farm. She's my best friend from university and Charlie's godmother. Charlie and Rich used to go and see her in the summer holidays and always came back *completely* wild. She's what you'd call a bit of a free spirit,' she confided to Daniel with a giggle.

'Charlie tells us you're a designer?' boomed Donald, steering the parental interrogation back on track.

Charlie sat rigid on her seat. She'd always felt nestled and secure in the bosom of her family home but now it seemed full of invisible mines and trip wires. She slipped off a shoe and stretched out her leg underneath the table to touch Daniel in a gesture of comfort. Daniel put his hand under the table and lifted her foot on to his crotch. She wiggled her toes and, with relief, felt his growing penis beneath his linen trousers.

'More peas?' Hazel smiled like her daughter and Daniel's penis throbbed beneath Charlie's groping toes. Daniel had said earlier that if you wanted to find out what the daughter would look like in twenty years, you should check out the mother. Charlie now watched him studying the 'so show me' line of her mother's eyebrows that Charlie had inherited.

Content with the information Daniel had given him and after Charlie's brief explanation of the current activities at Bistram Huff, Donald launched into a blow-by-blow account of the planned itinerary for their forthcoming golf holiday in Australia.

'Darling, can you give me a hand with the dishes?' asked Hazel when she could get a word in, and Charlie had no choice but to leave the table and Daniel's erect member. She leaned forwards to give Daniel the benefit of her cleavage and stared into his eyes.

'That was superb,' said Daniel.

Charlie's mother gathered the plates. 'Have you had enough?'

'I'm a hard man to satisfy, Hazel.'

'Then I can tempt you to some summer pudding?' Hazel cocked her head towards him as Daniel looked tempted. '. . . and cream,' she urged, as if promising an absolute treat.

'Hazel. You spoil me!'

'Do you play golf?' Donald was asking as Charlie followed her mother, picking the crispy bits from the bottom of the roast potato dish. Charlie grimaced to her reflection in the hall mirror. Poor Daniel.

'So? What do you think?' Charlie asked her mother as they stacked the dishwasher.

'He seems like a jolly nice young man,' said Hazel handing her a serving plate.

'Oh God! The kiss of death!'

'It's just, well, he seems a bit . . . showy. That's all, dear.'

'Oh, and you're not!' Charlie was indignant.

'There's no need to be so defensive, darling. If you're happy, that's the main thing.' Hazel slammed the dishwasher door repeatedly until it shut.

'I am happy, Mum. He's just so cool and he's great in bed.'

A cloud crossed Hazel's brow. 'You be careful. You are taking adequate precautions, aren't you?'

'Yes, Mum,' sing-songed Charlie. 'Stop treating me like a child – I'm a big girl now.'

'Oh, it's just that I do worry about you.' Hazel gave her daughter a protective hug.

Charlie kissed her mother, breathing in the Nina Ricci perfume she loved so much. 'Well don't.'

'I can't help it, you're still my baby.' Hazel squeezed her nose affectionately.

'Is it OK to go to the beach after?' asked Charlie, breaking away.

'Of course, darling. Do whatever you like. Perhaps we could all go?' she said, enthused with the idea.

'I think I'll show Daniel Devil's Dyke. He's got a stunt kite in the car.'

Hazel nodded and Charlie felt guilty, seeing the disappointment in her eyes, but the concept of her father driving while her mother tried to navigate around the sights of Sussex was too much.

'Well, whatever. Your Daniel doesn't strike me as the kite-flying type, though.'

'Mum, don't be fooled by appearances,' laughed Charlie.

'Oh I'm not,' said Hazel, squirting foam cream into a bone china jug.

*

At the top of Devil's Dyke, the wind was fresh and exhilarating. Charlie stood at the cliff edge straining against it, feeling the air swoop into her mouth, her teeth tingling. Daniel walked towards her, carrying the stunt kite and calling to Benson who was bounding in the opposite direction. Charlie curled her toes around the soft grass and stretched out her arms towards the horizon, her hair lifting in a halo around her head. She turned round to face Daniel.

'Isn't it wonderful?' she yelled, the wind gusting against her back, making her totter forward a few steps. Her eyes gleamed as she removed a strand of hair which had blown across her mouth.

'Stay there. I want to take a photo of you,' he said and knelt down, making a viewfinder with his fingers. Charlie laughed, posing for him.

He handed her the multicoloured kite. 'Hold it tight,' he said, and she pressed it to her as Daniel walked away, unravelling the strings from the red plastic controls.

She watched him retreating, looking behind him as he negotiated the gentle slope, trying not to tread on Benson who was running in circles around his feet. She hugged the kite. God, he was gorgeous. She wanted to cuddle him, to hold him for ever.

'Now let go,' Daniel yelled from the bottom of the slope, the strings between them taut. Charlie launched the kite, jumping with glee as the streaming red tail fluttered around her and swooped into the air.

She skipped towards Daniel.

'This is such a laugh,' she said when she reached him. 'I haven't done this for years!'

Daniel smiled and looked up at the kite. 'Here, have a go,' he said, handing her the controls. He stood behind her, his hands over hers as together they flew the kite in long swoops and tight spirals. Charlie felt safe and happy, her heart high as the kite above her. They laughed like kids as it ducked and shimmered against the blue horizon.

'How did I do with your parents?'

'Mum said you seemed like a "jolly nice young man"!'

'Oh no! Didn't she say I was a sex god?' he laughed.

'No. I told her you were, but I'm sure she must have thought it. I'm sorry if they embarrassed you about your family.' She looked over her shoulder at him.

Daniel looked up at the kite. 'It doesn't matter.'

'You don't talk about your family much, do you?' She leaned back into the warmth of his body to give him encouragement.

Daniel sighed. 'We're about the most dysfunctional family you could ever meet. I managed to rescue Angelica and Benson from Dad's abusive clutches,' he said, his voice sad.

'What about your mum?'

'Dad stole Mummy away from the thing she loved most. She could've made it right to the top as a ballerina but instead she got pregnant with Matthew. Then after the divorce she got cancer.' Daniel's voice sounded bitter and Charlie was shocked.

Fascinated, she cajoled him and sighed with sympathy as he told her about his childhood with his dying mother and alcoholic father.

'Matthew bore the brunt of it and he's more or less a recluse now. I've tried to look after him, but he's stubborn and eccentric like my father. They'd probably get on quite well if they ever spoke.'

'And what about you?' asked Charlie, her voice soft.

'Oh, I'm fine.'

'But what about your father? Surely family is family?' she persisted. She couldn't imagine never speaking to her dad.

'Blood can rot,' said Daniel morbidly. 'Here, let me have a go.' Suddenly he brightened up and took the controls from Charlie.

At last he'd opened up to her! She stood beside him, folding her arms against the fresh breeze, and felt a surge of maternal protectiveness. She'd told Rich so often that a man's way to a woman's heart was to show his vulnerability and, sure enough, her heart strings were jangling like a string quartet.

'You're not looking,' he said, turning to her. 'I'm writing you a message.' Charlie watched with delight as Daniel made the kite swoop, the flowing tail forming letters in the air.

She stared at him, her heart in her mouth.

'I'd love to be yours,' she gasped.

The kite was still now, buzzing against the wind. In the soft silence between them, Charlie could see her distorted reflection in the lenses of Daniel's sunglasses.

She ducked under the strings of the kite and put her arms around him, kissing her lover with all her heart, as the kite fluttered above them. Benson hurtled toward them and ran around their ankles, barking, and they both looked down and laughed. Then the kite was caught by a gust of wind and it nosedived, its crossbar shattering as it crashed into the green grass.

Charlie yawned and groaned. She had to face Rich. She stretched, remembering how Monday mornings used to be.

'Duvet Monster One – are you ready?' Rich used to yell from his room.

Charlie would pull her duvet on to her back. 'Ready,' she would yell back, the giggle rising in her as she crept to the door.

'GO!'

She used to race out of her room into the sitting room, shrouded in duvet as Rich ran out of his room, equally blind, making roaring noises. They'd stumble into one another and crash to the floor laughing.

Oasis was playing on the radio and Rich was cleaning his teeth. Charlie leaned against the frame of the bathroom door.

'Why didn't you tell me about Pix?' she asked, wondering why she felt so upset.

Rich's mouth was full of foam and he started to say something, but it didn't make sense, so he spat into the sink. 'I've only just started seeing her.' He rinsed his toothbrush under the tap. 'It's no big deal.'

He brushed past her and Charlie stared at him. Why couldn't he understand that his withdrawal of information was a total betrayal? All their lives, they'd shared everything.

That's what friends were for. She'd told him everything when she'd first started seeing Daniel and she swallowed back a thick clump of hurt as Rich tied his tie in the mirror.

'She seems nice.'

'She is.'

'I'm happy for you,' she said, pulling the dressing-gown cord tighter and feeling anything but happy.

Rich glanced up at her, but they both lowered their eyes, a wall of unspoken feelings between them. Charlie wished she could step towards him and hug him, but something stopped her. She was the one who had changed things between them so she'd have to live with it. She shuffled into the bathroom.

Rich stared at the closed door, hearing the song in the kitchen. 'There are so many things that I'd like to say to you, but I don't know how . . .'

Charlie stood by the fax machine, straightening the Bistram Huff embossed paper containing the contract and final schedule for the Up Beat promotion as it glided through. She should have checked the figures with Philippa, but even if her boss had been around, it would probably have been the wrong thing to do. She'd made it painfully clear that the promotion was down to Charlie.

The fax beeped and spewed out a receipt as Charlie picked up the papers and tapped them on the top of the reception booth. She checked the arrangements she'd typed once more. It was too late to change anything, but out of habit she scanned the neat paragraphs for spelling mistakes. It all seemed fine, but still her conscience nagged her.

She slotted the papers into a plastic folder. 'Sadie, you don't know when Philippa will be back, do you?'

'No. She's out at Up Beat, I think,' muttered Sadie, turning over the page of *Ms London*.

Charlie was surprised. 'She isn't because I've been speaking to Nigel Hawkes all day and he hasn't seen Philippa or had any meetings booked with her.'

Sadie shrugged and was silent, not meeting Charlie's eye. 'Sadie?' She sidled up behind her desk and bent down close to her ear. 'Come on, you can tell me. Where has the old battle-axe skived off to?'

Sadie gave Charlie a sidelong glance. 'Promise you won't say anything?'

'Promise.'

'She's gone to Chayney's. I booked her in for a massage at two,' said Sadie.

Charlie was unsure whether to laugh or scream at Philippa's audacity.

'Don't say anything. She'll freak if anyone finds out,' pleaded Sadie.

'Of course I won't.' Charlie patted Sadie on the shoulder. 'The cheek of it though! I'm here having a nightmare trying to get everything approved and the one time I need her, she's off spending the day in a health club!'

'Shhh! Keep your voice down,' urged Sadie, smiling at Charlie's outrage. 'Why did you need her anyway?'

'There were a few things I needed to check with her.' Charlie trailed off. She was thinking about Philippa and how often she must have used Up Beat as a cover to get out of the office. If Charlie hadn't spoken to Nigel Hawkes, no-one except Sadie would ever have known about Philippa's deception. As she walked back to her desk, it occurred to her that if Philippa's back-to-back meeting schedule was a sham, what else was she hiding?

'I told Bob he's got the job for the *Reporter* scratchcards,' said Bandit. 'And my lighter promotion has been approved. I think it's going to be a winner. I'm going out with Bob for a drink tomorrow night to celebrate. You coming, Pete?'

'I can't,' he mumbled.

'Oh?' said Bandit, his interest raised.

'I've promised Sharon that I'll go to an ante-natal class with her.'

'You're not!' laughed Bandit.

Pete frowned and held up his hands. 'Don't say anything, don't say anything!'

'How about you, Charlie?'

'No, I can't, sorry,' she said absently. She'd been so excited about taking Daniel to the 51 tomorrow night to meet Dillon and Kate and she'd set aside this lunchtime to find a new funky outfit. Now the last thing she felt like was shopping. Maybe she'd have a sandwich on her own in the park.

'What's wrong with her?' asked Bandit, watching Charlie go.

'Unpredictable? Irrational? Moody? I'd say her complaint is being a woman,' joked Pete. 'It's best to ignore 'em,' he added, standing up and walking behind Toff's desk and clipping him around the head for playing Solitaire.

If Philippa had been massaged all afternoon, it didn't show. She looked tense and the lines around her mouth stood out as if she had just bitten into a rotten nut.

Charlie saw her coming as she sat at her desk writing a list of all the calories she'd eaten that day, the Pret à Manger salad sandwich having been usurped by a baked potato with beans and cheese. She stood up as Philippa waved the copy of the Up Beat contract that Charlie had left on her desk.

'Can you explain, please, why this promotion has been agreed without my authorisation?' demanded Philippa, sucking in her cheeks and tapping her foot ominously.

Charlie winced. She'd expected Philippa to be cross, but she wasn't expecting a show-down. She kept her voice low as she explained that she'd been up against the deadline and she'd had to use Bob's quote for the printing with the usual agency mark-up. The agency would make much less than Philippa had been expecting, but Charlie had no choice.

'You stupid incompetent fool,' quivered Philippa. 'Haven't you ever heard of negotiation?'

'Yes,' bristled Charlie. 'However, we're up against a tight deadline.'

'So you thought you'd murder the margin – just like that! I want you to find another printer.'

Charlie looked over to Bandit for support. She needed him to tell Philippa that the job had been given to Bob, but Bandit lowered his eyes and said nothing.

'It's too late,' she said quietly. Philippa slowly turned, her sculpted eyebrows furrowed menacingly.

Charlie took a deep breath. 'We're printing at the end of the week, so I had no choice but to go with the printer that Bob has found. We'll still make money . . .'

'Jesus Christ!' exploded Philippa. 'I don't believe this.' She paced with her sleek hands on her hips, catching the attention of everyone in the room. 'First Daniel and his pathetic pranks and now this!' She threw her hands up. 'You are *so stupid*,' she spat at Charlie, who felt her cheeks burn in the silence of the office.

'If you'd been here then maybe the situation might have been different,' Charlie said, her voice husky as her chin started to quiver. She glanced over to the double doors and saw Sadie standing there, her eyes pleading with Charlie not to let out her secret.

'You're an account director. You're supposed to be able to make rational decisions. It shouldn't matter whether I am here or not.'

Charlie said nothing, feeling thirty pairs of eyes on her witnessing Philippa's attack. Please don't cry, please don't cry, she pleaded with herself, clenching her fists so that her nails dug into her palms.

'You should never have been promoted,' concluded Philippa, aware of the power of her words in the room full of Charlie's peers. 'For just how long are you going to keep fouling things up? Tell me that?'

Charlie looked up at her, jutting out her chin as waves of humiliation crashed inside her. Philippa shot her a disgusted look and, shaking her head, careered back into her office like a tornado.

The silence was like a vacuum. Charlie unhooked the jacket from the back of her chair, picked up her bag and car keys and walked out of the office. As she pushed open the door, Sadie put a hand on her arm.

'She's a bitch, ignore her.'

Charlie nodded, unable to speak.

The sun slanted through the office windows as she walked across the reception area. She couldn't stand and wait for the lift and her knees trembled with mortification as she stumbled into the fire exit. She clutched on to the metal rail and ran down the concrete steps, her shoes echoing like her heart.

In the car park she leaned back against the pillar and closed her eyes. It was so unfair. How could Philippa be so unprofessional? Anger and spite coursed through her, leaving her gulping for air, before the tears came. She wanted to be sick.

'You fucking cow!' she yelped through gritted teeth, wanting to hit something.

The sound of her own voice in the dark car park brought her to her senses and she fumbled for her car keys. She had to get out; out into the sunshine and away from Philippa's venom. She ran towards her car.

She stopped short when she saw it. The shiny green paint was covered in yellow Post-It notes. She dropped her bag, laughing and crying at the same time as she peeled off the notes, reading the messages that could only be from Daniel. 'You're mine . . . Kiss me . . . . . . Love you.' He loved her! He'd said it at last. She peeled off each note until she held a wad of yellow paper, then she opened the car door, a smile on her face.

Daniel's love was her armour against the world and with it she wouldn't be vulnerable. She looked at herself in the rear-view mirror and licked her finger, wiping away her smudged mascara, then she started the engine and stamped on the accelerator. The car roared in the car park and boomed out into the sunshine. Charlie cranked up the music. 'Sticks and stones may break my bones, Philippa, but words will never hurt me,' she yelled, sticking up her fingers in a V sign.

Rich stood nervously waiting for Pix. It was the Mathers Egerickx Lovitt annual summer bash. The trestle tables set out in Fountain Court were covered in pristine linen table-cloths and rows of bubbling flutes of champagne. In the middle of the gathering, the fountain gurgled with sedate charm and the Tudor clock chimed seven in the still summer evening. As if on cue, the string quartet tuned up and the balmy night was filled with Elgar's 'Chanson du Matin' . . .

Yet despite the refined company and the gourmet canapés, Rich was anxious. He should never have let Pix bulldoze her way into an invitation, but when she'd rung from the college payphone, he hadn't been able to think of an excuse before the pips cut her off.

Now he turned and watched with dread as she bounced towards him, her steel-capped Doc Marten's grinding conspicuously on the gravel path as she tripped past the immaculate pond. She was wearing a long tie-dyed skirt and a multicoloured velvet waistcoat with a fake ruby nose stud to match.

'You look great,' lied Rich, seeing that she'd made an effort, his own prejudices kicking him as she kissed him. He could feel the whispered comments of his colleagues and see the lulling conversations as they gaped at Pix's attire. All the other girls, without exception, were in elegant black cocktail dresses.

'Look at this place!' gushed Pix. 'I can't believe you work here. It's like something out of a Merchant Ivory film. I keep expecting some little chap in black robes to pounce out at me any second.'

'They do,' said Rich, noticing with a pang of fondness that Pix was wearing mascara and lipstick.

She grabbed a waiter as he went past. 'So talk me through all these suits then,' she said, waving the ornate canapé at the crowd.

Rich tried to steer her out of sight behind the fountain as he pointed out his colleagues and Sir Oliver Egerickx, the main partner in the firm, describing with a mixture of respect and jealous scorn Sir Oliver's extravagant lifestyle. Pix looked astonished as he recounted details of the private helicopter, lavish skiing trips to Klosters and the hundred and twenty foot yacht which Sir Oliver used for 'corporate entertainment'.

'Lucky bastard – and he's very good-looking,' said Pix, noticing Sir Oliver's swarthy face, salt and pepper hair and dimpled smile.

'All the girls in the firm fancy him,' said Rich, his face falling with horror as Pix smiled cheekily at Sir Oliver who started to walk over towards them.

'Come on,' he said hastily, grabbing Pix's arm, but she shrugged him off.

'Don't be rude. He's coming over to say hello. This could be my lucky day.'

It was too late. Sir Oliver was in front of them, bowing slightly, his hand-made suit falling perfectly over his tennis player's physique.

'Ah, Richard. I hear the PWL case is progressing.'

'Yes, sir, very well.'

Sir Oliver stooped slightly to look at Pix. 'And this is your charming companion, I presume. Delighted to meet you, Miss . . .'

Pix, who had shoved her index finger in her mouth to suck off the grease, now wiped her hand hastily on her skirt.

'Pix, call me Pix.' She smiled and Rich saw Sir Oliver notice the piece of lettuce which was stuck to her front teeth. Pix took their stares as her cue.

'Terrific food,' she said, grinning again. 'I had a drinks do like this in my housing association in Vauxhall last year for all the residents. We didn't stretch to a string quartet, but it still cost a fortune.'

Rich's knees locked.

Sir Oliver smiled graciously and rubbed the side of his tanned nose with his little finger, trying to cover his disdainful amusement. 'Ah well, er, Pix, we don't mind the expense, you see. Once a year, we like to show our appreciation to our staff and their partners for their support and encouragement.'

'If you don't mind me saying, you'd be better off showing your appreciation every day and stop making your staff work so hard,' said Pix, gulping down a mouthful of champagne. She held her nose and pulled a face. 'Those bubbles get me every time.' She looked up at Sir Oliver who was staring at her intently and Rich, who was glaring at her and making strange vibrating movements with his head.

'It's all very well throwing a party once in a while, but it doesn't make up for the hours people put in. You get dumped on all the time, don't you?' Pix stared at Rich for affirmation, but he was blushing to his bone marrow.

'It's not like that at all,' he said, hating himself for fawning.

'Yes it is,' said Pix, apparently oblivious to the fact that Rich was visibly crumbling with embarrassment. 'You said so yourself.'

Sir Oliver clicked his heels together like a German count and pinched his soft lips into a joyless smile.

'Well I must move on, I'm afraid, I've just seen the mayor. It's been extremely – ' he paused, choosing his words – 'enlightening to meet you, Pix. I do so hope you enjoy the rest of the party.'

'Thanks a lot,' said Pix, smiling at him widely as he turned away. 'You too.'

Rich covered his eyes. 'I can't believe you just did that. Tell me this is a bad dream.'

'What?' asked Pix innocently, loading up her palm from the passing waiter's tray.

'Don't you realise who he was?' hissed Rich.

Pix popped a pastry tartlet into her mouth. 'Sir Oliver. You said.'

Rich put his arm around her shoulders and frog-marched her around the fountain. 'You can't go telling people like him that I hate my job.'

'I didn't.'

'You told him I get dumped on. Dumped on! Pix, how could you?'

Pix was unfazed. 'But you do. You work far too hard for no recognition and if Sir Oliver Wotsit thinks he can soft soap you with a couple of glasses of champagne then he's got another think coming. If he's so busy flitting off into the clouds in his helicopter, someone's got to tell him what's happening down here in the real world.'

Rich was red in the face and he made a helpless whimpering noise.

'Don't be so melodramatic. I only told him the truth. He's a big boy, he can take it.'

'You can't tell him the truth,' exploded Rich in a contained whisper.

Pix raised her eyebrows at him. 'Then why do you want to work for this lot anyway?'

Rich pushed his glasses up his nose. Pix was so infuriating, he didn't know what to say. He was saved from making any comment by James Lovitt, whose plummy tones wafted over to him, compounding his misery.

'Rich, old chap!' James patted him on the shoulder patronisingly and the hairs on the back of Rich's neck stood up. He couldn't stand James Lovitt, who was only thirty-four and had secured a partnership by some very underhand means.

'Hello, James.'

'This must be the controversial young Pix. Sir Oliver thinks you're great, so I had to introduce myself,' said James. Pix smiled triumphantly at Rich.

'Bit of a surprise you didn't bring Charlie this year. Delightful filly, that one.'

Rich cringed, remembering how James had slavered over Charlie like a randy alsation at all the corporate events he'd brought her to over the years.

'She's very busy,' he mumbled.

'Just as well we've got Pix here to keep us all entertained,' snorted James. 'Come on, stop hiding round here, I want you to meet everyone.' He led Pix off into the judgmental throng and Rich wished he could dive under the surface of the fountain and disappear for ever.

It was Friday morning and Charlie was feeling subdued.

'Can you pass my sunglasses?' she asked Bandit. 'They're in the glove compartment.'

He turned the knob on the walnut dashboard and riffled about among crisp packets and parking tickets before retrieving the glasses and pulling the sticky plastic cover of a penalty notice from the lenses. 'You're such a slob,' he teased.

'I know.' She gripped the steering wheel and felt her head ache as she remembered the amount of cocaine and champagne she'd had last night with Daniel and how they'd made love all night, until she'd had to beg him to stop. She felt guilty now, scared at how out of control she'd become. Six months ago she wouldn't have dreamed of doing drugs, let alone on a week night. Bandit was right, she was turning into a slob. Daniel had made her throw all caution to the wind and she'd given up reading, seeing her friends, and even *Brookside* to join him on the front seat of his rollercoaster lifestyle. Now she felt decidedly dizzy.

'This is it,' said Bandit, pointing out the entrance to the south London industrial estate. Charlie peered out of the window at the grotty façade and graffiti-covered doors and turned the wheel too late so that the tyre smacked over the kerb.

Bandit covered his face with the A-Z. 'Jesus, you're dangerous.'

She stuck her tongue out at him and pulled into a parking space, letting the clutch out too soon so that the car juddered to a halt.

Bandit had made a big fuss about coming with Charlie to check the scratchcards on press and now, as they entered the warehouse, she was glad he had. Over the deafening clatter of the machines, she shouted to a man in grimy overalls who blew smoke in her face and waved a filthy hand in the direction of the office.

They waited in the empty room looking round at the tasteless posters, the beige plastic cups with fag butts in the bottom and the ringing phone that no-one answered.

'It's not what you'd call state-of-the-art,' said Charlie sceptically.

Bandit was immediately on the defensive. 'Bob says they're good. And anyway, they're cheap.'

After Philippa's outburst, Charlie had had no choice but to get Bob to find a cheaper printer to make sure they'd still make a decent profit. 'What if something goes wrong?'

'That's why we're here. Once you've signed off the running sheets, that's it. Nothing can go wrong.'

Jack Marsden, the printer, didn't inspire Charlie with the confidence she needed. When they stood by the huge steel machine, he coughed bronchially. 'We print the cards in two lots and interleave the winning cards with the duff ones later,' he said.

'Are you sure that's the way we're supposed to do it?' she asked. 'I thought they were supposed to be printed at random.'

The printer wiped ink from his fingertips on an old towel.

'No, love,' he said. 'Too expensive like that. We do scratchcards like this for everyone.' He winked. ''Course we're not supposed to, but I'm not saying nuffink.' He switched a light on above a scuffed drawing board and pinned up two running sheets of the Up Beat scratchcards. 'We put the silver latex on after we've printed,' he shouted as Charlie pored over the sheets.

'It looks fine to me,' shrugged Bandit, his attention diverted by the *Playboy* calendar which hung above the filthy sink and battered kettle in the corner.

Charlie pulled a piece of paper out of her bag and inspected it.

'These are the losing ones.' She pointed to the codes on the cards. 'You need to print five million of those,' she instructed and the printer nodded, unhooking some of his breakfast from his nicotine-stained teeth with his sausage finger.

Bandit glanced at the winning cards. 'These look fine too,' he said.

'OK. Print fifteen hundred of those,' she told Jack Marsden, pointing to them. 'You've got my fax and all the details so there shouldn't be a problem?'

The printer shook his head. 'Piece of piss,' he said. 'They'll be going on press tonight.'

Charlie checked the stock and looked once more at the running sheets. She frowned at Bandit, misgivings thumping inside her. Despite the fact that everything was in order, the printer seemed too slapdash for such an important job. Maybe she felt so odd because of last night.

'You're sure that Bob says these people are OK?' she whispered, wanting reassurance.

'Don't worry your pretty little head. It'll all be fine.'

'OK. Go ahead. If there are any problems, give me a call.' She handed the printer her card and for a second thought that he was going to use the corner as a toothpick. He nodded.

'Can I take these?' she asked, picking up the running sheets.

'Best not to,' he said. 'I'll check the colour against those later.'

Bandit, who had been jangling his keys in his pocket, accompanied Charlie back out to the car. 'I'll drive, I'm insured.'

Charlie started to protest, but after all it was a company car.

'Keys!' he demanded and held out his hand to her.

'Just this once,' cautioned Charlie and threw them over to him, wondering why Bandit seemed so pleased with himself.

At the 51 later that night, Charlie was about to moan to Kate about her dreadful week when she noticed her friend's sulky expression.

'What's the matter with you, misery guts?' she asked.

'It's Dillon. He's here all the time and I'm not getting enough attention,' moaned Kate, scowling towards Dillon at the bar. 'We haven't had sex for weeks and I'm going to explode soon. Anyway, I'm off to New York to cover the fashion show and while the cat's away, she will definitely play.'

'Kate!'

'Lighten up, for God's sake. I know we've always disagreed on this fidelity issue, but you might as well have a bit of fun. After all, what the eye doesn't see, the heart doesn't grieve over.'

'That's appalling, you should know better!' Charlie slugged her drink. 'Jesus, I sound like my mother.'

Kate held up her hand. 'You are your mother.'

'You can't do that to Dillon just because you're horny. He trusts you,' said Charlie, crossing her arms and leaning on the table.

'Fidelity has got nothing to do with trust,' retorted Kate.

'You say things like that to provoke me and because you want to have your cake and eat it.'

'What's wrong with that? Us girls are supposed to be like that these days. Don't look like that. I'm always going to be wicked. In fact, I'm probably much more wicked than you'd ever believe.'

Charlie frowned.

Kate polished off her second vodka and raised her eyebrows. 'So? I gather it's all going well with Daniel. I've hardly seen you.'

Charlie felt guilty. 'I know. I've missed you, but I've been so wrapped up in work and I've been staying at Daniel's house most nights. He's been such a darling, though. He sent me a huge fuck-off bunch of flowers yesterday. Rich said the only vessel big enough to hold them was the toilet!'

'He told us.'

Charlie was taken aback. 'I see.'

'He's been in here a few times with his new girlfriend. She's really sweet. Dillon gets on with her like a house on fire.'

Charlie folded her arms, feeling jealous. How dare Rich bring Pix to the 51 without telling her. 'He didn't mention it to me.'

'He said he hadn't seen you. Anyway, I told him we were meeting Daniel tonight.' Suddenly, Kate clutched Charlie's arm, making her spill her drink.

'Oh my God, is that him?'

'Yes,' said Charlie and waved. She groped in her bag and peered quickly at her face in the compact mirror. 'Oh no. Bad hair day!'

Kate rolled her eyes. 'You're a babe.'

'I don't feel like one.'

'You didn't tell me he was a ten!' Kate hissed as Daniel approached the table.

Charlie smiled, pleased that Daniel was obviously impressing Kate. He leaned down and kissed Charlie on the lips. 'I got held up,' he said, stroking her cheek. 'This place is a bit out in the sticks.'

Kate watched as Charlie's doe eyes turned like melting toffee towards Daniel's dimpled smile before she introduced him.

Daniel sat between the two girls, his arm resting on the back of Charlie's chair. As Charlie leaned back, Kate saw the way Daniel's fingers foraged into her hair and tickled the back of her neck and felt a stab of envy. Charlie giggled and Kate stared at her in dismay, watching her friend's feisty personality shrink, eclipsed by Daniel's hard-nosed charisma.

'So Daniel, I hear you're a fantastic lover,' said Kate, cutting the light chit-chat and hoping to catch Charlie's attention.

Daniel didn't bat an eyelid. He met her innocent little girl stare with a full look, like an open invitation. 'So I'm told.'

Charlie reached out and held his hands, laughing.

'Don't mind her,' she said to Daniel. 'It's her profession to try to shock people.' She leaned forward to Kate. 'You'll have to try harder than that with this one.'

'Just checking,' said Kate matter-of-factly and finished her drink. If Charlie was going to behave like this, the only thing to do was get very pissed, but then seeing Charlie so frantic for her approval made her feel guilty. As she ripped open her olive bread roll, she decided that she should make an effort.

By the time the starters arrived the three were laughing loudly. Daniel lapped up the privilege of being let in on a girlie chat and fell about at Kate's hilarious recounting of times spent with Charlie, and by the end of the main course Charlie was thoroughly enjoying herself.

There was still a smile on her lips as she watched Kate walk towards the kitchen to have a word with Dillon. She looked at Daniel who took a sip of wine. 'What do you think?' she asked, feeling light-headed.

'Is Kate always this flirtatious with your boyfriends?' he asked.

Charlie sat up. 'Flirtatious! What do you mean?'

'Oh you know, little looks, hand on my knee, that sort of stuff,' Daniel ran his finger and thumb up and down the stem of his wine glass.

'She's just like that,' said Charlie.

'Is she?'

'She's outgoing, that's all. She doesn't mean anything by it.'

'Well, whatever,' said Daniel, taking a sip of wine.

Charlie met his smile. 'Did you like the food?'

'Yes. Delicious. Although to be honest, I thought the sea bass was a little salty.'

'Don't let Dillon hear you say that,' whispered Charlie.

'Don't let Dillon hear what?' asked Kate, returning to her seat.

'Nothing,' said Charlie.

Daniel turned to Kate. 'I thought Dillon's food was delicious,' he said. 'He must be quite a treat to have at home.'

Kate made a face. 'He's not. I do most of the cooking.'

'Stop feeling so hard done by,' said Charlie.

'It's fine for you to say,' Kate drained her glass.

Charlie looked at her disapprovingly. 'I'm going to the loo.'

Daniel re-filled Kate's glass.

She took a sip and sat back in her seat, looking at Daniel. 'It's nice wine. You made a good choice.'

'I see you like it.'

Kate twisted her hair up into a pony tail.

'So have you and Charlie ever shared a lover?' he asked as soon as Charlie was out of earshot. 'You know, had a threesome.'

Kate looked at him, flushed from the wine. 'I don't think Charlie would approve of that sort of thing.'

'Avoiding my question. Good journalistic tactics.'

'I'm not avoiding the question.'

'So? You'd find it a turn on, would you?'

'In principle I wouldn't be against it. I guess it's about finding the right person and everyone being in the right mood.'

Daniel leaned towards her, mesmerising her with his gaze. 'You're horny, aren't you?'

She blushed.

'I know you're thinking about it,' teased Daniel. 'It wouldn't be disappointing.'

Kate picked up her glass, feeling unsteady and pissed. She shouldn't be having this conversation. 'Look, there's Dillon,' she said, waving to him excitedly and sending her wine glass flying. A quarter of a glass of Vouvray landed in Daniel's lap.

Flustered and gushing apologies, she picked up her napkin and doused the stain on his trousers.

Daniel held her hand, his eyes locking with hers. 'Don't worry.'

Kate broke away from him and groped in her bag for her Filofax. She pulled out a piece of blue paper and wrote down her number then thrust it at Daniel, avoiding his eyes.

'Look, here's my number. I'll pay for the dry cleaning. Call me and tell me how much it is.'

'I'll do that,' said Daniel, taking the paper as if she'd just consented to his suggestion.

Charlie stepped out of the cloakroom and walked towards the table. She saw Kate touching Daniel's leg and she strained her head forward, not believing her eyes. She couldn't hear anything but the pounding of her own blood in her ears as she watched Kate give Daniel a piece of paper and smile at him, leaning forward and stroking his leg once more.

Suddenly, her conversation with Kate took on a horrible new meaning.

'I see you don't waste much time,' she said as she approached the table.

Kate's cheeks flushed. Then they both looked down at the paper in Daniel's hand.

At that moment Dillon approached. 'Hey,' he said, stopping abruptly as he sussed out the atmosphere between the two women. 'What's going on?'

Charlie watched as the colour of guilt rose in Kate's face. She ripped the piece of Filofax paper out of Daniel's hand. 'Just what are you planning? Another one of your infidelities? Oh, I forgot,' she said. 'It's got nothing to do with trust.' She tore up the paper and hurled the pieces at Kate.

'What are you talking about?' asked Dillon angrily.

'I suggest you ask her that. Come on, Daniel.' Charlie yanked his arm.

'Don't be so ridiculous!' said Kate, jumping up. 'This is stupid.'

'Is it?' hissed Charlie.

'Daniel, tell her,' Kate implored. 'You've got it all wrong. Daniel is the one you can't trust.'

'Calm down, all of you,' said Dillon.

'Don't you dare try to blame Daniel!'

'I suggest that you leave,' Dillon said to Daniel, aware of the other diners, their forks and glasses suspended in mid air.

Daniel nodded to Kate, a smug look on his face as Charlie dragged him towards the door.

'Charlie, don't do this. You're making a huge mistake,' Kate pleaded, but Charlie was stomping towards the door. 'Charlie!' she shouted.

Charlie turned round. 'Actually, I think it's you who has just made the biggest mistake of your life,' she said and, taking Daniel by the arm to steady her trembling body, she stormed out of the 51.

'You bastard!' screamed Kate after Daniel, but Dillon grabbed her flailing arms and man-handled her into the kitchen.

In the car, Daniel put his arms around Charlie.

'I ruined your evening,' she sobbed. 'I can't believe she came on to you. She's my best friend.'

'Come on, cheer up. It's not the end of the world. You've still got me,' he said, lifting up her chin. Charlie's sobs subsided into occasional gasps and Daniel rocked her until she calmed down.

'I'm making you all wet,' she said, lifting herself away from him.

'It doesn't matter. I have to get this suit dry cleaned anyway.' He started the engine.

'I only mind so much because she could have anyone and she goes for you. I know you're irresistible and everything,' said Charlie, twisting the end of a piece of tissue.

'Shhh,' calmed Daniel. 'You're much prettier than her. I wouldn't go for her anyway. She's hard as steel. Not my type at all.'

'What did she say to you?' asked Charlie, regaining her composure.

'Nothing much. Well, you know. She made quite obvious suggestions and she gave me her number.'

Charlie sighed heavily and sniffed. 'I didn't over-react, did I?'

'Don't be ridiculous, you were just defending what is rightfully yours.' He squeezed her knee. 'You know, you are very, very beautiful,' he said, stroking the curve of her blotchy cheek as he stopped at some traffic lights. Charlie let his words nourish her wrenched emotions. 'I think so anyway.' He pulled her towards him to kiss her, but before he reached her lips, his mobile phone shattered the moment and Charlie shrank back.

Daniel sped away from the lights, his phone against his ear. 'Hey darlin',' he chirped as if nothing had happened.

Charlie bit her lip and looked out of the Porsche window.

'What!' exploded Daniel and she turned to face him.

'OK, what happened?' It was the first time Charlie had seen Daniel angry. 'The fucker. I don't believe he did that!' he shouted. 'Angel, baby. Stay where you are. No, just stay put. I'll be right there.'

Charlie clasped her hands between her knees.

'The bastard,' fumed Daniel, flicking off his phone.

'What happened?'

'Some bastard has pumped Angelica full of dud coke. She reckons it's crack or it's cut with something really nasty. She's pissed as well which doesn't help. I'll drop you off.'

Charlie stared out of the window, furious and disappointed. She needed Daniel now and Angelica should be old enough to know better.

Daniel glanced at Charlie. 'Don't be like that,' he snapped.

'Like what? I didn't say anything!'

'You didn't need to. She's my sister, for Christ's sake, have a little compassion.'

'Sorry,' said Charlie, worried that Daniel was turning his anger on her.

He cranked up the stereo and they spent the rest of the short journey in silence. It had started to rain and rivulets of water formed on the window. Daniel lit a cigarette and slid to a halt outside Charlie's door.

'I guess it's just not our night tonight,' she said over the growl of the idling engine. 'I hope Angelica is OK.'

'See you,' said Daniel, impatient to get away. She shut the door, her eyes brimming with tears. She leaned down to look in the passenger's window, but he didn't notice her and roared off into the night.

Bandit pulled into the same driving space that he'd occupied with Charlie twelve hours earlier and slipped into the warehouse. It took him a while to locate Jack Marsden. He found him watching a portable TV in the back room.

'Yeah?' he asked, lumbering out of the chair.

'Sorry to butt in,' apologised Bandit. 'It's about the scratchcards.'

Jack scrambled to his feet.

'There's been a mix up, so I thought I ought to come and tell you.'

'Right, right,' nodded the printer, scratching his head.

'I know it's a pain, but we got the two cards mixed up. What you thought were the winning cards are actually the losing ones,' he explained. 'I just came to say can you print fifteen hundred of the first sheet and five million of the second? Is that going to be a problem?' He smiled and looked the printer in the eye.

'But I've already started printing most of the first lot. Most of them have been chopped up,' he protested. 'It'll cost you.'

'I know. Don't worry, I'll authorise any extra expense.' Can you keep fifteen hundred of what you've printed already and get straight on to printing the other five million?'

'I suppose so. I guess it's not too late. Just as well you caught me,' Jack grumbled.

Bandit nodded and tapped his lips. 'This is a big promotion. I'm afraid I'll have to ask you to dispose of the cards that you've already printed as discreetly as possible. We really can't afford for any to be seen.'

'No problem. I'll take them down to Covent Garden. They

pulverise everything in the skips there at twelve o'clock after the market's finished. It's the only place in London you can get rid of stuff, even bodies they say,' he added with a macabre grin, unearthing a Rothman's cigarette from his top pocket.

'I'm so sorry to put you to all this trouble,' apologised Bandit. 'Charlie will be very relieved I've managed to sort it out.' He followed Jack through to the warehouse.

'Don't worry, mate,' he said, shutting down the grumbling intestines of the printing machine. He slapped his overall pockets trying to find his matches.

Bandit pulled out one of his promotional lighters and lit the cigarette for the printer, who looked at him, dismayed at such etiquette. He took the lighter out of Bandit's fingers and turned it over in his grubby palm, weighing the silver.

'Have it. I don't smoke,' said Bandit with a generous flourish. 'It's worth quite a bit.'

'You sure?'

'Absolutely.'

Jack smiled and put the lighter in his pocket. 'So you want five mill of the second sheet?' he said, resetting the machine.

'Yes. Thanks ever so. It's a bit embarrassing really. I'd appreciate it if you didn't say anything. You know, professional reputations and all that.'

'Say no more about it,' said Jack with a wink. 'These things happen all the time.'

Pix was reading Rich's palm when Charlie walked in. Rich, docked on the sofa like a refuelling jumbo jet, had his eyes closed and his fingers resting in Pix's small hands as she knelt by his side.

'You're going to have three kids . . .'

'God forbid,' laughed Rich.

'Poor kids. Let's hope they don't get your looks.'

'What else?' Rich glanced down at his palm as if it were a book he was trying to memorise. Pix traced a line along his hand and Rich giggled.

'That tickles!'

'Hold still,' said Pix, securing his hand in hers and peering at it. 'This one is your life line. You're going to live a long and healthy life. My intuition tells me that you'll live until you're eighty-seven.'

'Blimey.'

They hadn't heard Charlie and as she cleared her throat they looked up at her.

'Hi,' she croaked, trying to keep her head down so that they wouldn't see she had been crying.

Rich jumped off the sofa, wrenching his hand out of Pix's. 'How was your evening?' he asked, plunging his recently attended to hand into his pocket as if he had been caught with a stolen sweet.

'Not so great,' said Charlie, affording him a glimpse of her haggard face.

'What's happened?' asked Rich, touching her shoulder.

'Forget it. I'll be fine. I think I'll have a hot bath and go to bed. Hi, Pix.' She managed a half smile as she walked into her bedroom and closed the door.

Rich paced the room, beside himself with concern. 'Something has gone horribly wrong. I've never seen her looking like that. What shall I do?' he whispered to Pix.

'Go in and talk to her if you're that concerned.'

'I can't,' said Rich, giving up the struggle and plummeting on to the sofa. 'Let's watch TV.' He flipped on the screen and stared at it blankly.

'Until you find out what's wrong with her, you'll have no peace,' cautioned Pix, sitting next to him and folding her arms.

'If she wants to talk, she can.'

'Jesus, you're so stubborn!'

'Where are you going?' he asked, alarmed.

'To talk to her.'

Charlie felt like a refugee from some horrible disaster as she sat on her bed.

'Charlie?' Pix ventured, creeping forward into the room. Roused from despair and exhaustion, Charlie looked at her.

'Are you OK?' asked Pix, switching on the bedside lamp.

Charlie tried nodding, then shook her head, her eyes brimming with tears.

'Come on. Out with it,' commanded Pix. She picked up the box of Kleenex from the top of the chest of drawers and fed them one by one to Charlie as she recounted the horror of Kate's betrayal.

'I'm sorry to dump all this on you,' she cried, but Pix put her arms around her.

'You're not dumping anything on me. Crying is good for you. Your skin's going to look like you've just stepped out of a make-over tomorrow.'

Charlie blew her nose. 'I hate being miserable. Since I met Daniel I seem to have lost all my strength. Honestly, having a boyfriend is so annoying. I was fine before.'

'I know what you mean.'

Charlie sniffed. 'Surely things are going well between you and Rich? You seem really happy together.'

Pix sighed. 'Ah, he's a lovely guy and we have a great time, but it'll never be anything serious.'

'But he's really keen on you.' Charlie looked at her quizzically.

Pix shrugged. 'Not really.'

'Maybe you're being paranoid?'

Pix shook her head sadly. 'No. It's never going to work.'

'Why?'

'You of all people should know the answer to that one.'

'Know what?'

Pix scoured Charlie's innocent blotched face for a sign.

'What is it?' she asked, sensing Pix's nervousness.

'Nothing. Take no notice,' back-pedalled Pix, getting off the bed and edging towards the door.

'No, wait. Tell me. What's the problem?'

Pix looked at her feet. 'He's in love with you.'

Her simple sentence hung between them.

'What?' Charlie was stunned, her breath leaving her like a punctured football. 'In love with me. How do you know? Did he say that?'

'It's obvious,' murmured Pix, looking at her hands. 'I

thought you must know.' She looked up at Charlie without malice.

'No, no, I didn't.'

Pix shrugged and backed out of the room.

'One, two, three . . .' SLAM! Twelve glasses of tequila banged on the wooden table like a cannon blast. The celebratory meal in the Mexican restaurant just off Oxford Street was in full swing. In the dingy wooden-clad dining area, two girls wearing bandiers doled out the last of the tequila shots, ignoring the leers and gropes from the noisy tables.

Sadie screwed up her face. 'Lemon, lemon,' she urged, her cheeks blotched as she thrust the wedge toward Charlie.

'Where's my beer chaser?' shouted Pete, removing the remains of the salt from the back of his hand with dog-like licks.

The lemon stuck in Charlie's mouth like a pair of joke false teeth and she picked a clump of salsa from her hair. She swayed on her seat, her vision blurred.

'I think we should go clubbing after,' suggested Poppy. 'Daniel said he could get us into Orgasm. You're on for that, aren't you, Charlie?'

'I don't think so,' she said, remembering her night there with Daniel. She didn't want the memory sullied by Poppy's extrovert dancing. She'd hoped that Daniel would feel the same way.

Bandit lurched to his feet and banged the pepper grinder up and down on the table. Charlie watched the broken tortillas jump on the surface.

'Quiet, quiiiiiiet!' shouted Bandit, flailing his arms around like an airport traffic controller. 'I got sommink to say,' he slurred.

A collective 'Shh' went around the table.

'Unaccustomed as I am to public speaking . . .' he started and a roar went up. He raised his arms in defence, ducking the flying lemon wedges. He gestured to the bedraggled waitress who patiently placed a tray full of beers in the centre of the

168

table. 'As you all know the Up Beat promotion is going to be in the papers tomorrow and it's going to look the fucking bollocks and I want you all to raise your glasses to Nigel here.'

There was a round of applause for Nigel Hawkes from Up Beat, who'd been dragged out reluctantly and looked totally out of place. He was in his mid thirties, but could have passed for fifty in his grey suit and ugly thick glasses. He blushed, mumbling thanks.

'And let's not forget our Charlie,' continued Bandit.

Pete banged his fist on the table. 'Hear, hear.'

'Stand up, stand up!' Bandit tugged Charlie's arm. 'She's done an excellent job despite Philippa. What I say is fuck the lot of them!' He raised his beer bottle and swung it towards the centre of the table where it crashed into the other bottles.

Charlie wobbled on her high slingbacks. 'I couldn't have done it without you lot,' she shouted over the loud music, sweeping her beer bottle in the direction of Pete, Toff and Sadie.

Bandit stood up on the bench and climbed over the table. He plucked a carnation out of the vase.

'How about the last tango?' he asked Charlie, pulling her up on to the dance floor as she laughed and shook her head.

'Go on, go on,' her colleagues cheered, starting to clap in time to the music and reluctantly Charlie settled into Bandit's embrace. He put the carnation between his teeth and they tango-ed amongst the rowdy crowd. Bandit threw Charlie around, transferring the flower into her mouth and pulling her closer. As the track came to an end, he leaned her backwards over his arm in a dramatic finale. It was in this upsidedown position that Charlie spotted Daniel leaning by the door.

'Look, there's Daniel,' shouted Toff, gesturing him to come over.

Charlie staggered into an upright position and closed one eye in an attempt to focus. Daniel, sober and sophisticated, squeezed the top of her arm.

'Hi, Charlie,' he said. 'Having fun I see.'

'My body's come undone,' wailed Sadie, hooking her arm into Charlie's and yanking her away to the Ladies.

In the toilet, Sadie hitched up her tiny skirt and fiddled with the poppers between her legs.

Charlie stared at herself in the mirror. She was appalled by her three reflections. 'I'm pissed.'

'Me 'n' all,' said Sadie, straightening up. She upturned her black handbag. A Lancôme mascara and face compact, a tampon, keys, a packet of three condoms, a hairbrush and a huge pink nailfile clattered into the sink. Sadie picked up the tampon and marched into the loo.

'I'm glad Daniel's turned up, I was beginning to lose hope,' she shouted as she crouched on the toilet.

Charlie picked up Sadie's hairbrush and unearthed an earring from it before attempting to brush her hair.

'Why?' she asked and hiccuped.

'I didn't really fancy him at first, especially when everyone said he shags anything with a pulse,' Sadie continued, 'but you've got to admit he's great in the looks department. D'you think I should snog him? I mean, don't you ever wonder what it would be like?' Sadie flushed the loo and exited the cubicle, catching Charlie's blushing reflection.

Charlie shrugged and looked away.

Sadie unscrewed the mascara and pumped the wand into its slim pot. 'You fancy him, don't you!' she said, flicking the wand over her long lashes as she scrutinised Charlie in the mirror. Then she gasped, interpreting Charlie's bashfulness. 'Have you shagged him?'

Charlie swayed and looked sheepish.

'You didn't!'

'Sadie, don't say anything,' pleaded Charlie, hanging on to her arm and silencing her demands for more information. 'You are the only person who knows.'

The mascara wand stayed motionless in mid air. 'Blimey! I had no idea. How long has it been going on?'

'Ages.'

'Who'd have thought it? You're a dark horse, aren't you?' laughed Sadie, digging Charlie in the ribs.

'Shh. Please don't say anything, Sadie. Daniel would freak if he knew I'd told you!'

'So it was you – the Tipp-Ex crosses!'

Charlie shook her head. 'The security guards' joke. Sadie, don't look like that. You mustn't say anything. Promise.'

'Mum's the word.' Sadie grinned. 'Here,' she said, approaching Charlie with a compact. She opened it and daubed powder on Charlie's shining nose. 'A little dab of powder, a little dab of paint, makes a little lady what she really ain't!' Sadie winked like a pantomime queen, her wet lashes leaving black lines on her cheek bones. 'Gawd!' she exclaimed, spitting on her finger. Charlie smoothed her skirt over her hips, groped inside her bra to hitch up her breasts and held her head high. She was determined not to make a fool of herself in front of Daniel, but she realised that would be more difficult than she thought when she tripped and stumbled into the arms of Nigel Hawkes.

Charlie was dreaming about the hot summer of '76 and her shell necklace as she looked over the side of the rubber dinghy. She knelt up on the soft bottom of the boat and twirled around, hoping to catch Rich as he came up the other side. But still he didn't appear. She looked back towards the shoreline and to Mary Rose who was preparing sandwiches on the lid of the blue coolbox.

'Rich. Come back,' she called, her feeble voice lost in the sun, but still he didn't surface. It seemed like hours since he'd dived in. Maybe he had drowned, and if he had then it would be her fault. Fat tears started to plop on to her orange and purple bikini. Then the boat tipped. She screamed and plunged overboard, gulping mouthfuls of sea water.

She felt an arm around her as she rose, spluttering into the sunshine. Rich laughed while she coughed and clung on to the slippery overturned dinghy.

'Cry-baby,' he teased.

'I thought you'd drowned.' She blinked at him. Her long eyelashes clumped together in the water.

'Don't be silly, I was with you all the time, you just didn't see.' He punched her playfully on the armband.

'Don't leave me, ever again!' she said, trying to scold him while her eyes shone.

Charlie slid into consciousness. She raked her dry tongue along the roof of her mouth, thinking she must be licking an industrial sander and slowly woke up to the beating gong of her hangover. She attempted to open her eyes, but the neon sunshine burned into her over-exposed retinas and she squeezed them shut again, groaning as her poisoned body cranked into life with a crescending ache.

A pneumatic drill started up outside her bedroom door and she sank further underneath the duvet. Rich was Hoovering the flat. Now that she was awake, her bed seemed like a bouncy castle. Feeling wretched she sat up, groaning as her brain followed a second later. She stood up and steadied herself on the bedside table trampling off her clothes, furious that she had been too pissed the night before to get undressed. She twisted her bra around her torso, but coordination was not on her side and she collapsed once more on to the bed. The sound of the vacuum died, but the booming sound continued in her eardrums and Charlie moaned from her core and pulled the pillow over her head.

'I brought you tea and Resolve,' Rich whispered, creeping into her room and putting the mug and the fizzing drink on the bedside table. 'Do the Resolve first.'

Charlie was unresponsive. How many times had Rich done this before? How many Saturdays had he cared for her in this familiar routine? Countless times. Yet now that Charlie knew he was in love with her, she felt violated. Usually she would have rolled over and Rich would have sat on the bed as she told him what she had done the previous night.

'Charlie?' He put his hand on her shoulder and inwardly she squirmed.

Could he not feel her shoulder repelling his touch? Feeling annoyed, she grunted in acknowledgment and didn't move, hoping her lethargy would make him go away.

'That bad, eh?' he laughed, straightening the duvet on top of her before tip-toeing out.

Charlie rolled over on to her back and looked at the swirling steam from her favourite mug. How could she have been so naive? Rich had brought her tea every morning, had cooked her favourite food, been there whenever she needed him and, like an idiot, she'd taken it all for granted. Now she thought about it, his behaviour made it obvious that he was in love with her. Why hadn't she noticed?

She cradled her temples, her mind reeling. Usually she would have staggered from her room and wouldn't have thought twice about her scantily-clad form. Had Rich stared at her body all that time with longing? She pulled on her dressing gown inside out and groped for the door handle.

'Hail, shining morn!' teased Rich, taking in Charlie's sallow face, crumpled hair and half-closed eyes. Charlie scowled at him and he laughed as she dragged her queasy body into the bathroom for a twenty-minute cuddle with the toilet bowl.

As she vomited tequila-tinted bile into the S-bend she heard Rich tuning the radio into *Any Questions* as he faffed around in the kitchen and she wanted to scream at him to shut up. She realised, as her angry stomach contracted, that this was what he did every weekend. He hung around, waiting for her to announce her plans, scrutinising her every move and wanting to be her playmate. When did he become so doting and dependent? She flushed the toilet and swilled sweet-tasting tap water around her furry teeth.

Kate had always said that men don't have soft spots for women, only hard-ons, and Charlie had scorned her cynicism. She had held up her relationship with Rich as a shining example of an honest friendship between a man and a woman that didn't involve sex. Now Charlie wriggled with repulsion at the thought of Rich's secret admiration. At least Kate was no longer around to say 'I told you so.'

She had to get out of the flat. She scurried back to her room, and yanked on some mismatching clothes and rushed past the kitchen.

'I've made you a bacon butty,' yelled Rich above the

applause on the radio and Charlie cursed, stopping in her tracks. She poked her head around the door of the kitchen.

'How are we feeling?' He pushed the plate temptingly towards her.

Charlie gazed at him. Did he think he could buy her love?

'You don't look so great,' he said, wincing at her. 'Come and have something to eat, you'll feel much better.'

'I don't want anything to eat.'

Undeterred, Rich continued, 'You're probably still feeling a bit queasy.' He gave her a knowing nod. 'What you need is a hair of the dog,' he said, getting up to make one of his mega-strength Bloody Marys.

'I'm going out,' said Charlie. Without looking at Rich, she made for the door. The phone rang.

'It's Pix for you,' she said rudely, dumping the receiver down next to the phone.

'Oh,' muttered Rich, staring at her with bewilderment as she stomped out.

Dillon absent-mindedly rubbed off the silver lamination on the scratchcard as he read the review of London restaurants in Saturday's edition of the *Reporter*.

'They have absolutely no idea,' he tutted. He looked up at Kate, but his attention was caught by the scratchcard.

'Hey, look! I've won a free CD!' he exclaimed, handing the card to Kate. She took it from him, raised her eyebrows and handed it back without comment. Dillon stared at the scratchcard and turned it over a few times.

'I saw a whole load of these in Covent Garden,' he said. 'I helped a bloke with them. Do you remember? I told you about it.'

Kate pushed down the plunger on the cafetière.

'We put them in the pulverising skip. Masses of them. I was buying strawberries and I got chatting to him. He's a printer and I got his card for Pix. He might be able to print up her flyers,' he said and put the card down. He poured a cup of coffee for Kate and one for himself. She ignored him and continued to read the paper in silence.

Dillon glanced at her and broke open a steaming croissant. 'Are we going to talk about it?' he asked.

'Talk about what?'

'Charlie,' said Dillon, hoiking the croissant into his enormous mouth.

'No!' Kate shook her paper so that it straightened out and resumed reading.

Dillon sighed and bunched up his dreadlocks behind his head before letting them flop down his back.

'Come on,' he said. 'We haven't talked for days.'

'So?'

'Fine. Our whole relationship is in jeopardy, you're going away and you don't want to talk about it. Fine!' Dillon stood up angrily.

'Stop being so dramatic,' said Kate, putting down the paper. 'What is all this "in jeopardy" shit? Charlie is obsessed with the biggest dickhead in Christendom and when she sees the error of her ways and apologises, I will *think* about forgiving her. It's got nothing to do with you.'

'Oh no? How do you think I feel when your best friend–'

'Ex-best friend,' interrupted Kate, taking a sip of her coffee.

'Whatever. Your ex-best friend accuses you of *another* infidelity? Am I supposed to ignore her? How do you think I feel?'

'You're a bloke, you're not supposed to have feelings.'

'Yeah? Well I do,' said Dillon, thumping his chest, and for the first time Kate realised he really was upset.

She sized him up.

'Well? Have you been unfaithful to me?' Dillon's voice was wounded.

Kate swung back on her stool so that she swayed precariously on its two legs. She grabbed hold of the counter to stop herself tipping backwards.

'No,' she mumbled, 'but I've thought about it.'

Dillon let out a sharp breath as if he had been punched. 'What?' he gasped. 'Why?'

Kate banged the front feet of the stool down.

'Because you never spend any time with me. You should win an award for neglect, not for cooking,' she began, gathering steam and confidence as her complaints about their relationship flooded out. 'And we hardly have sex any more,' she finished with a final grumble.

'Oh I see. So going off and fucking someone else will solve all our problems, will it?'

'No,' she admitted, running her thumbnail along the edge of the chunky wooden counter. 'But you probably wouldn't notice anyway.'

Dillon slammed his huge hand down on the kitchen counter. He grabbed her wrist and looked into her face, his face contorted with passion. 'How can you do this to me?' he choked. 'Why didn't you say something before?'

'There was no point,' she said, frightened by the force of his grip.

'So if Charlie hadn't said anything, we wouldn't be having this conversation? Is that what you're telling me?'

Kate shrugged. 'It looks that way,' she muttered. Dillon threw her wrist away in disgust and put his palms on his forehead.

'I don't believe it. I don't believe you could be unfaithful to me.'

'Well believe it. It wouldn't be that difficult!'

He looked at her with hurt eyes. 'If you could consider it, you obviously don't care about our relationship.'

'That's rubbish, and anyway I haven't been unfaithful to you yet.'

'Oh well, don't let me stop you! No, carry on. Feel free to fuck your way out,' he exploded.

'Don't shout at me,' she shouted. 'I haven't done anything and if I did it would have nothing to do with you.'

'Do you know what that is?' Dillon leaned close to her. 'That's bollocks! And you know it. Your warped views on fidelity and your teenage feminist slogans are just a cover for the fact that you're scared of commitment.'

'Now that *is* bollocks,' she countered, pointing her finger at him. 'You're the one who's scared of commitment.'

'No I'm not,' retorted Dillon. 'I *want* commitment. I relish it. I want to bathe in it!' He waved his arms dramatically and marched around the counter.

Kate slid off the stool and picked up one of her papers. 'I'm not listening to any more of your egotistical ranting. I've got better things to do,' she declared and started out of the door, but Dillon grabbed her, pinning her arms by her sides.

'No way, lady. You're not running away from this one.'

'Let go of me,' she said, trying to wriggle out of his grip.

Dillon was silent as he looked down into her angry face. 'Marry me,' he said softly.

'I beg your pardon?'

'I know I can't stop you going off with other men if you want to, but I want you to know how serious I am about you. I want you to be my wife, Kate,' he said, looking into her eyes. 'I've always thought we belong together, right from the first day we met.'

She scrutinised his face for traces of a bluff.

'Will you?' pressed Dillon.

Kate's mouth fell open in shock.

'You don't have to answer me now. Tell me when you get back from New York,' said Dillon, backing away from her, as stunned by his proposal as she was.

'You've gone mad,' she said angrily, yet a warm feeling flowered inside her.

Pix bit into the apple she'd bought from a stall in Portobello market. She wriggled her hand into Rich's to stop them getting separated amongst the milling crowds.

'What's wrong?' she asked over the din. 'You seem distracted.'

Rich shrugged his shoulders. 'Nothing,' he said, freeing himself from her grip.

Pix took another bite and eyed him suspiciously 'Rubbish. There's doom and gloom written all over your face.'

Rich ignored her as they strolled across the road to listen to the buskers who were playing 'Yesterday' on steel drums. He stared glumly at the bright colours of the African's wool hat and sighed dejectedly.

'I think it's going to rain. Do you fancy a pint?' asked Pix, her Saturday free now that she had delivered the bundle of clothes she'd collected to the housing trust.

'Not particularly,' replied Rich. He felt as if his voice was coming from miles away.

'What's wrong?' persisted Pix, worried now. Eliciting no response, she stopped by a stall to look at some ethnic jewellery. Rich shuffled his feet together. Pix held some ear cuffs up to her ears and looked at them in the mirror. She caught Rich's eye behind her in the mirror and held his gaze.

'Are you still pissed off about that silly drinks party?'

Rich shook his head. 'No, it's not that.'

Pix snorted impatiently.

'It's Charlie,' he admitted.

'What about her?' Pix rummaged through the velvet tray of nose studs in front of her.

'I don't know. She's acting very strangely. She's not talking to me and I can't think what I've done.' Rich looked at the sky. It was the colour of a prison blanket. 'She didn't say anything. You know, the other night when you had a chat with her?'

Pix undid the jacket that was tied around her waist as it started to drizzle.

'Well?'

'Well what?' said Pix, glancing up at Rich and moving out of his gaze quickly. 'I guess that's the last of the weather. Winter is upon us!'

'What did she say?' persisted Rich.

'I don't know. Stuff.' Pix shrugged. The market-stall holders started to move fast as the rain grew heavier, erecting plastic covers over the hanging rails and pulling in stands under the cover of the tarpaulins.

'Why are you being so evasive?' Rich caught up with Pix in a doorway.

'I told you at the time. She was upset about Daniel and Kate.' She lowered her eyes.

'You said something,' said Rich, suddenly suspicious. 'You said something about me, didn't you?' His face was as solemn as the weather. Pix looked away into the scurrying crowd as the downpour began.

'Pix? Tell me. What did you tell her?' Rich grabbed her arm.

She looked at him, her forehead creased with concern. 'I told her the truth.'

'And what's that?'

'That you're in love with her,' she said.

'What?'

'You heard me.'

Rich paced out into the rain and paced back, his mouth opening and closing like a goldfish.

'Well it's true, isn't it?' She walked after him, her forehead wrinkling as the rain pelted down, flattening her hair against her skull.

'That's why you can't make love to me. That's why you go bonkers every time she's near. You're obsessed with her and you're using me as an excuse . . .'

Rich swirled round and grabbed Pix by the shoulders, shaking her angrily. 'How dare you. How fucking dare you!' he yelled. She rattled in his grip like a rag doll.

'Put me down,' she screamed, kicking him hard in the shins.

'You can't say things like that,' he stormed, his voice cracking with emotion.

'Just because you can't face the truth, don't take it out on me.'

Rich felt anger and humiliation swamp him.

'Oi! You leave her alone,' said a woman in fingerless gloves from one of the stalls, making for Rich with a broom and swiping at his ankles, so that he staggered backwards.

'Are you all right, love?' she asked Pix, who nodded and glowered at Rich.

'Go on. Hop it!' The woman advanced menacingly towards him as if he were a dangerous dog.

'Pix?' Rich reached out towards her, horrified that he'd shaken her.

She cowered away from him, tears mingling with the rain on her cheeks. 'Leave me alone. You're just the same as all the others.'

'Pix.'

'Don't ever come near me again,' she choked, before stomping away in her black boots, swiping angrily at her tears.

'That's right, you tell him,' rallied the woman, shooing Rich away.

Rich didn't feel the rain soaking through his suede jacket as he sprinted through the dripping antiques market towards Notting Hill. He felt like a shaken snow-storm toy. He hadn't wanted to admit his feelings for Charlie to himself, let alone to Charlie, and now Pix had blown it. As he'd feared, Charlie was obviously disgusted by the whole idea and he couldn't blame her. He was so angry with Pix. What was happening to him?

By the time he'd reached Notting Hill he was knackered. His hair was soaked with sweat and rain and he bent over, putting his hands on his knees, pulling in mouthfuls of car fumes and misery. He turned his head and, glimpsing his reflection in the glass of a shop front he straightened up, appalled by his own image. Then he re-focused his eyes and saw behind the glass a card advertising cheap flights to India.

A girl in a red and white blouse was thrusting her chin towards the small mirror in the compact to inspect her spots. She saw Rich and snapped on her automatic smile and the compact closed.

'Can I help?'

Rich shuffled, embarrassed by his drenched appearance. What was he doing in here anyway?'

'I saw the cards in the window.' He pointed lamely towards them and trailed off.

'We've got some excellent offers.' The girl gestured to the padded seat in front of her desk and Rich sat down. He placed his palms on the soaked legs of his jeans.

'Anywhere in particular?' The girl rattled the keys on her computer keyboard.

'What's that one to India?'

'The Goa break? Well, let's see. I think you'll be in luck and it'll be fantastic at this time of year.'

Rich felt a sudden chink of light in his despair. He could go away. Who was to stop him? And what did he have to stay for? Being in the flat with Charlie would be too difficult now. He wouldn't be able to look her in the eye and Pix would never forgive him for shaking her like a madman. His brain flipped through the organisation he'd need to do like a spinning card index.

'When do you want to go?'

In a dream state he sat, dripping, staring blankly at the travel agent. 'As soon as possible.'

'We have a flight to Goa on Tuesday. That's the soonest. Could you get your visa and jabs on Monday?'

Rich heard her from a mile away and nodded slowly.

'How will you pay?' The girl's fingers hovered over her keyboard waiting for his answer.

He reached into his jacket and took out his soggy wallet. Inside, the slotted leather housed rows of credit cards. He pulled out the Visa card. A small passport photo of Charlie was lodged behind it and it fell on to his lap as he handed across his card. He looked down at it and a large drop fell from his soaked hair and discoloured the surface, leaving a stain on Charlie's forehead like a faded ink blot.

'Are you travelling alone?' she asked, punching in his credit card number.

'Yes. All alone.' His voice was husky with the dull pain in his chest.

'I don't care if it's Saturday morning. Get your ass in here now!' Si spat into the phone and slammed down the receiver, ending his call to Daniel's mobile.

Despite her tanned face, Philippa looked pale as she perched one Armani-clad buttock on the corner of the boardroom table. Si tapped his lip with a sweating sausage-like finger and swivelled menacingly in the large leather chair. He glanced at the framed marketing awards adorning the walls.

'It could ruin us,' said Philippa, her gaze following his. 'If we let it.'

Si was silent and Philippa sensed the calm before the storm.

'It will just be a matter of how we handle the press.' She flipped off the table and, folding her arms across herself, started to pace.

Si watched her. His forefingers formed a triangle over his mouth which was pinched in a stubbly line of fury.

'You think it's my fault, don't you?' she said, as if Si had shouted at her. Si shrugged, holding her in his gaze.

'How was I to know that the wrong cards were printed? It's such a stupid mistake. But you were the one who insisted that Charlie was put in charge.'

'*You* were in charge,' Si interrupted her, his watery eyes piercing into her. 'She's just a kid.'

'I . . .'

Si pounced out of the chair, spitting his words at Philippa. 'You're supposed to oversee everything. Nearly every scratchcard is a winning one. Up Beat have been besieged by the public and today is only the first morning. They are going to lose a fucking fortune and we'll be responsible. Heads are going to roll over this one. We'll lose everything and I'll look a prize jerk. For fuck's sake, Pippa, how can this have happened?'

'I don't know.' Philippa looked up at him, her gaze like a matador's. Si's eyes locked with hers and he exhaled suddenly, turning away from her. He knew there was no use blaming Philippa. They had to present a united front. 'It's a bloody disaster.'

'You're sure Teddy Longfellow won't recall tomorrow's issues?' asked Philippa, wincing as Si flashed her a contemptuous look. He'd spent all morning on the phone to the *Reporter*, trying to get them to recall the papers so that they could remove the scratchcards, but it was too late. And worst of all, Teddy Longfellow now knew of the disaster and would surely set one of his other papers on the story to boost the circulation of the *Reporter* tomorrow. After all, Bistram Huff's mistake was doing the paper no harm whatsoever.

Si's eyes narrowed. 'Have you got a copy of the contract?' he asked.

'Of course. Hang on. We've still got the client copy here,' said Philippa, a flicker of hope igniting the spark of a plan.

Si caught her look. 'Where is it?'

'In my office.'

'Well what are you waiting for? Get it now. You and I are going to do a very clever Tipp-Ex job. I refuse to let this agency go under.'

Daniel walked in. He hadn't been to bed and his pupils were dilated from the night spent at Orgasm with Poppy and Will. Philippa stalked past him, looking him up and down and turning her nose up at his stale smell.

'Talk to Si. He's in the boardroom.'

Si looked at him and shook his head.

'What's going on?' asked Daniel.

'The Up Beat promotion has gone pear shaped!' he said.

Charlie pursed her lips in fury as she waited for Daniel. She'd gone straight to his place from the flat, stopping only for a coffee to settle her complaining stomach, to find he hadn't been home. Even though she'd been too drunk to contemplate clubbing, she was still angry that he'd gone without her. She turned over the page of the magazine, her attention caught by Angelica's conversation on the phone.

'Daddy, don't fuss, I'm fine,' she was saying and, despite her hangover, alarm bells sounded in Charlie's brain.

'How's Matthew? Is he there? Yes, I'll have a quick word. Hey pugs,' Angelica squeaked. 'Are you looking after the old man? It sounds like you two are having a blast. I wish I was there too. I miss you. Have a lovely time and don't forget to bring me a present. Put Daddy back on. I love you too. Bye!'

Moments later Angelica sauntered into the kitchen reading the *Reporter*. She pulled the scratchcard off the front and threw the paper on the counter.

'Daniel designed that,' said Charlie as Angelica scraped her French polished nail over the silver lamination.

Angelica looked closely at the card and resumed scratching. 'I've won a CD!' she announced.

'Let me see.'

'I found it, I'm keeping it.'

'You're welcome to it. I'm just surprised you won,' said Charlie. 'I arranged the promotion and there aren't many winning cards.'

Angelica raised her eyebrows. 'I thought you were the secretary!'

Charlie handed her the card, trying to keep her voice level. 'No, I'm the account director.'

Angelica flounced towards the fridge.

'Was that your father on the phone?' asked Charlie, her curiosity overwhelming her.

Angelica looked her up and down, swigging out a milk carton. 'Yes. So?'

'I thought you and Daniel didn't get on with him, that's all.'

Angelica licked her milk moustache. 'Oh, I get it, another one of Daniel's sob stories. Ha!' She laughed artificially. 'What else has he told you? No, don't tell me, something about Matthew being eccentric and dull,' she said, riffling through her bag on the counter to find a cigarette. She dumped a leather cheque book holder and a whole pile of flyers on the counter. The top flyer was for Space Odyssey and Charlie stared at it. It couldn't be, could it? Her illustration. How on earth . . .?

Angelica eased herself on to the stool opposite Charlie. 'Daniel does this big sob story with everyone.' She rolled her eyes. 'But you mustn't listen. Matthew is a hot-shot lawyer in New York and he owns this house. He'd freak if he knew that Daniel lives here. He and Daddy won't speak to Daniel,' she said, laying the bait. 'But I expect you know why.' Angelica's gleaming blue eyes bored into her as Charlie looked up.

'No, I don't. Why?' Charlie's voice cracked.

'Because Daniel had an affair with Pierre Derevara when he was seventeen and Daddy won't forgive him for being bi-sexual.'

Charlie put down the magazine which was shaking in her

hands and there was a silence as Angelica let the meaning of her words sink in.

'Daniel? Bisexual? Don't be ridiculous.'

'Don't worry, he's been into women now for a while. I'm surprised he hasn't told you. He said he was going to.'

Charlie felt as if an earthquake was starting in her legs. 'I don't believe you.'

'Believe what you want. It's no skin off my nose.'

Charlie slipped off the kitchen stool and steadied herself on the counter. 'Are you OK? You look like you could do with a bit of air. How about taking Benson out?' asked Angelica.

Charlie was so angry she couldn't speak. Benson scratched the back door.

'It's such a relief that Benson is a hit with one of Daniel's girlfriends,' said Angelica, getting up to open the door. 'Daniel bought him for Tamara, but she was so heartbroken she couldn't have any reminder of Daniel near her. Anyway he practically bankrupted her and she said she couldn't afford to keep the puppy. Poor old Benson has been a bit of a spare part ever since, haven't you, boy?'

Get out, get out, get out, Charlie screamed to herself, but she was trapped. Daniel's key turned in the door and he stepped inside.

Charlie's hand flew to her mouth to cover her quivering lips.

'See ya!' said Angelica, flouncing past them out of the open door, flinging her bag over her shoulder as she went.

Daniel retrieved his key from the door lock slowly. He looked after Angelica.

'Have you heard?' he asked, his eyebrows ruffling together.

Charlie nodded. 'Is it true?'

Daniel hung his head and fiddled with the keys.

'Why didn't you tell me?'

Daniel shrugged and looked up at her. 'You were going to find out soon enough.'

A sob escaped from Charlie's throat. 'I had to hear it from Angelica!'

'Angelica? How–' began Daniel, looking confused, but Charlie interrupted him.

'You lied to me about your father and your brother, not to mention Pierre. Just when exactly were you planning to enlighten me?'

'Charlie?' Daniel reached out for her, but she pushed him away violently and struggled for the door.

Daniel was speechless for a moment, confusion crinkling his smooth exterior. Then he flung his arms around her, pulling her away from the door, hugging her with such force that she was helpless to fight.

'Let me go,' she wailed.

'Oh God, oh God,' muttered Daniel, rocking her and covering her ears as if he could shield her from what she'd already heard. 'I'm so, so sorry,' he whispered. 'Don't believe her, please don't believe her.'

She struggled free from him.

'It's not as you think it is. Honestly.'

'Tell me it isn't true,' she pleaded, her eyes swimming with tears. 'Tell me. Just tell me.'

'I will, I will. But not here. Come on, get in the car.'

'Just another manic Monday, wish it was Sunday,' sang Charlie as she swung around the corner by the office. She was surprised to see some reporters outside the revolving front door of the mirrored glass building, but nothing could bother her this morning, apart from her bank balance. Then again, on reflection the weekend with Daniel had been worth it.

They had whizzed down the M40 as if by driving fast Daniel could break through the barrier of impending doom which had encapsulated them in London. Charlie sat on her hands most of the way, unable to ask the questions that whirled in her head as the stereo boomed out club music.

Eventually, the Porsche's tyres crunched over some gravel and Daniel stopped the engine.

'Where are we?' asked Charlie, gazing at the Bentleys and Rolls Royces surrounding them.

'Where nothing can touch us,' said Daniel, looking towards a willow tree which dangled over the perfect lawn. 'I want this weekend to be special. Just for us.' He patted her hand.

She pulled away, his contact stinging her.

He started to open the car door, but Charlie sat still. She'd worked out what she wanted to say, but now all she could utter was, 'How could you? How could you lie to me?'

Daniel sighed and sat back. 'Look, I know I've got some explaining to do. You have to understand, Pierre was a one-off thing. I was so confused at the time. Middle child syndrome, I guess.'

How were they going to talk about this? Charlie thought of Pierre and the secret he'd shared with Daniel for over ten years. She couldn't wrap her head around this unexploded missile of Daniel's past and she looked at him, thinking how she barely knew him. 'Go on.' She forced herself to say it.

'It's so difficult. I never took my sexuality for granted like other people. And I fell in love with Pierre. I thought I'd be gay for ever, but Dad and Michael put a stop to all that. They made me feel like shit.' He looked up at Charlie. 'I know now what they knew then – that I'm not gay. But they totally invaded me and now they are the ones who won't forgive. I had to shut them out, you've got to understand that.'

'But what about everything you told me?'

Daniel rubbed his forehead. 'I know. I knew I should have told you the truth. I've got such a well-rehearsed story and it just came out. Anyway, the truth seemed so sordid after seeing your family. I didn't think you'd find out.'

'Didn't you?'

'Yes. No. I don't know. I've never told anyone. It's not the kind of thing you can slip into conversation.'

Charlie pushed her head back into the leather headrest.

Daniel leaned across the gear stick and reached for her arm, forcing her to look at him. 'Charlie, I need you to understand,' he implored. 'You're the only person who can. I couldn't tell you before. I didn't have the words.'

She looked down, avoiding his gaze.

'It didn't seem important. It's ancient history. Whatever Angelica said, you know that she'd make it sound a billion times worse than it actually is.'

'Subtlety isn't her strong point.'

'Forget Angel, it's us that matters.'

'Is it?'

Daniel took off his sunglasses. 'You've changed everything round in my life. I used to be so alone with my secrets, but now I've got you.' His voice was soft. 'I should have told you, I admit that, but it wasn't important. I can't help my past, can I?'

Charlie softened.

Daniel looked at her. 'I don't care what happens. All I care about is that you're with me now. You don't understand, do you? You're everything to me. You mean everything they sing in all the lines of all the corny love songs ever written. Believe me. You've got to believe me.'

She looked at him.

'I love you,' he whispered, and she couldn't fight it. His words and his hands caressed her and she couldn't argue any more.

'Don't ever lie to me again. I can't bear it. Promise,' she said.

'I won't.' He kissed her nose, her eyelids and then her mouth with overwhelming tenderness until she melted into him.

'Oh, Daniel,' she sighed, hugging him awkwardly in the cramped car.

'OK now?' he asked, holding her face.

She groaned. 'Actually, I feel like shit. I've got such a bad hangover.'

Daniel laughed and put his forehead against hers. 'Come on. This is the best place in the whole world for a hangover.'

Charlie gasped as Daniel led her through the entrance hall of the Roux brothers' exquisite guest house. She stood by a majestic flower display as Daniel went to talk to the manager and, before she knew it, she was following the immaculate porter up an oak staircase to the blue suite.

As the door swung open, her angst vanished. It was like a dream. A magnificent four-poster bed was set in the middle of the panelled room which overlooked the walled rose garden.

'It's beautiful,' she sighed, her feet sinking into the rich silk rug. She turned to face Daniel.

'Am I forgiven?' he asked coyly.

She couldn't speak. The room was like something out of a fairy tale. In a trance she walked into the marble bathroom, gasping at the deep round bath and the cabinet crammed with luxury toiletries.

Daniel put his arms around her and nuzzled her ear, then carried her to the bed and laid her down so that she sank into its soft freshness.

Pulling away, he took his mobile phone out of his pocket and switched it off. 'There. We're all on our own,' he said.

She reached out to him. 'What shall we do first? she asked, as he bent towards her and kissed her.

They'd overdosed the tub with bubble bath and jumped into the foam peaks, scrubbing each other with long-handled back brushes. She slapped Daniel's bottom as he leaned over the edge and reached into the pocket of his jeans. Then, on the wide shelf beside the bath, he'd drawn out two lines of cocaine and Charlie submerged under the water as it hit her.

Her body tingled with pleasure as Daniel enfolded her in a thick dressing gown and she sat on the bed while he popped open the vintage champagne that had been delivered to their room. She sipped from the fluted glass and rolled over on top of him, taking him in her mouth and letting the cold bubbles fizz over his erection.

'Turn around,' whispered Daniel.

She knelt over his face as she roamed her tongue over his hardness, her head buzzing, rocking against him as her pleasure mounted. Daniel nuzzled his lips into hers and she leaned back towards him, feeling her nerve endings catch, grabbing on to the mounting sensations pulling her towards their summit.

Daniel slid out from underneath her as she shook in the aftermath of her orgasm.

'Stay there,' he rasped. She leaned towards him on all fours and he eased into her, filling her as he held on to her hips. Then she stretched out on the enormous bed and clenched around him until he came, shuddering and gasping her name.

They'd lazed for the rest of the day, nestled in luxury.

'Are you hungry?' asked Daniel, stretching across the bed to reach the room-service menu.

'Shall we go to the restaurant?' Charlie stroked her hand over his taut smooth buttocks.

'We can't. We're not dressed for it.' He reached up and sucked her nipple. She laughed.

'Good point.'

She settled into the crook of his arm and read the menu. 'I haven't eaten for ages. Not since last night. That seems ages ago.'

'You all seemed to be having a good time,' said Daniel, kissing her hair.

'We were. It was good to celebrate the Up Beat promotion. By the way, Angelica won a CD this morning.'

Daniel sat up and looked at Charlie, his eyes earnest. 'You know, we should have a chat about work,' he said, swallowing hard.

She smiled and reached for his face. 'Oh, babe. You're so lovely. I know the promotion's over, so I don't mind if we tell people that we're together. It's up to you.'

'There's quite a bit we should discuss. Repercussions and–'

Charlie sat up and draped her arms around him. 'Shh,' she said, 'I don't want to hear any more about work.'

'But–'

Charlie kissed him. 'Let's not talk about it.'

Daniel tried to pull away from her, but she straddled him. 'I said shh!' She moved down his body and licked him. 'Now then, what am I going to have for dinner?' She grinned wickedly and sank down to him, admiring his glorious penis.

'What's this?' she asked, inspecting a red patch and running her finger over it.

Daniel grabbed his penis away from her. 'What?'

'There, look.'

Daniel's face tensed. 'It's nothing. Must be a friction burn. You're such a sex goddess.' He lifted her up and hugged her.

'Is that all I am to you?' she asked, running her fingers over his chest.

'You guessed it,' said Daniel, drawing away from her and grabbing his cigarettes.

It was as if they were in a time capsule. Being isolated from the world had changed her perspective and as she wrapped her body around Daniel's, she felt like a queen.

The time sped by in a snoozing haze, and they hardly left the bed. She'd tried to chat to Daniel, but he just told her to be quiet and held her tightly. By the time they came to leave on Sunday, Charlie was dizzy with love. She flicked through the brochure in the foyer wishing they could stay longer, suddenly regretting that they hadn't used any of the facilities. They could have taken a long walk in the grounds, gone swimming or horse riding. Instead they'd got drunk, watched the porn channel and smoked cigarettes all night.

Daniel slapped his pockets anxiously. 'Shit! Shit! Shit!'

'What?' asked Charlie, her face relaxed in a dreamy grin.

'I haven't got my credit card wallet,' he said, looking anxiously towards her.

'Don't worry,' she said, reaching into her bag.

'I'll pay you back,' he said. 'I promise.'

'You'd better,' she said, gagging at the astronomic bill and hoping the cheque wouldn't bounce.

She was still thinking about it on Monday morning when she walked into the hushed building. Sadie wasn't at the reception desk and the switchboard was going crazy. Confused, she went into the office, but as she entered everyone turned away from her, their conversations dwindling.

Philippa stood facing Charlie in the silence, clenching and unclenching her fists by her sides. Charlie glanced anxiously at Bandit, but he was absorbed in his computer screen and ignored her. Toff lowered his gaze and scurried off. For a moment, Charlie thought that Philippa was going to hit her.

'Had a nice weekend?' she asked in an unusually squeaky voice.

That's it, thought Charlie. They've all found out about Daniel. She felt incredibly relieved now that it was all out in the open.

'Yes thanks,' she managed, the words seeming to stick in her throat. She unbuttoned her jacket and looked away from Philippa as she put it on the back of her chair.

'Get into my office.' Philippa's command hung like a death sentence in the air.

'OK,' said Charlie, brushing past her. This display of drama seemed ridiculous and she felt her hackles rising. What was Philippa going to do – sack her, just because she'd fallen in love with Daniel?

It was when Si came in that a wave of dread hit her and she felt her hand go clammy. 'Hi.' She smiled at him, but he shook his head and walked solemnly behind Philippa's desk. He was wearing a black pin-striped suit in which he looked absurd, like a lumberjack at a funeral. He flexed the folds of his neck in the restrictive white collar and avoided Charlie's eyes.

Philippa closed the door of her office.

'What's going on?' asked Charlie, her gaze yoyo-ing between her bosses in panic.

Si and Philippa exchanged a look.

'Let me,' said Philippa, turning to Charlie with python eyes as she explained the details of the disastrous Up Beat promotion.

Charlie sat in silence. Nothing had prepared her for the shock. An icy cold rush of panic prickled through her nerve endings. 'I checked the cards on the press,' she stuttered as soon as she could get a word in edgeways. 'Bandit was with me. They were right, I saw them.' Her eyes implored Si, who stood with his hands on the back of Philippa's chair.

'They obviously weren't right, were they?' he said, his voice cutting through her protestations.

'But . . .'

Philippa held her hand up and leaned forward. 'You were

in charge.' She jabbed her finger perilously close to Charlie's chest.

'Come off it. Surely it can't be my fault?'

'How could you be so careless?' asked Si.

Charlie was caught in the quicksand of disaster. No matter how much she flailed her arms, there was no-one around to get her out of this one.

'You shall be accompanying Philippa to an emergency meeting at Up Beat. I suggest that you try not to embarrass us further,' said Si.

'You don't believe that I did it deliberately, surely?'

'It doesn't matter. You weren't promoted to make deliberate *or* careless mistakes. The mess is equally bad. Excuse me. I am going to deal with the press.' He stalked out and Charlie felt nausea in her soul.

She stumbled out of Philippa's office and into Bandit. She grabbed his arms as if she were drowning. 'Tell them. Tell them we checked the cards on press. They were fine. The printer must have made a mistake and printed the wrong amounts.'

Bandit patted her arm as if she were a raving geriatric. 'That's what I thought. But I've spoken to Jack and he followed your instructions to the letter. It seems the codes were mixed up right from the beginning. It's not his fault.' He shrugged and turned away from her.

Pete frowned at Bandit's heartless attitude. He looked at Charlie sympathetically. 'It's not that bad, Charlie. It'll all blow over . . .'

'Not that bad!'

'Are you ready?' Philippa's scathing tones trapped Charlie like a caged animal and she looked around her frantically at the stony faces of her colleagues. There was no doubt about it. Everyone thought it was her fault.

Rich walked out of the office on Monday morning having spun a sob-story about mitigating personal circumstances to James Lovitt.

'Sometimes it's hard to take the pace, old boy,' he said condescendingly and Rich cringed.

'It's not that . . .'

'Just between you and me, I think we're going to drop the PWL case anyway. A shame after all that work, but it's good timing. You might as well have some time off. Best thing for you.'

Rich hadn't worried about sorting out his desk. He'd looked around the partitioned cubicle that had been his working environment for the last five years as if seeing it for the first time. There was so much kudos attached to working in the blue felt section by the partners' offices, but he saw it now for what it was: office furniture. There was nothing to clear up, nothing that marked the space as his own except a few strip cartoons cut out from the *Evening Standard* and a restaurant guide.

Now, as he was swallowed into Blackfriars Tube, he was stunned by how easy it had been to walk out. Part of him had wanted someone to stop him and ask him where he was going and why, or a concerned colleague to hand him a Styrofoam cup of coffee and engage him in a heart-to-heart. But no-one noticed him leave.

He'd hurried into the office every day on time, had worked weekends and left late, all in the name of 'getting on'. The higher his salary had become, the more he'd believed that he was a vital bolt in the well-oiled corporate machine of the firm. He'd been miserable, but he thought that if he rocked the boat and left, well, the whole department would collapse and he'd never be forgiven.

So he was shocked that when it came down to it, he'd been able to extricate himself from the corporate stranglehold in just one hour. Nobody seemed particularly bothered that he wasn't going to be there for the next month. They would muddle on without him. Walking down the escalator into the Tube, he realised that his cubicle would probably be filled by now, before his seat was even cold.

The doctor had looked disapproving when Rich demanded his jabs and he rubbed his sore arm as he packed the last of his stuff into a rucksack. He felt so depressed, he hardly cared whether he contracted typhoid. He felt as if he was dying and nobody was noticing.

All that was left to do was write a note to Charlie. He had rehearsed it over and over again in his mind. He chewed the end of the biro briefly before writing on the back of a bank statement envelope: 'Charlie – I've gone away for a while. I know it's sudden, but it's for the best given the circumstances. What Pix told you is true. I am in love with you and I know that you're with Daniel so I have to get away. I also know that you think I've betrayed our friendship. Maybe I have, and I'm sorry. Take cáre of yourself. Please understand that all I've ever wanted is for you to be happy. R. PS Si from the office rang over the weekend.'

Charlie felt like she was facing a trigger-happy firing squad as she sat through the quarrel in the boardroom of Up Beat's UK headquarters. All she could think was that she wished she had worn smarter clothes. She had stayed the night at Daniel's and, having over-slept, had flung on a pair of trousers and one of his old sweatshirts. She'd expected to spend the day making personal phone calls and sending chatty E-mails.

In Up Beat's meeting room, Nigel Hawkes' complexion had taken on a greenish hue. He glared at Philippa as she entered the room, but she ignored him. Charlie's mind was reeling. She went over and over her visit to the printers. She remembered checking the running sheets and making sure that the amounts being printed were correct. How could it have gone wrong? It didn't make sense.

'This is causing us significant financial loss and public humiliation and has seriously undermined our reputation in the marketplace, not to mention the fact that we're the laughing stock of the whole industry. Have you seen the *Sun* this morning?' railed the managing director of Up Beat.

'Actually, I think the publicity it has caused for Up Beat can only have a positive effect,' countered Philippa.

'Bullshit! Do you know how much we've lost?'

'I'm sure that the damage can be limited . . .'

'You bet your bottom dollar it'll be limited. I want full financial compensation from Bistram Huff.' He banged his fist on the table, making Charlie jump.

Philippa stiffened in her chair. 'I'm afraid that's out of the question.'

'Says who?'

Philippa pursed her lips. Taking her time, she swung her briefcase on to the table and opened the catches one by one. The clicks reverberated like a revolver being loaded. Charlie watched in dismay as Philippa retrieved the contracts from the briefcase. She'd typed them herself and she knew that the agency was liable.

'If you'd be kind enough to look at paragraph seven, gentlemen, you'll see that it states quite clearly that the agency is not responsible for any loss of revenue due to the promotion,' she said as she slid copies of the contracts across the table. Nigel Hawkes closed his eyes and shook his head.

Charlie glanced at Philippa. Was there anything to which she wouldn't stoop? The MD pored over the document and looked at the European group director.

'Jesus!' he swore, pushing back in his chair. He turned to Nigel. 'You signed this?'

'Yes, but I didn't . . .'

'I think you'll find that Nigel was fully aware of the contract and signed both copies,' interrupted Philippa.

'Did you check this with legal?' The MD shook the contract at Nigel who stared aghast at Charlie.

'I . . .' he began.

'OUT!' the MD railed. 'Get out!' He pointed to the door.

Nigel Hawkes stood up. He looked at Philippa who raised one eyebrow.

'It's just one bloody disaster after another! Right. We're going to have a full inquiry into how this happened. Hans here will be leading the investigation.' The MD nodded to the man in question who smirked with Teutonic charm towards Philippa.

Charlie watched Nigel Hawkes leave the room, her heart pounding. This was a nightmare.

'Obviously we will do whatever we can to help you,' purred Philippa. 'We are naturally extremely upset that this has happened and we will be doing our own investigation within the agency.'

She turned her glare towards Charlie. 'Since you were in charge of the promotion, do you have anything to say to these gentlemen?'

The spotlight was on her and Charlie winced under the five sets of angry eyes. There was a small silence while she groped for something to say. 'I don't understand how this can have happened,' she said, stopping to cough as her voice choked with nerves. 'I personally checked the cards at the printers.'

'Who printed the cards?' interrupted the managing director.

'Well, we were working within the budget and I, we, used a printer over in south London and I . . .'

'You chose some cowboy printer for a national promotion? Who made that decision?' interrupted the MD.

Charlie looked down at her hands. 'I did,' she said quietly, feeling her personality draining out of her into an invisible puddle around her feet.

'Tell me. Do you always have such competent people in charge of your biggest accounts?' he asked Philippa, his sarcasm biting into Charlie.

Philippa looked at Charlie as if she was rancid. 'Rest assured that if we find any member of staff to have been at fault we will not hesitate in dismissing them immediately.'

Charlie's heart banged inside her rib cage like a budgerigar having an epileptic fit. Philippa had as good as sacked her in front of a client. She had never felt more humiliated in her life.

That was until she heard Philippa say, 'We called an emergency directors' meeting on Saturday lunchtime as soon as the situation became apparent and we are all committed to finding out what happened. Our creative director, Daniel Goldsmith, is naturally very upset. He is fully aware of the implications of the situation and gave his personal commitment to sorting it out as quickly as possible.'

Bob watched Bandit pour chilli oil over his Four Seasons in Pizza Express. 'What's going to happen?' he asked. 'It's a right old hoo-ha, isn't it?'

197

'Obviously Charlie made a mistake. A very expensive one by the looks of it,' said Bandit.

'But the printer said you went to check everything on press with her.'

'I did.'

Bandit looked as if he had stepped off the pages of *Loaded*. He reeked of aftershave and had a new slick haircut. Bob had noticed the silk Armani label on the inside of his jacket. Bandit obviously thought he was going up in the world.

'What else did Jack say?' Bandit asked.

Bob cautiously spread the red paper napkin over his lap. 'He said that you'd gone to see him afterwards. After. Well, after everything had been agreed.'

'Oh? He must have been mistaken.'

'No, he was quite clear about it,' said Bob, the hairs on the back of his neck starting to bristle.

Bandit leaned forward over the table, flicking his head to draw Bob closer.

'I think you'll be forgetting what Jack told you. There's enough rumpus already without adding to it. And if I find that your tongue has been wagging, Bob, then I might have to have a tongue-wagging session with Amanda. Do you get my drift?'

Bob looked down at his pizza, his appetite deserting him. Bandit watched him. 'Come on. Eat up. I'm going to brief you on a piece of business this afternoon that's going to make you very rich.'

Charlie stood by the door of the creative department, finding it difficult to breathe. Daniel had taken her away for the weekend and all the time he had known. Known that this was going to happen to her.

The department was in full swing as Charlie pushed open the door.

'Where's Daniel?' she asked, feeling sick and stumbling towards the kitchen.

Poppy pulled a face at Will and ran after Charlie, but it was too late, Charlie had already recognised the pictures that adorned the walls. Above the photocopy of her labia was a large sign saying 'Name That . . . Hunt.'

'It was meant to be a joke,' said Poppy sheepishly.

'You knew? You knew it was me?' Charlie stared at the pictures, mortified.

Poppy lowered her eyes.

Charlie felt her knees shaking and for a moment she thought she was going to faint, before anger gripped her. 'Where is he?' she asked icily.

Poppy looped her thumbs into the hooks on her army trousers. 'You can't see him, he's in the dark room.'

But Charlie was already pushing past her. She ran to the corner of the studio and yanked open the dark-room door.

'What the fuck are you doing?' yelled Daniel, bathed in infra red light.

'You bastard!' she screamed. 'You lying bastard! You knew!' She picked up one of the plastic trays full of water and hurled it at him. 'You knew all about the promotion going wrong on Saturday and you didn't tell me.'

'Stop it! Stop it right now!' Daniel pinned her arms by her sides, halting her wave of destruction. He pulled the door shut behind her and they faced each other in the red glow.

'What difference would it have made if I'd told you?'

'All the difference in the world. You lied to me. After everything. You lied to me!'

'I didn't lie. I just withheld information, that's not lying.'

'Like you withheld information about the Tipp-Ex crosses? Like the information you withheld about Pierre?' She started to shake, the words rattling out of her like a choking engine. 'Like the photocopies of me going up on the kitchen wall?' She searched his face, feeling her heart breaking, cracking up like a melting glacier.

Daniel pulled down the ruined photographs from the pegs on the wire. 'You're getting hysterical about nothing.'

'Nothing!'

'Calm down. I felt sorry for you. You know how fond I am of you and . . .'

In the cramped space of the dark room she stared at him

across the vast chasm between them. 'Fond of me? You said you loved me, but I guess that was another one of your lies.'

Daniel tutted, rolling his eyes as if she were being ridiculous. 'Charlie,' he said soothingly, reaching out to touch her arm. She whipped it out of his reach.

'Don't touch me, you bastard,' she hissed, pushing him away. Daniel staggered backwards, slipping on the water on the floor and losing his balance. He crashed, upsetting the trays of chemicals over himself and gashing the back of his head on the corner of the bench.

But Charlie didn't stop. She yanked open the door and stormed past Will and Poppy. Daniel staggered out of the red glow of the dark room and leaned against the doorpost, his crotch soaked with developing fluid. Poppy grimaced at him.

'The problem with that girl,' said Daniel, 'is that she has no sense of humour.' Then he collapsed on the floor, blood seeping out of the back of his head.

'Call an ambulance, Poppy. Quickly,' said Will, rushing over to him.

Charlie sat in the oasis of silence at her desk, not caring about the rivulets of mascara that ran in trenches down her face. She sniffed loudly as she finished typing the e-mail to Si. Her hands flew across the keys, rattling out the facts about the promotion, the copies of the faxes to the printer, the copies of the original contract she had typed that Philippa had altered and the facts surrounding Philippa's duplicitous life. Surely, if he saw all the facts, Si wouldn't let Philippa get away with what she'd done. But before she could finish it, Bandit stopped her.

'Si wants you in his office,' he said.

Charlie turned to him, her eyes raw with scorn. 'I bet you're loving this, aren't you?'

Si sat at his desk, squeezing the bag of silicone that a breast surgeon friend of his had given him as a desk toy. Today it was of little comfort. As he listened to Poppy's dramatic account of Charlie's encounter with Daniel in the dark room, the compassion he'd felt for Charlie had deserted him. She wasn't the woman he'd thought she was. She was just a stupid, man-crazy slag like the rest of them and it galled him deeply that he had been such a bad judge of character.

'You'll be relieved to hear that Daniel is going to be OK. He's got a nasty gash on his head and bad burns around his groin area.'

Charlie breathed in deeply. She hoped his rotten stinking penis was scarred for ever, or better still melted off.

'Please let me explain,' began Charlie, but Si's look silenced her.

'Given the circumstances, I have no choice but to let you go. You have lowered the tone of this agency. I'm so disappointed in you.'

Charlie stared at him. There was no point. Si was as blinkered as the rest of them.

'You have to understand that I can't risk the agency's reputation any further. You've embarrassed us rather considerably, not to mention yourself. I wouldn't feel comfortable having you in charge. Not after what's happened.'

She curled her lip in disgust and, slamming her car keys on the table, walked out of his office for the last time.

Charlie felt calm, almost serene as she caught the bus back home. She looked out of the window, the carrier bag containing all the personal things from her desk perched on her knee. She jolted in her seat as people stepped on to the bus, but it didn't bother her any more. She watched the cold dusk settle across the bumper-to-bumper traffic and found herself humming.

She let herself in the front door of the flat and stood in the doorway. Something about being at home brought her to her senses and the numbness she had felt evaporated with each step she took up the stairs. Underneath it was a terrifying pain.

'Rich?' she called, her voice barely a whisper. She needed him. His warmth, his face. She needed to be enfolded into his hug and for him to tell her everything was OK. To soothe her, cajole her into humour.

The bag fell from her hand on to the sofa and she walked into the kitchen and turned on the light. She looked at the notice board and shook her head. The card she had made for Rich had gone. He'd given her drawing to Pix without even asking her. She steadied herself against the table and then she saw Rich's note, stark against the grain of the pine.

She picked it up and read it over and over again, the silence clanging around her as desolation swept over her. Then she slumped to the floor, her back against the table leg as huge, racking fat sobs rumbled up from her soul.

Eight hours later she woke up, crunched in a foetal position. Flexing her cricked neck, she saw Kev mewing around her and poking her with his wet nose.

She looked up at him and ruffled his fur and for a split second everything was normal. And then she remembered the events of yesterday and gasped as if she had been hit in the chest.

'Oh, Kev,' she whispered, the river of tears, dammed by sleep, flowing freely once more. 'You're the only decent bloke I know. And you're a cat.'

BOOK
III

Rich had no idea that Goa was so beautiful. As he sipped his Sandpiper beer, he surveyed Baga beach from the corner table of the Good Luck bar. It was two o'clock and getting hotter. Hip-swinging women in brightly coloured saris swayed through the heat haze with woven baskets on their heads. 'Pineapple, mango, coconut, watermelon,' they chanted, their soft voices lost in the heat. Occasionally they stopped by a sun worshipper and, in one graceful move, swung down their heavy baskets on to the squeaky sand and split open fruit on a muslin cloth.

Rich sighed and watched a brown cow wander past the bamboo haven, its black nostrils covered in sand. It nudged the dried seaweed, ribs visible beneath its sagging skin as it blinked away flies.

Draining the rest of his beer, he pushed the straw hat to the back of his head. He loved the way the brightness dazzled his eyes and the heat soaked him in lethargy. For the first time in years he was starting to relax and it felt strange. At first he'd woken up in the early morning, panicking that he had missed the Tube to work, or that he hadn't completed a review of a crucial legal file. Then the vocal limbering of the cockerel in the yard, the buzzing whine and honking horns of passing mopeds, not to mention chattering tropical birds in the coconut tree outside his window, reminded him where he was.

He would pull the thin cotton sheet over his head and try to go back to sleep, but the bustle outside defeated him and he'd get up and pad over the dunes at the back of the guest house and down to the beach, his old deck shoes filling with fine sand. After neatly straightening his towel, he'd arrange his suntan lotion bottles and, tightening the string on his baggy shorts, would dive into the waves. He'd tried to get a routine going, disciplining himself to swim for twenty minutes each morning and organising his day into informative reading periods, sunbathing, sightseeing and eating.

Yet the sun had banished any order and he'd given in and slept for hours each day, only waking to cool off in the water and eat. His mornings had become more and more lazy and instead of swimming, he'd found himself playing in the surf. He felt like a kid again as he jumped through the foaming white breakers, body surfing the more powerful waves, letting them carry him towards the shore, where they crashed over him, spinning him round until he stood up in the shallows, disorientated and with sand up his nose.

Rich smiled to himself, remembering how he'd played for an hour that morning. An hour! He billed clients £120 per hour for his time. He felt a stab of guilt. What was he doing here, running away from Pix, Charlie and Mathers Egerickx Lovitt? He watched two men playing bat and ball by the water's edge, the gentle pit pat close on the breeze, like applause in a cricket stadium.

He knew he needed space, but apart from playing in the waves when he succumbed to the power of the water, he didn't feel free. He had booked his holiday for a month and now he realised that wasn't long enough. In a month he'd be back in London and it would be a few weeks before Christmas. He hated the thought of the freezing drizzle and December gloom of London and he knew that he didn't want to go home. It would never be the same again. Charlie would probably have moved in with Daniel, Pix hated him and he would be alone.

Walking along the beach, he pressed his toes into the wet sand. The water squeezed away from under him as if a halo was forming around each foot. He tried to rationalise the events of the past couple of weeks and how his life had disintegrated around him.

He flopped on to the raffia beach mat he'd bought that morning from a young girl with white teeth and pleading eyes. He peeped through his fluttering lashes into the glinting white flashbulb of brightness and buried his hands and lifted them, sieving the soft sand through his fingers. Feeling the sun sink into him, warming his bones, he sighed, and, as he closed his eyes and pulled his hat over his face, he couldn't fight the wave of sleep that lulled him.

Charlie slumped in front of the television. She had been in her nightie for days, with a pair of Rich's large welly-socks and her threadbare dressing gown. She stared blankly at a daytime television chat show as she shovelled crisps into her mouth. She looked listlessly at the label. She didn't even like this flavour! Being miserable was supposed to make you thin, but Charlie had been bingeing on a steady stream of un-comforting junk food. Yet still she couldn't connect with anything. She felt as if her skull had been clobbered with a mallet.

She stood up and paced around the flat. She definitely felt ill, and there was something else. Something she could no longer escape. She thought she was sore from the frenzied love-making with Daniel on Saturday. Yet Saturday seemed like a million years ago and the sore, tingling sensation was still there. Maybe Daniel's friction burn wasn't friction after all. How could she have been such an idiot? She covered her face, but there was no escaping the nasty truth: she had to go to the VD clinic and she had to go soon.

In the GU department of the local hospital, Charlie pulled out her numbered ticket from the red machine by the reception desk as if she were buying cheese. She supposed that VD must affect all sorts, but she still felt like a leper. She shrank down in her seat, wishing it was her coffin. When her number came up, she approached the reception desk.

Behind the glass, the receptionist flicked over the page of a magazine and looked up, boredom making her features droop. 'Go and wait in the other waiting room. Someone will see you shortly,' she said with complete indifference and Charlie felt like beating her fists on the glass. Couldn't the silly cow see that she was having a silent nervous breakdown?

Stop the world, I want to get off, she thought as she clutched her pink ticket, pushed through the double doors and saw that the next waiting room was also full. A young girl sat huddled in the corner seat, weeping on her pimply companion. Next to her, oblivious to the snivels, a middle-aged woman sat with a plastic co-op bag on her lap. A strand of baby yellow wool jerked from its interior as she clacked her knitting needles.

Charlie squeezed past the traffic jam of pushchairs, and sat beside a neatly dressed businessman who was mostly hidden behind the *Independent*. Out of the corner of her eye, she read the headline of one of the articles on the front page: 'Up Beat promotional fiasco' and quickly picked up the cover-less Reader's Digest. It had reached the national newspapers. What if someone recognised her?

She couldn't pretend to read and stood, trembling by the wall rack of leaflets. A gaggle of Middle Eastern women covered from head to foot in black chadors were huddled in the space by the coffee table arguing in babbling Arabic. A small boy emerged from under the table and started tugging at one of the women's skirts. Charlie saw the woman's eyes flash with anger as she turned round and whacked him. She felt the little boy's sense of injustice and when he started wailing, she wanted to join in.

The woman caught Charlie's desperate stare and glared at her through her rectangular slit. She started talking to the other women who all looked over in Charlie's direction. She lowered her eyes to the leaflet she was holding with 'Understanding Genital Warts' on the front and hastily shoved it back in the rack. What did all these people think she had? Syphilis, gonorrhoea, HIV, genital warts? She didn't know herself. All she knew was that she must have the most ghastly of all diseases emblazoned in neon just above her head: stupidity.

She flicked through the leaflets warning her about safer sex, remembering her conversations with Daniel about how appalling condoms were. But however much she hated Daniel, she had only herself to blame. She'd been the one who had made the decision to have unprotected sex because she'd thought it would disappoint Daniel if she didn't. She hadn't thought twice about it, but now she'd found out he was bisexual and that he was the world's biggest liar, she probably had AIDS and God knows what else. Terrifying thoughts of dying alone in a hospital bed, or worse, having to tell her parents stabbed into her and she felt the inside of her nose pricking with anxious tears.

'Number fifty-one.' The junior doctor stood in the doorway of the consulting room and Charlie slotted the leaflet back in the rack. She looked at her ticket, thinking of the irony of it all as she walked into the room to expose her shame between the waiting stirrups.

It was eleven in the morning and Rich was sitting in the bar at the far end of the beach, devouring a banana and ice-cream pancake, when he saw her. She was way out on the sand bank, standing with her back to him, her hands stretched in a praying position above her head. A thick rope of pleated white blonde hair slithered down her back and Rich watched her fold forward, her walnut buttocks stretched towards him from the green material of her g-string leotard.

He breathed in with wonder as she raised herself into a perfect handstand. Her front was visible now, her full breasts nestling in her leotard. He couldn't take his eyes off her as he hurried back to his beach mat and lay on his stomach, hiding his embarrassing desire.

He tried to read his book, but when he glanced up, she'd opened her legs out horizontally and he was mesmerised. The azure sea glinted in the morning sun between the V of her contoured legs and he imagined her to be a sea goddess, enticing the gentle waves on to the beach.

He hunched his shoulders and rolled them back. He was stiff from his tormented sleep and his sunburn had woken him up at the crack of dawn. It had been impossible to get back to sleep and when the generator had cranked into a gurgling drone, he'd got up and decided to hire a moped.

He'd walked through the town to the church at the other end of the bay, watching the women washing their clothes and the locals swerving on their ancient bicycles. In the bright sun, a warped recording of Bing Crosby's 'I'm Dreaming of a White Christmas' blared out from a loudspeaker.

'You want moped. I make you cheap price.' A man in a dirty striped shirt, grey trousers and spanking new flip-flops approached him with a big smile. Rich found himself nodding and being led to a dusty graveyard of bikes by the main lamppost in the village.

The man told Rich to wait one moment and twenty minutes later produced a set of keys and an old Honda moped with two stickers on the plastic petrol-tank casing. One declared 'Jesus Loves You' and the other simply said 'Dream Lover'.

'This is perfect,' laughed Rich and handed over the money. 'Can you teach me to ride it?'

'No problem, no problem.' The man grinned. 'Get on behind please,' he said, starting the engine as Rich clambered on. He shot across the road, through a ditch and swerved to a halt on what must be the local football pitch, where he handed over the keys.

'Give it more of the right hand,' encouraged the man, making vrooming noises as Rich wobbled away across the dried mud.

'That's it, you have it, sir,' he shouted, and clapped his hands as Rich speeded up.

Since it was Wednesday, he'd gone to explore Anjuna market. He'd wandered through the bustling crowd, in amongst the walls of panelled bedspreads hanging like washing, fending off the little girls with their big smiles who recognised him from the beach and enticed him to inspect their silver bracelets. He lingered at the spice stalls, laden with hessian sacks full of bright powders, and was followed by two eager drum salesmen, who ran their hard thin fingers across the drums' hide surface to make a swooping, sliding skin-on-skin noise. Rich looked up appreciatively.

'I make you very cheap price.' A drum was thrust towards him.

'No. I don't want one.' Rich was swamped by bartering children, holding out colourful soft cotton lunghis, silver trinkets, hats, beach mats, bedspreads, bongs and ornaments of every description, and yet more drums. Soon, the clamouring for his attention was more than he could bear and he blundered into the shade of the make-shift café and collapsed on a cushion.

How stupid he'd been to get into such a state about his life. How pointless his law career seemed when he saw the eager faces of these poverty-stricken children, peddling their wares for pennies. And yet they all seemed happy. All had their place in the dusty, bright market where nothing seemed too serious.

'You want happy cake?' He heard the American's voice behind him. He turned to see a lanky brown man, covered in henna tattoos and wearing loose Indian print shorts. Two tiny dots in the centre of his irises were all that was left of his pupils. He carried an ancient tape recorder on which an ambient trance tape played and he swayed in time to the music.

'Hey man. You look like you could do with some happy cake. It's totally happy and fluffy. You'll be happy and fluffy all day,' he tempted, gyrating his washboard torso and swirling around Rich.

'No. I don't think so,' began Rich, feeling prim.

'Hey, loosen up, bro'. What have you got to lose?'

'No, I don't, well, I don't do drugs,' he stuttered, feeling ridiculous.

The man laughed. 'Then you need some.'

Rich thought about it. It wasn't like taking mixed-up drugs in London. This stuff was bound to be pure and surely there was no harm in trying a bit of banana hash cake. Why was he being such a prude? Impulsively, he handed over his fifty rupees and stuffed the cake, wrapped in smudged newspaper, into his knapsack.

Feeling reckless he bought some new clothes: a red and yellow embroidered hat with mirror shapes on it, two lunghis, a new pair of baggy shorts and a light purple cotton shirt. It was the best shopping spree he'd had for ages and he felt pleased with himself as he negotiated the bumpy road back to Baga.

Now as he watched the supple limbering of the woman, he remembered the banana hash cake and furtively removed it from his bag. He lay back on his elbow, eating the cake and watching her finish her yoga session.

When the chocolate-eyed Indian man approached him on the beach and offered him a price for a massage, Rich already had a big grin on his face. What the hell? He felt like spoiling himself. In the shade of a bamboo hut, he felt the man's expert fingers knead coconut oil into his parched pores, and as his head span and his body relaxed, Rich moaned contentedly and decided that he was in heaven.

Charlie's mouth dropped open with shock. 'There's no cure?'

The doctor shook his head. 'No, but you will be able to manage the symptoms more with time and the attacks should become less frequent. A lot of people only have one attack. Just take the tablets five times a day and you should be back to normal in a day or so.'

Charlie hardly heard him. She felt sick. This couldn't be happening.

The doctor patted her hand. 'Are you OK?'

She had herpes. An incurable reminder of Daniel for ever. For ever! At home, she stared at herself in the bathroom mirror, not recognising her face. Herpes? Who had herpes these days? It was ridiculous. She'd never be able to have another lover, she thought, crouching in the bath, roughly washing her body as if it had betrayed her. She wrapped herself in towels and lay on the sofa, staring at the flaking ceiling. She couldn't even be bothered to take an overdose.

The phone rang for five rings before the answer machine clicked on and she heard her mother on the fuzzy long-distance line.

'Oh, you're not in. You're probably at work. I just called to say that we're having a splendid time in Australia. We're in Melbourne at the moment and Dad and I are going to Sydney tomorrow. Hope you're well. Love to Rich. Cheerio darling.'

Charlie turned into the back of the sofa. Maybe if she lay still enough, the shame would go. She felt hot tears plopping on to the pillow and ached for Kate. Now that she realised what a shit Daniel was she couldn't believe she'd accused Kate of betraying her. She'd put Daniel above everything and everyone else, and ruined her relationship with her best friend in the process. How many times had she promised Kate that she was more important than any bloke would ever be? And how quickly had she thrown it all away? No. She couldn't possibly expect Kate to forgive her.

Hours later, Charlie was roused from her pit of self-loathing by the door buzzer. She pulled the tear- and snot-stained cushion over her head and groaned. Her head thumped and her back ached and she shivered. But the buzzer kept on buzzing and the noise pierced her head. She hauled herself from the sofa and went over to the doorphone in the hall.

'It's Pix, let me in.'

'Rich isn't here.' She spoke into the receiver, her voice barely a whisper.

'Let me in. I want to talk to you.'

Charlie cradled the answerphone against her chest and took a deep breath. She felt wobbly and ill. There was no way she could see anyone. She let the phone dangle by its beige curly cord and padded away from it as Pix's dismembered voice pleaded through the small flower-pattern of holes in the mouthpiece.

Then the banging started. Charlie put her hands to her temples. Was there no peace? She went back to the phone and hung it back on the wall and pressed the open door button. She should have known that Pix was too stubborn to do something normal, like leave her alone.

Pix stopped at the top of the stairs, her mouth falling open at the sight of Charlie cowering by the kitchen door in her tea-stained nightie, her hair in a tangled matted knot. Deep purple bags lurked below her red-rimmed eyes and her complexion had erupted into spots. Pix stared at the woman she had formally revered as beautiful.

'Sweet Jesus! What happened to you?'

Charlie turned away from her into the kitchen and stood against the sink. Pix followed her, hopping through the debris of empty vodka bottles, crumpled crisp packets, pizza boxes, discarded clothes and ripped-up photos.

'What do you want?' asked Charlie, her hostile eyes making Pix recoil.

'I had an argument with Rich and I . . .'

Charlie shook her head and looked down. 'I don't want to hear about it.'

Pix approached cautiously. 'What's wrong?'

'Rich left a note,' she said. 'It's on the table.'

Pix gasped as she read it. 'Oh God. I'm so sorry. I had no idea. He's gone because of me.' She put her hand on Charlie's back, but she flinched away.

'I had no idea you'd be so upset.'

Charlie sneered in a bitter laugh. 'It was the straw that broke the camel's back. But hey, it's the least of my worries.' She brushed past Pix and flopped on to the chair. 'Don't worry, I'm over it.'

'You don't look like it. You look terrible.'

'Thanks!'

'Sorry – I–'

'As you can see, Rich isn't here and I can't help you so maybe it's better if you leave. And I'd appreciate it if you could make it out of the door without stealing any of my illustrations.'

'I can explain.'

'Don't bother,' snapped Charlie rudely, circling her temples with her forefingers and pulling up her cold feet to the edge of the kitchen chair.

'Can I do something?' said Pix desperately, noticing Charlie's voice growing hysterical.

'I don't need you to be my mother.'

Charlie put her hands over her ears as Pix ran the tap into the spout of the kettle, not knowing what to do, her emotions raging in turmoil. How dare Pix be so presumptuous. Couldn't she see that she had lost the plot completely? Couldn't she see that she didn't need anyone . . .

'What's wrong?' asked Pix, touching Charlie on the shoulder.

'I want my mummy,' gasped Charlie, fat tears overflowing from her eyes. 'I want my mum,' she wailed. 'I'm so pathetic!'

'You poor lamb,' soothed Pix, rocking her back and forth as Charlie sobbed out the events of the last week.

'Oh, Pix. What a mess. What a fucking horrible mess I've made of it all.'

'It's not your fault.'

'It is. It's all my fault. The promotion going wrong and Daniel. I just can't believe it. He's a psychotic control freak and I didn't even notice. I'm so stupid.'

'You can't blame yourself.'

'I've driven everyone away, even Rich. And there's nothing I can do.'

Pix stood up. 'There is something you can do.'

Charlie blew her nose. 'What? Just tell me, Pix, because I'm at a dead end here.'

The kettle clicked off. Pix went over to the window and pulled up the blind, letting the weak grey sunlight filter into the dank kitchen.

'I'll tell you. You can make a choice. You can either be a victim in all of this, or you can fight for yourself.'

Charlie groaned and flopped her elbows on to the table, burying her head on her forearms. 'You don't understand.'

'I do. You've been shat on from a great height, but that doesn't mean you have to give up your life.'

'But I feel such a fool.'

'You're not a fool. Those silly people in the office are.

Daniel is.' She put some herbal tea in front of Charlie. 'You've been a victim of injustice. It's disgusting.'

Charlie took a sip of the tea. 'So is this.'

'Come on. Have a shower and get dressed. We're going to get a plan of action together.'

Charlie moaned. 'I can't. Leave me alone. I can't face anyone.'

Pix started to tug her arm to raise her from the chair.

'I said leave me!' Charlie snapped away from Pix and a large red slug of blackcurrant tea spilled out over Rich's letter.

Pix put her hands on her hips and shook her head sadly. 'I thought you were made of sterner stuff.'

Charlie put her head in her hands. 'Yeah? Well you thought wrong.'

'You've got all these people who love you and look out for you . . .'

Charlie looked up, her bloodshot eyes bitter. 'Like who?'

'Like Rich. Your parents. Loads of people. Me!' she said accusingly. 'And everyone will go on loving you, even though life has dealt you a few blows. You've got so much going for you, but you refuse to see it.'

Charlie let out a cynical laugh. 'Oh really? Well how come everything I touch goes wrong?'

'It doesn't. You're really talented. Just take your illustration. It's been a complete success. I know I shouldn't have taken it without your permission, but Rich said it'd be OK.'

'Well it wasn't.'

Pix took a deep breath. 'I know you're upset, but once your head clears you'll see that you could do something with your talent. You don't want to work for sharks like Bistram whatever they were.'

'And what the hell would you know about what I want?'

'I'm a woman too,' said Pix quietly. 'I know you want recognition at something you enjoy . . .'

Charlie slammed out of the chair. 'Don't you dare give me all this feminist bullshit. What the fuck do you know? Get out and leave me alone.'

Pix exhaled impatiently and put her hands up in defeat. 'If that's what you want.'

'Just go.'

Pix turned on her plimsolled heel and headed for the door, then she turned back to Charlie. 'I know you're lashing out because you're in pain and I can see that. But I can help you and it seems to me that there doesn't seem to be anyone else around who can.'

Pix was nearly out of the flat before her words sank in and Charlie raced after her.

'Come back,' she begged, scuttling down the stairs. 'I'm sorry. I'm being such a bitch. I think I've had a personality-ectomy by mistake.'

Pix smiled and Charlie's eyes filled up with tears at the compassion she saw. 'I need you. Will you help me? Please?'

Pix smiled. 'Aye. 'Course I will.'

Rich floated down the beach. He was stoned. Stoned and supremely relaxed. He collapsed on to his beach mat and rolled round his head. He felt so supple and light after his massage, it was as if his whole body had undergone an MOT. The masseur had even crunched the tension out of his ears!

The man at the market had been right. It was happy fluffy cake. He felt superb. He was too stoned to read and instead he walked out over to the rocks. Crouching down by a rock pool, he stared into its clear depths. It was like the staging for a play, the shells clamped to the sides of the pool like scenery, while vertical fronds of seaweed floated up towards the surface.

'Hi.'

Rich heard the voice behind him and looked up. The yoga woman stood before him, blocking out the sun. From his squatting position he ran his eyes up her long firm legs to the crotch of her bikini, up past the toned flatness of her stomach to the ripe, oiled breasts in their crochet cups. Was he having an hallucination?

'I saw you having a massage. I thought I might have one myself. Was he any good? The masseur?' She crouched down on the other side of the rock pool. Her white gold hair was parted in the middle and she had loosely plaited the two sides of her fringe, looping them around the back of her head. The rest of her hair hung in gentle waves over her freckled shoulders so that she looked like a seventies model, yet her face was scored with deep laughter lines.

Rich wondered whether his tongue was visibly out of his mouth with lust. He'd obviously stumbled into a slow-motion sequence of *Baywatch*! What felt like forty-five minutes later, he found his voice.

'Excellent. Although I smell like a coconut macaroon now!' He sniffed his arm and pulled a face and the woman laughed, her polished white teeth glinting in the sun.

Rich had spent over a week on his own. Now, as he started pointing out the intricacies of the rock pool to the woman, he realised that he craved human contact. He didn't stop talking. He watched her mouth as she rocked her head back and laughed at his unstoppable babble.

They strolled back along the beach and Rich found an old, hollow horn sticking out of the sand. He washed it in the waves and gave it to her before they stopped in a beach bar for a freshly squeezed mango juice. Something about the happy fluffy cake was working. He was making the woman laugh and he liked the way he felt with her.

'I saw you doing yoga this morning,' said Rich. 'I'm so impressed. I'd never do anything like that.'

'Why not?'

'I'm built for comfort, not speed. It all seems a bit athletic to me.'

'You're mistaken. Yoga isn't athletic. It works from the inside out and if you don't like speed, then it'd be perfect for you. Why don't you come along and try it?'

Lulled by her intriguing accent, Rich found himself agreeing. He looked out to sea. He felt more relaxed than he could ever remember. 'Don't you love that? In the afternoon, when the sun makes the water go all golden?' He pointed to the shimmer on the water and she nodded.

'Why are you here?' she asked softly and he realised she had been studying him.

'Oh, you know. I felt like a holiday and . . .'

The woman stared at him, her clear green eyes demanding the truth.

'If you must know, I'm running away.'

She nodded. 'You picked the right place to run to. Just make sure that you remember to leave one day. Quite a few don't.'

'I can understand why.'

She stood up. 'I'm going to a party at Little Vagatour tonight. You'll come?'

'I'd love to.'

'I'll meet you here at nine. I want my massage now.'

Rich looked after her and realised he hadn't found out anything about her. 'I don't know your name,' he shouted after her.

'Does it matter?'

Rich looked at her perplexed and she laughed at him. 'I'm Tanya,' she said and waved before walking off, her feet swivelling as she strode through the sand.

'Tanya,' said Rich to himself, rubbing his eyes. God, he felt strange.

She never thought she'd leave but, as Pix saw her off from King's Cross on the train, Charlie knew it was the right thing to do. She leaned out of the window of the train door.

'Promise you'll look after Kev?'

'Charlie!'

'I know. I know you will, but remember that he hates Whiskas. He's the cat that dares to be different!'

'Go and relax. Don't come back until things have died down. Kev will be fine with me.'

Charlie rubbed the corner of her watering eyes. 'Oh, Pix. You've been so wonderful to me. I'm sorry I've been such a mess.'

'Ah go on with you. For a stupid cow, you're not so bad. Now stop apologising. Just go.'

The train started to pull out of the station and Charlie waved. Pix had kick-started her into action and it was only through her efforts that she was on the train at all. Pix had cleaned up the flat while Charlie had a shower and then ordered her to get her address book. She pulled off one of the thongs around her neck and held it with her thumb. The wire-enclosed crystal swung like a pendulum over the book.

'What on earth are you doing?' asked Charlie, yanking a comb through her wet hair.

Pix closed her eyes. 'Asking the universe to point you in the right direction.'

Charlie was too tired to argue.

Then Pix flipped open the pages and it fell open. 'Who's Mary Rose?'

'My godmother.' Charlie looked at the address.

'Then she's the one.' Pix handed her the phone and, before Charlie could protest, she was booked on the train to Aberdeen.

Charlie had to take her hat off to Pix. She'd dismissed her as a New Age hippy type, but she was actually extremely practical and down to earth. Lurching towards the buffet carriage, she couldn't help thinking that it was a shame things hadn't worked out with Pix and Rich. Why didn't Pix blame her, especially after reading Rich's pathetic note? How could she be so gracious?

As the train rumbled through the suburbs, Charlie kicked off her shoes and pulled her feet under her. She opened the brown paper bag on the table in front of her and pulled out the bacon and tomato roll, but the smell was deceptive. It had the consistency of cardboard and it singed the tastebuds from her tongue as soon as she bit into it. Why were even the simple things in life a let-down? Despondently, she discarded it and rested her head on the cool glass.

What was she doing? She'd been willing to let Pix take over all her decision-making processes, but now she thought about dumping herself on Mary Rose and felt apprehensive about what her godmother would make of her failures in London. Mary Rose had always had such high hopes for her. How could she possibly explain what had happened?

It had started to rain and Charlie stared out at the bare

trees, thinking of Daniel and everything she'd lost. When she caught her reflection in the glass, her tears were indistinguishable from the rain on the window.

Rich studied his face in the cracked mirror above the Victorian porcelain sink in the apartment. Would Tanya ever find him attractive? He rubbed the peeling skin on the end of his nose and was delving into his washbag to find his sandalwood aftershave when his fingers touched the moonstone Pix had given him. He'd completely forgotten about it and he washed it under the tap and held it, its smoothness reminding him of the smell of tarmac after rain.

Poor Pix. He closed his eyes, clutching the moonstone, his heart lurching as he remembered the pain of leaving London. He mustn't think about it. Mustn't dwell on what he'd lost, or he'd never enjoy his holiday. He looked at himself sternly in the mirror. Don't think about it. Shut it out.

Tanya was waiting for him on the beach. She was a vision in a tight vest with a damask lunghi casually draped around her supple hips and Rich was glad that he was wearing his new shorts. Tanya waved and walked towards him, her ankle bracelets tingling and an image of Pix flickered into Rich's mind. He quickly swiped it out.

'We'll go on my bike, if you like?' he suggested. 'You'll have to look out for me. I'm a beginner.'

Tanya clutched him round the waist. 'You'll be fine,' she said with such conviction that he didn't remember to breathe in.

She clung on to him as he sped off on the moped and, in their shadow, Rich could see her white gold hair flying out behind her. He felt as if he was in a movie and he laughed, the warm air buffeting his clean-shaven cheeks. By the time they reached the old bridge across the river, the sun had dropped behind the horizon and night had slunk amongst the trees.

'Hold on,' yelled Rich, tightening his grip on the throttle and hurtling down the dirt track into the unlit palm tree grove. 'Oh my God,' he screeched as they swerved in the deep sand and wobbled round the tall tree trunks, but Tanya just laughed.

'You're doing fine,' she said, patting him reassuringly.

The new moon party at Little Vagatour was in full swing. Rich's legs were shaking as he stopped at the top of the cliff and took the keys out of the ignition. On the beach below, trance music boomed out across the rocks from the bamboo and mud huts. A small crowd milled about on the dark sand and out on the rocks some jugglers and acrobats threw flaming batons up into the night sky.

Tanya swung off the back and re-tied her lunghi over her tight stomach. Rich watched her, wanting to stroke her flesh and ease his hands under her vest to feel the shape of her rib cage and the underside fullness of her breasts.

'New moon.' She nodded to the sky. Rich blushed and put the bike keys in his pocket, staring at the perfect silver crescent and the bright star of Venus shining out beside it. He remembered that someone had once told him that a new moon brought luck, as long as your first glimpse of it wasn't through a window. He felt the moonstone in his pocket. Perhaps it was a good omen.

'Come.' He looked around and saw Tanya waiting for him, holding out her hand to lead him down the winding, rocky cliff path, through the cold grass underneath the silvery palm trees and into the crowd.

It was seven o'clock and dark by the time Charlie reached Hill Farm.

'Here we are,' said Jamie, the cab driver Mary Rose had sent to pick Charlie up from the station. He swung the battered Volvo into the lane and Charlie leaned forward to see the lights in the old granite farmhouse. He stopped the car in the drive, the tyres crunching on the rough pebbles, and Charlie stepped out into biting wind and spattering rain.

The heavy oak door in the gable end of the farmhouse swung open and Mary Rose hurried towards her, her head-scarf flapping around her small ruddy face as she shouted at the dogs. It was no use. Jakey-Boy and Spoof jumped past her little legs and skittered towards Charlie, who almost lost her balance as they sprang up at her.

'Hello boys,' she said, ruffling the soft ears of the border collies.

Mary Rose padded towards Charlie, her ancient green wellies clacking as she waved. 'Put it on my account, Jamie.'

'Right-ho,' said Jamie, touching the rim of his tweed cap and getting back in the car.

Mary Rose bustled round Charlie, picking up her heavy holdall in one neat move. 'Hello darling, you must be exhausted. Come on inside, quickly now,' she said, striding back towards the house. Even though Charlie was three inches taller than her, she had to trot to keep up.

'Ghastly weather,' announced Mary Rose, dumping Charlie's bag in the large porch. She shut the door and immediately the sounds of the blustery night were muffled. Charlie noticed the gun propped up in the corner. 'They say it's going to get worse,' she continued as Charlie followed her through to the kitchen, past the rack of coats and hats, churning washing machine and a crusty bowl of cat food on the window sill.

The farm kitchen was lit by a harsh fluorescent strip which showed up the mug stains on the plastic tablecloth. A fat black cat jumped off the side by the rickety gas cooker and landed silently on the stone flags, disappearing through the cat flap in the steamed-up glass door. In the corner an ancient boiler whistled; beneath it a sideboard was piled high with various bunches of keys, bottles and gardening tools. Pots of pruned geranium plants were lined up on the big stainless steel sink, next to which sat a huge chopping board and a butcher's knife and a mug tree with an odd assortment of chipped Royal wedding mugs.

Mary Rose unknotted the scarf below her chin and patted her permed grey curls. She was only fifty-one, the same age as Charlie's mother, but she looked older than Charlie remembered. Her round cheeks were reddened by the elements and wrinkles fanned out around her sharp brown eyes, while the skin around her rosebud mouth was puckered with lines.

'Now, how about a gin!' Mary Rose unscrewed the lid of an optic-sized green bottle and took down two glasses from the shelf. Not waiting for an answer, she deposited two inches of the oily liquid in each glass and a dash of tonic from the fridge.

'No lemons, I'm afraid.' She handed one of the glasses to Charlie. 'Chin-chin.'

Charlie took a sip of the gin, its fumes making her eyes water. 'I'd forgotten your gins,' she coughed and Mary Rose smiled.

'Let's have a look at you then,' she said, inspecting her in the harsh light. Her wispy eyebrows furrowed together. 'When was the last time you saw a vegetable?'

'Does pizza count?'

'Definitely not,' said Mary Rose, squeezing her cheek. 'Not to worry, we'll have you right as rain in no time.'

The lid of the bubbling pot on the stove lifted and puffed and Mary Rose put her glass on the table and marched over to it. Charlie sipped her drink and looked around for a place to sit. The chair nearest her was covered in a pile of newspapers, another with a horses bridle.

'I hope you don't mind me intruding like this,' she said.

'Don't be silly. I can think of nothing better and there's plenty for you to do. You can stay for as long as you want, but I can't say I've got much in the way of entertainment. It's very boring here compared to your glamorous life in London.'

'It's hardly glamorous.'

Mary Rose caught her look. 'I can't believe that. How's Rich? Behaving himself, I hope?'

Charlie fiddled with her glass. 'He's fine, I think.'

Mary Rose looked at her in alarm.

'He's gone away for a while,' Charlie explained, her breath catching in her throat. Seeing Mary Rose made her miss Rich and a wave of guilt swept over her. 'We sort of fell out.'

Mary Rose hung the oven mits over the oven door. 'Oh dear.'

'There's so much to explain. It's all been a bit . . .' Charlie looked down into her glass, feeling fragile and tearful.

Mary Rose nodded. 'I've put you in the top bedroom,' she said. 'Why don't you get settled and then we can have a nice long chat.'

Charlie pushed open the heavy kitchen door, bending her knees to stop the dogs running into the lounge. A black log burner glowed red and crackled under the granite chimney breast. A worn chintz sofa, a rocking chair and an old-fashioned Singer sewing machine covered most of the rug space. In the far corner, a grandfather clock ticked slowly. Charlie pulled back the thick curtain to look at the view down to the valley, but all that was on the other side of the glass was pitch black night and she shivered.

The house was at least two hundred and fifty years old and the treads of the stone stairs were worn and blackened. Upstairs it was cold and Charlie's teeth chattered as she hurried along the creaking floorboards to the end room, reacquainting her senses with the atmosphere, feeling like a nine-year-old again as she lifted the latch of the bedroom door.

It was smaller than she remembered and she had to crouch down as she entered the room to stop her head banging on the beam. She walked down the steps to the sheepskin rug which had yellowed with age and noticed that the familiar watercolour of a hunting scene had a well-established cobweb on it. The iron-framed single bed was draped in a faded patchwork quilt and she sat on it, sinking into its duck feather softness as the springs creaked.

The room was so familiar and yet so strange. She had come back to it a different person. She looked across at the dusty bookshelf filled with faded blue and red hardback books and saw the battered copy of *The Magic Faraway Tree*. She went to the shelf and flicked open the Brownie Guide annual. 'I promise that I shall do my best to do my duty to God, to serve the Queen and help other people and to keep the Brownie Guide law,' she read, and a bitter laugh escaped her for her lost innocence.

As she re-entered the kitchen, the phone rang and Mary Rose pulled out the bent aerial, putting her ear to the receiver.

She banged it on the heel of her hand. 'Yes, Hamish, hello there.' She donned her large plastic-framed glasses and took hold of a leaking red biro which was bound with Sellotape on to a length of string by the kitchen calendar. She scanned down the rows of spidery writing.

'Yes. Eight-thirty tomorrow. I'll see you there. Oh, and I'm bringing a guest.' She glanced at Charlie. 'My goddaughter. Yes, yes. Up from London.'

Mary Rose smiled at Charlie as she replaced the receiver. 'Hamish, the vet. We're going to an auction tomorrow and he's coming as protection.'

'Protection?'

'You'll see,' said Mary Rose. 'You'll like Hamish. He's a lovely man.'

'I'm off men.'

Mary Rose flicked off the fluorescent strip lighting and pulled down a lamp over the table so that its warm glow changed the room and the clutter was obscured in dark shadows.

Charlie peered at a photo on the wall of Mary Rose at the Burleigh horse trials. 'Is there anything I can do to help?'

Her godmother sat her down and dumped a saucepan of water and a bag of potatoes on the table. 'You can do these if you like. Now then, I want to hear everything.'

Charlie held a potato in her hand. 'I don't know where to start.'

Mary Rose put the bottle of gin down beside her. 'Just talk,' she said.

And so Charlie repeated the repeatable bits of the disastrous Up Beat promotion, her relationship with Daniel, Rich's flight and, worst of all, losing Kate.

'They sound like a thoroughly incorrigible bunch to me,' said Mary Rose sternly, refilling Charlie's glass. 'And as for Daniel, well, if I so much as laid eyes on him I'd give him a round of the horse whip.'

Charlie's eyes filled with tears. 'I was in love with him and all along he was lying to me. I feel such an idiot.' She put her hand on her forehead, the potato peeler jutting out.

Mary Rose sat down. 'You listen to me, young lady. You're better off without them.'

Charlie shook her head and sniffed. 'How could I have made such a stupid mistake?'

'We all make mistakes.'

'Not this big.'

Mary Rose reached up to the side and grabbed the kitchen roll, tearing off a piece for Charlie. 'Maybe you were set up.'

'Who would set me up?' Charlie blew her nose.

'Any one of them. They've all got a motive if you think about it. One thing I've learned is that jealous people always cause trouble.'

Charlie looked pathetic as she blew her nose and Mary Rose cocked her head.

'It's one silly promotion with one newspaper. It's not exactly the end of the world.'

Charlie looked up at her, her eyes swimming with tears. 'It feels like it. I feel so humiliated. I can't believe how much I trusted them all, not least Daniel.'

Mary Rose waved her hand dismissively. 'Pah! Daniel. You're far too good for him. A bit of farm air and you'll see it all differently.'

Charlie resumed peeling. How could Mary Rose say that? Her life had completely collapsed. Nose-dived into oblivion. As if fresh air could cure her yoyo emotions.

'I know you think I'm harsh,' said Mary Rose, as if reading her thoughts. 'But moping around and feeling sorry for yourself is not going to help. You'll soon forget.'

Charlie dug a black eye out of the potato with the end of the peeler. 'I don't think my bank balance is going to forget.'

Mary Rose took off her glasses. 'Are you into trouble?'

'Daniel practically bankrupted me and now I've lost my job, I don't know what I'm going to do.'

'Men! They're all the same,' said Mary Rose, scraping back her chair. 'Tell me how much and I'll give you a cheque.'

Charlie blushed and looked up from her peeling. 'Mary Rose, don't be ridiculous. I didn't tell you because I thought you'd bail me out.'

'Hush. What are godmothers for? Your parents are on the other side of the world. What else are you going to do?'

Charlie shook her head and swiped away a tear from the corner of her eye with her wrist.

'Exactly. We'll send some money to your bank and you can pay me back when you can. Or think of it as earning your keep. I'll make you work hard, mind.'

Charlie felt her bottom lip trembling. 'Enough of that,' scolded Mary Rose.

'Sorry.'

'You'll be fine. Just remember that life is like riding a bike. You don't fall off unless you stop pedalling.'

'Here,' Tanya passed Rich the bong, holding the muslin gauze over its base. Rich scrunched up his eyes as the acrid smoke smouldered towards his eyes. He put his lips over the base and inhaled.

He coughed out thick grey smoke. 'What do they put in these things?' he asked.

'All sorts. I think this stuff is opiated.'

'I'm not used to smoking,' he said, passing the bong on and thumping his stinging chest with his fist. 'I had some hash cake from Anjuna market earlier. I'm really sorry. When I met you, I was completely off on one.'

Tanya laughed. 'You were sweet.'

'I enjoyed it. I felt very relaxed – especially after my massage.'

'You looked it. But you have yet to discover the greatest drug of all,' said Tanya, leaning back and looking up at the universe of stars which seemed tantalisingly close.

Rich followed her gaze to the moon, which wobbled. He looked through one eye in an attempt to even it out. 'What, you mean like Es and whizz?'

Tanya laughed and stretched out her perfectly toned legs towards him, her full breasts pressed against the fabric of her vest as she looked up.

This woman was so desirable it almost took his breath away. He longed to know everything about her: where she was from, where she lived, what she was doing for the next sixty years. Yet the ritual of questions he usually asked when he met girls seemed totally out of place here. He had no choice but to chill out. And as he looked at her, he knew that whatever she had, her mystery quality, her peace, he wanted it.

She hugged her knees to her and took a sip of beer. 'What's in your mind?' she asked.

'That I don't know anything about you.'

'You know more than you think,' she said cryptically as if she could see into his mind and Rich blushed unexpectedly.

'At last. Here comes Jeff,' she said, looking over his shoulder at the approaching throng.

Jeff was possibly the coolest man Rich had ever met and he sat, feeling like an idiot, as Jeff flopped into a lotus position on the sand and began drumming on some bongos. There wasn't an ounce of fat on him and Rich choked with envy as he stretched up to kiss a girl revealing a concave chestnut stomach, ruffled with bleached-blond hair.

Jeff's bongos were the call to his disciples and within minutes a large group had gathered around them on the sand. Tanya explained that Jeff had lived in Goa for years and owned the strange tepee he had noticed in the palm trees. He could speak Portuguese and Hindi, knew all the mafia, made sure the drugs didn't get too dirty, looked after the place during the rainy season, ran yoga and t'ai chi courses, played his bongos, sired local children and administered tattoos in return for tapes of the latest dance music. Rich scanned the biceps, ankles and backs of the assembled crowd. They had all been recipients of Jeff's flourishing art form.

Jeff shouted to the DJ and a new tune thumped across the beach. He jumped to his feet and the crowd cheered as he flung his arms out towards the horizon, his bare feet trampling the sand. Rich watched, but the dancing was infectious and he stood up and started jigging, trying to copy Jeff's fluid movements. He made dancing seem like a martial art.

Tanya smiled at him and swayed her hips. 'Forget it! Just be yourself!' she shouted above the music.

Rich shrugged, accepting her advice. Here goes then, he said to himself and flung his arms out, whirling around like a spinning top.

Dizzy but euphoric, he came to a wobbling standstill. The horizon zig-zagged across his vision.

'Hey!' Jeff's guttural tones resonated in Rich's ears. He put his arm around Rich's shoulder and laughed. Rich felt immediately balanced. This must be what it felt like to be blessed by the Pope. He grinned at Jeff who, to his astonishment, kept his mahogany-solid arm draped around him and they danced together. Rich grabbed on to him, lifting up his legs and copying Jeff as others joined in.

The music grew louder and the crowd melted towards the soft kiss-chase ripples. Suddenly Jeff slipped out of his shorts and stood in the moonlight, magnificently naked, his sand-coloured curly hair falling in a pony tail down the rippling muscles of his back as he stretched out his arms to the moon. 'Come on,' he yelled, and before Rich knew it he too was yelping as he dived through the dark waves.

He held his hand out to Tanya, his desire fighting with the cool water, and she swam towards him through the phosphorescence.

'Let's float,' she said, lifting her legs to the surface. Rich watched her blonde hair spread out in the water, her beautiful breasts buoyant as she lay in the cradle of the sea as if it were her personal water bed.

Rich stretched back in the gentle waves and took her hand, his ears filling with salt water and his eyes relaxing into the galaxy of stars above while his mind drifted away into the planets. What was the point of getting stressed out about a legal case when he was a tiny speck on the world and the world just a tiny speck in the galaxies?

Suddenly they were both splashed by a wave. He reached out instinctively to Tanya and pulled her upright and for a moment he held her naked body against his as his toes danced against the sandy sea bed. He could feel her long legs around him, silky smooth in the water, and as her womanly belly slid across his groin he shivered with desire. But in a moment she had flipped round and was gone, sliding through the water to the others, and Rich felt as if he had just touched a mermaid.

Later, back on the moped, they shivered in the dawn light, their hair still damp. 'Did you enjoy the party?' she asked when they emerged on to the road.

'I loved it.' Rich breathed in the cool air and looked out across the paddy fields.

'Look at this place, it's beautiful,' she sighed. 'I love dawn.'

Rich stopped on an old bridge and as he cut the engine, peace fell. Tanya kept her arms around him and he put his hands over hers. Staring through the avenue of trees Rich could make out the silver ripple of the tide on the beach.

'Mary Rose,' he said quietly. He reached behind him and rested his hand reassuringly on Tanya's thigh. 'It was Mary Rose who said about the new moon being lucky.'

Back at Baga, Rich parked the bike near the apartments.

'Where shall we go?' he whispered, not wanting to leave her.

'The beach.'

He took her hand as they padded through the thick sand. She shivered in the morning mist. Rich walked over to one of the dug-out coconut trees that made the local fishing boats and began to pull off its faded tarpaulin.

'Stop.' Tanya flicked her head to tell him to come away.

'But it's freezing.'

'Shh. You have to warm yourself from inside.'

She beckoned him to a white patch of sand and folded her supple legs beneath her. Leaning forward, she patted the sand in front of her and he sat down.

'What a night,' began Rich, starting to make conversation in the silence, but Tanya put her finger on her lips. She stared at him, her eyes serious yet soft in the milky light, then took his hands and put her palms against his.

Rich giggled nervously and looked about him. As if reading his thoughts, Tanya pressed lightly against his hands. 'Don't doubt it. It works. See?' And she stared at him until he was swallowed into her gaze. He felt her heat emanating into him and, enthralled, he held her gaze until he was lost in connection with her. When the sun rose higher into the sky, the fishing boats headed back to shore, their outboard motors breaking the stillness as the day began.

Rich shook himself as if from a trance. Tanya's cheeks were flushed and he touched her hair, feeling the fineness of the golden strands as if they were priceless. She smiled at him, her eyes as clear as the sky, and he reached out to hug her, feeling as if they'd just made love. He knew that, despite himself, his frozen core was defrosting.

Charlie's stomach growled for the breakfast she'd missed as Mary Rose turned off the bypass and pulled into the huge car park by the auction house. Although it was only eight o'clock, the place was heaving and they had trouble finding a place amongst the Land Rovers, lorries and horseboxes. So much for quiet pastoral living, thought Charlie.

The ugly concrete auction house was the size of an out-of-town multiplex cinema and was filled with hard-faced farmers as Charlie and Mary Rose pushed through the dirty doors.

'Gird up your loins and stay close,' instructed Mary Rose, puffing out her chest. Setting her face in a determined look, she marched towards the auction ring. Charlie had never felt as conspicuous and, taking up her ringside position with Mary Rose, felt sure there was a slight lull in the colossal noise.

They must have been the only two women in the whole place, including the sheep who bleated loudly, waiting their turn in the wooden stalls. Charlie rubbed her eyes, feeling tired and weird. She felt as if she was in an automatic car-wash, helplessly trapped by the overbearing whirring brushes of life that were sweeping over her. How the hell had she landed up at a sheep auction?

On a high platform, the auctioneer adjusted his tweed cap and boomed through the microphone to call the next lot. Above him the black and red digital display was as illegible to Charlie as his voice was impossible to understand. The steel gate clanked open and the reluctant sheep were booted into the sawdust arena, accompanied by a rumble of conversation as the gnarled farmers inspected them.

Suddenly the bidding had started, the auctioneer yelling what sounded like gibberish at breakneck speed. The price was obviously going up, but as Charlie stood on tiptoe and watched the crowd, it was impossible to tell who was bidding. In a few minutes a loud bell sounded and the huge farmer herded the jittery sheep back to their stall.

'Mary Rose? Hello!'

Charlie spun round to identify the owner of the voice and saw a tall man shouldering through the crowd, nodding to farmers who stood aside in grudging respect.

'I'm sorry I'm late,' he said, taking off an oilskin trilby and ruffling his cropped ginger hair. 'Got held up at the surgery. Hello there,' he said, extending his freckled hand.

Hamish Hamilton had a Sean Connery accent, friendly pale blue eyes beneath long, curling ginger lashes and was wearing a checked shirt and soft Aran jumper. Charlie smiled shyly as she introduced herself.

'Angus Wilson has a good Border Leicester. I thought we'd go for that. What do you think?' asked Mary Rose.

Hamish looked in his programme. 'It's a bit of a gamble, but we'll see what we can do. He's coming on next. Are you going to bid?'

'Will you do it? You know how they ignore me.'

Charlie looked puzzled and Mary Rose explained that because the Hill Farm ewes were the most maternal, and therefore successful, the other farmers ignored her.

'And you're a lady and I'm sorry to say these boys live in the Dark Ages,' added Hamish.

'Why doesn't Charlie have a go?' said Mary Rose suddenly. 'Me?'

Hamish chuckled. 'It's worth a try. Come on.'

He pushed a path through the crowd and Charlie followed him, climbing up on the bottom rail of the steel barriers. The noise and the smell were unbearable and Hamish had to stand right behind her, guarding her from the jostling farmers.

'What shall I do?' asked Charlie, feeling completely perplexed.

Hamish put a protective arm around her and gripped the rail. 'Just follow my instructions. I'll tell you when to bid. Just nod your head.'

'Will they see me?'

Hamish put his foot on the railing next to hers. 'Believe me, they'll see you,' he laughed.

Charlie leaned over the railings, scratching her head so that her blonde curls frizzed out. She could see the farmers across the ring observing her sceptically, but she ignored them and watched as the large ram was shunted forwards. He had a bold Roman nose and a high carriage and looked disdainfully at the auctioneer as he strutted into the centre of the pen.

The bell sounded and the auctioneer was off. Hamish leaned in close to Charlie, talking into her ear and giving her the cue to bid. Charlie's gaze flitted between the auctioneer, the crowd and the ram as the bidding continued. Hamish's lips were practically tickling her earlobe now.

'Hang on in there. We've nearly got it. OK, now,' he said. Charlie flicked her hand, the auctioneer nodded to her and the bell sounded.

Mary Rose slapped Hamish on the chest with her programme as he announced the news that they'd outbid Finlay Macintosh, Mary Rose's cantankerous neighbour, and that she was now the proud owner of a new tup.

'You'll bankrupt me yet, Hamish Hamilton,' she said. 'Let's hope for your sake he's randy.'

Hamish looked at Charlie. 'Once he sees his new owners, I'm sure he'll be so horny he'll be only too happy to oblige your girls.'

Mary Rose tutted and laughed at the same time as Hamish waved goodye and his green Barbour was lost in the crowd.

The new tup, however, was far from happy when Charlie and Mary Rose picked him up from the pen and it took all their efforts to manhandle him to the bottom of the ramp at the back of the Land Rover.

'Do you want the front or the back end?' asked Mary Rose,

her cheeks red with exertion and fury, studiously ignoring the group of farmers who rested on the wooden pens lazily watching and smoking roll-ups.

Their new ram glared at Charlie and bared his rows of white teeth and she sidled to the back while Mary Rose fastened a rope around its neck. She felt too exhausted and cold to deal with this and she longed to close her eyes.

'Now push,' said Mary Rose, hopping into the Land Rover and pulling the rope, forcing the sheep up the ramp. Charlie surveyed its back and, gingerly placing her hands on his rump, pushed.

'Harder,' yelled Mary Rose. 'Give it some welly.'

The farmers whispered as Charlie heaved the sheep up the ramp and burst into gales of laughter when its back leg kicked out. Charlie felt as if she'd been karate chopped in the shin.

Trying not to show the agony, she helped Mary Rose push the wooden ramp into the back of the Land Rover and, glowering at the farmers, she limped to the passenger's door.

'Why are they so hostile?' asked Charlie.

'Take no notice. They're jealous,' said Mary Rose, starting the engine. The tup bucked and writhed in the back and she looked through the grille.

'Shut up back there and behave,' she commanded and for a moment the animal was silent. She crunched into gear and sped back on to the bypass.

Charlie put her boot on the lurching dashboard and rolled up her jeans leg to inspect her shin.

'That's a corker,' said Mary Rose.

Charlie looked dismally at the throbbing bruise. 'And I was sober.'

'What do you mean?'

'I used to wake up with bruises after a good night out. We used to call them UPIs.'

'What's a UPI?'

'An unidentified party injury.'

Mary Rose laughed, but Charlie stared forlornly at the road. 'At least, that's what Kate and I used to say.'

Mary Rose glanced at her and changed the subject, briskly informing her about the tupping season and all there was to be done on the farm. Charlie didn't have time to think about Kate as Mary Rose bombarded her with new information.

By the time they turned off the road, back on to the lane, the tup was battering the sides of the Land Rover, playing havoc with the suspension.

'What shall we call him?' she asked.

'Let's think.' Charlie tapped her lips and then hastily removed them, remembering where her hands had been.

'What do you call an expensive, arrogant, randy, stubborn, moody, shin-kicking ram?'

Charlie looked out of the window and then turned to her godmother. 'Daniel, of course,' she said and burst into tears.

Tanya strolled around the exercise mats under the bamboo canopy.

'Good. Now we're going to do Suryanamaskar B. Stand at the front of your mats and don't forget to concentrate on Mula Banda, Uddiyanna Banda and Uijayi breathing,' she said.

Sweat trickled down Rich's temples as he centred himself on the soles of his feet and looked out through the palm trees to the sea. It was half past six in the morning and the air was fresh and cool. There were six other people in this, his third Astanga yoga class.

Tanya was demonstrating and he watched in awe as she sprang her shapely legs back and formed a graceful chest press. 'And inhale,' she instructed, rolling over her toes and scooping her body forward in one fluid movement. 'And exhale into downward dog.' She pushed backwards on her hands and feet into a breathtaking inverted V shape.

Rich was determined to be good at yoga. Something about these early morning sessions made him feel spiritual and cleansed, as if he should be wandering around saying 'Om'. And maybe one day he'd have a physique like Jeff's, then he'd never fail to pull the girls! However, there was a long way to go. After only two repetitions of the posture Rich pressed the side of his face into the blue mat, panting as sweat ran across his forehead.

'I'm broken. No. In fact I'm dead,' he said as Tanya approached. He rolled over and looked up at her. There was no way she was going to be impressed with his physical prowess after this disastrous display. He was hopeless. She laughed and extended one of her perfect toes to jab him in the stomach.

'You'll get the hang of it.'

'This is worse than rugby training.'

'It's a lot better for you. You're not so bad. Remember, practice, practice, practice,' she said, taking his arm and hauling him up.

'You're a hard woman,' he said.

'And I'll make you a hard man.' She raised her eyebrows at him as she went back to instructing.

Was she? Was she flirting with him? Rich bent forward and looked behind him between his legs, but he didn't have time to dwell on the subject as Tanya continued with the seated postures. He'd get the hang of this yoga lark if it killed him.

By the time they got to shoulder stands, Rich was exhausted but feeling amazing. Tanya stood over him and pulled at his legs to make them straight.

'I haven't done this since I were a lad,' joked Rich with difficulty as his chin pressed into his chest.

'It shows.' She hoisted him up and Rich yelped as his back straightened. His poor body didn't know what was going on.

Tanya smiled at him as she let him go, and flipped his feet over his head. 'Now hug your ears with your knees.'

Rich curled himself in the backward ball, his legs round his head, his navel at closer proximity than ever before. Another couple of inches and he'd be able to give himself a blow job.

'Visualise yourself doing yoga,' Tanya was saying as she finally went into the finishing sequence.

'Who me? After today? You must be joking!' he said.

'Imagine yourself on the beach doing a sun salutation.'

'Never.'

'Just picture it. Go on!'

Rich closed his eyes. His mind was filled with the ever-present image of him ripping off Tanya's leotard and nuzzling into her breasts.

'I'm having a problem.' He squinted up at Tanya through one eye and she shook her head and went off to attend to the other beginners.

At last the finishing postures were complete and Rich lay back on the mat relaxing. His body tingled with the exertion of the first exercise he'd done in years. Still, it was a start. Then the image came to him. He saw himself, brown and toned, sitting in a lotus position on the beach, looking out to sea, next to a beautiful woman. And as he felt the breeze on his face and the sand in his hair, he knew that he was filled with deep contentment. He smiled and, in his vision, turned to Tanya next to him. But the face that turned to him wasn't hers, because the woman in his vision wasn't Tanya.

Mary Rose wiped her oven glove over the kitchen window as the boot green Range Rover loomed like an army tank into the yard. 'It's Valerie,' she said. 'Quick. Get the jug out of that cupboard.'

Charlie yanked open the slatted door. Inside the jug was hidden behind jars of home-made marmalade, their grease-proof paper tops secured with sticky elastic bands. 'It's hideous,' she said, lifting it down.

'I won it in her raffle,' said Mary Rose, dusting the jug down with the cuff of her jumper and placing it in the centre of the table. 'I won't hear the last of it if it's not on show.'

'Cooee.' Valerie's shrill voice was accompanied by a yapping Jack Russell who darted into the kitchen like an Exocet missile. Mary Rose pounced towards the back door and slammed it shut, almost catching the dog's nose.

'In here,' she shouted, patting her grey curls as the dog started sniffing the skirting board like a Hoover nozzle.

'Lancelot, come here!' Valerie entered the kitchen, a towering spike of a woman, and slapped the dog with a gigantic blue-veined hand. 'You bad boy, Lancy!'

'Leave him, he's fine,' said Mary Rose, advancing towards

Valerie who dumped her wicker basket on the table and proffered a powdered cheek.

'I was just passing and I thought I'd pop in and say hello,' she said, looking Charlie up and down. 'I'm Valerie Packenham,' she added, offering her hand.

'From the manor house?'

'You've been doing your homework!' she said appreciatively and Mary Rose winked at Charlie.

'This is Charlie, my goddaughter. She's up from London for a while,' said Mary Rose gravely as if Valerie didn't already know everything there was to know about Charlie. 'Will you stay for a sherry?' she urged, pulling back a chair for Valerie to sit down.

'Well all right then. Just the one.' She sat, still transfixed by Charlie. 'Marcus is in a terrible state about the point-to-point and I must go to the village.'

Mary Rose reached up for the chipped sherry glasses, while Valerie's plummy tones filled the kitchen as she recited the village gossip. She clinked glasses with Charlie and downed the sherry almost in one.

'How long are you in sunny Scotland for?' she asked. 'Because we're having a little New Year's Eve gathering. I'll be sending you an invite, but you will come, won't you? I want you both there.' She wagged a knobbly finger at Mary Rose. 'No excuses this year.'

Charlie leaned back against the counter. 'I don't know whether I'll still be here . . .' she began, looking frantically at Mary Rose.

Valerie swiped at the air in front of her. 'Silly me. Social engagements in London and a nice boyfriend, I expect!' she said, clucking at Mary Rose and waiting for her suspicions to be confirmed.

'Charlie will probably be in LA by then.'

'LA? America?' gasped Valerie.

'Oh yes,' said Mary Rose in dramatic hushed tones. 'Her fiancé is a big director over there. Huge.'

Valerie's hand flew to her pearls as she turned to Charlie, her eyes glittering with the gossip. 'My, oh my!'

Mary Rose burst into giggles as Valerie reversed out of the yard. 'That'll teach her to come snooping around here,' she said, handing a washing-up bowl full of scraps to Charlie. 'She was probably seeing if you were the marriageable type. She's got a son she can't wait to off-load on to some poor, unsuspecting girl.'

'What's wrong with him?'

'Ask Hamish,' said Mary Rose, pulling on her ancient blue Puffa. 'You will stay for Christmas though, won't you?' she added. 'I need the extra set of hands.'

Charlie sighed. 'I should be heading home, although I'm not quite sure where home is any more.'

'You always have a home as long as you're at home within yourself. Then you're never lonely,' said Mary Rose.

'Yes, but I'm not like you. I'm not self-sufficient. I've always had people looking after me and now they've all gone, I don't know how to cope.'

'Yes you do. You've got grit.'

Kate's Saturday afternoon wasn't going well. In the bridal department, the wedding dresses hung like collapsed hot-air balloons, muffling the piped Vivaldi. Behind the velvet curtain, red faced and bad tempered, she struggled with the zip of the designer dress and swore.

'Can I help you?' The pin-lipped manageress poked her head around the curtain.

'I can manage,' said Kate scowling, yanking once more at the stuck zip.

The manageress barged into the cubicle and with the authority of a headmistress turned Kate round by the shoulders and untangled the silk rose from the zip.

'When is the happy day?' she asked sourly, tucking Kate's bra strap into the scooped neckline of the dress and drawing back the curtain.

Kate stepped out into the carpeted area and scowled at herself in the mirror. 'I don't know yet,' she said, pulling up the billowing ivory skirt to reveal a pair of Minnie Mouse socks.

The manageress fiddled around her. 'It gapes a bit here,' she said, pinching a couple of inches of boned bodice. 'Obviously these dresses are individually made.' She unhooked the white tape measure from around her neck as if she was going to whip Kate with it. 'It looks lovely.'

'It looks terrible,' shot back Kate. 'I look like a giant meringue.'

The manageress drew such a haughty breath that her conical breasts lurched chin-wards under the uniform shirt. 'I think you'll like it more once it's fitted at the waist,' she snapped.

Kate jerked as the manageress pulled the dress and pinned the material, wishing she'd never bothered to try it on. She had spent a fortnight in New York and the puffiness of her face was testament to a string of late nights and never-ending booze.

She'd tried to escape the fact that she'd made up her mind to marry Dillon. Despite her aspirations to be a wild child, she knew that she loved him. Yet she couldn't bring herself to tell him. Every day she'd spoken to him and they hadn't mentioned his proposal and she wondered whether he knew that she was terrified of the decision she'd made. At night she dreamed of her wedding plans, the party, the dress, the cake and she'd even booked her flight back to London early so that she could get to the shops to try on a dress, just to see how it felt before she gave Dillon her answer. She'd expected it to be fun, but it was quite the reverse.

She watched in the mirror as a heavily pregnant girl in a blue anorak lovingly fingered the white netting of a frilly wedding dress. 'Look, isn't it gorgeous?' said the girl, pulling out the dress and holding it over her bulge.

Her boyfriend slouched on one of the stools. 'We can't afford it. We can't get married and have a baby.'

'Why not? Most people do.'

'I'm not made of money.'

'Pete. Please?'

'No.'

'But you promised we'd get married.'

'And we will,' he said wearily. 'Things are so up in the air at work at the moment. Since Charlie went, everyone is keeping their heads down. I don't even know what's going on with the agency. I might be out of a job soon.'

'Do you really think it's that bad?'

'That scratchcard promotion has rocked the boat, big time.'

'Was it her fault?' asked Sharon, putting the dress back and browsing through some more.

Kate padded back into the cubicle and stood miserably as the manageress unhooked the floppy roses on the back of the dress. She listened in to the conversation beyond the curtain.

'No, not really. I can't believe she'd muck up a promotion deliberately. It doesn't make sense. She was always so conscientious and she wanted to get on in Bistram Huff. You could tell. Come on, love, let's get going.'

Kate went cold.

'You miss her, don't you?' asked Sharon as they walked away.

'Yes. I wanted to call her, but I don't know what's happened to her, nobody has heard from her since she was fired.'

Kate held her breath. Surely not? Surely they couldn't be talking about her Charlie? But she could tell from the lurch in her gut that they were.

'Wait!' she screeched, shoving the manageress aside and, with the wedding dress half off, ran after Pete and Sharon. She hurdle-jumped over the thick red rope which cordoned off the wedding section, tripping over the acres of dress around her.

'Stop! Stop that girl,' shouted the manageress.

Kate looked around frantically, but Sharon and Pete had disappeared in the Saturday shopping crowds. Then she saw them getting into the lift, the doors closing. She ran through the crowd and banged on the closed door of the lift with her fists. She had to find out what had happened to Charlie. She tore down the wooden stairs, slapping her palms against the wall to steady herself.

Billowing like a ghost, Kate skidded to a halt as the lift arrived. Gasping for breath, she grabbed Pete as he escorted Sharon out of it.

'Wait,' she panted, pulling the puffy shoulders of the open dress roughly over her shoulders, her underwear exposed to all the shoppers in the scarves and belts department. 'Charlie. Were you talking about Charlie at Bistram Huff?'

'Yes, why?' asked Pete, surprised. Sharon tugged at his arm.

'She's my best friend,' panted Kate frantically. Pete stared as the security guard and the manageress lunged at her, each grabbing an arm. Kate shook them off.

'She was doing a runner,' said the disgusted manageress.

'I think you ought to come with us,' said the security guard, pressing buttons on his hissing walkie-talkie, 'Roger. Roger. Assailant detained,' he shouted as if he were a member of a special vice squad.

Sharon tugged at Pete's arm, embarrased by the scene. 'Come on,' she urged.

'Wait,' shouted Kate as the security guard hauled her into the lift, the manageress apoplectic about the state of the wedding dress.

'I'm Kate Freelan. Please, could you wait for me by the main door . . .' shouted Kate, but the doors of the lift were closing and, flanked by her jobs-worth guards, her words were lost.

'Do you have to be so noisy!' The shirty manageress scowled at Kate. 'Talk about drawing attention to yourself. Really!'

'Oh, piss off!' said Kate, irritated. She marched out of the lift and back to the bridal department where she stepped out of the dress and, scrunching it into a great ivory ball, threw it at the manageress.

'Oh Charlie, my Charlie, what have you done now?' she muttered as she ran to find Pete.

Charlie was caked in mud, her hair matted and her numb fingers stiff as she propped her glove in her armpit and pulled out the furry Lipsyl from the deep pocket of her coat. She ran it around her lips and tried to smear them together, but they were also stiff with cold. She looked down the field to the sea of slow-moving ewes which she was shepherding down to the lower field to be covered by Daniel.

Charlie shook her head to remove the hair which had stuck to her lips in the howling gale. The bare trees were stark against a grey sky and the fields rolled at a steep angle to the farmhouse. To the west, the view down the valley was clear for the first time in days and Charlie could see the winding road to the village and the roaring river. Across the valley, she glimpsed the chimneys and folly of the Packenham estate, above dense fir trees. The only sign of human life was the smoke which billowed from the chimney of the village pub and Charlie shivered, longing to be by a crackling fire.

She still felt numb inside. Every morning she woke up hugging the cold hot water bottle in the creaking single bed, the silence and her loneliness crashing around her. Her limbs ached and she felt too miserable to move as she lay in the dark, staring into the void of her life, until Mary Rose bustled in and switched on the light, reminding her that she was still alive.

This morning she'd been up since dawn, constructing the mating pen with Mary Rose, splitting the skin on her palm as she wielded the mallet and drove heavy stakes into the hard ground. And just when she'd thought it was breakfast time, Mary Rose had given her a pitchfork and she'd had to hump bales of hay to line the pen. Still, she might as well be working since there was nothing else to do. Mary Rose's black and white television set had appalling reception, the radio only picked up the shipping forecast and the raciest reading material the village shop could offer was a battered selection of Mills and Boon romances, and even those made her cry.

Spoof and Jakey-Boy were brilliant sheepdogs, but it still took ages to get all of the ewes safely into the pen and Charlie was shaking by the time she found Mary Rose in the barn.

'If I hold him, can you do the honours?' she asked from the corner stall, wrestling with Daniel, who was almost as big as her.

'What do I do?' Charlie fought back her exhaustion. Mary Rose had so much stamina, it put her to shame.

'Put on those gloves and fetch that bucket of dye.'

Charlie did as she was told, Daniel's bleats becoming louder as Mary Rose got him on to his back. Charlie entered the stall gingerly, wrinkling her nose at the horrible smell and the disgusting sight of Daniel's undercarriage.

Mary Rose was holding the ram down with all her might. 'I want you to paint in between his front legs.'

'Why?'

'So that we'll know which ewes he's covered because they'll all have blue bums.'

'Very sophisticated,' said Charlie. She picked up the brush in the bucket of dye and squeamishly dabbed it on to Daniel's chest.

'Hurry up,' panted Mary Rose. 'You'll have to be more vigorous than that. There's got to be enough dye to mark every one of the girls out there.'

Charlie coated the disgruntled ram and then jumped aside, flattening herself against the wall as Daniel wriggled and righted himself, bleating angrily.

'Right!' said Mary Rose, wiping her hands on her trousers. 'This is his big moment.'

Charlie still held the paintbrush in her hand. 'Let the mating begin.'

They stood watching Daniel terrorising the ewes who scuttled to the sides of the pen as he chased them.

'Poor things,' said Charlie, wincing as Daniel mounted a complaining ewe.

Mary Rose laughed. 'Come on, let's leave him to it and get some breakfast.'

Charlie trotted beside her. 'I don't think I can eat after seeing Daniel's apparatus.'

'You're such an innocent! Don't be squeamish. It's the law of nature.'

'I guess that's a bloke thing.'

Mary Rose laughed. 'Exactly.'

Charlie watched Mary Rose striding along in her corduroy

trousers. 'Why aren't you with someone? Why didn't you get married?' she asked suddenly.

Mary Rose looked across the valley to the bruise-coloured cloud shrouding a hilltop.

'I made a mistake,' she said simply, and swallowed. 'When love comes along for you, you must open your heart. Don't turn away and look for an ideal that exists only in your head.'

Charlie longed to find out more, but she knew the subject was closed. 'I don't think I'll ever fall in love again. It hurts too much.'

'Rubbish. You'll find someone as long as you don't look too hard. The most priceless gems are always dirty on the outside.'

'Think!' Kate paced around the white tiled floor of the 51's kitchen. 'You said you saw some scratchcards in the skip. When you won the CD?'

Dillon levered the lid off a huge tub of olives. 'Yes, I remember. They were in Covent Garden.' He popped an olive in his mouth.

Kate leaned on the polished stainless steel. 'You're not listening. I think Charlie's in trouble. Pete said she was really traumatised when she left and she's not at the flat.'

'What about that schmuck Daniel?'

'I don't know where he lives.'

'He's lucky. I wouldn't like to be in his shoes.'

'What an arsehole. Oh poor, poor Charlie.'

'You're really worried about her, aren't you?'

Kate shrugged. 'I can't get married without her.'

Dillon stopped and turned to face her. 'Does that mean you'll marry me?'

She smiled slyly at him.

Dillon bent down and peered at her, searching her face. 'Say it.'

'Dillon, I'd love to marry you. If you'll have me.'

He let out a whoop, picking her up and swirling her around in the kitchen. 'I love you, I love you,' he shouted, before holding her face in his giant hands and kissing her with such tenderness that Kate's knees quivered.

'We'd better find Charlie,' he said.

Kate nodded. 'We will,' she gasped, reaching up to Dillon's mouth for another kiss.

He moaned and lifted her up, sliding her back on the counter.

'What are you doing?' Kate slid her fingers into his hair as his hat fell to the floor.

'Starting as I mean to go on,' he grinned, pushing up her skirt. 'I'm never, ever going to take you for granted again.'

Rich turned his face up into the sprinkle of the shower, letting his mouth fill up and overflow with water. His mind was filled with images of Tanya, bending over, stretching back, flipping her hair, swimming naked in the moonlight, and he thought his balls were going to explode with desire.

He pulled on his shorts and shirt, slapped a wedge of rupee notes in his pocket and locked his room. As he made his way through the rubble in the courtyard, he caught his reflection in the glass of the tuk-tuk. His skin was tanned, his hair sunkissed and shaggy and he was glowing with health. He walked down the street in the starlit balmy warmth of the evening.

The street market was still open and the little girls ran around him, holding out their palms and pulling him towards their stalls, ensnaring him with their giggles and doe-eyes of disappointment. He held up his hands in surrender, committing to a dozen promises as he broke through the throng to the bar where he would devour a delicious spicy korma in the company of Tanya.

Typically, he'd become her friend. He'd spent the past week bathing in her earthy sexuality as they strolled in the moonlight or relaxed on the beach. He had stayed with her, watching her, waiting for her, wanting to be like her. She was so relaxed, so confident of herself, so unconcerned about what other people thought, that he couldn't help changing in her midst. Apart from his nagging ache to make love to her, he felt more at peace with himself than he ever had.

He strolled along the dusty road and tentatively, as if testing a mending limb, allowed himself to think about Charlie. He thought about the self-pitying note he had left. Was it true that he was in love with her, or was it just that he couldn't have her? He put his hands in his pockets and thought about it. Then he thought about going home and a shudder ran through him.

If he admitted it, he missed Charlie. He thought about Daniel ensnaring her, trapping her with his mock-sophistication and arrogance. He'd been so quick to judge. So hasty and childish in his jealousy. He knew Charlie better than Daniel ever would and hadn't he promised that he'd always be there for her? His mind started to rush ahead. What if she needed him and he wasn't there? But then, what about all the times that he'd needed her and she hadn't been there for him? Panic and confusion engulfed him.

He'd reached the restaurant. Tanya sat beneath a hanging lamp watching the flying insects buzzing around its glow. She looked like a butterfly herself, with a diaphanous shirt draped over her tanned shoulders, and Rich stood by the wall, observing her and calming down. As ever in tune with her sixth sense she looked up and smiled, the lines around her eyes bunching together.

'You look distracted,' she said. 'What's on your mind?'

'Need.'

'What kind of need?'

'Every kind. My need for curry in my tummy,' he joked, picking up the sheet of roughly typed menu.

'You and your defences,' said Tanya, reaching out to touch Rich's cleanly shaven jaw.

He looked at her. Once again, she had floored him. It was impossible to be brash in her company. 'I was thinking about going home.'

'Oh?'

'I'm supposed to be leaving in a couple of days.'

'Do you want to go home yet?'

'No.' He placed the menu on the rough table. 'But that doesn't matter. The ticket is booked and I have to go.'

'If you're going home to slip back into everything you did before you left, make the same mistakes and feel just as miserable, then don't go. Go home when you feel a shift.'

'What do you mean?'

'There are times in life when something shifts inside. Your perspective changes and you're set free from everything that ties you down.'

'Well maybe, but I don't have the luxury of waiting for that to happen.'

'Why?'

'Because I have to go. I've got to go back to work.'

'Says who? Who's in charge of your life?'

Rich shuffled in his seat, feeling pressurised.

'Do you want to be doing that job?'

'No,' he said, surprised by the force of his feelings.

'Rich, this isn't a dress rehearsal. This is your life. Live it, before it's too late.'

He exhaled and rubbed his head. 'You don't understand. It's not that easy.'

'Why? What's so difficult?'

Rich looked away. As if reading his thoughts, she leaned closer to him. 'I'll tell you what's so difficult.'

'What?'

'Fear!'

Rich's face was burning. 'Rubbish,' he snorted.

She thumped her fist on the table, making the insects flit around the light. 'What's your problem? Why can't you tell the truth about how you're feeling?'

He stared at her, alarmed at her outburst.

'Say the truth.'

'I can't . . . I . . .'

'Why?'

'You'll think I'm stupid.'

She laughed with exasperation. 'Will I? Did you ever think badly of anyone for telling the truth?'

The waiter came over to the table, but Tanya waved him

away. She took Rich's hand across the rough wooden slats.

Rich thought about Pix and realised Tanya was right. He was scared of the truth, but as he looked at her he realised he couldn't run away any longer. He took a deep breath. 'I'm terrified of going home and terrified of drudging to work every day and hating it, but I'm more terrified that if I stay and give up everything that I've worked for, then I'll have failed . . .' He trailed off. 'It's ridiculous isn't it?'

'No,' she said quietly.

'On the one hand I feel as if I've wasted my life. I've chosen the easy path and now I've reached somewhere I never wanted to be in the first place. I look at all the people above me at work and I don't want to be like them in ten years' time, but then, I can't just drop out. I don't know how to do anything else and I've got used to my lifestyle.'

'What lifestyle? You sound miserable.'

Images of the office, of the flat and Charlie flashed through his mind. He shook his head. 'I've got responsibilities.'

'What about your responsibility to yourself?'

Rich exhaled wearily and gazed up at the night sky. 'It's all very well to think all this when I'm here and London seems a million miles away, but it's different when you're there.'

'You're choosing to be trapped.'

Rich withdrew his hand from hers. 'You don't understand.'

She smiled. 'Of course I do. You're scaring yourself with all the "what ifs". What if I don't have the job, the money, what if, what if, what if! It's like you're teetering on the edge of a diving board, too frightened to jump or to look down.'

'There may not be any water at the bottom.'

'There's always water at the bottom. It's much more scary dithering about whether to jump or not. Just do it. Have some faith in yourself.'

'I wish I shared your optimism.'

Tanya flung her hands up. 'Why don't you start making some choices for yourself? Start saying what *you* want.'

'I do . . .' he started, but she interrupted him, her eyes flashing.

'You don't.' Her eyes challenged him.

A tense silence fell. He couldn't deny her accusation. He was too scared to tell her how he felt. She shook her head in disappointment and swivelled on her seat. 'I guess it's your life,' she said flatly.

Rich grabbed her arm. What did he have to lose?

'Wait. You can't go. Not until I've told you how I feel.'

She looked at him impatiently. 'I thought that was your problem, that you don't know what you feel.'

'I do, I–' Rich dropped her arm and took a deep breath. 'The truth is that I think you're amazing and wonderful and from the first moment I laid eyes on you, I've wanted you so much it hurts.' But Tanya stopped his words as she leaned across the table and kissed him gently on the lips.

'See, that wasn't so bad,' she said softly and, taking his hand, led him out of the restaurant.

Charlie rubbed her hands together and stamped her feet, wrapping her arms around her in the cold as she jumped down from the tractor and straight into a frozen puddle. It had grown much colder overnight but, as Mary Rose pointed out, the weather was no excuse for laziness and she'd dispatched Charlie to feed the ewes in the top field.

She hauled the bag of feed from the back, her breath billowing out in a cloud in front of her, and her knees buckled as she dragged the sack across the frost-encrusted grass to the trough. She stood up, pressing her hands into her lower back, and watched the sheep, huddled together against the white-tipped trees of the coppice. The lights of Hill Farm were only just visible through the swirling early morning mist and Charlie shivered. She might as well be on a different planet. Up here with the biting air and the harsh realities of farming, her life in London seemed like a distant dream. Who am I, she thought, trying to remember what her concerns had been before her exile. Well, there was one thing to be happy about. At least she wasn't a sheep!

Sniffing the droplets on the end of her nose, she split open the sack and, with difficulty, tipped it into the trough. The sack buckled and half the feed fell on the muddy ground, but she was already trapped by the deluge of sheep, pressing against her legs.

She held the sack above her head as the last of the feed scattered everywhere.

'Excuse me,' she said, gingerly stepping through the sheep, the cold fleeces squashing her legs so hard that in the end she had to shove the ewes aside. She swore and stumbled her way out of the crowd, looking back to see them barging each other with their blue bottoms. She pulled at her anorak and made for the tractor.

Charlie had all the confidence of a nervous beginner skier as the tractor rumbled and jolted beneath her. How did Mary Rose manage this all on her own?

She was at the bottom of the field when she saw the old caravan and, leaving the gate, she went over to it.

Inside it was musty and smelled of damp and she could see her breath in the cold air. Mould crept up the walls and a rusty bucket had overflowed from the drips in the ceiling and soaked the carpet. She ran her hand over the familiar sunflower unholstery and, bending down, sat on the bottom bunk. As she did, the jack collapsed and the caravan lurched, throwing her back in the bunk, her arm crashing into the wall. She yelped as her head hit a wooden plank. For a moment she was dazed, too scared to move as she looked up at the bottom of the top bunk, her heart pounding.

She stretched her legs and rubbed her head and was pulling herself up when she saw the corner of a notebook poking out between the top bunk and the wall. It must have become dislodged in the jolt. She reached for it, easing the wire spiral binding free from the upholstery. The cover was torn and damp, with a pastel illustration of a cartoon dog. It was one of her old holiday diaries. She edged to the corner of the bunk and opened the relic from her past.

The lined pages were covered with childish writing and her eyes filled with tears, bittersweet nostalgia flooding over her, as she flipped through the book, smiling at her sketches of beach scenes and Mary Rose and the dogs.

In the centre pages she stopped to read the faded pencil thoughts. 'Today we went to a castle. When I am grown up, I will be a princess and Rich will be the king. In the day I will eat ice cream and paint pictures and look after all my people and play with my puppy.' She couldn't read further – her eyes were bulging with tears and she hugged the book to her chest, rocking back and forth on the bunk. Where had she gone so wrong? How had she lost her dreams?

She put the book in her pocket and crawled off the bunk. What had she expected? That she would come to Mary Rose's and step back into her childhood and all the hurt and disappointment would vanish? Angrily she clawed her way out of the caravan and looked towards the tractor.

The sheep, energised by their breakfast, had flocked down the hill to the open gate. 'No!' yelled Charlie, running towards the gate, slipping on the icy puddles. She reached the gate and barged her way through the jostling sheep to pull it shut. One was caught in the lower field and as Charlie tried to run after it, it scarpered in the opposite direction.

'Come here!' she shouted, pounding after the bulky ewe, but she only succeeded in frightening it. She slipped and fell forwards, the mud splattering her face and coating her hair. Swearing with frustration, she hauled herself up and it was then that she saw Hamish walking up the field, looking warm and cheerful.

He laughed when he saw Charlie's hot cheeks and angry expression. 'Want a hand?' he asked.

Charlie sucked in her breath and put her hands on her hips. 'I'm not being a very good sheepdog.'

Hamish squeezed her shoulder gently. 'There's a knack.'

With maddening calmness he guided the sheep back to the right side of the gate, shooed the ewes back up the field and drove the tractor through the gate for Charlie.

He jumped down from the cab. 'You have to watch them, they're tenacious buggers when they want to be.'

Charlie squeezed the mud from her hair and Hamish pulled a face.

'Not so much Wash and Go as Go and Wash,' he said and

Charlie laughed. It was the first time she'd found anything amusing for weeks.

'You're right. Thank you so much, Hamish,' she said, accepting his hand and getting back into the tractor.

Hamish smiled and raised his hat slightly like a city gent. 'My pleasure. It takes a while getting used to all this.'

'I'll never get used to it.'

'Well, to give you some light relief, why don't you come for a drink with me tomorrow night?'

Charlie looked down at his kind face. 'You know, Hamish, I'd really love that,' she said and set off, feeling calmer now that the weak winter sun had burnt off the mist and she could get her bearings.

Rich stared at the sky through the rattan roof of Tanya's hut. As much as he felt like a feather floating gently down to earth, he also wanted to jump up and beat his chest like a gorilla.

He looked over at the supple globes of Tanya's brown bottom and felt more contented than he ever had in his life. She knelt beside him, her blonde hair ruffled and curly with sweat, and ran a finger down his nose to touch his lips. He kissed her fingertip.

'You sleep,' she whispered.

'Where are you going?'

'I want to do a session on the beach.'

'After that, you're going to do yoga?' Rich was incredulous.

'Of course.'

He sank into the cushion. 'You can count me out. I'm knackered.'

She smiled enigmatically and he rolled on to his side and watched her as she pulled on her leotard and combed her hair. She dipped a length of muslin into an earthenware bowl of water and twisted it.

Rich propped himself up on his elbow. 'Do you want me to come with you?'

'No. I need time to re-connect and I want to be alone.'

'Fair enough.'

She dabbed the damp cloth over her chest. Rich watched the dribble of water trickle between her breasts and found himself becoming aroused again. 'You're like Eve,' he observed, reaching out to touch her. 'You are the earth, wind and fire, but most of all you are the flesh . . .'

She looked at him. 'Is that a song?'

'No, it's the beginning of a dreadfully naff poem that I'm writing for you,' said Rich. He reached out and circled her waist, pulling her back towards him.

Eventually she left, after the sun had risen and Rich's insatiable loins had sunk into submission. He lay back on the embroidered cushions and sighed like a sultan who has just sent off his harem. The aura of sex hung around him and he stroked his fluffy navel wondering why it had taken him so long to discover the joys of sex.

He laughed, looking round him at what Tanya had explained was her magic circle. At first he'd been dismayed when she led him into the beach house. He'd been so eager as he tried to kiss her, but Tanya had pushed him away. She'd made him sit cross-legged on the low mattress while she opened a carved wooden box. From it she'd taken seven brightly coloured scarves and twisted them in a circle round the bed.

'These represent each chakra,' she said as she laid them down.

'What?' asked Rich, perplexed.

She'd smiled at him. 'You'll see.'

Then she took four heavy stones and weighted down the scarves.

Rich scratched his head. 'What are those for?'

'These stones represent north, south, east and west, so that we are the centre of the universe and can resonate with the astral network.'

'The *what*?'

Tanya ignored him. On the east side of the bed she covered a low box with an elaborate Indian cotton scarf and on it placed a small bell, some feathers and a cheap Buddha statue, the type Rich had seen in Anjuna market. Next she'd taken the horn that Rich had found on the beach and held it above her head before placing it on the table. She reached up and took two candles down from the window sill.

'These represent our spirits,' she said, lighting them.

She arranged the objects, inspecting her work.

'Is that it?' asked Rich, his voice tinged with amusement.

'I need a crystal,' she said, looking round the simple room.

'Here.' Rich took the small moonstone out of his pocket and gave it to her. She turned it over in her palm.

'Perfect,' she said, placing it at the feet of the Buddha. Then she took the final item out of the box – a grotesque statue of what looked like a character from the *Kama Sutra*, holding his enormous penis.

Rich put his hand over his mouth to suppress his giggles.

Tanya was solemn as she bowed to the altar. 'Let's energise the magic circle,' she said, her voice husky.

Rich stroked his cheeks, trying to rub out his smile. 'Listen, Tanya,' he said, getting to his feet. 'This is all very nice, but I'm not really into all this kind of stuff and . . .'

'Follow me,' said Tanya, picking up the drum by the door. She walked around the outside of the scarves beating the drum.

'Tanya!' protested Rich, tripping after her.

'Let all negative energies depart,' she declared loudly. 'Let anger, sorrow, self-doubt fly away.' She stopped at the altar, picked up the small bell and handed it to Rich.

'Other way,' she coaxed, pushing him gently. 'Ring the bell.' Reluctantly he started walking round the bed, feeling like a stroppy teenager who was joining in a barn dance.

'Let wonder, compassion, patience and pleasure live within this circle,' chanted Tanya.

Rich rang the bell, feeling foolish and expecting a thunder-bolt to strike him down at any second.

When they had circled the bed three times, Tanya drew him towards the centre and Rich tripped over the crumpled sheet and dropped the bell. Tanya didn't seem to mind. She put the drum down by the altar and picked up the bell. Holding

Rich's hand, she guided him round to face the door. The bell tinkled in her grasp.

'We call upon the wind and air to bless us with clarity and vision. Teach us lightness of being.'

Rich shook his head and grimaced. She squeezed his hand and turned round to face the other end of the room, then closed her eyes and took a deep breath. Rich watched her breasts heave and didn't know whether to run away or drag her down on the mattress.

'Gentle south, we call upon the water and ocean to open our heart to playfulness and joy and to give us courage to let our feelings flow freely.'

She rang the bell and looked at Rich, her skin clear and her eyes shining. 'West,' she said.

'Right,' said Rich, turning to the altar and closing his eyes, but Tanya was in the other direction. He scrambled round as she rang the bell again. 'Mother Earth, give us strength and health and fill our beings with sexual vitality.'

'I'll second that,' he said, immediately regretting his flippant comment as Tanya spun round and faced the altar. 'We call on the guardians of the east to bring us the flames of life and lust so that our spirits will burn bright. Teach us to be passionate.'

She replaced the small bell on the altar. 'Stop being so sceptical. What harm can come to you?'

Rich wasn't sure; his only concern was that Tanya was close to him and, as if her spell had been cast, he felt himself become overwhelmed with sensuality. He reached out for her, taking her in his arms and hugging her tightly. She seemed to melt into him and he sighed as they sank on to the mattress. He stroked her face, tracing his finger over the line of her fine eyebrows and felt her hair between his fingers.

'I don't care what spells you cast, you're beautiful,' he whispered.

She pressed her lips against his and Rich felt electric shocks of desire tingle through him as his tongue found hers.

Tanya slowly undressed him and he moaned at the caress

of her soft fingertips, burying his nose in her neck and smelling the sweet fragrance of her skin. He felt his erection straining towards her, but Tanya pushed him away gently.

'Show me. Show me how to please you,' whispered Rich and she smiled at him.

'I will,' she whispered, letting her shirt fall from her shoulders. Rich gasped as the fullness of her breasts jutted towards him. He wanted to feel her erect nipples in his mouth, but Tanya had other plans.

She'd taught him more about sex in one night that he'd known in his entire life. Caught in her spell, he'd lost all his shyness as he'd exposed himself to her. She'd stroked and licked him, tickled him, teased him and introduced him to erogenous zones he never knew existed. And in turn, she'd spread herself before him and given him an erotic, sensual geography lesson of the female anatomy.

Fascinated, Rich had explored her as she guided him to the heart of her pleasure. She had made him lie back on the cushions and time and time again she brought him tantalisingly close to orgasm, but stopped him coming.

'Breathe deeply,' she instructed as his body relaxed. At first Rich had been frustrated and eager, but each time Tanya resumed her caresses, his pleasure became more intense. 'Let your sexual energy rise through your chakras,' she explained.

Rich looked confused and she nestled into his embrace.

'If you climax now, it will be with the energy still locked in here,' she said, cupping his balls. 'You have to let it flow through you to here.' She traced a line up his body and pressed her hand on his chest. 'Eventually the energy travels to your seventh chakra in the crown of your head and when you come, you can release your vision to the universe.'

'Blimey,' said Rich.

Tanya smiled and kissed him. 'If you want to, you can transform your life through sex. You can use your power to change the universe.'

'I'm pretty transformed already,' said Rich, sinking down and sucking her large nipples.

Finally he'd entered her. Breathing and moving together

in the stillness of the night, Rich had forgotten who and what he was, his whole body filling with desire and his heart swelling with joy. At last, as Tanya held him, her lithe body arched and tensed against his, she'd whispered his name and Rich felt white light filling his head as sensations ricocheted over his body, his nerve endings bathing in wave upon wave of throbbing ecstasy. He held Tanya close to him, their heartbeats thumping in unison in the aftermath of their orgasms.

Rich sat up and stretched, feeling his stomach contract at the memory. He felt light and excited. After all, as Tanya had said, last night was just the beginning. He looked over at the Indian statue on the makeshift altar. 'I know how you feel, mate,' he said.

Kate put the phone down to Sadie and wound up her hair, skewering it with her chewed pencil. At last she was getting somewhere.

'How did you get on?' she asked as Dillon came through the door. He held down the heel of one of his boots with the toe of the other and levered his foot out of the expensive leather.

'Our mystery is solved, my darling.' He hopped on one foot as he wriggled out of the other boot. 'I found the card the printer had given me and went to pay him a visit. He runs a very dodgy printing shop down in south London. Anyway, I got chatting with him and it turns out he'd been bribed not to say anything, but some short guy turned up and made him change round the cards on the press, after Charlie approved them.'

'Oh my God! Did he know who it was?'

'No, but he'd been there with Charlie that day, so it must be one of her colleagues.'

'Yes, but how are we going to prove it? Did he bribe the printer with money?'

'He gave the printer this lighter. Here.' Dillon delved into the pocket of his sheepskin coat and pulled out the silver promotional lighter which he threw to Kate. She caught it and turned it over in her hand. 'He's very proud of it. I feel quite guilty because he dropped it and I picked it up and I was about to give it back when I realised it must be evidence.'

Kate smiled. 'You Sherlock Holmes, you.'

'I could get into being a private investigator,' agreed Dillon, kissing her nose.

'What do you think?'

Dillon shrugged. 'All I know is there was some big conspiracy afoot to get rid of the cards sharpish. I smell a rat.'

Kate padded around the kitchen in her checked pyjamas, holding on to the lighter. 'So Charlie was set up! I wish I knew where she is. She must be feeling terrible.'

'You've tried her parents?'

'Hazel and Donald are in Australia and I can't find Rich.'

'Don't worry, she'll turn up and when she does we'll be able to tell her the happy news, won't we!' He circled his hands underneath the top of her pyjamas.

'You've got cold hands,' she squealed, laughing and trying to pull away from his grasp.

'So? I've come to the right place to warm them up, haven't I,' growled Dillon, cupping Kate's breasts in his cold hands and she smiled as she wiggled back against him.

The rain was hammering down on the roof of the car as Mary Rose stopped outside the village pub.

'Go on, he'll be waiting,' she said.

'I don't want to go.' Charlie checked her reflection in the mirror on the passenger seat sun visor, but it was showing more silver than reflection. 'I look awful and I've got nothing to say.'

Mary Rose tutted. 'Go on, you'll enjoy yourself.'

'I won't. I've forgotten how to.'

Her godmother leaned over and opened the car door. 'Then it's time to start remembering.'

Charlie pulled a face at her, then sprinted for the old oak door.

The Haystack, the local pub, had a roaring log fire and a low beamed ceiling from which tarnished silver tankards hung above the bar. There wasn't a juke-box or games machine in sight, just the relaxing rumble of conversation and the crackling of the fire. At the bar Libby, the ancient landlady, talked to the few men slouched on stools. An enormous Labrador snoring at her feet.

The conversation stopped when Charlie blustered through the door and Libby's drawn-in eyebrows shot towards her purple rinse as Hamish waved from the corner table. He was half-way through a pint of beer, with two tumblers of whisky lined up, and he rolled his eyes as Charlie approached. He was having his ear bent by one of the locals.

'You know Charlie, don't you, Jack?' asked Hamish.

'I don't think I do,' said Jack sourly, his few remaining teeth yellow with age and nicotine. He tapped the peak of his worn tweed hat as Charlie smiled.

'Shan't be keeping you,' he said in a gravelly voice before shuffling off to the bar with his silent companion, who viewed Charlie suspiciously as she sat down opposite Hamish.

'That's Jack,' he said, sipping his pint. 'Our local poacher and ferret keeper. He insists on buying me a couple of shots each time I see him.'

'What is it?' asked Charlie, picking up one of the glasses and sniffing the dark liquid.

'The local poison. It's lethal, but it tastes quite nice. Have one of those if you dare.'

'Thanks.'

'You know what they call it in Glasgow?'

Charlie shook her head. 'Electric soup,' said Hamish as she took a slug and her eyes watered with the fumes. She slapped her chest, gasping for air as the whisky burnt a layer off her throat.

Hamish laughed. 'Och, you town folk,' he teased.

Once Charlie had got used to it, though, the local whisky was quite drinkable and after two more glasses her cheeks were rosy in the warm glow of the fire. Hamish kept her amused with stories of his various patients and, more importantly, their owners in yarns that would have put James Herriot to shame.

'You make it sound like great fun,' said Charlie.

'It is, if you like the countryside and a simple way of life.'

She sipped her whisky and caught Hamish's eye. Self-consciously, she tugged at the hem of her short skirt, wishing that Mary Rose hadn't persuaded her to change out of her jeans.

'So when's the big marriage to this Hollywood mogul of yours, then?' asked Hamish.

'Is nothing sacred around here?'

'Nothing. You can't keep a secret in these parts. The trees have ears, you know.'

'It's Mary Rose's little joke. She thought it was a ploy to keep me away from Valerie's New Year's Eve bash.'

'Very wise indeed, but you won't get out of it. From what I hear, Valerie won't hear a word against you and she's desperate for you to meet Gerald.'

Charlie raised her eyebrows. 'I came here to get away from being gossiped about. Has everyone been talking about me?'

'Of course! You're the most exciting thing to happen round here since Gerald came out.'

'Gerald, Valerie's son? He's gay?'

Hamish laughed. 'Absolutely. He's the local shirt-lifter, but Valerie won't hear a word of it. It's very behind the times here.'

Charlie looked at Hamish. 'I can imagine Valerie being horrified.'

'Aye. She'll have to get used to it. There's quite a few who bat for the other side when no-one's looking,' Hamish winked. 'There's quite a few who bat for both sides, come to think of it.'

Charlie drained her glass. 'Don't I know it!'

'Och, that sounds ominous.'

'It is. Well, it was.' She paused and looked at Hamish's huge, kind ginger face and, fortified by the alcohol, she told him the story of her humiliation. It was the first time she'd recounted the facts without crying.

To her surprise, Hamish chuckled heartily and dabbed the tears out of the corners of his eyes with huge knuckles.

'It's not funny,' she said, smiling despite herself.

'It's hilarious. What did your friends say?'

Charlie's face was solemn. 'I don't know. I drove them all away because I was so blind about Daniel. My best friend Kate will probably never forgive me after what happened. And Rich . . .' Charlie trailed off, astonished by the clump of hurt which choked her.

'Nonsense, don't worry about Kate,' said Hamish, patting her hand. 'If there's one thing I've learned about girls, they love a friend in a crisis.'

Charlie wondered what else Hamish knew about girls.

'You should call her, tell her what's happened. Go on, do it right now.'

Charlie sighed. 'I can't.'

'It's making you sad, I can see that. Life's too short to be miserable about disagreements. Here, give her a call, it'll make you feel loads better.' He thrust some change into her hand and pointed her towards the pub's ancient telephone booth.

Charlie looked at Hamish through the glass as she picked up the old-fashioned receiver. He nodded eagerly and waved her on. The money clonked into the worn apparatus and she dialled Kate's number, her mind reeling with what to say. The answer machine clicked on at the other end and she felt a rush of disappointment, but hearing Kate's voice was enough. She swallowed an unexpected sob and took a deep breath.

'It's me,' she said and then paused, remembering what it was like to be cocooned in a group of people who knew her voice, knew what she was doing and how she felt all the time. What could she say now she'd left that cosy place and exiled herself in the country? How could she possibly tell Kate the heaviness of her heart?

'I miss you,' she choked and hugged the receiver, closing her eyes and bowing her head as the pips sounded and the connection was broken.

*

'Philippa is a right old bitch,' said Sadie, sipping her café latte in the Dôme. ''Course I shouldn't be saying this.' She sniffed loudly, the latest victim of the flu bug which had hit most of the staff at Bistram Huff.

'No. It's OK. I won't say anything.' Kate filled up her wine glass. 'Tell me again what happened when the promotion went wrong?'

She listened as the story unfolded, guilt and concern overwhelming her as she heard the exaggerated version of the show-down with Daniel and Charlie's dismissal.

Kate shook her head. 'I can't believe it! Poor, poor Charlie.'

'She really liked Daniel.'

'Yes, but they only had one thing in common,' said Kate.

'What was that?'

'They were both in love with him.'

Sadie laughed. 'You're not wrong there. Do you think she's OK?'

'I've heard from her at last. God knows where she was calling from. She sounded a bit pissed, but she's still alive.'

Sadie nodded and flicked open a box of Silk Cut. 'I must give up smoking,' she said, putting a cigarette between her lips.

Kate brought out the lighter and lit it for her.

'Hey, where d'you get that?' Sadie took the lighter from Kate and examined it. 'Did Charlie give it to you?'

'No. Why?'

'We did a promotion and produced all these lighters.'

Kate leaned forward, her eyes wide in anticipation. 'Go on.'

'I'm really surprised you've got one, that's all. They're very exclusive and we only gave out a few.'

'Did Charlie have anything to do with the promotion?' asked Kate.

'Sort of. No. It was Bandit who sorted it all out.'

'Who's Bandit?'

'David Delancey. He was in Charlie's account team. They were quite good mates. Only if you ask me, there's something funny about him.'

'Why?'

'Well. Since she left, that lighter promotion he did has been a big success and he's been all pally with Philippa. They've made him account director in Charlie's place.'

Kate leaned forward in her seat. 'What does Bandit look like, Sadie?'

'Cropped hair, flashy, quite attractive despite the fact that he's short.'

'Did he go with Charlie to the printers to check the scratchcards?'

'Yeah, that's right. How did you know?'

'Oh my God, we've just found our culprit!' gasped Kate, explaining how the printer dumped the scratchcards.

'How can we prove it? Who else but the printer would have known?'

'Bob maybe?'

'Would Charlie have kept records of everything?'

'I guess so. They're probably still on her computer.'

'Come on,' said Kate, standing up. 'It's time to get to work. We're going to nail these bastards once and for all.' She grinned with excitement. This was it, she'd found the story she'd been waiting for to launch into mainstream journalism. If she could find out all the facts and get in to see Teddy Longfellow at the *Reporter*, she'd be laughing. She'd have an exclusive on her hands, then people would take her seriously and she wouldn't have to write about the Spice Girls any more.

Charlie rifled through her make-up bag and pulled out her foundation. She stared at it as if it were from a different era then studied herself in the framed mirror on top of the mahogany tallboy. Her face was pale with two red spots where the wind had whipped her complexion and her lips were chapped. She peered more closely, wondering how she had let her appearance slip so drastically. Her eyebrows were unplucked and bushy, her hair was unkempt and curly, the yellowing blonde gaudy against the dark roots.

She had shut out her memory and all thoughts of vanity as

the weeks went by at Hill Farm. She'd been determined to earn her keep and help Mary Rose, even though it had taken every ounce of her strength. Yet Mary Rose had been right. Each time Charlie did something brave, like going out on her own into the dark fields, she felt as if she was scoring points for herself. Restoring her heart, ready to fight again.

And now here she was, worrying about what she would look like for Hamish. She thought of his face and the way he had started to hold her eye contact for longer than he should and she felt herself waking up in the light of his attention. She desperately craved his approval and each time she watched him stroking the dogs or tenderly lifting the cat, she longed for him to take her in his arms and pay that kind of attention to her.

She looked around the room. Mary Rose must be a good influence. She had never been this tidy in her life. Her jumpers were folded neatly in the cupboard and she even made the bed each day. She thought of her silver hipsters on their clip hanger in the flat and felt a pang of homesickness. How could life change so completely, she thought, pulling on her favourite jumper.

It was the one that Rich had bought her back in February. As the lambswool stroked her cheek, she breathed in its scent, hoping to recapture the time before her life had tumbled into disaster. Rich had insisted on buying it because it was the same colour as her eyes.

'It's shopping therapy,' he'd said, pulling his Visa card out of his wallet.

'We're supposed to be on shopping therapy for you, not me.'

'Same difference. Anyway, I like impulse buying.'

'I like it too. When you pay!' She'd stood, cuddling the soft jumper in the shop in Covent Garden, then tiptoed up to kiss him on the cheek.

He'd blushed in front of the sales assistant. 'Proof! The way to a woman's heart is through a Visa card!'

Charlie remembered how she had slung the rope-handled carrier bag over her shoulder and pulled open the shop door for Rich. 'Did I tell you yet today that you're fantastic?'

Rich had stood on the threshold and rubbed his jaw. 'Now let me see.'

Charlie had giggled and, looping her arm through his, bounced down the street. 'Well you are.'

They'd ambled through the main plaza, watching a clown busking in the last of the daylight. He wobbled on his unicycle, his music system clashing with the two violinists playing Bach down the stairs.

'What now? Shall we buy you something?'

Rich had groaned. 'I'm knackered. Can't we go home and get a vid?'

'Yes, but only if I can choose it.'

'No. I don't want girly, gushy stuff. I want a man's film. Action. Shagging worthless whores, that kind of thing.' Rich puffed out his chest.

'So we can't get an old slushy one like *Ghost* then?'

Rich had stopped in his tracks. 'Don't. Not that bit at the end when she says "Ditto" and he goes up to heaven?' He'd crammed his knuckles in his mouth, faking tears. 'I love that bit.'

'Come on, you old softie,' Charlie had laughed as she bundled him back into the Panda.

She hugged the jumper to her. How could she have been so blind and so stupid? She had let down the one person who'd always stuck up for her. She'd been so angry with Rich when she'd fallen for Daniel and he was trying to protect her from him all along. Then she'd made a fool of him, dismissing his care and concern and making him feel as if he was the one in the wrong. Now that she thought about it, he must have felt appalling to have just taken off and only left a note. It was completely out of character. She looked out at the moon through the crack in the tartan curtains, her heart hurting as she wondered whether Rich was safe under the same moon and whether they'd ever mend their friendship.

Kate pulled the bench in closer and leaned over the thick table in All Bar One towards Pete and Bob, who was rattling peanuts in the palm of his hand.

'I still can't believe it. You're sure Bandit set her up?' asked Pete.

Kate nodded and flicked her hair over her shoulder. 'He swapped the cards on press for sure. It's just a matter of how we prove it.'

'The sneaky bastard. I thought he was Charlie's friend.'

'People like Bandit have such big egos that they don't need friends.'

'Why do you think he did it?'

'Jealousy probably.'

Pete sighed. 'You could be right. He was desperate to get the promotion to account director and ever since Charlie left he's been larging it about the office like he owns the place.'

'He's been a pig,' chipped in Sadie.

'And he's dumped a load of work on to you, hasn't he?' Pete nodded to Bob who shuffled sheepishly in his chair.

Bandit had been doing more than dumping work on to Bob. He'd blackmailed Bob with the threat of telling Amanda, his wife, about his infidelity, to the point where Bob had been forced to slash his print margins to keep him quiet and was virtually working round the clock for no money. Bistram Huff was bleeding him dry, but he couldn't see a way out.

Kate studied him closely as he nodded. 'You knew about Bandit swapping the cards on press, didn't you, Bob?'

'Now just hang on a minute,' he began, but Kate cocked her head at him, looking surprised at his reaction, and his protest faltered. He blushed.

'You must have known,' said Sadie triumphantly, looking smugly at Kate. 'You've worked with Jack Marsden for years.' She seemed to be enjoying her role as detective's assistant.

Pete looked at Kate and then at Bob who was going redder. 'Bob? What's going on?'

Kate knew she was on the right track. 'You were covering up for Bandit, weren't you?'

'Blackmail!' said Sadie and Kate put a hand out to quiet her.

Bob took a deep breath and looked up at Pete and Sadie apologetically. 'I couldn't say anything. I wanted to, but he's got me by the balls.'

'Oh Bob.' Kate reached out across the wide table and touched his arm. 'Listen. I don't know how he's got you, but you can't let this happen. Charlie got sacked and her career is ruined, but this is about more than that. This whole industry is being tarnished by agencies like Bistram Huff. I'm determined to let people know about it, but I need your help.'

'I'm really sorry about Charlie, but I can't do anything,' said Bob.

Pete and Kate looked at each other.

'Why don't you tell us what Bandit's been up to?' asked Pete. 'We might be able to help.'

Bob shook his head. Despite the fact that Caroline's pregnancy had turned out to be a hoax, he still felt hopeless. 'He knows something. Something that could ruin my marriage. Oh God, it's all such a mess.' He rubbed his forehead.

Pete was aghast. 'Do you honestly think that Bandit could split up you and Amanda?'

'He could if he tells her what he knows,' said Bob.

'And will Amanda believe him, if we prove in front of everyone that he's a liar and a cheat?' Kate raised her eyebrows at him. 'Surely Amanda wouldn't believe anything he had to say. After all, who does she love?'

Bob sighed. 'Me.'

'Well then. Let's nail David Delancey once and for all and then you'll have nothing to worry about.'

'You might get Bandit, but you'll never get Bistram Huff. Philippa's sunk her fortune into the agency and she'll never let it go down.'

'She hasn't met me yet,' grinned Kate.

'What about our jobs?' asked Pete.

Kate nodded and looked serious. 'Don't worry, I'll think of something.'

'You can count me in, then,' said Pete.

'And me,' said Bob, visibly relieved. 'But how will we do it?'

Kate looked at Sadie and smiled. 'I have a plan.'

Rich sat on the edge of Chapura Fort beneath the crumbling lighthouse. He dangled his legs over the weathered stones and surveyed the vista before him. In the afternoon haze he could see for miles, down to Vagatour and up around the peninsula to the white sand of Anjuna. Behind him in the shadow of the ancient fort was a new white hotel complex. Rich peered between its re-rooted palm trees and saw the glitter of the empty swimming pool, sealed off from poverty.

Squinting against the warm hairdryer breeze coming straight at him from endless miles of blue Indian Ocean, he understood why people wanted to fly. If he had wings, he would launch himself right now from the fortress wall and soar like a seagull over the rubbly sheer drop to the crashing waves below.

He breathed in. He felt calm and free. He'd found a fax machine in the back of one of the local kiosks and had faxed a letter to work saying he wouldn't be returning. He swung his feet, his sandals kicking the worn stone. He felt as naughty as a schoolboy. Right now, he should've been in work. A shudder ran through him as he imagined his jealous and uninterested colleagues briefly questioning him about where he'd been, then updating him about the petty office politics. He thought of his in-tray and as the sun sank to the horizon, he smiled with the knowledge that it was no longer his problem.

He was on top of the world, his eyes relaxing with miles of view, his skin tanned, his muscles supple and his ego pampered. He didn't care what his bosses thought of his fax. He felt reckless and free and as he looked out over the shimmering ocean, he wondered why it had taken him so long to realise that he didn't want to be a commercial lawyer. In fact, he couldn't think of anything more pointless.

Hearing voices behind him, he watched as two young men and a slim girl clambered on to the wall near him and lit up a joint. Rich smiled and said hello.

'It's great here,' said the dark-haired boy to Rich, gesturing to the view.

Rich nodded. They all seemed too young and so pale! 'It's lovely,' he agreed, putting his feet up on the wall and turning to face them, his lunghi flapping in the breeze.

'Better than being in England, the weather's crap,' said the girl, taking a drag on the spliff and looking at Rich with flirtatious eyes.

'I was just thinking that,' said Rich. 'Are you on holiday?'

'Yeah. We're travelling round a bit,' said the first guy. 'But we've only got two weeks, so we'll stay here mostly. The night life's good and everything. Everyone's really laid back.'

'You here on holiday?' asked the friend, putting his arm around the girl protectively, having sensed her attraction to Rich.

'Sort of,' said Rich.

'From England, are you?'

'London.'

'What do you do?' asked the girl, handing Rich the joint. He shook his head and she passed it on to her friend.

'I'm a . . .' Rich stopped himself and felt a rush of excitement. 'I used to work in the city, but I hated it, so I've left. I'm planning what to do next.'

'Good on you,' said the first bloke. 'That's really cool. I wish I could leave my job. I hate it.'

'Are you staying for Christmas? We've heard it's a right laugh,' asked the girl's boyfriend.

'I expect so.'

'If I were you, I wouldn't go back to England. I'd stay here all the time.'

Silence fell over them as the sun sunk to the horizon. Rich felt himself absorbing the view. He remembered his conversation with Tanya.

'Stop. Let life come to you. Absorb it. Don't chase it, because it'll just get further away,' she'd cautioned. Now he knew what she meant. He'd never noticed how beautiful the world was until now. He had limitless choices and all that remained was to follow his instincts to his future. He climbed down from the wall.

'I'm heading back to Baga before it gets dark. I'll see you around maybe. Have a good time,' he said, jumping down into the grass.

He re-tied the knot in his lunghi and strolled away. The breeze blew down the conversation from the wall behind him.

'He's cool.'

'I thought he was gorgeous,' said the girl, but the rest of their conversation was out of earshot as Rich strode through the grass and rubble which had once been a garrison's banqueting hall.

He smiled to himself. Once he would have been ecstatic, overwhelmed that a young, pretty girl thought he was gorgeous and the guys thought he was cool. But now, as well as being flattered, he knew it to be true. He felt fantastic and it must show to everyone around him. As he kick-started 'Dream Lover' and sped along the bumpy winding road the cool shadows of the trees flashed across his path.

Revving up, he flew along the potholed road, the plastic 'Jesus loves you' sticker glinting in the shimmering light. He shook his head, the warm breeze blowing through his hair. Spotting a cow in the middle of the road he slowed down and, as he carefully drove round it, Rich could have sworn it was smiling. He laughed and let out a whoop of joy, breathing in the balmy air, and promised himself that he'd remember this moment for the rest of his life.

'Wake up!' Mary Rose's worried features blurred into Charlie's vision as she squinted open her eyes. She sat up in bed, her mind cloudy with sleep, but panicked by the tone in Mary Rose's voice.

'What's the matter?'

Mary Rose was throwing tights, jeans, socks and jumpers on to the bed. 'The weather's come down. We've got to rescue the ewes.'

Charlie drew back the curtain, but the slanting window

was obscured by a thick cover of snow. She pulled on her clothes under the blankets, her teeth chattering.

'Come on. We haven't got much time,' insisted Mary Rose, her little face creased with concern.

Charlie grabbed her scarf which had been drying on the radiator and tucked its warmth around her neck before pulling on her boots in the porch. Mary Rose lifted down another Drizabone from a hook.

'Put this on. You'll need it,' she said.

Charlie gasped as Mary Rose yanked open the back door. Outside it was pitch black, the snow cascading horizontally in the screaming gale. Charlie yelped and fell backwards as the freezing wind slapped her in the face.

'We can't go out in this! Look at it. Surely the ewes will be OK until the morning?' she shouted, fear gripping her as she squinted out into the darkness.

Mary Rose grabbed a shovel and thrust it into her hands. 'There's no time,' she shouted grimly. 'If they get stuck, we'll lose them. We'll take the tractor.' She stepped out into the blizzard.

The wind stung Charlie's face and it took all her strength to follow Mary Rose through the snow to the tractor. This had to be a nightmare. Even the tractor could hardly move through the blizzard. Its windscreen wipers were doing double time, swiping away the icy splats of snow.

At the top of the first field, Mary Rose stopped, leaving the lights on. They'd never get through the gate which was half buried in a snow drift.

'Look at it!' yelled Charlie. 'We have to turn back.'

'It'll be OK. Let's go up and see. The wind might not be so bad in the top field.'

Charlie's teeth seemed to freeze as she took the torch from Mary Rose, her fingers already numb beneath her woolly gloves. She pushed open the door of the tractor with all her might and jumped down into the snow which piled over the top of her wellies.

The beam of the tractor lights illuminated a tunnel in the darkness as Mary Rose helped her over the gate, her coat flapping around her as the wind whisked fresh drifts across the field. Charlie followed Mary Rose's deep imprints, the snow splattering against her, dragging her down. The tractor lights were dimmer now and they turned on their torches like intrepid explorers.

'Can you see anything?' shouted Charlie.

Mary Rose was just a dark shadow. 'It's much worse up here than I thought. We need to get help. I'm sure the girls are at the top, but we'll have to dig them out and we need light. If this weather carries on, it'll be too late by the morning.'

'What shall I do?'

'There isn't much time. I'll carry on. You go back down to the house and phone Hamish. He'll know who to call. Stay in the house until help comes.'

'I can't leave you,' shouted Charlie.

'Don't be silly. I've done this before and once I've reached the top, it'll be more sheltered by the trees.'

'Are you sure?'

'Yes. Now go and be careful.'

Charlie's heart hammered with fear as she trudged back through the snow. Would Mary Rose be OK? She looked around and squinted, the icy wind whipping the snow up around her so she couldn't see which way she was going. She concentrated on walking through the snow, which was so deep now she could hardly move. When she next looked up she realised that she couldn't see the tractor light and that the footprint track she'd been following had disappeared.

Holding her hat on her head, she crouched against the force of the gale as panic gripped her. She looked around her, but there was only darkness and snow. She felt the vibration of her voice in her chest, but she couldn't hear anything. She was lost in a tunnel of swirling snow and she suddenly remembered the entrance to the dance floor at Orgasm. How had she got from there to here? What terrible thing had she done that fate had left her alone on a mountainside in a blizzard?

Her knees were rattling now and she hugged herself, the cold biting into her. She'd always been scared of the dark, and as the blackness enclosed her she imagined something jumping out to grab her, but she was completely alone, a prisoner of the elements.

She talked to herself out loud, desperate to think of a plan. She had to reach the house; she couldn't just stop, or she'd freeze to death. 'Please, please, someone help me,' she wailed as she blundered on through the dark, the torch beam only illuminating the next step.

Fear hammered into her, she was out of breath, blinded by the cold and snow. 'Keep going,' she shouted to herself and thoughts of dying and being found frozen in the snow poisoned her mind. Then she stumbled into a drift of powder snow and her hand hit something hard. She reached out and found a post. Thank God, this must be the fence of the lower field. Blindly she climbed over, falling down into the thigh-high snow on the other side, crying with the cold.

The snow found its way inside her clothes and she whimpered. It was like swimming in ice-cold water. 'Don't stop,' she said, her voice swallowed in the blackness, the weak beam of her torch flickering as she groped blindly for the line of the fence, but the snow was too deep. She was hopelessly disorientated and she spun around, willing her eyes to see some lights through the blizzard, but there were none.

She shivered, her lips going blue, shouting for help. She longed for London, desperate to be in a town in a comfy flat away from the ravages of the elements. The snow piled up against her knees as she trudged on, knowing it was useless to stop, but clueless as to where she was heading.

Just when she was about to give up, her foot hit something that moved and she shone the torch down on the mound of snow. It moved again and she held the torch with her teeth as she dug down with her hands. It was Daniel, the tup.

She sank to her knees with relief, her mind suddenly focused now that she wasn't alone. She had to save him and by the looks of it she'd reached him in the nick of time.

'I'll get you out,' she muttered, freeing Daniel's face and brushing his nostrils which were clogged with snow. He was hardly breathing and she dug at the snow around his enormous bulk and flung herself on to him, rubbing his flanks with all her might, clinging to him for shared warmth.

'Come on! You can make it. Please, come on,' she begged, rubbing him all over to revive him.

Eventually, Daniel bleated pathetically and Charlie laughed. Breathless with exertion, she sank back on to the snow while Daniel shook himself. It was only then that she noticed that the snow had eased and first light was creeping over the horizon. She squinted hard, knowing that she must be in one of the side fields if she had found Daniel. The farm couldn't be too far away.

She untied her scarf from round her neck, the snow from her hair falling down her back, making her yelp. She was sweating with exertion, her extremities still stiff with cold, but she had to get back to the farm. Looping the scarf around Daniel's neck, she dragged him through the snow, stumbling as she dug a path for them through the field.

As the weak light filtered into her consciousness, the snowflakes fell gently and she lifted her face up into them, catching them on her tongue as the farm buildings came into view. She left Daniel in the near field, where the snow wasn't deep, and lunged for the gate, realising she hadn't been that far from the tractor after all.

Finlay Macintosh, Mary Rose's neighbour, was driving his huge JCB into the yard when Charlie eventually arrived.

Mary Rose ran towards her, crying with relief. 'I thought we'd lost you.'

Charlie hugged her. 'I found Daniel,' she gasped.

'Where do you want me?' asked Finlay, gruffly tramping over to them.

Mary Rose clutched his arm. 'Finlay, thank you so much. But everything's all right now.'

'Are you sure? I can go up into the fields, if you want.'

'No. Everyone is safe.'

Finlay grunted. 'Well, I'll be off. Merry Christmas,' he said.

As Charlie sat in the kitchen, her feet immersed in hot water, cupping a Lemsip, cuddling a duvet round her shoulders, she'd never felt happier.

'I can't forgive myself for letting you go like that,' said Mary Rose, fussing round her.

'You were the one I was worried about. Did you find the ewes?'

'Yes. They're not as stupid as they look. I found them all huddled together in the coppice. Those girls have got a good instinct for survival.'

Charlie sneezed loudly. 'I guess we all have,' she said.

The sales promotion industry 'Oscars' were held every year at the Hyde Park Hotel. In the ballroom, huge Christmas trees were loaded with thousands of silver baubles reflecting the sprung floor crammed with laden tables. Over the piped carols, champagne corks popped and conversation rumbled. Everyone was de-mob happy. This was the last event before Christmas and the hangover from the night's champagne was expected to last into the New Year.

In the centre of the room, at the Bistram Huff table, Si dabbed perspiration from his forehead with a linen table napkin and whispered to a waiter to deliver a bottle of champagne to the prestigious client on the BFK table. Philippa, elegant in a white backless dress, surveyed the room with hawk eyes and nodded to several acquaintances.

'If you'll excuse me, I'm going to powder my nose,' said Daniel, fingering the wallet of cocaine in the pocket of his DJ.

'Don't be too long,' said Bandit. 'The awards are going to start any minute.'

Philippa smiled at him. 'You seem very excited,' she said.

'You never know what will happen,' he said, shrugging and sucking in his cheeks confidently.

'Yes you do,' said Philippa, raising her eyebrows, and turned away to talk to the marketing director behind her.

The room went quiet as the lights dimmed and the director of the Institute walked on to the stage and tapped the end of the microphone speculatively. 'Testing, testing, one, two, one, two.' He met with a round of applause and jeering.

In the toilet, Daniel chopped up cocaine on the porcelain cistern and inhaled the fine powder. Smoothing down his hair in the mirror, he smiled at himself.

Outside, Kate bustled out of the taxi with Bob.

'I can't do it,' he said, holding on to the door.

Kate grabbed his arm, pulling him up the steps and past the porters in grey top hats. 'We've been over this a hundred times. You don't have to say anything. You just have to be there.'

In the main hall, Daniel made his way back to his seat through the twinkling table candles. He staggered slightly and steadied himself.

Kate slipped behind the buffet tables at the back of the hall, telling Bob to stay back as he perched the video camera on his shoulder. She felt apprehensive as she surveyed the room filled with hundreds of people in evening dress. She spotted Daniel straight away and, as if sensing her nervousness, he turned and looked in her direction, but his pupils were dilated and, if he saw her, he didn't recognise her. Kate shrank from his gaze and nodded discreetly at Sadie, who sat on her hands, chewing her lips.

The introduction of the best promotion took ages. Slides were shown of various work, but it was Bandit's lighter promotion that won. Kate heaved a sigh of relief. If Bistram Huff hadn't been selected, her plan wouldn't work, even though Pete had informed her the whole thing was rigged and that Si had paid a fortune to make sure that Bistram Huff won an award to repair its damaged reputation.

She watched as Bandit and Daniel mounted the steps to receive the award and was filled with revulsion. The two of them were as bad as each other. Poor Charlie.

'This is it,' she whispered to Bob.

'Go for it,' he said and, spurred into action, Kate began her walk through the tables to the stage. At first everyone ignored her, but as she mounted the steps Bandit wavered in his speech. Then Daniel recognised her.

'Ladies and gentlemen, excuse the interruption,' said Kate, grabbing the microphone from Bandit. She cleared her throat, looking out at the room full of curious faces. This was more difficult than she'd thought. 'I have a few things to tell you all that I think you need to know about Bistram Huff and the unprofessional practices that are tarnishing the name of the whole industry.'

'What the fu—' Bandit seized the microphone from her, but she yanked it back and pushed him away with all her strength.

An astonished hush fell over the room. This was the industry that loved gossip and every one of Bistram Huff's rival agencies was straining to hear what Kate had to say.

At the Bistram Huff table, Si and Philippa faced each other as Kate's calm voice soared out above the silent guests, recounting Bandit's swapping of the scratchcards and the agency's cover-up.

'I think you'll agree it's a disgrace that this has been allowed to happen and that this deplorable agency has not been penalised.'

Philippa scrambled out of her chair as the room erupted into frenzied conversation. 'Get her out!' she shouted.

Si held on to her arm, but Philippa brushed him off and strode to the stage.

'Ah, Ms Bistram,' said Kate calmly as Philippa stormed towards her.

'She's got no proof,' said Bandit, angry and humiliated.

'Oh, but I have,' said Kate, beckoning Bob and Sadie to join her.

'That's enough!' Philippa screamed, hurling herself at the microphone.

An official launched himself on to the stage, the tails of his evening suit flapping like wings. 'Ladies, ladies,' he said, trying to break up the scene.

Kate could scarcely remember what happened next. Philippa lost control and slammed her fist into Kate's face. She staggered backwards into Daniel.

'We meet again,' he said and giggled, and she saw that he was high as a kite.

Si was shouting and all the other agencies were gossiping

furiously. The official managed to remove Philippa from the stage, tugging at the back of her white dress as she flailed her arms.

Bandit picked up the microphone from the floor. He straightened his jacket.

'Sorry about this unfortunate interruption, ladies and gentlemen,' he began farcically. 'As I was saying, I am delighted to accept this award on behalf of Bistram Huff.' But he never had a chance to finish his sentence as the compère snatched the award out of his hands.

Then it started, the slow hand clap and the long boo. Pete and Sadie were on their feet rallying the crowd. Bandit stared out at them helplessly for a moment before he stormed off stage, following the path of Philippa who had been dragged blaspheming through the double doors. Kate waggled her aching jaw and staggered to her feet, reaching out her hand to Bob, who had filmed the whole incident and was completely over-excited.

'You can turn it off now, Bob,' said Kate groggily. 'I think that's most of the action.'

Bob, who'd been looking through the viewfinder, came to his senses and put the camera on the floor, forgetting to turn it off. He helped Kate up. 'You were brilliant. Did you see their reaction?'

'Guilty as sin,' said Kate as she took Bob's arm and went to find Pete and Sadie in the crowd and answer all the questions.

Only Daniel was left on stage, giggling ridiculously like a child.

'You stupid fucks! All of you!' he railed like a hysterical drunk, in between bouts of laughter. But no-one was taking any notice of him except the scornful eye of the abandoned video recorder.

Rich knocked on the door of Tanya's hut and hesitated on the doorstep, holding the bunch of flowers he'd bought her from the market. They were spectacular and he almost wanted to keep them for himself. He'd never bought flowers as a Christmas present before, but he'd been driven by an impulse to please his lover. He pushed the door cautiously.

Inside, the air was hot and heavy with dust. Rich looked at the swirled sheet on the bed, dishevelled from their night of passion. He put the flowers in Tanya's jug and smoothed down the covers. Beside the bed, he saw her multicoloured money belt and he straightened it as he faffed around. Some coins fell out and he picked it up. He'd buried himself into Tanya's most hidden parts and yet her money belt was private. But curiosity got the better of him and he peeked inside the zip and saw her passport. He knelt on the bed, sweating in the heat of the room.

She'd changed his life and made him see things from a whole different perspective and yet he knew little about her. Pulling out the passport, he thought how lucky she was still to have an old-style black British one. He flicked through the brittle, crumpled pages marvelling at all the faded stamps and visas and a trickle of pale sand fell out from between the pages like an hour glass.

He turned to her passport photo in the front. Behind the yellowing plastic, Tanya stared out at him with short spiky hair. He chuckled to himself, thinking how different she looked. Then he read the smudged details and his heart jolted. The knowledge felt shocking, like the taste of ink. Tanya was forty-five. He'd been shagging a forty-five year old.

Charlie took the matches off the shelf. 'OK. Lights, Hamish,' she said and tried to strike the match in the darkness.

'And action!' She put the lit match to the Christmas pudding and it burst into blue flames. As she picked up the dish and carried it to the table Mary Rose and Hamish burst into a round of 'We Wish You A Merry Christmas'.

Mary Rose clapped her hands as the blue flame died and Hamish lit the angel chimes, bathing the table in soft light.

'Happy Christmas,' he said, raising his glass, and Charlie smiled at him in the soft glow. It looked so cosy in the kitchen, especially now that she'd drunk a bottle of claret and was well into the port. Hamish picked up the card she'd made him from the table and studied her painting. 'I love my card,' he said.

Charlie smiled and felt proud of herself. After rescuing Daniel, she'd spent a week nursing her cold, feeling delighted to be alive and not to have to go out into the fields. She'd spent her days pottering round the house, studying the pages of Mary Rose's thick cookery books until she'd made an edible batch of mince pies to impress Hamish.

She felt guilty that she wasn't helping Mary Rose and she'd decided to make Christmas as special as possible, decorating the tree and painting Christmas cards while she listened to the radio. She felt happier than she had in months, but as she prepared for Christmas on the farm, she missed shopping with Kate in Harvey Nichols and the slush around the big tree in Trafalgar Square.

Hamish had called every day, and she'd regaled him with stories of Christmases past and wrapping presents with Rich in the flat and the parties in the 51.

But now, as Mary Rose finished the last of her pudding and clattered her spoon into her dish, Charlie looked at her face and knew it had all been worth it.

'I never thought I'd say it of one of your creations, but that was a wonderful Christmas dinner,' she said.

Charlie smiled and reached out for her arm. 'Are you OK? You look exhausted.'

Mary Rose yawned. 'I am,' she said.

She'd been up all night battling with the snow and Charlie, seeing her so tired, had volunteered to cook Christmas dinner, but it was gone nine when they'd finally got to eat.

'Do you mind if I turn in?' asked Mary Rose, looking between Hamish and Charlie.

'Not at all,' said Hamish.

Charlie got up and hugged her godmother.

'Thank you so much. I couldn't have got through the last few weeks if it wasn't for you,' said Mary Rose. 'Don't stay up too late, you've only just got over your cold.'

Charlie laughed. 'I've got more stamina than you think.'

'I know,' said Mary Rose. 'Night, night.'

Later, after they'd washed up, Charlie sat cross-legged on the floor in front of the wood burner and put the two glasses on the rug. She felt excited – alone at last with Hamish.

'You've really cheered this place up,' said Hamish, looking at the Christmas tree and the tinsel over the door. He sat beside her on the rug in the warmth of the fire. 'You're looking better,' he said.

'I feel better. I was really scared out there. For a moment I thought I was a goner. It puts everything into perspective.'

Hamish smiled and was quiet.

Charlie suddenly jumped up. 'I forgot,' she said, rummaging under the tree and producing a sprig of mistletoe. She sat back down and held it above her head, grinning at Hamish, but he didn't move.

She looked up at it. 'Aren't you going to kiss me?' she asked flirtatiously, but Hamish's face was solemn.

'There's nothing I'd like more than to kiss you,' he said. 'But the thing is . . .'

'What?'

'You don't really want me to kiss you.'

Charlie shook her head and laughed. 'Of course I do.'

'Not really.'

'It's not as if I'm going to kiss anyone else around here.'

'That's not the point.'

She put the mistletoe down. 'Then what is? I'm not going to bite you.'

Hamish sighed. 'I've dreamed about kissing you from the first time I saw you, looking like a lost Hollywood superstar in that grisly auction.' He took her hand. 'It's not what you want.'

Charlie rolled her eyes, refusing to take him seriously. 'What do I want then?'

'Rich.'

She backed away. 'You're jealous of Rich?'

'Yes, actually, I am.'

'That's ridiculous.' Charlie stood up and folded her arms and Hamish scrambled to his feet.

'Is it? Do you realise that you talk about him all the time?

You're always comparing us. Every time I do something for you, or I say something funny, you compare me to him.'

Charlie gasped. 'I don't. Rich is just a friend, he's . . '

'He's not.' Hamish put his hand on his chest. 'He's in here, only you refuse to see it.'

Charlie stared down at her hands. 'You're just using Rich as an excuse.'

Hamish grabbed her shoulders and forced her to look at him. 'Can't you see I'm being honest with you? If I thought you belonged in the country and your heart was here, I wouldn't be kissing you under the mistletoe, I'd be proposing to you. I'm not rejecting you, I'm trying to make you see what's so bloody obvious to everyone else and it's tearing my heart out.'

Charlie watched the door close behind him then she sat down by the flickering wood burner, inexplicable tears pouring down her face.

The air hostess's blonde hair was sprayed solid into an immobile fringe. Rich gulped down the last of the Temazepam he'd bought from a chemist in Calangute with the dreadful white wine and handed his food tray to her. He pressed the button on the arm of his seat and pushed back. He reclined half an inch and, pretending to be comfortable, closed his eyes.

Christmas in Goa had been fantastic. After finding out Tanya's age, he'd sat on the beach for hours, trying to make sense of it all. Could he really ignore her age? Or didn't it matter? Tanya might have a few years on him, but she was comfortable with who she was. She didn't have to define herself by her age, just as he wasn't defined by his job any more.

As he floated idly in the sea, he thought about it. He couldn't be cross with her for lying about her age, because she hadn't. He'd taken her for what she was and she'd done the same for him, setting him free just to be himself.

But finding Tanya's passport had jolted him into reality and he knew the time had come to make some decisions. He could stay on in Goa or travel round, but he knew this wasn't his world. He loved it, but he would only really succeed if he could feel like this when he was at home.

Actions were what mattered, he thought as the waves bounced him about. He could do anything. His bonus from last year was still safely tucked in the building society, so he'd have enough money to live. Maybe he'd set up with Dillon and they could run a restaurant, or perhaps he'd go back to college and study again. It didn't matter. His perspective before had been so limited, but now he realised there were endless possibilities as long as he followed his heart.

He jumped about in the waves, feeling absurdly happy, and then it came to him. There *was* something he was passionate about. Something that he'd never lost, all the time he'd been in Goa, and he refused to ignore it any longer. He strode out of the water, feeling more purposeful than ever before, and went straight to the village to book his flight home.

When he'd met up with Tanya later that evening for the Christmas Eve party, she only had to look at him once to know what he'd done. She'd nodded at him and hugged him tightly. 'You're right, it's time.'

On Christmas Day, they'd dined in style in the local restaurant, singing Christmas carols in their bathing suits and playing drinking games with coconut cocktails. He'd spent Boxing Day chilling out and playing backgammon with Tanya on the beach, topping up his deep tan. He smiled, remembering the surprise leaving party that Tanya had thrown for him and her affectionate farewell, but the sleeping tablet faded out his memories and he was comatose until Gatwick.

It was the day before New Year's Eve when the flight arrived and Rich's heart was racing as he climbed out of the cab outside the flat. Charlie was bound to be back in London if she'd been away for Christmas. Still wearing his embroidered Indian cap, he breathed in the soggy December air and looked up at the windows. There were no lights on. Maybe Charlie was in the kitchen. He imagined her drinking tea, her feet up on the edge of the kitchen table as she painted her toenails. He would walk in and confront her. He would be honest. Tell her that he had been in love with her, well besotted actually, and that he realised she was right, that he'd needed to get a life, and he had. Then he'd play the rest by ear.

He rummaged for his keys in the depths of the sandy pocket of his rucksack. Maybe she would get up and hug him. He could imagine her clear grey eyes. 'Oh Rich, I've missed you,' she would say and Kev would wind round his legs as she went to run him a bath. Everything would be cosy and warm and they would see New Year in together, just as they always had.

The dank air inside slapped Rich into reality. He shivered in the cold hallway and leaned against the door to push it open against the backlog of mail on the mat. He bent down to pick up the mound of letters and junk mail, seeing his frightened breath in a vapour before him.

In the dark, rank-smelling kitchen he let the thick straps of his rucksack slither from his shoulders and his heavy load slumped on to the lino with a thud. Kev's cat flap was taped up with masking tape, his precious weeping fig looked as if it had wept itself into extinction and all the appliances were unplugged at the wall.

The hair on the back of his neck was already up and he shuddered with foreboding as he pressed the play button on the answer machine. Every message seemed to be the same. The last message was from Daniel.

'Charlie, I think you've still got my keys. I'd be grateful if you'd send them back, recorded delivery if you can. As soon as possible.'

Rich's hackles rose at the sound of his cruel voice. What had happened? He grabbed the phone and punched in Charlie's work number, surprised that it was still in the subconsciousness of his fingertips. The phone rang and rang. Eventually an answer machine clicked on. To his surprise, it was Si's voice on the line. 'Thank you for calling Bistram Huff. Our press conference will be held in the new year.'

Press conference? What was going on? Rich replaced the receiver slowly and ran his hand over his aghast face. Whenever he'd pictured coming home, he'd always imagined

Charlie being there. It hadn't occurred to him even for a moment that she might have disappeared. He shivered and sneezed. Something was really, badly and horribly wrong and Rich felt the possibilities festering in his gut.

He opened the fridge and toppled backwards away from the stench of furry olives and rancid milk. Panic gripped him and, leaving the door ajar, he tore through the flat, upturning everything looking for clues. It was only when he sat down defeated at the kitchen table that he spotted the cellophane cover of *Marketing* in amongst the mail. He edged out the magazine from the pile and read the headline before tearing open the wrapping. And there in the centrefold was a blown-up picture of Charlie and columns of smug copy telling the whole sad story.

Mary Rose stood on the top step of the ladder and peered into the darkness of the loft. 'Can you find it?' she called.

Charlie took the torch from between her knees and quickly replaced the bundle of love letters back in the trunk.

'I think so,' she replied. 'I won't be a minute.'

She pulled out the antique silk dress and coughed in the dusty air. She couldn't wait to get it into the light.

It had been Mary Rose's idea to find the dress. Charlie had been cooking supper when her godmother came in looking tired. She laughed as Charlie fussed round her.

'I could get used to this. I can't remember the last time I had someone to look after me.'

Charlie sliced the bread on the counter. 'You need it. Everybody needs a bit of TLC now and then and you've been rushed off your feet.'

Mary Rose rubbed her forehead. 'I'm terribly worried about Daniel.'

Charlie placed the breadboard on the table and touched Mary Rose's shoulder sympathetically. Hamish had diagnosed pneumonia since the ram got stuck in the snow and neither he nor Mary Rose held out much hope.

Mary Rose nodded. 'I can't go to Valerie's and leave him.

What if the snow comes? No, I'll stay here. New Year isn't such a big deal anyway.'

'You're not going to make me go on my own?' asked Charlie.

'Hamish will be there.'

Charlie served up the casserole. 'I know.' She hadn't told Mary Rose about her chat with Hamish. He hadn't been around for days as he was overseeing Archie Packenham's hunting party as it tore around the countryside. 'But I can't go. I've got nothing to wear.'

And that was when Mary Rose had suggested a trip into the loft. Charlie was amazed by the amount of junk up there. There were more battered sewing machines, an old brass bedstead, a couple of sets of bookshelves and two large trunks, covered in dust and to her surprise stuffed full of memorabilia. There were sewing patterns from the sixties, half-finished knitting projects, books, postcards and letters, most of which were from a guy called Derek. Charlie laughed at the image of Mary Rose in a mini-skirt and sixties' sunglasses.

Mary Rose held the ladder as Charlie came back down carrying the dress in a bundle. She slid the hatch cover across and stepped on to the landing, brushing dust from her jumper.

'You've got a treasure trove up there. That bedstead would sell for a fortune in Fulham.'

But Mary Rose was fondling the material of the dress softly.

'Look at this old thing. I never got to wear it,' she said, her voice husky.

Charlie stooped to look into her face. 'What happened?' she asked, thinking of the bundle of love letters.

Mary Rose shook her head sadly. 'I don't really know. I was supposed to be going to a ball in London and I was waiting for him, but he never came. That was New Year's Eve too.' Her voice trailed off.

'Who?' Charlie touched her arm gently, astonished that Mary Rose could be so sentimental.

Mary Rose looked at her and smiled sadly. 'Oh, just some ghost from my past. It's ancient history now.'

'Did you love him?'

'Who, Derek? Of course I did, but I never realised it at the time. It was only when he got tired of waiting and married someone else that I realised. I've kicked myself ever since.'

'He never came back?'

Mary Rose shook her head. 'That's why you must always regret the things you have done and not the things you haven't.'

Charlie held the dress to her. She wanted to know more, but Mary Rose had resumed her bustling manner and was heading downstairs.

'Come on. Let's see what it looks like on you. And by the way, I bought you a rinse in the chemist. I think it's time for you to lose the blonde. It really doesn't suit you.'

'Aha, the wanderer returns!' Kate's voice came down the telephone like a balm.

Rich smiled, cheered by the triumphant tone in her voice. 'Kate, oh, Kate, what's happened? Where's Charlie?'

Kate smiled. 'Wherever she is, she ought to be very proud of us.'

'Why?'

'We've stitched up Bistram Huff. Charlie was set up by this bloke Bandit who fixed it so that the Up Beat promotion went wrong and she got the blame, and now I've got a fantastic new job at the *Reporter*.'

Rich sat down. 'I'm lost. Start from the beginning.'

Kate quickly told him what had happened, adding that now, before New Year, she wanted to find Charlie to tell her the good news and make up with her, especially after discovering what Daniel had done. She told him about Charlie's message. 'She didn't say where she is. You've no idea where she could be?' she asked.

'None. I know her parents aren't due back till the New Year, so she can't be there.'

Rich put down the receiver burdened by his knowledge. He

sat for a long time letting Kate's news sink in before the scraping at the back door entered his consciousness. Unable to find the keys, he ripped off the masking tape from the cat flap and, like a rat, Kev flopped over the threshold.

Rich picked him up, twirled him round and kissed him. 'Am I pleased to see you, fella! Where've you been?' he asked, tickling the soggy smelly bundle.

Kev scrambled out of his embrace and stalked across the kitchen floor leaving muddy paw prints in his wake, before collapsing on to the sofa into a deep sleep. But Kev's return only brought temporary solace. Rich could hardly sleep. By five a.m. he was manically vacuuming the flat and by nine he'd been shopping and was ringing round everyone he could think of who might know Charlie's whereabouts.

When the doorbell rang, Rich's heart leapt into his throat. He ran down the stairs and flung open the door, his face animated with anticipation.

On the doorstep, Pix stood wringing her hands. 'I've lost Kev,' she said. 'Charlie gave him to me to look after, but we got thrown out of Vauxhall and I've had nowhere to stay . . .' Her voice trailed off as she followed the clearly disappointed Rich up the stairs.

'Don't worry, look over there,' he said, nodding to a fluffy Kev who was gorged with smoked salmon and sprawled in front of the heater.

'Thank God for that! I thought he'd been run over.' Pix picked up Kev and muzzled her face into his fur. Eventually she returned the pampered cat to his warm cushion and straightened up.

'How was your trip?' She looked Rich up and down. 'You look fantastic.'

Rich put his hands in his pockets. 'It was great. Just what I needed, only I got back yesterday to find that Charlie has disappeared.'

Pix warmed her fingers in front of the heater and gently stamped her cold feet. 'She went to Scotland.'

'Scotland?'

'Her godmother?'

Rich slapped both hands on his head. 'Why didn't I think of Mary Rose?'

He raced out into the hall, returning with his electronic organiser. He flipped it on and scrolled through the information, but could only find the address. Frantically, he rang 192, but Mary Rose was ex-directory.

Pix scowled at him and pulled her woolly hat over her ears. 'Well, I guess I should be going then,' she said, shuffling towards the stairs.

Rich pounced towards her and grabbed her arm. 'No! Wait. Please don't go.'

Pix sucked in her cheeks and folded her arms.

Rich rubbed his forehead. 'I'm being such a klutz. Pix, I have to talk to you. I've been feeling terrible about what happened. You were right to tell Charlie. I would have done if I'd been in your shoes, but I should never have lashed out at you. I'm so, so sorry.'

She stared at him, her eyebrows raised.

Rich exhaled, getting it off his chest. 'You didn't deserve to get hurt and I hope you'll forgive me, Pix, because you're fab and I really want you to be my friend . . .'

'I see.'

Rich put his hand on her shoulder. 'Oh Pix, I've been such a fool. Will you ever forgive me?'

She shrugged. 'You hurt me.'

'I know. I'm sorry. I was hurting so much myself, I lashed out at the nearest person to me and that was you.'

Pix put her hands on her hips and looked at him. 'So how do you feel about Charlie now?'

Rich smiled at her, his tanned face crinkling with affection. 'Don't worry, I've got over my obsession. I learned so much about myself when I went away,' he said quietly. 'All I know is that I have to get her back. Life feels wrong without her.' He sighed. It felt great finally to admit to Pix how he felt.

Pix reached up and touched his cheek. 'What are you standing here for then?'

Rich held her cold hand against his face and they smiled at

each other, then she put her hand on his chest. 'It's good to see you at long last,' she said.

The Panda was on its last legs as it rattled into the drive of Hill Farm. It wheezed and coughed when Rich turned off the ignition key.

'Thank you,' he said to the car, patting the dashboard gratefully.

His knees trembled as he stumbled out of the car, rubbing his tired eyes. It had been mad to drive to Scotland and it had taken him over eight hours. Yet he'd barely noticed the time or how hungry he was; he had only one thought on his mind. He had to get to Charlie before midnight.

He looked round him as the smell of the air reawakened the atmosphere of childhood and for the first time he felt nervous. What would Charlie say? Would she be pleased to see him? What if she'd found someone else? Faced with the reality of the situation as he knocked on the door, he wanted to bolt. But he had to know. Had to see her face again to know if he was crazy or not.

The light in the kitchen was on, but no-one seemed to be home and he knocked on the window. He looked at his watch. It was gone eleven and he'd blown his chances. They must have gone out.

'Shit!' he said, pulling his overcoat around him, then started calling Mary Rose.

Then he saw her at the door of the barn and ran towards her, waving frantically. He stopped, the smile fading from his face as he saw Mary Rose's grim expression.

'You've come,' she said.

'What's wrong?'

'It's Daniel. He's in terrible pain.'

Rich's heart jolted with panic. Daniel was here, after everything he'd put Charlie through? His spirits slumped. Charlie wouldn't want him here now. He shielded his eyes from the headlights as Hamish pulled up beside them.

'What's going on?' asked Rich.

'It's too late,' said Mary Rose sadly, but Rich had already

broken away from her, his heart thumping as he sprinted into the barn.

'Charlie?' he shouted.

But the barn was empty apart from the shivering ram who lay on its side in a pile of straw, beseeching him with exhausted eyes.

Mary Rose came in with Hamish. 'He's here,' she said, pointing to the ram.

'That's Daniel!' exclaimed Rich, relief flooding his face.

Hamish knelt down in his kilt, the dagger in his green woollen sock bulging as he tenderly took Daniel's pulse. 'I'll have to give him a shot of the stronger stuff. I'm afraid it's going to finish him off.'

Mary Rose nodded sadly.

'I'm going to get my bag. You can have a few moments to say goodbye.'

He drew Rich away.

'Is there anything I can do to help?' Rich asked, concerned by Mary Rose's distress. Hamish shook his head sadly and Rich followed him out to the muddy Range Rover. 'I'm Rich, Charlie's friend,' he said.

Hamish stopped and looked at him for a long time and nodded slowly. 'I know,' he said eventually.

Rich was confused by his look. 'Have you seen her?'

Hamish nodded. 'You'll find her at the ball. You can see the lights from here. It's the manor house on the other side of the valley. But you'd better hurry, it's nearly midnight.'

'I don't know whether the car will make it.'

'Take this. The keys are in the ignition,' said Hamish.

'I'm sorry about Daniel,' Rich said as he opened the driver's door. Poor Hamish, he looked really upset.

Charlie could hear Valerie screeching with laughter as Archie led the conga of jostling, stumbling guests out of time with the music. He had taken off his dinner jacket and his bow tie was skew-whiff as he shuffle-kicked through one set of French doors on to the patio and back through the others into the main room, his orange paper hat falling over one eye, a blob of trifle on his purple-veined nose.

Charlie picked at the fingers of the local farmer who was gripping her waist so tightly that she could hardly breathe and extricated herself from the concertina line, standing aside before she was dragged back into the ballroom.

'Join in, Charlie,' yelled Valerie, looking slightly the worse for wear as she followed up the line.

Charlie tried to look as pathetic as she could and waved her hand in front of her face.

'I need a bit of air,' she said. 'I'll just go to the folly and back.'

Valerie hopped past her. 'Make sure you're back by midnight.'

Charlie smiled. 'Of course.'

She shivered in the cold air and as the conga snaked back into the ballroom she searched around for something to cover her. She unhooked a sheepskin from the wall and draped it over her shoulders. They wouldn't miss her for a few minutes.

Yet as she slipped down the patio on to the crunchy, frost-covered lawn, she knew she had no intention of going back to the party. She looked behind her at the manor house, its lighted windows bright in the ivy-covered walls. In the ballroom, the yokel tones of the band's lead singer announced 'The Birdie Song', his lips pressed against the microphone as he cranked up the drum machine, and Charlie could see the adults and children alike wriggling their bottoms. A plastic banner saying 'Happy New Year' in bright primary letters had come unstuck from the antlers over the huge mantelpiece and draped down towards the roaring fire.

Charlie had to smile. So much for a rave New Year's Eve. She looked up at the pincushion of stars and watched her breath. She had to be alone when New Year sounded, even if Hamish came back from wherever he'd rushed off to. Much as she appreciated being belle of the ball in her dress, she couldn't face standing in a circle overlapping arms with the village locals and Valerie's posh friends pretending that she knew the words to 'Auld Lang Syne' while the bagpiper deafened them all.

She bunched up the silk skirt of the dress and ran across the rolling lawn, hearing the raucous noise of the party recede, and felt a rush of excitement as she was enveloped into the thick silence of the night. The dark firs were tipped in silver and on the mirror of the lake a lone swan glided in the reflected moonlight.

As she approached the folly, birds took off from the top of the trees flapping the scent of the night towards her. Nearby an owl hooted. Charlie twisted the ancient metal loop and pushed open the creaky door.

Inside, the folly was dark except for narrow slits of silver light which illuminated the dust and spider webs. For a moment, her old fear of the dark gripped her stomach, but Mary Rose was right. She had nothing to fear but fear itself and she found herself panting with excitement as she clambered up the stone steps to the trapdoor at the top.

She breathed in and huddled against the cold stone, looking up at the wispy clouds passing across the moon. She tipped her head back, letting her eyes get lost in the stars.

She thought of Daniel and how much she'd changed since she'd been at Bistram Huff, and she thought of Kate. Dillon would probably be throwing a party in the 51 right now. She imagined Rich and Kate cracking open the champagne and she longed to be with them.

She hugged the sheepskin around her. It was the dawn of another year and she knew as she stared up into the heavens that the time had come for her to reclaim her life.

The crunch of the Range Rover on the drive and the glare of its headlights brought her round. That would be Hamish and he'd find her and she couldn't bear his hurt look.

She wanted to spend these moments alone, to savour her memories and the possibilities for her future. She crouched in the crystallising snow, hardly daring to breathe.

'Charlie?'

Rich's call flew through the moonlight to her heart and for

a moment she thought she must be dreaming. When the call came again, she jumped up. Rich was standing by the French doors, peering out into the darkness. For a moment she couldn't believe it was him, but when he called out again, she threw her arms up in the air.

Rich saw her pale face illuminated at the top of the folly as she leaned on the rough brick and he ran towards her. Inside the music stopped and Charlie could hear Archie announcing the countdown to New Year through an antique megaphone.

'What the hell are you doing here?' she asked as she peered down at Rich.

'I've got this thing about rescuing princesses, even if it does mean freezing my nuts off,' said Rich, cramming his fists into his armpits.

Charlie laughed. The countdown began and Rich looked behind him towards the party. 'Stay there, I'm coming to get you.'

Charlie pressed her hand over her mouth, the sheepskin falling away as Rich bounded up the steps and appeared through the hatch.

From inside the cheer rose for New Year and they stood opposite each other in the night, the noise of poppers and cheering breaking the shy stillness between them.

He shook his head, gazing at her.

Tears pricked her eyelids. 'You look gorgeous,' she said.

'So do you. The blonde's gone, I see.'

Charlie bit her lip, her eyes shining. 'We all make mistakes.'

'It's all right,' said Rich quietly, taking her hands and squeezing them.

'I'm so sorry. I've been such a dope,' she began, but Rich put his fingers on her lips to silence her.

'It doesn't matter. All that matters is now. Right now.' He gently pushed a lock of hair behind her ear.

'Oh Rich, Rich, I've missed you so much.'

Inside the house the guests began to sing 'Auld Lang Syne' their voices soaring out in unison.

'Come here.' Rich pulled her towards him and she fell into his arms. Closing his eyes, he breathed in her perfume. He kissed the top of her head and then put his cheek on it. 'Shall I take you home?' he whispered.

Charlie laid her head on Rich's chest, her arms holding the one person she loved more than anyone in the world, and the realisation hit her. 'I am home,' she murmured.